Bride Flight

MARIEKE VAN DER POL is the author of the prize-winning script for the international hit movie *The Twin Sisters*. This, her debut novel, has also been made into a film in the Netherlands.

COLLEEN HIGGINS lives and works in her adopted country of the Netherlands and also spends time in her native state of Minnesota in the USA.

Bride Flight

Marieke van der Pol

Translated from the Dutch
by Colleen Higgins

Portobello
BOOKS

Published by Portobello Books Ltd 2010

Portobello Books Ltd
Twelve Addison Avenue
London
W11 4QR

First published in Dutch by De Arbeiderspers in 2007

The publication of this work has been made possible by
financial support from the Foundation for the Production
and Translation of Dutch Literature (Nederlands Literair
Productie-en Vertalingenfonds).

A CIP catalogue record is available
from the British Library

9 8 7 6 5 4 3 2 1

ISBN 978 1 84627 172 4

www.portobellobooks.com

Designed and typeset in Minion by Patty Rennie

Printed in the UK by CPI William Clowes Beccles NR34 7TL

1

THE NEWS OF FRANK'S DEATH reaches the three women at more or less the same time. For a brief moment, it seems as if the breeze is carrying with it the dizzying bouquet of a blood-red wine, and they grope around for support. I have to go to the funeral, all three of them think; I should be there. Maybe me more than anyone.

In Auckland, the lights aren't yet on in the bridal salon when the death announcement lands on the doormat along with the other post. The mannequins in wedding dresses stand in the dark, elegant and lifeless. The windows are covered with heavy blue velvet curtains in front of lavishly pleated lace ones, which keep out the daylight and the noise from the street. There is no display window, because the shop doesn't depend on people who just happen to be passing by. It isn't long before Esther emerges from her rooms at the back of the salon. She clears her throat, and has already smoked her first cigarette. She got up late again this morning; she's a poor sleeper who has to make do with the final hours of the night, once her spirit has stopped resisting the childlike trust that falling asleep requires. Her clients know that Lady Esther Bridal doesn't open until ten. Oh dear, she groans, stooping down to push a plug into an electrical outlet, whereupon the fluorescent lights in the suspended ceiling flicker on one by one with a buzzing sound. The index finger she uses to push the buttons on the stereo system is adorned with rings. Soft muzak wafts through the salon, a breezy samba. She hums along, her voice deep and throaty and rather off key, *mas que nada*, as she walks through her shop over the thick blue carpeting, turning on all the switches until the room is bathed in the glow of a combination of neon light and chandeliers. In spite of her age and the early hour, her clothes are dramatic, a skirt and blouse she made the previous autumn from deep purple cotton-Lycra jersey, a fabric she also sells. The three strings of plump pink pearls around her throat attest to her zest for life. She enjoys looking in the mirror and still applies her make-up with care, although poor eyesight means that nowadays she occasionally pencils in her eyebrows with lipliner. She has her hair dyed mahogany brown every three weeks, and wears it pulled back as tightly as possible – 'my natural facelift, dear' – and fastened with a tortoiseshell comb. Her lipstick is always applied just so, the whole day through; there's no-one she has to kiss, and anyway, in her world you plant your kisses in the air. Today her lips have an aubergine undertone because of the pink and purple.

Just as she does every morning, she goes over to the mannequins that are lined up on either side of the wide passageway. Artifical women, with their heads inclined slightly, their arms slightly curved, and each and every one of them wearing one of *her* wedding gowns, *her* creations. Here and there she pushes a satin strap back up over a slick shoulder, or smoothes out an imaginary crease from the tulle with the lace appliqués. She calls it inspecting the troops. Behind the mannequins are racks that hold the rest of the gowns – so many dresses, but she just can't stop – and the heavy lengths of fabric that have to be hung out flat. Throughout the room, showcases made from dark wood display an extensive array of accessories: wedding shoes, corsages, and hats, gloves, hosiery, undergarments, sequins, beads and pearls, feathers, ribbons of satin and lace, tiaras, necklaces, and earrings – there are hundreds of kinds of earrings alone. Esther holds sway over these things, she knows where to find each item because she carefully placed it there herself. She moves through a hushed dream world, but does so briskly as she begins an ordinary workday in her shop. On the way to the entrance she straightens the piles of bridal magazines in the sitting area where she receives her clients, the young women who look at her anxiously, as if hoping that Lady Esther can not only design the most wonderful day of their lives but also the indistinct years yet to come. There is a suite of furniture, like you might find in the Palace of Versailles, which she visited before the war with her parents and Sal; he'd run through the rooms on his short little legs. For years afterwards she'd dreamt about this in well-defined images, and behold: golden baroque chairs, their seats covered with deep blue velvet, placed at a round table with a glass top to protect the floor-length velvet tablecloth from the hundreds of cups of coffee and the occasional glass of liqueur. She slides the open magazines across the glass towards the hopeful expression on her client's face. 'Have a look, I had something like this in mind, no, I wouldn't go two-piece if I were you, you need to be taller for that.'

She's an authority, people listen to her, and if not she's always willing to let a girl try on a two-piece first, immediately followed by something like an elegant, svelte A-line. Well, it would be highly unlikely for her to be proved wrong.

As she passes, she runs her hand absently over the black wooden counter, where stacks of soft yellow, pale pink, and ivory lace lie behind the glass front, with bolts of fabric leaning up against the wall at the back – there are at least a hundred – and above them, shelves with rayon, satin, and voile. She passes the wooden stands with rounded tops over which white lace floor-length veils are draped, so that they resemble a group of veiled Arab brides waiting bashfully for their bridegrooms. And then she's at the door with the massive locks – Auckland is a big city, and so many strange people have come to New Zealand over the past few years. Just like every other morning, she bends over – oh, dear – towards the doormat and picks up the pile of letters, but the moment she sees the black-edged envelope with the Druivebloed crest in among the bank statements and advertising flyers she knows this won't be a day like any other, and that her shop will remain closed.

3

In the affluent Dutch town of Blaricum, Marjorie crashes to the ground near the rhododendron, her mobile phone still held to her ear, because Captain Cook hears branches snapping at the bottom of the garden and tugs at the leash with unexpected force. She shouldn't have allowed herself to be talked into a male. That wouldn't have happened if Hans had been there. The thought had come up again this morning when they were out for their walk over the heath: this dog is too strong for me, too wild, the training hadn't been very successful, and as happened so often nowadays, she made her way back home filled with self-pity. She's been a widow for four years now and refuses to get used to the idea. That's not how things were supposed to have gone. Hans took care of her and she was his princess, his diva if you will, that's the way things were, and everyone was happy with the arrangement. Dying in the middle of the night hadn't been part of the plan.

Back at the villa with the thatched roof, she takes the post out of the letter box by the gate and, wouldn't you know it, at the very same moment her phone starts ringing in the pocket of her duffel coat. She slips the loop at the end of the leash around her wrist, clasps the post under her arm, and somehow manages to get the irritating thing out of her pocket in time.

'Mrs Doorman speaking.'

From the other side of the world, the past comes rushing in.

It's a rather undignified spectacle – a heavyset elderly woman falling flat on her face into the crocus bed – and for a second, even though she feels the bone in her wrist snap, she thanks her lucky stars that the large garden is densely wooded and well enclosed so no-one can see her. But then she starts to moan, and feels very much abandoned as she struggles to get back on her feet, in so much pain and so filthy, reeking of the manure she has spread in the garden every spring and that hasn't yet sunk in. Why isn't Hans here? To move her wrist even slightly is excruciating:

4

it's probably broken, no, it's definitely broken, because she can't move her fingers. She's got to call Bob, but she can't do that with only one hand. Blast it all, this jacket has only just come back from the cleaners. Bob has to come right over, but he can't leave just like that, of course, and it's her right wrist, too, how will she manage? Hans should never have abandoned her like that. She sobs out loud. Right now she couldn't care less, let them get an earful, because worst of all is that behind the news, behind that wretched phone call from New Zealand, waits an important decision she now has to take all by herself.

*

It's raining in Greymouth. The postie didn't manage to get the payment reminders, the church magazine, and the death announcement through the letter box before they got wet. I did a better job of it in my day, thinks Ada. For years, in driving rain and blustery winds, she used her body to protect the post and kept the letters dry. She had always done her duty.

Because Derk keeps watching her from the doorway with that special look of his, she gets up from her chair at the kitchen table and crumples the announcement into a ball, which she throws into the bin, to show her indifference: look at this, it means nothing to me, Frank is dead, but who is this Frank anyway, how many decades has it been since I last thought about him, I wouldn't dream of going to his funeral, why would I? She reinforces her trustworthiness by the way in which she sits back down at the table and picks up the potato peeler, but she can tell by the look on his face that Derk doesn't believe it for a minute. All that dutifulness has made a liar out of her. She watches him go, her husband, how he shakes his head as he walks away down the hall, back to his chair by the window in the living room. His bony, stooped back, the sunken neck, his shuffling gait. She notices that she tends not to lift her own feet, either; it's like we're afraid of leaving the earth. She waits until he gets to the living room, then stops peeling. She fishes the announcement out of the bin, wipes off the coffee grounds, and hides it in her apron pocket.

She spends the rest of the morning in the backpacker cafe on the corner near the river, right beneath a large wooden insect that hangs on the red wall. No-one would think of looking for her here. The furniture in the cafe dates from the sixties, and she runs her chilled hand over the Formica tabletop. It's 'retro', her grandchildren have explained to her, but she sat at a kitchen table exactly like this one for years. No-one seems surprised by her presence; maybe the young travellers even think it's cool, an elderly woman like her who doesn't mind their music. Children, she thinks tenderly, they're still children. What about us back then, we were the same age, but were we ever so young? Just look at them, they come from all over the world, meet each other in places like this and speak the same language with each other. They're not afraid. Or who knows, maybe they are, but they don't let that stop them. Keeping their fear at bay by escaping on to the internet, there's no harm in that, why shouldn't they? Those first few years I was always wanting to write letters, too.

Derk had discouraged this.

For a long time, she sits and watches three Japanese girls giggling in front of a computer. The crumpled death announcement burns in her jacket pocket. Without realizing it, she keeps twirling the same unruly lock of white hair around her finger, which makes it seem like she's pondering something. But she's made up her mind. When she's gathered enough courage, she gets up cautiously, but even so, the shooting pain in her knees takes her breath away.

As she expected, Derk is furious. In the end he falls silent, and sits in his chair staring out of the window, with the rain lashing against the window-panes. He doesn't respond even when she comes in with her jacket on, puts down the cup of tea next to him, and plants a kiss on the top of his head. It's not that I don't love you – she'd like to say something along these lines, but she can't break through the wall of resentment and embittered silence. Trumpet blasts may have brought down the walls of Jericho, but she'd never had enough breath to produce a good, strong tone. So instead she softly strokes his thin hair and tries to leave the room in the most ordi-

6

nary way possible, while doing her best to ignore her jangling nerves. Derk hasn't even moved. Outside she can feel him watching her as she rushes to cross their street – so as not to get too wet – and walks to the bus stop. Why is he so upset? I'll be back in a couple of days and everything will be back to normal. Which gives her the courage to turn around and look right at him. To wave. He doesn't wave back, of course. The person she's best at deceiving is herself.

*

Unbalanced, Marjorie observes as she passes through the no-man's-land above the clouds on her way to New Zealand, I'm unbalanced. It's dark and quiet in the large aeroplane. Her son is asleep next to her. They're travelling business class – Bob didn't think someone her age should still be flying economy, and though the seats are indeed wonderful, she can't sleep, it's all too much. She looks at her boy, a middle-aged man – unbelievable – with a successful career and three beautiful daughters, her granddaughters. With her good arm, she arranges the blanket around his shoulders and – like she'd read somewhere – tries to turn and calmly face the fear that has been besieging her with increasing frequency the last few years. What she really wants to do is shake his arm, wake him up, they have to talk, it's vitally important. Instead, she pushes a button and a moment later the stewardess appears.

'Could I get some more water, please?'

She takes two painkillers. Her wrist did indeed turn out to be broken, and while the doctor set the bone and she cried out in pain, Bob sat in the waiting room with his laptop looking for the fastest way for them to get to New Zealand. He was going with her, and that was final. He wasn't sure why his mother was set on going to the funeral – as far as he knew, they hadn't stayed in touch with Frank de Rooy – but it was clear she'd made up her mind, and she couldn't travel on her own with one arm in a cast. He wouldn't budge, was just as stubborn as she was. And he also wanted to have another look at the country he'd lived in till he was nine. This is meant to be, she thought, it's a sign, and she stopped protesting. He had no way of knowing that his presence certainly wasn't going to make her mission any easier.

He couldn't be allowed to know this.

To make things even worse, he'd emailed Hannah, who'd been travelling around since she passed her final exams, to say that her dad and grandma would be in Martinborough in two days' time. If you get off to a running start, he wrote, you should easily be able to jump from Australia to New Zealand, and otherwise I'll pay for your ticket. Bring liquorice, she'd emailed back. The Dutch are so fond of their liquorice. And although Marjorie was delighted at the prospect of seeing her youngest granddaughter again, the news had come as yet another shock that she could share with no-one.

She and Bob left that same evening at half past eight. He's working on a museum (she so enjoyed mentioning this to her friends and acquaintances, my son, you know, the architect, she would say modestly, he's involved in *such* a wonderful project), but has enough people on staff who can take care of things for a while. Vera had driven them to Amsterdam's Schiphol Airport in her fast Audi, and Marjorie had waited impatiently while her son and his wife embraced ardently at the kerb. You're jealous, Hans had always teased her, you want him to stay your little boy for ever. Which was nonsense – it was more that she found Vera to be a bit possessive at times, I mean, really, when you've been married for twenty years you can leave each other alone once in a while; most people were divorced by then.

Tonight had been no different. When they'd finally got their luggage onto the cart and were walking towards the departure hall, the whole waving ritual started again. And Vera kept blowing kisses the whole time and calling out like a Yiddish mama, telling him he should phone when they got there. He seems to enjoy it, he's always been good-natured, even as a child. A brave, strong, cheerful little boy who excelled at rugby and loved to swim. Yes, he was indeed *her* little boy, who'd been so upset when

8

they came to Holland and he found himself going to indoor chlorinated swimming pools and in a football culture to boot. Football was for sissies! He was beside himself as he stood stamping his feet in the kitchen, and she hadn't dared look at him.

'Aren't you glad for Daddy then?'

That had been a low blow, but it was the only thing she could come up with. Of course he was glad for Daddy, he'd got a better job in Holland. He trudged off to his room with his shoulders hunched; he couldn't play outside in this country, and hadn't made any friends yet. They'd failed to teach him Dutch. We failed, failed. The word goes round and round inside her head and thankfully soon loses its meaning, becomes a strange word.

At the airport, she finally put her good arm on her grown-up son's back and pushed him through the revolving door. These days you have to check in two hours ahead of time and it seemed they were very strict about this. Vera came running up in the departure hall, out of breath, because the bag of liquorice for Hannah was still in the car. Imagine, said Bob with a smile, she came all that way just because of the liquorice.

The painkillers are working, and she feels her muscles relaxing, but she can't let herself fall asleep. She has just over twenty hours to reflect on this, a little less if you don't count the time it will take to change planes tomorrow in Kuala Lumpur. Twenty hours to take a decision that will turn everything on its head, and she will need those hours, because right now her thoughts are flying all over the place, and every time she wants to grab on to one of them it vanishes like a dream upon waking.

*

Ada's daughter drives her to the small airport in Hokitika. The day before, she'd taken the bus from Greymouth to Julie and Gary's house, and candidly told her eldest child the whole story when they went out for a walk after supper. They wandered down the beach, between worn grey stones and bleached branches and tree roots that lay there as if they'd been flung cruelly out of the ocean and left behind, dead. The wind had howled around their ears, so that they'd had to look down at the sand and didn't have to look at one another. Occasionally Julie took her hand and gave it a squeeze, but when Ada finished her confession, her daughter burst into tears. There is no Father Christmas.

Ada had rubbed Julie's back, grown old before its time, and wondered why she felt relieved instead of guilty. Almost cheerful, like a young girl who finds life incredibly exciting. I'm not as sweet as everyone thinks. As she rubbed she looked around, at the ocean, the towering waves, this rugged beach – she has never been insensitive to the beauty of this coast, this desolate place, but for the first time she looked at it with the eye of a traveller who would soon be leaving it all behind. It's all very beautiful, but I have to be going… tra-la-la-la, she'd nearly added, and shook her head to rid herself of the thought, because she loves her children as well, and doesn't like to see them cry.

Now, at the airport in Hokitika, her exuberance is gone. Walking through the hall towards the entrance to the airport's small apron, she feels her daughter's eyes on her from behind the glass wall. It makes her nervous, and in her haste she can't find her ticket, pardon me, she murmurs to no-one in particular, looks first for her spectacle case and then drops it. Impulsively, she gives her handbag to the friendly steward, then he can look for the ticket himself, and in the meantime she gives Julie a thumbs-up to show her everything is under control. But she can see from her daughter's face that she has her doubts. Do Pete and Dan know? she'd sobbed.

'No, love. Only you right now.'

'When are you going to tell them?'

She will have to visit her two sons and their families in Auckland and Kerikeri and tell the whole story again. 'Can I tell Gary?'

During the night she'd heard whispering, and this morning at breakfast her son-in-law had made a point of being jovial, which she'd found both annoying and touching. Take care, Mum. A wink. It was all just awkwardness.

Esther tries to walk right on top of the blue line that's taking her around to Domestic Flights. The airport in Auckland is large and international. She walks past the buses ready to provide the stream of travellers with transportation to the city, and defies the looks of the waiting taxi drivers who gaze at her exotic clothing. She knows she won't see any hint of desire in those eyes, like in the curious looks she used to get in the past because her appearance exuded the thrilling prospect of eccentric behaviour, of jazz and drink, of European morals. She still swings her hips, exactly like she used to show her models how to do, but nowadays it's considered an affectation. What the hell, all that face powder has given her a thick skin, and she walks into the wind with her head held high. She's followed along the blue line by clattering – little Sal on his old tricycle on the pavement in Amsterdam – because she's pulling an elegant black wheeled case behind her, which contains the exquisite dark grey pinstripe suit she would wear to the funeral, she'd chosen it with care, maybe a bit too warm, but she doesn't have to put on the jacket and can just wear the blouse that goes with it, made from the most extraordinary deep red silk, the colour of dark blood, of pinot noir; she thinks about things like this. She's also packed her dress shields, because perspiration shows on silk. She's pleased with herself as she heads for the low Domestic Flights building. Her only concern is that she should stay on the blue line: to the left of this yawns a diabolical furnace, and the shrieks coming from within – no matter how horrific they may be – might lure you into the flames once and for all; to the right, a little girl stands wailing on an immense expanse of ice, softly but incessantly. It was enough to drive you mad.

*

Luck would have it that although the three women are spending the night before the funeral in the same hotel in Martinborough, they don't run into each other. They make the same movements, doing the things you do in a hotel, but they do so at different times. And because each of them knows that the other two might also be there, the hotel's sumptuousness doesn't fully register with them – which is a shame, because in spite of everything, they've looked forward to the crisp bed linens and the deep armchairs.

*

Country sophistication is the nicest kind, Esther thinks to herself. She looks at the hotel as the taxi driver takes her suitcase out of the boot. There's none of the arrogance of urban sophistication. It makes no excuses about delighting in its gleaming polished copper, its paintings and English antiques, no matter that they're out of date. I'm like that, too.

As she follows the man into the hotel, they pass a heavyset woman seated at a table outside, clumsily jabbing at a pie with the fork in her left hand, and with her right arm in a sling. Oh dear, capri pants, and bare legs at that. She's never been able to understand why elderly people – people her own age, but of a different sort – would choose comfort over elegance, and why on warm days they put their withered legs, where veins meander like blue rivers through the scaly landscape of their skin, out in full view. Why do we have to look at this? Why not a gorgeous pair of *cool wool* slacks? Are they trying to tan that ancient skin? Do they think it will make them look more attractive? Maybe they think they're entitled to it. Amazing, all the things we're entitled to these days. You get to see all my rolls of belly fat because I think I should be able to wear a bikini.

Give me a break.

She enjoys talking to herself, a habit that emerged from being on her own for so long, during the many hours she spends bent over her sketchbooks, always coming up with new bridal designs, during the many years, decades now, that she's kept her large bed to herself, making no attempt whatsoever to find a lover. She talks to herself from the moment she gets up. Late, but never reluctantly. I'm a walking wonder, she says to herself. Every night I'm excited as a little child because tomorrow will bring the start of another day. They didn't manage to spoil that. But oh, am I old. These are her standard lines when she first looks into the big bevelled mirror in the morning. It never ceases to amaze her: how do you get such a young person into such an old body? Like a cushion that's been sat upon too often, that's my face, full of creases and worn spots, I can't go out in public any more. I never was a beauty – those dark circles have always been there – but have a look at this. You can colour your hair mahogany till you turn into a tree, powder your face and paint your lips till you die trying, but there's no way you're going to fix that face, because it's an old face.

She finds this tremendously satisfying.

Talking to herself has become the accompaniment to her daily activities, and more and more often she turns off the music when there are no clients in the shop. The slick sambas intrude upon the conversations she has with herself. Oh, Lady Esther, she might say as she works on a bridal gown for a woman who flew to Auckland all the way from London for one of her divine creations, oh, Lady Esther, you're the only designer who uses my own body as the starting point for your designs. She goes on repeating this endlessly, like a mantra, until her assistant comes in and sees her look up in annoyance over the gold half-moons of her glasses.

'You're not allowed to smoke here,' says the boy who carried her suitcase up the stairs at the hotel. 'All our rooms are non-smoking.' Esther takes a deep drag on her cigarette and pauses dramatically.

'I have a blood clot in my heart, I could drop dead any minute.'

Even though it's true, she always enjoys the effect this has.

'Oh...' he says, inching back towards the door, 'I'll ask if... maybe you can...' She gives him a generous tip and shuts the door with a smile. The fact that every cigarette might be your last does wonders for the taste. Living like this suits her, she's well acquainted with it, because she's had very little faith in the future for a long time now. Although she'd left Europe far behind, she found it hard to imagine that life somewhere else would be safe and secure, even on the other side of the world in a country

13

where everyone greeted each other with 'Having a lovely day, dear?' Even there, something formless was breathing down her neck, something that at most she sensed as a jet-black shadow in the corners of every room she found herself in, but which nonetheless made her driven, and greedy. And so she has remained.

Now she's tired. She had flown from Auckland to Wellington during the hour she would normally have been taking her afternoon nap. And then there was the taxi driver, who had dispensed his body odour and dull chatter all the way to Martinborough. She lowers herself back onto the bed and looks straight at the smoke alarm on the ceiling.

*

Three rooms down, Ada rubs her frozen feet over the bottom sheet to warm them up. She has brought the cold along with her from Greymouth, as if her body can't yet grasp that here on the North Island it's a lot warmer than down on the West Coast. Next to her lies a young man with grey-green eyes and an intense expression. A lock of brown hair falls over his forehead. He sniffs, stretches his arms, and folds them snugly behind his head with a complacent smile, she doesn't need to look at him to see it. To see the movement of his muscles under the skin on his chest.

I'd almost forgotten about you, I nearly managed.

His smile broadens. He turns onto his side and studies her, uses a finger to draw a leisurely line over her forehead, nose, mouth. The finger lingers at her lower lip, she opens her mouth, arches her neck and gives a little whimper, like a puppy.

Liar, he says, you've never forgot about me, not for a single day.

In spite of the thick down comforter on the hotel bed, she can't get her feet warm. She needs more than that at her age. She gets out of bed carefully and goes to the bathroom. Time and again she's promised her daughter she'll buy thermal underwear – Mum, there's no reason for you to be cold – and every time Julie finds her half frozen she has to admit she forgot again, and she laughs as she shakes her head and thumps her chest

14

with her hand, this getting old is for the birds. But the real reason is the money. These kinds of undergarments are expensive. They can't live on Derk's pension, and he won't let her mention it to the children. Just like before, it's all the fault of the union, the railway, the local council, all those scoundrels who made his job intolerable. And as for claiming a pension from Holland, he refuses, over my dead body, it isn't his country any more.

She has secretly been putting aside some money, for unforeseen things, for the grandchildren, for a little something extra. As she waits for the tub to fill with hot water, she looks out at her hotel room. Maybe she'll spend all of the money here: she's not as sweet as everyone thinks. The entire king-size bed for her alone. The past few years she's been waking up in the middle of the night and listening to Derk – listening to him scratching the skin on his scalp with his fingernails, to his intense, infuriated sleep, grinding his teeth with the few molars he still has left while his dentures wait for morning in the glass.

*

They say a criminal always returns to the scene of the crime. In spite of the scrumptious pie – that's what I've missed the most, the pies – Marjorie shifts back and forth uncomfortably in her chair, making the wicker creak. It doesn't help matters that she has to eat with her left hand. She shouldn't have come. It had been stupid of her. She tries to recall the moment when the decision was finalized, when it suddenly became clear that the idea she'd been so anxiously entertaining had turned out to have already been decided.

'Is it good, Mama?'

She nods furiously, waves with exaggerated enthusiasm – don't arouse any suspicion. Her son walks on, down Kitchener Street in the direction of the park. There's not much to see in Martinborough, but he's capable of enjoying anything. He gets that from his father. She angrily prises a large piece from the pie; a pea shoots over the edge of her plate and falls onto the ground. Everyone is dying on her. She shouldn't be drinking wine, in the sun and with jet lag, she should keep her wits about her, stay alert, she has to think things through. But the pinot noir is heavenly and you're in a wine region, after all. 'Truly glorious, the prince among reds' the menu says. She had immediately looked for Frank's label, 'Druivebloed' in simple black lettering against a pale yellow background above a drawing of a magnificent country house. The waiter obligingly filled her glass half-full and didn't mention the death of Frank de Rooy – how could a tourist understand what a loss this was for the region? If only you knew, she thinks. Maybe everyone should know at last. Or maybe not. All these wretched doubts. She beckons to the waiter, indicates that her glass is empty again, her left-handed gestures awkward and stiff. Her wrist, was that one or two days ago now? They lost some time along the way; this really is her last glass. And Bob should come and sit with her. She'd like to take a nap for an hour or so, no-one enjoys a good sleep as much as she does, but because of that stupid arm of hers she can't lie on her favourite side, and her sensitive airways immediately announced there were too many soft furnishings in the room, and then there's the nuisance of getting undressed with a cast. She puts her left elbow on the table and leans her head against it. It's useless to think about all of the consequences, too much wine, too tired from travelling. Later. Later on she really has to think things through. Because *she* has to decide – this still manages to filter in through the heavy curtains. If you don't decide, someone else will do it for you – she hears the tinkling of bracelets, and a deep, husky female voice says: oh, dear. Then she curls up comfortably in the warm orangey light behind her eyelids.

*

Considering their age, it goes without saying that at some point they will all be taking an afternoon nap in their room at the same time.

These days, that's when Esther catches up on the sleep she's deprived of at night.

Marjorie has set her travel alarm to stay a step ahead of the jet lag, following the advice she'd read somewhere. She also likes to eat early, so at six o'clock she's ready and waiting in the large dining room, keeping a nervous eye on the other guests. Although her son is no longer used to eating at that hour, he *is* still used to letting his mother have her way. He spent the whole afternoon visiting the vineyards in the rental car, like most of the visitors to this region, and tells her about his experiences. Everything has changed so much, he says, and makes large, enthusiastic gestures as he speaks.

Ada decides to have dinner in her room. She says she's pampering herself. The truth is that she dreads sitting in such a sophisticated restaurant by herself. There are things she hasn't mastered, like using a fish knife and choosing a wine. She eats in her room in front of the television.

After dinner, Marjorie and Bob – who now feels just how tired he is – go for a stroll. Occasionally they recognize the Martinborough of forty years ago and reminisce about the past. Marjorie leans heavily on her son's arm. Without any warning, her eyes fill with tears. Have I been a good mother? she asks. It must be the jet lag. It makes him laugh, and he teases her.

It's dark when Esther wakes up. She doesn't mind, she always eats late. In the dining room she tells her entire story to a blonde woman who works in television and regularly spends a few days in this hotel. Her entire story – everything, that is, except the parts she's not allowed to tell. Not a word about Frank de Rooy. The woman finds it all incredibly interesting, says it would make a wonderful film. This makes no impression on Esther – she's heard this a number of times before and nothing ever comes of it. After the blonde woman is gone, she panics for a moment. In her room she alternates between watching television and reading her book, but nothing seems to sink in. She goes out onto the balcony to smoke, and looks out over the park. She thinks back to a walk she went on long ago, along the Avon River, to her bare feet dangling stubbornly in the icy water, and the grey-green eyes that watched this. The weight of the dead increased by one. Forgive me, she asks silently, even though she doesn't believe in life after death. In the next room she hears a man's voice talking on the phone, a cheerful low droning. It sounds like he's speaking Dutch.

Marjorie has been asleep for some time, in the room right above Ada's.

Ada wakes up in the middle of the night. Since Derk isn't there she could turn on the reading lamp, but she's too tired to read. The words and images arrive in the dark. There are only a few and they've never changed; they can still pick her up and carry her off. She masturbates, no-one there to notice. Her body still works. Beautiful, full, shapely thighs, a deep voice says to the girl she has now become. Afterwards the melancholy sets in. She lets the tears run slowly down her cheeks, something she can otherwise never allow herself to do. Gradually she falls asleep.

The next morning she has her breakfast brought to her room. Although this feels like a defeat, she enjoys it nonetheless.

In the breakfast room, Marjorie is again one of the first people to arrive, which means that Bob is, too. The tiredness has finally caught up with them and they're both a little subdued. Marjorie is wearing her black suit, the same one she wore for Hans's cremation. Four years on, she can no longer get the jacket closed, and is only able to button the skirt with difficulty. After breakfast she goes back to her room.

Ada takes her time bathing and getting dressed, as if she were in love and going out on a date. She even brought along her paua-shell necklace, which brings out the blue in her eyes. She does up her silvery white hair with great care, and it shows. Strange, she thinks, as she tries to look at herself from all sides, people always told me I was beautiful but I could never see it myself. Now there are spots in bizarre places on her skin, a benign kind of cancer, her hair has become thin and lank, there are wrinkles around her mouth from the disappointed silences, and around her eyes from the pent-up tears, but when she looks in the mirror these days, she sees a beautiful woman.

Bob is reading the newspaper in the lounge when Esther walks by on

18

her way to the breakfast room. They nod to each other pleasantly, good morning. He watches the elderly woman in the dark trouser suit for a moment, as if he recognizes something in the way she moves her hips.

Esther is the very last guest to come in for breakfast, and around her the tables are being laid for lunch. When she's finished, she takes a walk down the high street. She goes into a boutique to look over the clothes, which are intended for very young girls. When she notices the salesperson staring at her, she explains that she is Lady Esther, 'of Lady Esther'. The girl gives her a blank look.

Outside it's warming up fast. Esther walks to the square where the taxis are waiting. Marjorie and Bob are already on their way to Frank's vineyard in the car.

Ada has decided to walk. She wants to feel the warmth of the sun — something that anyone who lives on the West Coast of the South Island will understand. It's quiet except for the occasional car speeding by. Her pace is slow, and this becomes progressively slower as her knees start to protest and the patent leather of her new black shoes blisters her feet. She passes one vineyard after another, field after field, but she only starts paying attention to her surroundings when she sees a sign with the Druivebloed crest, and becomes confused because she remembers Frank's property as being much smaller. Over the years he must have bought up a lot more land. Seemingly endless fields with straight rows of grapevines. Once in a while she hears a dry crack, bird shooting, she thinks, and in her mind's eye she sees a man's hips, wearing a sturdy leather belt hung with dead birds. Two hands slowly unbuckle the belt and place it on the ground beneath a crooked tree. There you are, says a deep voice.

She's hot, and takes off her sweater before walking on. In spite of the blisters and the stabbing pain in her knees, she unconsciously starts to walk faster. At last, close to where the mountains begin, a magnificent white country house built in colonial style appears on the horizon. She recognizes it from the tourist brochures on the reception desk at the hotel. Good God, she murmurs, good God, and walks on quickly until she reaches the entrance. As she stands there panting she looks around, then crosses the road to the bus stop, where she sits down on the bench. She's weighed down by a good many years and ailments, and memories that today seem heavier than ever. While she tries to catch her breath, she looks at the vineyard.

The sun casts the fields in the low, blazing light of autumn. Miles of white netting have been draped over the grapevines, like an endless bridal veil. The surplus is stuffed in between the vines like that very same veil after a disenchanting night, shoved all the way to the back of the wardrobe. Loss hangs in the air. She suspects that his footprints are still there on the paths.

Tall marble pillars flanked by trees stand on either side of a wide gravel road that leads directly through the fields to the winery and the house in the distance. A wrought-iron arch with a beautiful rendering of the Druivebloed crest spans the space between the two pillars. Ada can't help but feel proud. She leans her head back against the glass wall of the bus shelter and closes her eyes. He washed his garments in wine, and his clothes in the blood of grapes.

*

Upon reflection, it has more to do with disposition than with luck that their paths don't cross. Luck is a poor choice of words.

2

ON A PALE SPRING DAY in 1953, in a rush of pity, Ada van Holland bestowed her virginity on a God-fearing, strict Reformed farm boy who afterwards held this very much against her, especially when she didn't get her period some weeks later.

She'd seen him in church a few times. He was a new face, and people spoke in low voices as they told how he came from the town of Oude Tonge, one of the unfortunate souls who'd lost everything in February of that year in the terrible North Sea Flood, that they'd sat on the roof of their house in the cold for two days, and that his mother had screamed the whole time because her baby had slipped into the water, and when the tide surged in at the end of the second day, the roof ripped off like it was made of paper. And Derk – that was his name – was the only one in the family who'd managed to stay afloat by clinging to a beam. Ada couldn't keep her eyes off him, the tragedy of it all gave him a marvellous glow, like a film star, even though if you looked at him closely he was rather plain, and when he finally spoke to her, outside after the church service, she had been filled with the desire to comfort him as best she could. In the spiritual sense of the word.

He'd already applied to emigrate to New Zealand and his departure was imminent. On one of their outings he'd taken her to the tram station at the landing in Zijpe, where a temporary cemetery had been set up following the disaster. 'Unknown girl' said the cross where Ada paused.

'We're not in this world to enjoy ourselves,' he shouted into the wind, 'but if you have to work so hard here, and have so little to show for it, it's time to leave.' Ada nodded, repeated it under her breath, she learned sentences like that by heart.

'At this rate you could be engaged for ten years, because where are you supposed to live?'

It was all due to the housing shortage, the lack of jobs, the government, the rules and regulations, the bureaucracy. His voice grew increasingly angry as he explained all this to her, as if he was being forced to leave the country against his will and she was part of the conspiracy.

'Everything was going to get better after the war – but, well, things are just awful.'

Her head turned to one side, she watched him as he flung a handful of sand away from his body. The time they spent together was somewhat strained, and then there was that strange accent of his, but his anger touched her, and after all, she'd resolved to be supportive. 'Not that you don't have to work hard there, too, but at least you can get somewhere.'

She hadn't counted on the power of her own flesh. When he took her to Oude Tonge and they stood before what remained of the house where he'd lived with his parents, when his closed face suddenly burst open and she couldn't help but put her arms around him at seeing his tears, she found that her body responded of its own accord to his hands, which searched for comfort everywhere, and as if it were only natural she offered him her mouth, and of course he could then no longer resist all of that carnality, all of that tempting voluptuousness, and because of this what happened next was all her fault.

A week later she went with him to the *Waterman*. Their parting at the dock was awkward because her sin was there between them. She watched him as he went up the gangway, a thin, angry young man with sandy hair on his way to a better future.

Ada, who feared it was useless to beg the Lord to forgive her for a sin of this magnitude, pushed the entire incident far away. With her vivid powers of imagination she would have been able to believe it had never happened, maybe would gradually have even been able to forget about the boy with the sandy hair, if only that same self-willed body of hers hadn't put a stop to that. Five weeks later, when her period was long overdue and she awoke one morning in a sweat because she'd dreamt that a naked newborn baby kept slipping out of her hands and falling to its death on the tile floor, she knew her fate was sealed.

It hurt her to see her parents suffer because of her lapse. In their eyes she saw her suspicions confirmed, that she was indeed a child of the Devil, that she was damned. It was the woman's duty to keep the man from being tempted. Their daughter had offered herself up as a snack. Used goods, her mother sobbed. She had to confess her sins in church and repent openly before God and His congregation. It was a nightmare she seemed unable to wake up from. A shame-filled letter was dispatched to New Zealand. She received a short, stiff reply, and they were married by proxy with a distant cousin standing in for Derk. She wasn't allowed to wear white, and the pastor predicted that God would punish her directly or through her children. The neighbours talked about her. She had to get away as soon as she could.

∗

'How would you like to fly in an air race?' the emigration official asked. He placed his cigar in the ashtray with a flourish, leaned towards her, and took her hand. This was clearly something special. 'Instead of six weeks by ship.'

She didn't dare pull back her hand. Yes, she nodded, of course.

It was like this, the man explained. The province of Canterbury in New Zealand was celebrating its centenary. And so the capital, Christchurch, and the authorities wanted to celebrate this with an international air race, the London-to-Christchurch race. KLM Royal Dutch Airlines was going to take part in the handicap section with a cargo plane that had been converted to a passenger plane for the occasion. They could take sixty-four passengers, and right now everyone who came to apply for emigration was being asked this question and almost all of the places had now been spoken for. They were mostly young women like herself, on their way to join their fiancés who'd gone on ahead to look for work and somewhere to live.

An aeroplane full of brides, the official said with a wink.

The chosen ones, he called them, because their trip would take two days at most and they would be the centre of attention. This would be the first time in history that passengers would cover such a huge distance in such a short period of time. She was one of the chosen ones, he said as he stroked her hand with his sweaty fingers.

*

Whether she was damned or chosen, there was a great deal of fuss about the race. From August onwards it was all over the newspapers, and nearly every day she received official forms and advice in the post. Around her she could feel the condemnation give way to admiration and pride, and she breathed a sigh of relief. Her little brothers cheered whenever there was news. The idea that one of their own – it could have even been them – was going to get on a real aeroplane and fly twelve thousand miles around the world! They cut out everything related to the air race and pasted it into an exercise book, talking excitedly about what route the plane might take (which wouldn't be announced until the day itself) and about the bird, the Douglas DC-6A Liftmaster *Dr Ir M. H. Damme*, otherwise known as *The Flying Dutchman*. They said those names out loud as often as they could, stumbling over the syllables; it dominated their boastful childish conversations – not the fact that she was going away never to return, but the air race.

'Bird' was their word, a word boys used.

A journalist and a photographer came to their village to interview the emigrant Ada van Holland, who at eighteen years of age would be the youngest person on board. The photographer, a tall man with a pock-marked face and a prominent Adam's apple, set up his tripod and didn't take his eyes off her.

'Well, we certainly don't need to go to Hollywood to find a face with star quality.'

Her mother coughed. Ada didn't dare move while she was posing. That night she looked in the bathroom mirror and tried to see what the photographer had meant. Her mother suddenly opened the bathroom door. She who could look right through you knew that her daughter had been flattered by the photographer's words. She took Ada's chin in her hand. She never had to use force, because you wouldn't dream of pulling away. 'Child,' she said, 'you have an ordinary face, don't go getting any ideas into your head.'

Ada nodded, mortified. The face with the star quality melted away.

*

At the end of September, KLM's final letter fell onto the scrubbed tiles in the narrow hallway. It was handed to her that evening at the table after grace, to read aloud.

'The day of your departure to the country where your future awaits you is fast approaching.'

Her throat was squeezed shut, which made it hard to speak.

'You will soon board the aircraft in Amsterdam in order to make your way to the metropolis of London, from where you will actually depart for New Zealand.'

When talking about British territory, KLM thought it would be better to address her in the language of her future home. From that point on, the letter was in English. Of the three pages filled with information about what their programme would entail, the only words Ada recognized were England, Holland, London, New Zealand, and hotel. She wouldn't be able to understand anyone or anything. She fell silent, her eyes burning as she turned the pages, pretending she was thinking, buying time, struggling.

Her father broke the silence; he pushed his chair back over the wooden floor, stood up, and took the Bible down from the mantelpiece. It was time to pray.

'You can ask the teacher,' he said.

*

The teacher's house smelled like old people. Ada was shown to the straight-backed chair. The teacher sat down opposite her in a low-slung armchair and took her time as she read the letter. The scandal filled the room, there was no need to mention it. The only sound was the ticking of the clock. She fixed her gaze on the print above the mantelpiece, a picture of a skull that stared out at you from hollow sockets. If you stood up close to it, it turned out to be a drawing of a frivolously clad young woman, seated in front of the mirror of her ornate vanity table. It alarmed her that she was drawn to this scene in particular, and she forced herself to look at the skull.

'Well, well...' muttered the teacher. KLM was going to do everything in its power to make their short stay in London an unforgettable one.

'But what if you don't speak English?'

The teacher didn't answer, nor did she look up from the letter, just as she always used to do at the primary school, frightening into silence the child who had dared to speak and who would then await the reprimand that was sure to follow with cheeks gone bright red. Ada murmured an apology, but the woman expertly allowed the silence to continue. Then she cleared her throat and pushed back her glasses. After landing at Heathrow, the passengers would be given fifteen minutes to freshen up, for powder and lipstick, it was right there in the letter. Ada looked at the old, disapproving mouth. She'd once seen such a gold tube in the bedroom of one of the women she worked for; she twisted it open, sniffed at it and then smeared it – what on earth am I doing? – on her lips. She did so awkwardly and was terrified she would break it, because it had been shaped into a slender slope of wicked red. The girl that looked back at her from the mirror brought a warm heaviness to her thighs. Indians had tied her to a tree, and her breasts protruded between the ropes. This was how the hero found her. Immediately her heart started to pound, because God can see everything and she thought she heard the front door. She wiped off the lipstick on the inside of her skirt, a stain that would never come out. No-one had noticed at home, because she herself had been doing the washing since her mother developed arthritis, but the stain was still there as a warning.

Translating the letter seemed to be something of an effort for the teacher. Ada needed some air, but didn't dare ask whether they might open a window. *I wish she'd hurry up.*

'Before long,' the teacher read aloud, 'journalists will be plying you with questions about your future life in far-away New Zealand. They have a job to do, so please do not be offended if they sometimes ask you questions which seem rather personal. Remember, you are front-page news and this is the price you pay for fame.' The grey head was rocking back and forth almost imperceptibly, so Ada kept her excitement about these lines to herself.

As she cycled back home, she went over the programme. It was blowing steadily and she had the wind against her on top of the dyke. You always had the wind against you on the dyke. She pedalled hard, because it was dark and late and someone had been cycling right behind her the whole time. When she reached the big curve, she looked back and saw a formless figure with a heavy coat and a fleshy face. She didn't know him. As though taking her glance to be a sign, he started to overtake her. He nodded at her. She nodded back. Then he placed a heavy hand on her thigh and continued to ride alongside her at the same speed. Her throat constricted. She wanted to scream, but that might be rude, because what did he mean by this exactly? Nevertheless, a yelp slipped out. The hand stayed put and the man said nothing. The two of them rode on in silence, bent over their handlebars, straining against the wind, there was something almost companionable about it. 'Hey!' she shouted suddenly, and could hear how feeble it sounded. But then more sound thrust itself out of her throat. '*Heeey!*'

Without a word, the man removed his hand from her leg and increased his speed. He rode out in front of her for several minutes and she watched him anxiously, her heart racing. On both sides of the dyke, dark, formless journalists climbed up to the road. The price you pay for fame. She sobbed tearlessly, even once the houses appeared at last and the man went down the embankment to the right and disappeared into the darkness.

After crossing the square in front of the church, she rode quickly over the unlit path behind the church; she was out of the wind for a moment and able to catch her breath. The uneven paving stones made her teeth chatter and she clenched them together. At the narrow bridge over the channel she had to get off – that's how hard the side wind was tugging at her bicycle – and she walked it the final hundred yards home. There was a light on in the kitchen. She put her bicycle in the shed and ducked to avoid a cobweb. It would soon be winter. Without her. Inside the house they weren't allowed to light the stove yet because coal was so expensive. Just like every year, the damp would continue to make the wallpaper curl away from the wall. But New Zealand was so terribly far away. She wiped her cheeks and walked to the kitchen door.

*

On the 7th of October, the time had come. Her parents went with her to Schiphol Airport, and she began to feel nauseous on the bus. Her mother ran with her through the warm, congested hall to the ladies'. She retched above the toilet bowl, but nothing came out.

'It's not so bad. It will pass. Try to look at it like that...' Her mother dug a handkerchief out of the bag with the sandwiches. Ada walked to the washbasin and saw herself in the mirror. The face of a stranger, teary-eyed and sniffling, the thick blonde hair a tight mass of curls after a night rolled up in rags. She turned towards her mother.

'How? How do I have to look at it?'

The handkerchief had taken on the smell of the sandwiches, and she was finally able to vomit. She felt her mother's hand on her back.

'Love will come. It has to grow. What's important is to be a good wife. With God's help.'

She already knew this. She already knew everything.

'Ye shall be one flesh. Your father and I were… We had…'

She flushed the toilet, didn't want to hear about her father and mother as one flesh.

'Pray often… The church… And children. That's what you need. The rest… will come.'

Silence, nothing but the water. The hand withdrew. Her stomach relaxed.

*

'So,' her father said later, when the names were being called off the list and everyone had to say their goodbyes, 'it's time.'

Her kiss landed somewhere on the side of his neck; she smelled his tobacco, felt the hard stubble on his cheeks. He placed his calloused hand on the back of her head and she lost her balance; he didn't know his own strength.

'Well then, all the best.'

He sniffed hard and let her go. They stood facing each other like this, father and daughter, her disgrace between them.

'Keep to the straight and narrow.'

She had never planned to do otherwise. Her mother's kiss was warmer, a Judas kiss. The embrace went on, and she endured it because of the occasion.

'Be a good wife to Derk. A good mother to his children.'

She could smell her mother's saliva, and furtively wiped her cheek as she walked to the plane. For a moment it seemed like she was electrified – look at me, here I go. A bungalow with big windows and a sunny garden. There she is, walking through the sunlit rooms, a grown-up, Derk's good

wife, his children's good mother, her wide summery skirt swirling gracefully around her calves, who knows, maybe even high-heeled shoes, why
not, suddenly anything's possible, they tap pleasantly against the tiles on
the wide pavement, someone lifts up the skirt, she's happy because she and
Derk are now man and wife and live in a country where the sun always
shines. In their atlas at home, she'd looked at pictures of New Zealand,
with lakes and mountains and forests. She'd read about the people and the
climate, that the North Island was warm, almost tropical. One sentence
had stayed with her: In Auckland, the roses bloom all year round. At home
the windows were fogging over, but *she* was headed for everlasting spring.

She squeezed in among the chosen ones. The reporter for the *Polygoon
Newsreel* motioned to his cameraman and raised his microphone. 'All
around me I see happy faces and eyes glistening with anticipation...'

Emboldened by her freedom, she tried to flash a film-star smile, and
she was amazed at how well she was able to produce the requested waving
motions, smile *cheese!* for the photographers, a row of gabardine raincoats
with cameras around their necks, *cheese!* over and over, just like the other
young women around her. Indeed, it was striking, as if KLM had selected
them because of this: although there were a few married couples, a brother
and sister, a group of journalists, and a young man on his own, all the
others were girls – of every shape and size, glowing and giggling, with bags
and coats, their hair freshly curled, young brides on their way to their
fiancés, a planeload of rosy cheeks, *cheese!*

'Fleeing from the housing shortage and unemployment, they expect
their lives to be a hundred per cent better!'

During the Wilhelmus, the Dutch national anthem, she couldn't make
out her parents among the people on the viewing platform.

'I will remain true to my homeland until my death.' She sang along,
scanning the crowd all the while, they couldn't have left already.

'...Could it be that right now these young people are being plagued by
doubts? What are they leaving behind? What is the likelihood they will
ever see their beloved families again? New Zealand is so far away, and the

journey by sea is a long and expensive one. No, this could very well be the last time they will ever see their fathers and mothers, their sisters and brothers…'

While waving goodbye as they walked up the steps to the plane she thought she saw her father's head for a moment, behind all of the other heads. Why were they squeezed in at the back? Their poverty, their small-ness, struck her like a lightning bolt and paralysed her. Even so she kept waving, with a supreme effort she made the same enthusiastic motions as her fellow passengers.

Later on, as the *Abel Tasman* was flying over Haarlem and everyone around her was exclaiming about the miniature city down below, a mist of tears obstructed her view. Anyway, she didn't dare look around because if she did the plane might fall out of the sky.

*

'Dear Father and Mother,' she wrote on a postcard as she sat in the hotel, crying tears of remorse at her haughtiness, her ingratitude, 'dear Father and Mother, soon my long journey will begin, everyone is in good spirits, and London is a beautiful city. I miss you already.

'Think of me, your daughter Ada.'

3

IN THE FAITH IN WHICH Ada was raised, you never knew for sure whether you were damned or chosen. Even if you'd led an exemplary life of pious devotion and never missed a church service, you only knew for certain where you were headed on Judgement Day, when God would point to His chosen ones from among the departed believers, and provide new bones for their wasted bodies, new flesh, strong muscles, and healthy organs, and cover it all with glowing, wrinkle-free skin. He would lead the fortunate into heaven and allow them to spend eternity in His presence, singing psalms and waving palm fronds, dressed in white robes.

Unfortunately, some believers were born damned, and eternal suffering awaited them. Nothing could be done to change this, it was predestined. But because you never knew for sure during your lifetime, you had to do your best anyway. Ada did her best. Deep in her heart, she feared for the worst. She had an inborn tendency for that which was sinful.

On bright summer days, her mother would put the white laundry out to bleach on the grass. She bent down and stood up, and every time she did, the pleats of her multicoloured striped skirt would move along with her. The little girl toddled blissfully behind her, drunk with the smell of the grass, the washing, and sweet Mother. When she bent down again to spread out a sheet, the girl grabbed on to the hem of those cheery colours with her chubby little hands. And as her mother straightened up, she lifted the skirt up in the air as high as she could and stepped into a deliciously warm tent. The sun filtering through the fabric made the light there enchantingly beautiful. Her mother's strong bare legs held up her tent. She crowed with pleasure, but at the same moment the skirt above her was yanked back, and a vice-like hand grabbed her by the neck, shoving her head forward and shaking it back and forth. 'Don't you ever, ever do that again!'

Her mother's voice was shrill and high with shock.

A dark force kept sabotaging her. She drew pictures on the blank pages of her old school exercise books; for hours on end she would fill the pages with fairytale figures that her imagination brought to life. But when she turned twelve her pencil started to stray and she drew naked women. She took her time filling in the triangle with tiny lines. She carefully placed the two dots on the half moons. Even before the pleasant warmth could spread through her body, she was seized by fear and ripped the page out of the exercise book, distraught. Although she could destroy that filthy piece of trash so her parents would never see it, God saw everything and never forgot. In this way the stains on her soul accumulated, one after another.

*

When they arrived in London, the sixty-four passengers were taken around the city by bus and brought to a big hotel, where they shuffled awestruck through the plushly carpeted halls. This was followed by a press conference, and at eight o'clock an official dinner, sumptuous and elegant. Some mild grumbling ensued – in Holland you eat at half past five. Three long tables, beautifully laid, with special menus which they all took away with them, because everything was a souvenir. Such things would become precious, even more than they could imagine. They were served turkey. Ada, her stomach empty from vomiting, ate hungrily and stared at the glass of red wine on the table in front of her. She tried to keep to herself as much as she could, afraid she might have to talk about herself. She shared her hotel room with a remarkable-looking girl who had dark curly

33

hair and a deep, husky voice, and who disappeared into the city after dinner with a few of the journalists. Ada lay awake in the unfamiliar room, staring at the antique linen cupboard that was illuminated by a street lamp. It was nearly four when someone fumbled with the lock and the door opened softly. She closed her eyes and pretended to be asleep, and although she couldn't see anything, she caught a whiff of heavy, sweet perfume mixed with the smell of liquor. A woman's deep voice hummed in the bathroom, 'Don't fence me in...', a song everyone knew. The next morning her roommate didn't partake of the sausages and baked beans. Ada wondered if she was Jewish and whether she had suffered. After breakfast there was to be a boat trip on the Thames, but in addition to the dark-haired girl, there were a few more who hadn't made it out of bed yet so the activity was dropped. In the end, they were all brought back to the airport in buses, where they were weighed and given their tickets. Then at twelve o'clock there was lunch, with the press in attendance and KLM's chairman of the board in the middle. 'The trip won't be an easy one,' he predicted, 'but you're young and aren't yet bothered by rheumatism. The most important thing is to get to Christchurch.' The emigrants were blinded by flash bulbs, and questions were put to them in English – the price you pay for fame. Ada made herself invisible and plucked at the embroidery on the tablecloth. The programme unfurled of its own accord, like a huge wave rolling in, and she had to tell herself to keep breathing.

At around two o'clock, they were driven to the apron, where the planes taking part in the race were waiting and the Duke of Gloucester was being introduced to the pilots. A brass band was playing. Although Ada had never been away from home overnight, none of this seemed to really sink in. Maybe the magnitude of all of these festivities was too much for her.

They had to wait again on the apron. It was overcast and raw, and they all agreed it was the perfect day to emigrate. A tiresome, noisy October wind tugged at the coats of the emigrants and at the last of Ada's curls. A deafening roar like that of Judgement Day, the wind and the aeroplane engines, a sound that seemed to her to be heralding something irreversible, an end, or was it a beginning – something that would change everything.

*

To hide her own awkwardness, she joined a group that was watching a lanky girl in a wedding dress pose in front of their plane beneath 'Flying Dutchman' in large letters and the number 21, which was their number.

The girl was clasping a bouquet in one arm and with the other she waved at the invisible people at home, and every time she raised her arm in the air the wind would take hold of her veil and send it fluttering out in front of her face. The gabardine raincoats, who'd come along with them, looked down into their cameras and cried out for more, and each time, the girl would wave and the veil would wrap itself around her face; it was quite a tussle, but her enthusiasm was undiminished and she smiled and waved, pulling back the white tulle tirelessly, though Ada could see her cheeks were getting redder. Towards the back stood the solitary young man, one hand placed loosely in a trouser pocket. He smiled as if to say he thought all of that posing business was ridiculous. He looked as if he was cold, the way he rolled his cigarette between his fingers before taking a puff; he reminded her of one of those photographs in the display case of the pub in their village, where on Saturday night they would show films she was never allowed to go to. She had studied those photographs end-lessly, leaning against her bicycle, until she was sure she knew which story was behind them. He was someone with a story. She watched him as he strolled off in the direction of a man at a painter's easel who was immor-talizing their Liftmaster in oils.

To the left of the Liftmaster stood the Viscount from England, and to the right, the Hastings from New Zealand. This was the entire handicap section; some countries had dropped out, she didn't know why, hadn't read all of the newspaper articles or listened to all of the speeches. An incessant, deep rumbling came from the planes, as if they were impa-tiently pawing at the ground with their wheels, as if the fuselage was

35

flexing its frame to prepare for take-off, which was getting closer and closer. They were going to win, people were saying, KLM had calculated it all very precisely; you might say that a race like this was actually won on paper. She'd read this somewhere, another sentence that had stayed in her head. 'You might say that a race like this is actually won on paper,' she would sometimes say to herself offhandedly. Saying this out loud to another person without blushing required more courage than she possessed.

In a handicap race, being the last to arrive doesn't mean you've lost. They were heavily laden – sixty-four young people full of hope – and so had a handicap, like a kind of hunchback or clubfoot that brings all kinds of advantages along with it. The ancient market gardener in her village whose body had grown into a ninety-degree angle was allowed to sit in the front during band rehearsals.

Even though the Liftmaster was the favourite, all the speeches had made everyone nervous – you didn't know what was going to happen along the way, and the honour of their country was at stake. Everyone seemed to be so caught up in it all that Ada was ashamed of her own indifference. She kept trying to find the right facial expression so she wouldn't stand out amidst all the excitement.

A long way off stood the five Canberras – *bombers!* her brothers had whooped – small, streamlined jet planes, two from Australia and three from England. That was the speed section, which didn't involve them.

She shivered and pulled her jacket more tightly around her.

Behind the ropes at the air terminal the spectators waited, people who lived in the terrifying city of London and considered this to be quite normal. Her world was the path that led to the church, the dyke, the green, the windmill, the cattails and the Westplas, the lake whose muddy bottom you could feel beneath your feet in summer. So quiet you could hear the occasional car coming from miles away. The only violence was perpetrated by the pike, which would pull the baby ducklings under (*plop!* right before your eyes, from one second to the next the little creature would vanish and all that remained would be a little ring on the water, that was it, the mother duck just continued on her way, didn't even notice she only had three ducklings left, and shortly thereafter, even the ring would have disappeared). And the thunderstorms in the middle of the night, when roof tiles would fly through the air and her father would herd everyone into the living room in their pyjamas, and somewhere out in the fields there would always be a cow that had been struck by lightning. Sometimes, in her ears, the sermons that thundered out of the pulpit into the church. But there had been times when she'd had to close her eyes to the city of London; it was incomprehensible that, in that tangle of streets, in the rush of all that traffic, in among the tall buildings, there were people who knew the way and moved along looking relaxed. But there they were behind the ropes, in their thousands, all of them trying to catch a glimpse of the Duke of Gloucester holding the green starting flag – because how many times in your life do you get the chance to see a real duke, even if he does look like any other man in a suit?

*

It was after four when the officials put their empty champagne glasses back on the trays. The three captains and their co-pilots posed one last time, as the heroes they already were, while the names of the Dutch emigrants were called out. They had to assemble on the steel aircraft steps, which were too narrow for so many people and resulted in jokes and fits of laughter. Ada was exhausted and stayed at the bottom of the steps to avoid the crush; she could see how insignificant they all were beneath the plane's gleaming belly, beneath the propellers. Her roommate with the dark curly hair came walking up, swinging her hips, wearing a pair of wide trousers; she returned the curious looks that came her way, seemed to be used to it. This morning when Ada saw her lying in bed her face had been drained of colour, but now the first thing she noticed were her lips, which had been painted a bold shade of deep red – she couldn't take her eyes off them.

The last to arrive was the lanky girl, who came running up, flushed from exertion, the wedding dress in a garment bag over her arm. A section of the veil stuck out of her blue case, which pitched from side to side. KLM had handed them out, their bon voyage cases. The girl tried to squeeze in among the people on the steps, but it was too crowded. So, when the final photograph was being taken, the three found themselves standing next to each other out in front.

'Did you see me just then?'

The girl had to raise her voice to be heard above the din; she coughed.

'For the *Illustrated Catholic Review*, exciting, huh?'

Once more they waved to the invisible people at home, said cheese, stretched out the corners of their mouths.

'I'm going to be on the cover, too. Pa's going to send it to me.'

The people at home who before long would open the newspaper and see you waving so bravely, and who would then be sorry they'd let you go so easily. Ada knew for certain they'd be able to spot her, being right down in front like that. How sweet she looks, her father will say, look at her waving. Her mother leans over his paper, sees her duckling – too late.

'And a women's magazine is also interested.'

Her arm was like lead and she had to lower it. She bowed her head, and breathed through her mouth, nauseous from the smell of fuel that hung about the plane. A string of little whimpering sounds slipped out, which were fortunately lost in the roar. The route they would take had now been announced, and the names throbbed inside her head. Rome, Baghdad, Karachi, Rangoon, Jakarta, Darwin, and Brisbane, these were the places they would stop along the way, and then over the Tasman Sea to Christchurch. She fought back her tears valiantly, fussed with the strands of hair that had escaped; not one of her curls had withstood the gusts of wind. Mama, Mama, I'm drowning, everything's so unfamiliar, where am I headed?

Just then, someone behind her leaned over her shoulder and she heard a man's voice in her ear. 'Before long, everyone in Holland will be sitting in front of the radio so they can follow this race...' She turned around and looked into the face of the lone young man. Grey-green eyes, an intent expression. A somewhat prominent nose. He smiled pleasantly, self-assured, pushed back a brown lock of hair that had blown onto his forehead.

'This is a historic moment. And you're there.'

He kept looking at her, waited patiently for his words to register. The noise receded. She grew in the silence, stretched out and filled up, was lifted far above the throng, with a new, velvety skin.

He pointed to the distinguished man with the green flag on the apron. 'How many people can say they've stood face to face with the Duke of Gloucester and that the man waved an old handkerchief at them?'

She burst out laughing. 'I can!'

Next to her, the lanky girl turned and looked at them curiously, and from the other side a deep, throaty laugh came from between the red lips. All three of them turned towards the lone young man.

'I'm Frank,' he said. They all shook hands. Bracelets tinkled. 'Esther.'

The lanky girl with the funny face was called Marjorie. She pronounced her name as if she were English instead of Dutch, and Ada saw Frank's eyes light up with mild derision.

She was the last one to say her name. 'Beautiful,' he said, and kept hold of her hand, covering it with his left one for a moment. He savoured her name, which she only now heard properly. 'Ada van Holland... beautiful... a wide river... the bow of a ship through the water.'

Above their heads, a sign came from the open door. The chosen ones could go inside.

4

SO THIS WAS IT, THEN, the ship, their ark, this silvery grey cabin with curved walls, the carpeting in the aisles a soothing blue, three seats on the left and two on the right, all the way back to the tail. Welcome on board. Two stewards and a stewardess, their uniforms the same familiar colour, took their coats and stowed them quickly and efficiently in a cloakroom at the back, and showed the passengers to their seats. The operation had been well thought out and this instilled confidence; within ten minutes everyone was seated. Of course, the seats had been assigned to them by name, maybe even according to their weight, but other rules seemed to apply to the young man called Frank. With a steady hand, he steered Ada to two seats somewhere in the middle, placed her next to the window, and sat down beside her as if it had been planned that way. Esther and Marjorie plopped down behind them without a second thought, and Ada knew for sure it was because of this boy, as if they didn't want to let him go now that they had found him. It took a little persuasion, others had to move a bit further to the back, but it wasn't a problem, everyone was too excited to make an issue of it. The journalists made straight for the tail and opened out the tray tables for their typewriters.

Their hand luggage went into the nets above their heads; they had to stow their bon voyage cases under their seats. Marjorie opened her case to repack her veil. Ada, who still didn't know how to cope with the nearness of the stranger beside her, turned around in her seat to watch. This is me, this traveller who's casually leaning over the back of her seat. Marjorie smiled at her. 'Pretty, isn't it.'

Ada nodded, even though it hadn't been a question.

'New Zealanders seem to have quite conservative taste,' Esther said, as she examined her neighbour's wedding veil with her fingers, 'I'm going to take advantage of that.' The verdict in her eyes did not escape Ada. She'd never seen a woman like her up close before.

Marjorie folded and stuffed until the yards of wandering netting bent to her will. And how did Esther plan to do this, take advantage of that conservative taste? The long black eyelashes opened and closed coolly, you couldn't call it blinking. 'I'm a fashion designer.'

In the picture with the skull at the teacher's house, the woman powders her nose one last time, rises from her stool, gracefully sweeps back the wide folds of her evening gown, and trips off to the theatre, where there isn't a skull in sight.

'Are you going to get married?' asked Marjorie.

'That's the plan.'

'And what if you have a baby?'

Esther pushed away the last of the unruly tulle, her bracelets tinkling fiercely. 'I might even design fabric,' she said.

Let me be by myself in the evenin' breeze…

*

Newspapers and packs of chewing gum were handed out. One of the stewards walked to the front: 'Good afternoon, ladies and gentlemen… I don't know if you can hear me all the way at the back, but in any case I would like to welcome you on board on behalf of the entire crew…' The cabin crew was working at full speed, a well-oiled machine, they had a reputation to uphold and the chewing gum was part of this, but its meaning eluded Ada.

Her new acquaintance noticed this.

'For your ears, when we take off.'

Ada was puzzled and stared at the package, trying to imagine how that worked.

'Is there something wrong?'

She hated her own ignorance.

'Do you have to chew it first?'

He kept looking at her, and his eyes started to twinkle.

'Yes.'

The only thing she could do was to pay attention to what the others did. She turned towards the window, saw the Duke of Gloucester by the chalk line and pointed outside in relief, look!

Frank leaned forward in front of her, and she held her breath. A chiselled profile, maybe even an arrogant one, his nose not prominent enough to be considered a hook nose, but prominent enough to command respect. The face of a ruler.

Others had spotted the duke as well, and everyone tried to watch what was going on through the small windows, their noses pushed up against the glass. Marjorie tapped them on the shoulder, did they know he was Queen Elizabeth's uncle? In New Zealand, she was going to be their queen too. The stewardess walked to the open doorway, waved at the photographers one last time, and shut and secured the heavy door. They were alone.

Gradually, all the overhead lights came on in the cabin.

The aircraft jolted, the rows jerked – *The Flying Dutchman* taxied ponderously to the starting line. The three planes competing in the handicap section were to take off in five-minute intervals, and they were first in line. From inside the small windows, the travellers waved again. Not Ada, she'd done enough waving at people she couldn't see, and Frank didn't wave either.

The plane came to a halt at the chalk mark, and for a moment everyone pitched forward, suspended in their seat belts. Outside, the duke raised the green flag. An odd, edgy silence filled the cabin. Then the sound of the engines swelled, deep and dark. Ada closed her eyes. Our Father who art in heaven. The stewardess was the last to sit down and hastily buckled herself in. She pointed at her watch for the people sitting nearby. 'Seventy seconds to go.' Ada moaned softly and Frank took her hand, but because this wasn't proper she carefully withdrew it, feeling as though this wasn't proper either. Luckily there was the duke.

One moment of supreme suspense, then down came the flag.

'Step on it,' said Frank.

They lunged over the starting line with an enormous jolt, past the men with the walkie-talkies, down the runway. Pressed back against her seat, she endured this powerful force for the second time, while her heart beat wildly inside her chest. Our Father who art in heaven. There were thuds and thumps coming from under the plane.

'We're in the air,' cried the steward. 'Twenty-five seconds after the start and we're in the air! Not even halfway down the runway!' The plane tilted, wobbled, dropped and climbed. The same awful feeling in her stomach as yesterday.

'Ten thousand galloping horses are pulling us into the sky,' said Frank.

But hooves should be able to throw off sparks. She saw horses pawing at the void, falling straight out of the sky, a bloody mountain of broken bones and shattered skulls, with bits of brain spattered everywhere. Thy will be done. She squeezed the armrest and focused on the part of the wing she could see. They were hanging at an angle. Something was wrong. The idea that people can fly was an arrogant mistake. Forgive us.

The sound of singing girls rose above the roar of the engines. Some merry souls had adapted a familiar Dutch football song for the occasion. It was normally sung when the national team played – although they hadn't been able to achieve much on the football pitch, maybe Holland could become the champion up in the sky. From behind them came a throaty laugh. 'Such a modest song.'

Frank grinned. Marjorie joined in at the top of her lungs. No-one else seemed to notice anything. We're turning upside down, she wanted to scream, but her jaws wouldn't budge. She was glued to her seat by a spasm of fear and could feel the aircraft vibrate helplessly as it struggled during its final moments in the air.

'What is it?'

She couldn't look at him, because that would mean taking her eyes off the wing.

'Are you afraid?'

She nodded almost imperceptibly towards the outside of the plane.

'We're making a turn, that's all.' He kept looking at her. The plane tilted, levelled off, then tilted again. 'Nothing's going to happen. It's fun if you just give in to it. Just like at the fair.' She was dying, and in the distance someone was saying something about a fair.

'Do you think we'll crash if you talk?'

The rustling of a wrapper as he opened the gum. 'If your ears start to bother you, just chew on this. Here.' He held something in front of her mouth, she shook her head, no, she couldn't, not now. He laughed and put it is his own mouth.

'All right then…'

His hand slid calmly over hers, which was clamped talon-like around the armrest; she felt a pleasant, dry warmth.

'You just go ahead and concentrate, then at least we'll stay up in the air.'

She cautiously moved her eyes in his direction. He patted her hand amicably.

'I hope you can keep it up all the way to Christchurch.'

By now many of the others had also joined in the chorus, and things were loosening up. Frank joined in good-naturedly, chewing gum, singing bass. Once in a while he gave her an encouraging nod.

She loosened her grip on the armrest and tried to reflect. But the plane jumped and bumped through the clouds, which didn't make reflection any easier. Only when the last frothy wisps of clouds slid off the fuselage and they flew into a dazzling new world, a world in which the aircraft seemed to calm down and which bathed the cabin in brilliant white sunlight, only then did Ada let out a sigh. She finished her prayer, relaxed her fingers, shut her eyes, and let the sun glide over her face.

*

There was something about this stranger. Less than half an hour later – by this time they were flying at cruising speed and it turned out they were two minutes ahead of their own flight plan – Esther was sitting on his armrest on the aisle, and Marjorie kept sticking her head in between their seats. Ada was glued to her seat again, because she'd noticed that some of the panels were shifting slightly and what's more, thin curls of smoke or steam were coming in here and there. The sound of the engines remained deep and threatening, sometimes starting to whine for no clear reason. Everything in the cabin was vibrating. It kept her busy, and she latched on to the smile on the stewardess's face. But all the animated buzzing around the young man did not escape her notice.

Marjorie held out a photo of her fiancé.

'His name is Hans. Hans Doorman. Handsome, isn't he. He's been there two years now, and I got a letter every week. He's got very beautiful hands. He's working as a carpenter. He's not really a carpenter, you know, he went to college!'

Ada tried to imagine Derk's hands. She'd felt them on her body, the groping hands of a drowning man.

'He had to sign a contract, two years as a labourer, wherever they want to send him, otherwise he wouldn't have got the subsidy.'

Frank passed the photo on to Ada. A young man in plus fours stood on top of a dune looking off into the distance, deep in thought. 'I'm under contract, too. A "scheme emigrant", they called it. It's the same for me, I just have to wait and see. "Schemer," the official said. I'm a schemer.'

Esther leaned towards him and said in a husky voice that he didn't look like one. She took the photo from Ada, but barely glanced at it.

'I don't want to have to work just anywhere,' said Marjorie. 'I mean

45

really, I've got my nursing diploma.' She gave an indignant sniff. '*To be honest*,' she said in English, 'I don't want to work at all, I want to get married... and as soon as we've got somewhere to live, we'll have children.'

'You've ordered them already?' asked Esther.

'It's all the same to me,' said Frank, '*to be honest*. I'm in no hurry. I know what I want.'

Marjorie snatched the photo away from Esther. 'Do you know they don't have prams there? They carry their babies on their backs!'

Esther leaned even closer to Frank, and although Ada could smell her perfume, she didn't allow herself to be distracted, because she had just realized that the smile on the face of the stewardess could just as well be a frightened grimace.

'What do you want, then?'

'My own farm,' said Frank.

Now would have been Ada's chance to make a good impression because she came from a farming community, but what if a strange sound were to come out of her throat and everyone were to look at her, then there would still be fifty hours to go in which she wouldn't have the courage to go to the lavatory. So instead, she stared at the stewardess who was handing out packages, and acted as if the conversation didn't interest her.

'Do you come from a farming family?' Esther asked.

He shook his head. 'My father was a doctor in the Dutch East Indies. But I want to become a farmer.' She'd spent countless hours on the farm where her father worked as a farmhand, fascinated by the wide leather belt the farmer wore around his waist when he was driving the tractor, and the smell of the gigantic pig that was kept in a separate shed and was no longer able to stand up.

'So you didn't go to college,' Marjorie said.

'May I present this to you on behalf of KLM?' The package for the women was considerably larger than the one for men. Ada stuck in a finger and felt a skein of wool.

'Colonial School of Agriculture in Deventer,' said Frank. 'I wanted to go back to the East Indies...' He fell silent, ripped open the paper – it contained a KLM necktie and a blue cigarette case. '...but that's out of the question now, with everything that's happened there. And Holland is too cold for me. So I thought, emigrate – then I can put it to good use.'

'Good plan, schemer,' Esther said. She was totally uninterested in the package on her lap.

Frank gave his cigarette case a quick once-over. 'I'm in no hurry.' Then he suddenly turned to the person who hadn't spoken yet. 'And what about you?'

'I do,' Ada said. 'Come from a farming family, I mean,' she said. Her cheeks turned hot and red, she picked at the wool, but noticed how he was looking at her.

Marjorie held up a brooch. 'Did you see this? Would you look at that, it's darling. I'll bet it's real silver.' Three charms dangled in front of her eyes: a little wooden shoe, a tiny sailboat, and a miniature windmill.

*

The band of clouds beneath the Liftmaster gradually thinned out and in the end disappeared entirely. The plane droned on through a deep red evening sky. She was getting a bit used to it already. The stewardess, who was handing out the meals, gestured gracefully in front of Frank, pointing to the ribbons of lights they could see down below. 'On the left you can see... on the right is... and there just beyond: *voilà Paris.*' She was French by birth, she explained, as she slightly exaggerated her coquettish accent.

There were four courses: first, soup – consommé, Ada's menu called it, then pork chops with mushrooms... She couldn't believe it, she was flying to Paris through the most exquisite sunset and they were being served a four-course meal with strawberries for dessert, provided by a Dutch grower for the air-race passengers, followed by coffee and ginger tarts, just as if they were well-to-do. From now on, everything would be different.

Every foot this plane travelled was bringing her closer to her better future. Above the bowl of soup, she closed her eyes and gratefully folded her hands. Next to her, Frank had already started eating. He put down his spoon, murmured an apology and waited. Now matter how hard she tried, she was finding it impossible to devote her thoughts to God as long as this stranger was sitting so close to her that she had to angle her legs towards the window to keep from touching him. She kept her eyes closed for a while and then opened them again. He was watching her with interest.

'Was anyone home?'

She was sitting next to a heathen.

*

The first leg lasted three hours, three hours in which Ada reconciled herself to the undulating ship, the constant vibration. But just before Rome, the plane went into a steep dive, bumping and bouncing. It headed straight through an unstable layer of air, and her fear returned in all its intensity. It was nothing, said the stewardess with the French accent, just ordinary turbulence. A stack of trays clattered noisily to the ground, and Marjorie let out a lively little yelp. Frank joked with Ada to take her mind off things, but she was in tears by the time she was able to make out the lights of the landing beacons, and when the door was opened after landing, letting in the cold night air, she would have liked nothing better than to get off the plane and walk back home. They weren't allowed off, she knew this, the stopover was only for refuelling. Outside, the refuelling trucks were already standing by, and airport personnel ran to the plane with hoses.

'Eleven thousand litres of fresh fuel,' said Frank. He said it as though he would have enjoyed a taste. The Italians shouted and cursed as they tore about, and the captain rushed out to keep the ladders from damaging the wings. Before they knew it the chocks were being removed from in front of the wheels. A short time later, Ada squeezed the armrest as Rome faded away beneath them.

'Fourteen minutes.' Frank was keeping track of the race.

Everyone was elated: forty minutes had been scheduled for this stop, which meant they were now thirty-five minutes ahead. Ada had no time for gladness – she was battling the turbulence.

*

Then night came. Although she would have liked to have slept – the heavy plane was steering a smooth course towards Baghdad – she couldn't sleep; no-one could, the excitement was too intense. The cabin started to resemble a cosy living room where people played games while outside it was dark. Everywhere people were reading or talking quietly. Esther was playing cards with the journalists in the back for a bottle of whisky. Marjorie was practising new English words out loud.

Frank was reading a book about the Spanish Civil War and writing down details of the flight in a notebook. In his deep, pleasant voice he told Ada about Java, how as a little boy he'd seen the Uiver fly over and how he'd hoped he would one day be able to fly in an air race himself. About their large tropical garden, with behind it the jungle, inhabited by animals that made mysterious noises. About the enormous bushes with flowers that could intoxicate you with their smell. Ada asked questions and she could see it all right there in front of her eyes. To give herself something to do, she picked up the blue KLM wool and knitting needles and started to cast on, but couldn't decide what to knit or for whom. So she just kept casting on until there was hardly any room left on the needle.

He saw this and fell silent.

'Casting on,' she said, and had to laugh at the puzzled look on his face. 'That's what you call this. This is the only way I know how to do it. My mother is going to…'

She faltered. Put down her knitting needles. She would never see any of them again.

'Your mother is going to?'

'Teach me another method.'

49

'Right,' said Frank.

They kept looking at each other, while their ship travelled relentlessly on through the night, with no way back, further and further away from mothers and different knitting methods. 'This one seems to work well enough,' he said softly.

He brushed her face with the palm of his hand. She wanted to nuzzle her face in that hand, like a puppy. Now they were both bashful. He picked up the other knitting needle and studied it. Ada recovered and took up her knitting. The touch still burned. She reached casually for the needle in his hands.

'May I?'

He held it away from her.

'You've already got one,' he said. She tried again.

'I want two.'

'Don't be so greedy.'

'Give it to me.'

She couldn't get it away from him, he was faster than she was and she got the giggles. He taunted her with the knitting needle, moved it in front of her face and pulled it back again just in time, poked her in the side with it.

'Ow!'

'I can have one, too, can't I?'

'No!'

'Why not?'

'Because I said so.'

'Suit yourself,' he announced matter-of-factly, and all at once pulled the other needle out of the stitches that had been cast on with such care.

She let out a cry and took a swipe at him. He fended her off, grabbing her arm and pulling her towards him, their faces close together. She was gasping from laughing so hard, but wasn't ready to give up.

'I'm going to call the captain.'

'Can he knit?'

'He'll throw you off the plane!'

She felt an incredible urge to fight with him well up, to grab this heathen and squeeze the air right out of his chest, to push him down into the aisle, to fall on top of him and keep him down with all her might, her knees on his upper arms, rolling mercilessly over his muscles like her brothers sometimes did, pinning his hands to the ground with all the savage strength she possessed, panting and moaning, muscles quivering, her face just above his, beg for mercy, say it, it had to hurt and be a real struggle.

'What are you doing?' asked Marjorie.

*

There was quite a strong depression over the Balkans, they were told. This prospect had kept her from falling asleep, but the foul weather was so long in coming that she finally closed the blue curtain and leaned up against the wall with her head on a pillow made from the same fabric, exhausted like everyone around her. Everyone except Esther, who was beating the journalists at cards. Marjorie was snoring, softly but unmistakably.

Frank had been in the cockpit. They were too heavily laden to fly over the depression, and although the plane was strong enough to fly right through it, the captain had decided not to – people might get sick, not everyone had a strong stomach, so he was carefully leading his flock around the thunderstorm. If Ada had stayed awake, she would have seen the menacing clouds in the distance, and the lightning flashes that lit up the clouds. But she was asleep. It was warm and close, she moved restlessly, and dreamed she was locked in a classroom with a group of prisoners and that they were being guarded by soldiers. One of the soldiers raised his gun above her head, and she woke up at the moment the rifle butt hit her skull. She saw that her neighbour was watching her in the half-light.

'Not so bad, eh? The weather.'

She nodded drowsily. It was incomprehensible that he hadn't looked away. This man did things that were not done. But he did them so naturally that you started to doubt yourself, and wonder whether there was perhaps nothing unusual about looking at a woman you didn't know as she slept in the darkness. Or whether it might even be considered to be an expression of friendliness. He had a broad, high forehead and full eyebrows that sloped downwards, which might have made him appear somehow sad had it not been for the self-assured look in his eyes. She became aware that the buttons on her dress had come undone and that her slip was showing, and who knows, maybe even her brassiere. As she slept her dress had slid up and exposed one of her legs – she could feel the air on the bare skin above the top of her nylon stocking. Inwardly, she swiftly set everything right, covered herself and turned away, but her body didn't move. The straight and narrow was getting broader, and she was powerless to change it. She closed her eyes and went back to sleep.

*

In the middle of the night, the lights came on and they were served cold orange juice and strong coffee in preparation for the descent into Baghdad. Where are we? mumbled Ada. They had just flown over the Lebanese coast near Beirut, said Frank, and she wondered whether he'd been watching her all this time.

'Good morning, ladies and gentlemen...'

The steward announced that the Hastings, the plane from New Zealand, had run into the storm and was now forty minutes behind *The Flying Dutchman*, news that was greeted with cheers from the creased, sleepy faces. A report had come in that the English Viscount was about to make its first stop halfway down the Persian Gulf – the plane had flown straight through from London to Bahrain, carrying extra fuel tanks and only a few passengers. You could see that KLM had its spies everywhere. From the back of the plane, Esther returned to her seat unsteadily, yawning as she tidied her curls.

Frank talked Ada through the descent. That night he'd spent quite a bit of time in the cockpit, and he told her that according to the instructions there would be four twenty-five kilo bags of ballast waiting at the airport in Baghdad, along with a main refuelling truck and one in reserve. There'd be a special brand of hydraulic fluid, and all kinds of testing equipment and three sets of universal steps and wheel chocks and fire extinguishers (there was no need to worry, because this was a precautionary measure and in fact nothing ever actually went wrong, it just showed how thorough KLM was being, she should bear this in mind), a starting unit and a lavatory truck and so much more. Everything had been put down on paper: twelve bottles of beer, twenty-four bottles of juice, five hot-water containers, three large cold-water tanks. 'They'll unload four racks of dirty sherry glasses and bring in four racks of clean ones. Seventy-six plates, seventy-six cups, seventy-six saucers... shall I go on?'

Yes, he should go on. She wasn't listening, but the pleasure in his voice took away some of her fears, and the touch of his hand on hers was a friendly gesture. It would be impossible to find this offensive, should you happen to see it.

Months in advance, bulky sets of documents had been delivered to all the landing sites and to the alternative airports, containing mimeographed sheets of all of the separate instructions. There were detailed drawings of the aeroplane, with all the tanks and their access points. There was a complete technical supplement, it was a battle plan, you know, and had been worked out to the last detail. The procedure had been rehearsed a hundred times at every airport. While they were on their way to their next stop, hundreds of people were already there and waiting for them along with full tanks of fuel. Frank's just a little boy, thought Ada. Beneath her, in the first red light of dawn, she could see groups of palm trees like those in the Bible in an otherwise barren, arid landscape.

*

In spite of hundreds of rehearsals, it seemed to be just as chaotic in Baghdad as it had been in Rome. The passengers were to remain seated. A few girls gathered around the open door to catch a glimpse of a country they had never been and would never see again. They waved at the members of the local Dutch community, who stood behind the barriers holding flags, at a little boy who was dressed in a traditional Volendam costume for the occasion, with wide wool trousers and a little black cap.

When Esther complained that she wanted to go outside, Marjorie set her straight: it would take too much precious time from the race for such a large group to leave the plane and get back on again, she had to understand this, they'd all wanted to be part of the race, right? Ada studied the dark-skinned mechanic who was sitting outside her window on the wing, his energetic gestures, the sweat on his brown face, the black hair on his arms. He crawled back to the ladder and suddenly looked right at her. A wide grin appeared beneath his black moustache. He placed his right hand on his heart and bowed, then disappeared from view. 'Yes,' said Frank, 'you're more beautiful than the Empress of Persia.' She tingled with warmth; he shouldn't be saying things like that. It wasn't true anyway. So she was glad of the commotion when a man in a turban presented a large bunch of dates to the steward, who'd had to accept the gift so as not to seem rude. There was nothing about dates in the instruction manual. The bunch weighed several pounds. Everything had been included in the calculations, right down to the curtains on the windows. The passengers had been required to provide their weight on their application, and had been put on a scale at London Airport. (Ada had gained quite a bit of weight; someone had made a joke about this, but no-one could have suspected how close they'd come to the truth.)

They would just have to take the dates along and leave them in Karachi. When they were airborne, the dates were placed on the empty seat next to Marjorie, while Esther was sitting on the lap of a journalist at the back of the plane, speaking into a microphone, giving her own personal account for the radio. A couple of hours later, the stewardess paused next to the seat with the dates, and arched her thin French eyebrows: 'What do we have here?'

Ada turned around. Marjorie blushed a deep blotchy red all the way down her neck.

'I ate a few, there's no harm in that, is there?'

The stewardess tactfully held her tongue, and took the half-eaten bunch of dates away with her. Marjorie stared out the window in indignation. We won't be getting rid of that weight anytime soon, Frank murmured in Ada's ear. A laugh came bubbling up inside her, and she wished she could stay on this ark with him for ever. Then she decided that her knitting was going to become a sweater for Derk. She worked diligently, or at least more diligently than she had at first.

*

The third leg was another six-hour flight, and then the whole operation was repeated in Karachi on Friday afternoon at half past twelve local time. When the door opened and the desert heat poured into the cabin and settled inside the skulls of the chosen ones, Ada – just like all the others – would have given anything to be allowed to go outside. Onto the apron where the people from the Dutch embassy were standing in the shadow of the hangar and where, in spite of the heat, dark-skinned men worked like horses to get fifteen litres of soup, a hundred and sixty pieces of fruit, twelve litres of soda water, seventy-six main courses, a hundred and fifty pats of butter, and eighty-four hard-boiled eggs into the plane in less than twenty minutes. And just like all the others, she couldn't suppress a sigh of disappointment when it was announced they'd only completed a third of their journey. It became stuffy and close. Their feet were swollen. To cheer them up, they were told they would be able to get off the plane in Rangoon. They said goodbye to the cabin crew that was being replaced right now – *au revoir*! And they got rid of five kilos of sand, because the new stewardess had generous hips.

The flight to Rangoon would be the longest so far, and Ada wondered how long she would be able to hide the twinges of pain in her belly and back and the waves of nausea from the smell of coffee and why she'd done so till now, why she hadn't said a word yet about Derk, not one word. Oh, to be someone else, someone like Esther, who seemed so outspoken and who made jokes about everything. A bold girl like that, who throws back her head and laughs out loud like she's the only person on earth. That's the kind of person she would become. As she served glasses of sherry to their guests in her light, modern bungalow, she would be someone like that.

*

Seventeen minutes after their arrival, the wheel chocks were rolled away and Frank held her hand during take-off as they'd become accustomed to doing (although each time Ada hoped no-one else would see). It was sweltering, like flying inside an oven, and while they were still over Pakistan curtains were being closed left and right and people fell asleep, exhausted from being up so late and from all the emotions. When they woke up, they were flying above the Gulf of Bengal inside a velvety black star-filled dome. They were served a meal and were no longer sure if they were eating breakfast, lunch, or dinner. In this dazed, lethargic state, Ada van Holland and Frank de Rooy turned towards each other and talked quietly.

'Who'll be waiting for you when we land?' he asked.

'Derk Visser,' she said hoarsely, and asked him the same question.

'No-one,' he said. There had been a girl, from Utrecht, a medical student, blonde, just like her, but she didn't want to emigrate. So he'd broken it off.

'Didn't you love her enough to stay?'

His desire to leave had been stronger. 'I don't feel like a Dutchman.' He'd been seventeen when they had to return to the country of his parents and he couldn't get used to the cold, to the mentality, the polite distance between people. A cold, damp country. Although he spoke of this calmly, his eyes grew dark. He had never forgotten the smell of the Javanese earth, and homesickness had become his constant companion. 'But I'm not Javanese either.'

He made a silly face. 'I'm going to become a Kiwi.'

They'd had to fend for themselves when they came back to Holland on the ship. People were too busy licking their own wounds. He fell silent, and shrugged. 'That's how people are.'

She wondered if he'd been in a camp. She'd seen pictures in the newspaper. The Japs were just as cruel as the Krauts, it had said. But you don't ask questions about something like that. 'And God?' she asked.

He took her hand and stroked it as he thought about this; she allowed it because she could see he was going to give her an answer she wouldn't like and was trying to find a way to tell her this as gently as he could.

He didn't believe in God.

She'd expected this, but it was a shock to hear the words spoken so plainly and at such close proximity, and she sent up a silent prayer, a small, swift prayer for this young man, forgive him, save him.

He'd never believed in God. It hadn't been part of his upbringing. It was unlikely he would ever come to believe in Him.

'Bad, eh?' he said cheerfully. 'And now I can only hope that He believes in me.'

Her heart contracted with fear on his behalf. It was as if he were walking through the countryside, whistling a tune, and hadn't noticed that a boulder was hurtling towards him down the mountain. He saw the look on her face and apologized, he shouldn't be making jokes about something she took seriously. 'What are you?'

'Reformed.'

Beneath her feet she could see the grey rectangular gravestone, worn and faded, that made up the floor of their church along with all the other old gravestones. A date in Roman numerals and the name of an unknown dead person from an unknown century, a name you sometimes still came across in their village. She sat between her parents on a straight-backed wooden chair with a prickly rush seat, and felt the cold of the ancestors creep up into her soul by way of her thin calves. It was dark in the church, and wet snow slipped down the steamy windows.

'And what does that mean for you, religion?' he asked.

That she was ravenous as she sat there on the rush seat. That she had to pee. That she was bored and deeply unhappy at the prospect of an entire Sunday during which she wouldn't be allowed to do anything, not play outside, nothing, except in the afternoon to go and sit again on top of the dead for hours and defend herself against their malicious chill. That she got a stomach ache from the cold and the fact that she wasn't grateful like she was supposed to be. But religion just *was*, she'd never had to think about it. Like a coward, she took ready-made answers down off the shelf.

'That I'm never alone, because the Lord is always with me.'

It didn't sound right. She blushed and pulled back her hand, which only made her feel more embarrassed, so she ran her hand under the damp hair stuck to the back of her neck, as if that was why she'd done it.

'Is it nice, the thought that God is always with you?'

In her belly was an unborn child that had been conceived in sin. No-one had been there but she and Derk. There would be no talk of it in New Zealand. When the baby was born, a few eyebrows would be raised as people recalled the date of their wedding and did the sums, but the rumour would gradually fade away. The real day of reckoning would come on the day when God opens his books, He who sees everything and forgets nothing.

'What do you think?' she said. 'Of course!'

He didn't say what he was thinking, but the look in his eyes made her giddy. She had to come up with something better than this. 'Sometimes I'm not able to…'

She stirred blindly in her empty teacup.

'What aren't you able to do?'

'It's not always easy to…' He waited patiently.

'To keep to the straight and narrow.'

'Hmm?'

'To be virtuous. A good Christian.'

'No?'

58

'We're all sinners,' she whispered. Although these words were common ones, they brought forth a wave of fear in her throat. Silence. To escape his gaze she drank the last drop of cold tea, with the spoon sticking out of her cup past her eye. Then she ran out of ideas, and because he still hadn't spoken, she turned towards him.

In a soft, solemn voice he said: 'Aside from that, you seem like a very sweet girl.'

Tears stung behind her eyes. She and this nice young man, who was sitting so close she could feel the warmth of his skin, were miles apart. This was the first time she'd ever spoken with a non-believer, and his tranquillity confused her, he didn't seem to be afraid. But people who don't believe in hell were in for a surprise. It was pointless to warn him about this, and that made her sad as well. Everything made her sad.

'Is something wrong?'

She said she was tired, and was going to sleep for a bit. She turned around. He was silent. After a while he got up and went to the back.

*

Seven hours and eighteen minutes after their departure from Baghdad, the captain landed the Liftmaster in Rangoon and allowed the door to be opened for his chosen ones. By now they had been confined to their cramped seats for twenty-four hours straight. They had to hand in their passports. Stiff and stumbling, they made their way down the steps into the humid tropical night, where they were welcomed by a panting KLM manager in a lightweight white suit and women in sarongs who offered them cold drinks, while behind them people worked furiously to carry out the by now familiar operation with the aircraft. They were given half an hour.

'This is so incredibly interesting,' said Marjorie. Then she let out a yell and jumped, slapping furiously as an insect that looked like a large grasshopper climbed up her leg. Near the small airport terminal, the captain gave a press conference for the Burmese press, a timid bunch compared with their own boisterous journalists, who kept buzzing around queen bee Esther on the apron. They took turns lighting her cigarettes, and they laughed at her remarks.

Ada gazed up wide-eyed at the starry sky, which far exceeded her wildest imaginings, and wondered how you could behold such splendour and not believe in God. He telleth the number of the stars; He calleth them all by their names.

Frank hadn't come back to his seat for quite some time. Maybe she'd disappointed him. She'd dozed off with an unpleasant mental image of herself. When she'd woken with a start as they began their descent, he was there again. Like a gentleman, he opened his hand so she could place hers in his. And she was glad, there was nothing she could do about it. During the entire landing they sat in companionable silence and her heart swelled with friendship.

Now she saw him walk to a garden next to the terminal and lean towards the tropical flowers, which hung on the bushes like white lanterns. She saw how Esther broke away from the group she was with and walked towards him, swinging her hips. How he straightened up when he noticed the click-clack of her heels. How he smiled. She turned away sharply from the scene, for it was none of her business, none at all.

'Funny, isn't it?' Marjorie whispered in her ear. 'She's engaged, you know, just like us. There'll be someone waiting for her when we land in Christchurch. Do you think the poor devil knows what he's in for?'

Ada stared at her open-mouthed, too shocked to reply. On no account was she to hold the young man's hand again, no matter how rough it got. The Lord will protect me. She'd been lucky and no-one had seen it, but just imagine, just imagine. There would be a stain on her new life before it had even begun. What's the matter with me, anyway? She'd been carried away by her fear of flying, the unknown, travelling on her own, something like that – it couldn't happen again, not ever. People would talk about her, just like Esther. She stayed close to Marjorie as they strolled over the apron, keeping just behind her and speaking shyly with a Dutchman who worked there. She didn't look over at the garden again.

Twenty minutes later, the perspiring KLM manager was allowed to call off their names, something that clearly filled him with pride. Inside, the ashtrays had been emptied and the cabin was clean. Marjorie plopped down next to her – she was bored stiff, she grumbled, that Esther didn't say a thing, and she sat with the journalists more than she did in her own seat.

Ada didn't object.

'Just this leg,' Marjorie said to Frank.

He gave Ada a curious look and sat down behind her with no further comment. Esther slid in next to him. 'Watch this,' Marjorie whispered, 'the press can forget about it from here on in.'

The flying time to Jakarta was estimated to be six and a half hours. Jakarta, that's Java, thought Ada, and she glanced back at Frank, but he was busy fastening his seat belt and his face revealed nothing. They were expecting to run into turbulence, a word that produced a dull fear. No-one seemed to be worried about this, so she kept quiet. As they took off, she tried to imagine that Derk was holding her hand. It didn't work. I don't know who he is.

'Oh, this is so cosy,' Marjorie said contentedly, and fell asleep.

It was the middle of the night and oppressively hot in the plane. Immediately after take-off, most of the chosen ones leaned back onto their pillows without a glance at the exotic sky full of stars. Their tiredness had caught up with them, and the novelty of flying had worn off. It was actually dreadfully boring.

*

Maybe it was the heat, or being half asleep, or the constant vibration of the plane: in her loins she could feel a warm sensation arising. The same one she'd been able to produce as a child by swinging in a certain way, something that had started to happen more and more often of its own accord over the past few years, sometimes even in church during the summer months, when the singing was beautiful and stirring and the sun would shine in through the windows at the same moment and warm her. Scraps of a story belonged to this, specific images, the hero lifted her up, 'his strong arms lifted her up and carried her to the hayloft'. She'd read this in a library book she should never have set eyes upon. Although there were plenty of haylofts in their village, they weren't anything like this one. The hero lifted her up, she'd gone all soft inside and arched her body with desire, every which way. She wasn't wearing much, either. The lifting, the carrying, and the laying down in the hay repeated themselves endlessly, and were charged with the anticipation of what would happen next, there in the hay. That part was still unclear to her. In the local bakery she'd once watched while the baker kneaded the dough for his stollen, his broad hands making delicate movements, gently, tirelessly, so attentively that the dough beneath his fingers gave up all opposition and allowed itself be twisted and turned in all directions.

The incident with Derk was unrelated to any of this and didn't interfere with her fantasies. It had just happened.

There were small stones in the grass that pressed painfully into her skin and she was a little cold. Derk, the orphan with the gruesome images burned into his memory, sobbed as he yanked down her panties, his face contorted so strangely that she didn't dare look at him. He'd had to identify his entire family; it was weeks before they found his father in the mud. While she made comforting sounds, she peeked curiously at what appeared from behind his fly. It was the first time in her life she had seen a grown man's sexual organ, having only ever seen those of her little brothers. She also knew about the forbidden word 'prick' and had always found it to be vaguely arousing. So that's what it looked like. More wilful than she'd expected. The thing came quivering towards her, unstoppable, Derk himself was attached at the other end, and was being dragged helplessly along. She saw the glistening tip of a penis and a droplet of fluid, it was becoming very realistic all of a sudden. Then she became frightened. Not for the pain, she knew it could hurt a little the first time. She knew much more than her mother would have ever thought

possible, knowledge she'd acquired during whispered conversations with her
girlfriends on summer evenings after supper, when they were allowed to go
out for a bit and lean over the railing on the bridge.

A little pain, she'd been prepared for that. Not for haste.

'I'm... I'm...'

I'm a virgin, she'd wanted to say. But she said nothing and he heard
nothing. The wind howled around them, and her hair blew in front of her
eyes and into his face. She wanted to stop and tried to pull herself out from
under him, but only made it halfway. He clung to her. She understood. In the
end, she just let it happen, as if she herself had stepped out for a moment and
was waiting patiently for it to be over. It didn't take long. His body relaxed
and he started crying again, more softly now, with his face against her neck.
She stroked his bottom, and for a moment they could have been man and
wife. They didn't look at each other as they hurriedly straightened out their
clothes. When she got on the bus to go home, she was certain the driver could
see she was an adult woman, and this filled her with pride. When she got
home, she washed herself and her soiled panties thoroughly. For days she had
to hide the bruises on her arms. She tried not to think of the incident itself,
and not long afterwards the fantasies about strong arms and haylofts
resumed. What would happen there in the hay was still full of promise.

She sighed. Next to her, Marjorie was sleeping like a child might do, a
thin stream of saliva running out of the left side of her open mouth.
Behind her, Frank and Esther also seemed to be asleep. When she turned
around she could see his arm on the middle armrest; he'd taken off his
jacket and rolled his sleeves up past his elbows, to the middle of his upper
arm, and she could see the muscles beneath his smooth skin and the bulge
on his forearm in the bend by his elbow.

Now she closed her eyes and leaned her head against the window. She
rubbed the top of her left arm softly with her right hand, so it was quite
by accident that this very hand moved over her nipple too. In the hay, the
lovemaking would go on for hours and her happiness would never cease.
Someone was running a moist paintbrush lightly over her skin. With

difficulty – it was cramped, and everything clung to her in the tropical heat – she crossed her legs beneath her dress, because she knew that this would heighten the pleasant sensation to the point where a shiver would move down through her body all the way to her heels, and she could relax. Because she didn't need to use her hands, she considered it permissible. Although it didn't always work, it often did, even in church, as long as the sun was shining and the music was stirring. It wasn't self-abuse, because she didn't do anything. And it just wasn't possible to keep those images from coming up.

She shifted into the right position. Arms with strong muscles beneath smooth skin lifted her up. 'You're more beautiful than the Empress of Persia.' They had all the time in the world.

Afterwards she fell asleep, just like everyone else. And when they flew through thunderheads for several minutes she, too, barely opened her eyes.

*

At Jakarta's Kemayoran Airport, *The Flying Dutchman* was greeted with music. It was Saturday morning there, and as they landed they set their watches ahead by another half an hour. They got rid of time as if it were sand. The musicians in white uniforms paraded over the apron while airport personnel sweated blood to get the plane ready for take-off. In the cabin, people gathered round the open door to catch a glimpse of the lost colony. Frank made no attempt to have a look at the country he came from. Ada wondered why this was, and would have liked to have sat next to him and hold *his* hand for a change. Thank heavens he would never find out about the role he'd played as she dozed in her seat. Still, she had the strong suspicion he actually *was* aware of this, so that every time she turned around and their eyes met, she blushed all the way down to her throat.

'Let's get going,' grumbled Marjorie, who had woken up during their descent. 'I've had enough.' Her breath smelled slightly sour.

We're starting to smell, Ada thought. We'll reek by the time we arrive.

There was news about the race. The Viscount had landed on the Cocos Islands. The Hastings had run into monsoons over Colombo – according to the crew, it was the worst storm they'd ever been in – and they'd almost crashed at Negombo Airport during the torrential downpour. The engine had been damaged beyond repair, and they'd had to withdraw from the race. This would mean one less plane in the race, but it was sad all the same, and the captain sent his counterpart from New Zealand a telegram expressing his regrets. The fast Canberras had already landed in Christchurch. England had won. When the British pilot was asked what he wanted more than anything else, he'd answered, 'I believe I'd like a cup of tea.'

The words 'storm' and 'crashed' kept going around in her head. Until now all had gone well, but they weren't there yet. Behind her, Frank started talking with a heavyset man from the aircraft factory, who was pacing up and down the aisle to get some movement back into his stiff muscles. They were talking about the engines.

'They're beauties, sir,' the man said.

Frank wanted to know all about them.

'Pratt & Whitney, nothing ever goes wrong with them. They're overhauled after every twelve hundred hours of flight time, but nothing ever needs fixing.'

'Have they ever had to run so long at a single stretch before?'

'They never run for more than ten hours at a time.'

God help us.

'And now it will be at least fifty hours,' said Frank, as if he had read her mind. She wished she didn't have to listen to this conversation. The man mopped the sweat from his brow. 'The trouble is, they don't get time to cool off.'

'They're being pushed to the limit.'

'That's the trouble. They should get the chance to rest a bit.'

After seventeen minutes, the Liftmaster was in the air again, flying low

65

and in daylight. The most beautiful leg of the race so far, above the Indonesian archipelago. Ada saw the long chain of high volcanoes on Java, with green lakes within their truncated tops. Behind them lay Bali and the other Sunda Islands – names they'd learned by heart at school – because their course was taking them over the entire length of the archipelago. The steward pointed and explained, everyone was enjoying themselves, and even Marjorie woke up briefly. Frank, though, was engrossed in the newspaper that had been brought on board, which contained the first reports of the race written by their own group of journalists. He didn't even look up.

*

No-one was hungry, and the meals went back half-eaten. In fact, the only thing they were was thirsty. Their bewildered bodies thought it was midnight and were still tired. Marjorie yawned and turned over for the umpteenth time, it was impossible to get comfortable. 'I'm really looking forward to seeing Hans again,' she said, 'just not like this, so dirty and sweaty.'

By the time the sun was high enough to cast a shadow of the plane on the glistening water, there where the Indian Ocean became the Timor Sea, everyone around Ada was dozing again. Although a new front had been forecast, till now it hadn't been too bad, and because she didn't have the energy to be the only one on the alert, she surrendered to the arrogant notion that it would stay like this all the way to Christchurch. They would arrive in their new country without any unpleasantness. A young man on the plane had been very kind to her.

5

SHE STOOD IN THE AISLE in her stockinged feet. She had squeezed out over the sleeping Marjorie to go to the toilet. An undulating floor, sloping walls, that hole in the toilet bowl through which her urine was whisked away with a terrible whoosh into the vacuum below.

She walked unsteadily back to her seat, past Esther and Frank, who lay with their eyes closed. She lingered in the aisle for a bit, and tried to stretch away her stiffness.

'You're a gorgeous girl,' said a husky voice: Esther was awake. She lay there looking at Ada as if she was seeing something other than the cheap cotton floral print clinging to her hips. She shyly lowered her arms. Luckily Frank was asleep.

'Can't you sleep?'

'I know what I'd do with a figure like that,' Esther continued, stabbing a finger in her direction. 'Dior,' she said decidedly, 'ta-ta-ta-taaa!' It sounded like she'd won a battle. 'With a skirt like an explosion, to just above the ankles. Can I design a wedding dress for you? Are you getting married?'

Without waiting for a reply, she got up out of her seat.

'Wait…'

'Come with me.'

You didn't say no to a girl like Esther. Before Ada knew what was happening, she stood teetering in her underwear in the small cloakroom, which held sixty-four coats and a number of wedding dresses in garment bags. In her hands Esther was holding a cream-coloured affair, and she bent down to help her into it. Ada was glad she wasn't showing much yet. She'd filled out somewhat, but people who didn't know her wouldn't notice. Her breasts had started to swell before anything else. Esther tugged the dress up; she might not be able to get it closed all the way.

'If you like, I'll make one like this for you.'

Confident hands turned her around, and as many buttons as possible were being pushed through tiny loops at the back of the dress. She held her breath and looked straight into the mirror that hung next to the coats. The dress had a plunging neckline. Her breasts were partially visible above a gauzy shawl collar that left her shoulders exposed.

'I don't know if Derk…'

'My sewing machine is coming on the ship,' Esther said.

They'd all been allowed to send a crate with their possessions. The dimensions had been specified, and her father had built it during the evenings, his way of saying he forgave her. The ship would arrive in Lyttelton harbour near Christchurch in about six weeks' time and from there go on to the various harbours in New Zealand, so that the far-flung newcomers could collect their things. Her mother had her bewildered daughter put piles of diapers into the crate, and tiny vests, caps, socks, sheets, blankets, and buntings. Ada washed, ironed, folded, and piled, and tried to keep from actually seeing the tiny things in her hands.

'I don't know if Derk…'

'When are you getting married?' Esther asked, pulled the décolleté even lower.

'No!'

'Show it all off, why not?' She ran her hands through Ada's hair, shaking a few limp curls back to life, and pushed the whole thing off to one side and added a comb with white feathers. She inspected Ada from head to toe, closed one eye, and pursed her red lips in concentration.

Something was missing. 'Wait,' she said, 'a petticoat.' Then she left Ada alone with the mirror.

It took only a few minutes. In the meantime, it grew dark outside. She'd got used to their ship's unstable floor, this floating funfair. She didn't notice it was getting bumpier. She was looking at herself, and what she saw left her breathless. It was gorgeous. Gorgeous. Here she was, in this warm little cave, the girls' changing room, safely shielded from view by a heavy curtain, in a film-star dress that was beyond compare. Safe from the wrath of God – after all, she would never wear this dress. She was looking into another life, at a woman of glorious style and refinement. That she was beautiful… well, who wouldn't be beautiful in a creation like this? She pressed a finger against the swell of her breasts, which had been pushed up by the buttons at the back; cursing under her breath, Esther had managed to get all of them closed. She carefully touched the gossamer collar, soft folds of delicate white, wide around her shoulders, tapering off towards the centre. This woman would be loved. In soft swirling dresses she would walk in the evening sun on the arm of her husband, who loved and protected her. Esther was an enchantress.

*

This time the captain decided to fly through the front. Now that their most serious rival had dropped out, their main objective was to catch up with their own flight plan. The plane suddenly dropped a few feet before levelling off again. Ada got much more of a fright from Frank, who pushed aside the curtain and stumbled in.

'Wait a minute…' he said, laughing. 'She said I could… she said…' He closed the curtain. She tried with all her might to tug up the top of the dress. 'Don't,' said Frank, 'don't.'

She lowered her arms. They stood facing each other in the cramped space. She was once again struck by the calm way with which he regarded her. And once again, her body responded with a warm heaviness that kept her from taking action.

'Ada van Holland,' he said, and fell silent. His eyes grew dark.

'Yes?'

'I wish you would...'

'Yes?'

The curtain was pushed aside. Esther came in with her arms full of petticoat. Marjorie's sleepy face appeared just behind her. 'What are you doing?' She gazed in astonishment at Ada in the wedding dress and Frank so close to her. Were they coming back? There'd been a warning, and the 'no smoking, fasten seat belts' sign had come on. Esther shrugged. For one indecisive moment, all four of them stood together in the small space. Then it seemed as if the plane lifted up and rose above itself. It lasted an eternity, or a single second. Sighing deeply, as if it had lost all its nerve, the plane subsequently fell a thousand feet or more into the depths. It all happened so fast that in their minds they were still standing in the same position when their bodies grazed the closet walls in a confused tangle of arms and legs and exclamations of surprise and shock came from their mouths. Ada hit the back of her head against the coat rack and pulled several jackets down with her as she fell. Frank slammed into her, with Esther and the petticoat on top of him. Marjorie grabbed on to the curtain and hung there in a daze, swinging back and forth. She didn't keep it up for long – the curtain slipped out of her arms and she bounced on her knees over the floor, the floor that might have been the wall, or the ceiling.

The plane climbed and capsized, over and over, barely able to recover in between. The movements increased in intensity. From the cabin came frightened moans and shrieks – suddenly everyone was wide awake – and the crash of falling dishes in the pantry, suitcases dancing out of the luggage nets.

'Fasten your seat belts!' The steward's voice was not reassuring.

Before anyone had time to get over their fright, the plane was lifted up again and hurled into the sky. They managed to stand up in the lull between two of the jolts. Ada stepped on the inside of the dress, grabbed on to the coats, and fell for a second time. Frank pulled her up and clamped his arm so tightly around her waist it hurt. They slid along the wall behind Esther and Marjorie, who were trying to stand up again in the aisle, looking for support from the armrests to help them make their way to the front, to their seats. Once again the aircraft fell into the depths and once again they lost their balance. The panic in the cabin grew, and all around them people were screaming, and crying out for gods and mothers. A typewriter clattered towards them. Stumbling and sliding, they could see the steward buckling himself in at the front as he gestured wildly to them and shouted that they should stay there, stay there!

'Go back! Hold on! You'll be on the ceiling before you know it!'

The plane vibrated and bounced from left to right, shaking from the incessant stream of jolts. The engines roared, doing battle with an invisible force. Pushed to the limit, she thought suddenly. They've been pushed to the limit.

*

Frank didn't let go of her. He put her between himself and the wall, and pulled Marjorie back into the cloakroom. Then he leaned forward and reached his hand out to Esther, who'd slid halfway under a seat. But Esther shook her head no, she wanted to stay there, and she used the armrest to pull herself halfway up, slipped back, and hit the side of her head on the steel used to fasten the seat to the floor. Again she shook her head no, she would stay there. Frank didn't insist, and turned back to Ada. She'd clamped herself around him with a vice-like grip, her hands riveted together behind his back, and though her fingernails were digging into her skin, she felt nothing. Over Frank's shoulder she looked at the journalists, who were being tossed to and fro like rag dolls, straining against their seat belts.

Funny.

The looking took all her attention. She searched for a window and saw the darkness beyond, followed by the dazzling flashes of lightning that attacked them relentlessly. For a moment it seemed as if blue-green tongues of fire were flickering around the wing. We're burning up.

'Oh God… oh God…' Marjorie wailed behind them.

In the plane people were throwing up, screaming, cursing, crying, and praying, but a great calm descended inside Ada's head. They capsized again.

Frank had to use all his strength to keep them both upright. She felt his muscles turn rock hard and start to quiver, felt his chest pumping. She was leaning against him with her full weight and looked over his shoulder along the wing, which was pointing almost straight down. She saw ships on the ocean when the lightning flashed. Others had seen them as well.

'Look!' shouted the steward to reassure them. 'So many ships! If we crash, they'll pick us up!' The plane dropped. Her mind became soundless. Everything slowed down. She saw shoes and packages of wool flying through the cabin at a leisurely rate. Then she pushed her face into his neck and squeezed her eyes shut. She could smell the damp earth in a tropical garden with a statue of two lovers going together to their doom in the middle of a slow, silent hurricane.

*

It passed. As the last wisps of clouds slipped by the Liftmaster, they could suddenly see the northwest coast of Australia. No-one reacted. No-one looked. Some of the women were sobbing softly. The fat aircraft specialist was still vomiting, leaning forward in his seat.

Ada, Frank, Marjorie, and Esther stood next to each other at the back of the plane in a daze, hollow-eyed from fright. They didn't speak. The steward, pale as death and sweating profusely, came to get them and led them back to their seats.

'You see?' he said cheerfully. 'It was a front, only a front.'

It didn't matter that Ada was still wearing the wedding dress. No-one noticed. They'd started their descent and there was no time to change.

Their final approach to the airport was routine. Throttle back. Approaching from the sea, the plane descended in stages and headed straight for Darwin Airport. The cabin was filled with the acrid odour of fear and vomit. Even of excrement.

'Ladies and gentlemen,' the steward called out, 'on behalf of our captain I would like to express the hope that you didn't get too much of a fright, because that would be unfortunate. And unnecessary. As you will have noticed, our Liftmaster is second to none, and well able to handle difficult conditions...'

Frank had sat down next to her again as if it were a matter of course. Ada leaned up against his chest, her face buried in her hands. Something terrible had made its way into her befuddled brain. Frank, who was unaware of this, kept his arms around her.

'We'll be landing in Darwin soon...' the steward went on. There was no reaction whatsoever, as everyone was too busy recovering. 'I've never been so frightened in my life,' she heard Marjorie say to Esther. 'I'm shaking all over. Feel my heart – it's beating like crazy. Look at this... ow... that's going to be a bruise, all black and blue...'

There was no reply.

'After perhaps having a bit of a fright, I can imagine you'd like to get some fresh air,' the steward said, 'but on account of our schedule, the plane will take off again after a maximum of fifteen minutes...'

Ada was staring into her own black soul the whole time.

She hadn't given God a thought. In her hour of need, she hadn't turned to the Lord, not for one second. Instead, she'd pressed herself up against the ribs of a heathen, and had floated away on the rhythm of his breathing. The storm had been a warning. She had strayed. She'd looked admiringly at her own reflection and hadn't seen the skull sneering out at her.

'...Too many precious minutes would be lost just getting such a large group on and off of the plane.' She wrenched herself out of Frank's arms.

*

Saturday afternoon at half past four local time, the wheels bumped down on the hot red Australian earth. Although the hoses were immediately

73

attached so the plane could quench its thirst for fuel, their door remained hermetically sealed for a time. Outside the sun beat down on the plane, and the temperature in the cabin shot up. The captain, his tanned face a little more serious than usual, came into the cabin to personally reassure his deeply shaken chosen ones about the past few hours. With this fantastic aeroplane, they hadn't actually been in danger, although he had to admit that even for an experienced pilot like himself, the weather had been exceptionally bad. But they were flying in a thrilling handicap race, and if things went on like this, they might land in Christchurch hours ahead of schedule.

'Then there won't be anyone there to meet us,' Marjorie said dolefully.

The stewardess opened the door slightly and an Australian in a white jacket slipped in. 'Good afternoon,' he said politely, and methodically worked his way from back to front, spraying a fumigant over their heads with a Flit gun. He explained that this is how they kept the country and livestock free of diseases that might otherwise be brought in. He said goodbye and the door was secured once more. Five minutes would be sufficient, he'd assured them. If it had to be done, it had to be done. The stewardess looked at her watch, and everyone covered their noses and mouths.

Ada found it hard to breathe through her folded hands, and stared at the blue seat back in front of her. The storm had been a warning. She was a sinner, and remained a sinner. Look at her sitting here, gasping breathlessly in a wedding dress that's too tight for her and with her breasts half hanging out, with torn stockings, and her pregnant body aching with adulterous desire.

The chemical smell made her dizzy and nauseous. She moaned softly into the hollow of her hands. Frank looked at her. She didn't know what he saw. She sat up; it was now a matter of self-control. He took his hand from in front of his face.

'Still alive?'

She nodded aloofly, yes she was.

'We're tough bugs,' he said, smiling.

Love sliced right through her and took her breath away entirely.

*

This is how it came to pass that the soldiers in their shorts and the spectators who had waited in the shadow of the hangar for the arrival of the Dutch plane were treated to the sight of a bride running down the steps in her stockinged feet as soon as the stewardess threw open the door of the gigantic bird. Shouts went up over the apron, people pointed at her, look! The mechanics crouching over the open wing tanks straightened up in surprise. Two steps down she bumped into the men from the ground crew, who wanted to bring food and drink onto the plane. Three crates fell, and hundreds of apples rolled down the stairs. She stumbled, managed to grab on to the railing, and kept running. Someone shouted something at her in English – she wasn't listening, and ran blindly on through the hot tropical air in the direction of the crowd.

Inside the plane, she'd run into the steward, who had come out of the pantry carrying a bucket of soapy water. The passengers had been expressly requested to remain seated and not to congregate around the door, so the cabin crew could do some quick cleaning. 'Watch out!' he cried, but she slipped through the aisle like a silverfish on her way to the exit.

Now she ran panting over the apron towards the hangar. The hard red earth was on fire and seared the soles of her feet. She didn't know why she was heading for the hangar. It was the running that mattered, to get as far away from the plane as possible, and figure the rest out later. With both hands she tugged at the gown's gauzy collar, trying to support her breasts, which were swollen as a result of the pregnancy and hurt from all the bouncing. Everything was so terribly wrong. When she reached the hangar she couldn't stop. She could feel the difference in temperature through the soles of her feet, and saw the astonished looks on the faces of those who moved aside to let her pass. For a moment she became aware of how she must look in this dress. She saw the photograph in the display case, a still from the film she was acting in.

She couldn't stop running here. Not with these people. So she ignored the stabbing pain in her side and kept on running till she reached the back of the huge hangar, where a small steel door stood open. She was heading for light, for air, an exit.

The people got a run for their money. Just before escaping from the darkness into the sunlight behind the hangar, she heard someone call her name. Frank had come after her. Outside the hangar, she ran in pointless circles, until pain and shortness of breath forced her to stop. She retched as she bent forward, she was nearly suffocating. The same words continued to rack her overheated brain: the storm had been a warning. A warning. A warning.

'Ada!'

The ground was so hot she couldn't stand still. She saw him step out of the hangar as she hopped back and forth, her hands tucked under her armpits to keep her breasts in place. The low sun shone right in his eyes and blinded him. With his hand shading his eyes, he looked for her. The hero scans the prairie. Finds the girl.

'Hey.'

'I'm not getting back on!' She heard herself shouting. Her nose was running, and she wiped it with a wild gesture. Beads of sweat stung at the corners of her eyes and blurred her vision.

He approached her quietly, like you would approach a wild animal, or a lunatic. 'Nothing ever goes wrong,' he said. 'Never. It always seems worse than it is. You're not used to it, that's all.'

'I'm not going back!'

'All right. What would you like to do then?'

She looked at him as she danced crazily to and fro. He spread his arms towards the red expanse of earth. 'Do you want to stay in Australia?'

The heat was making her head boil over, she couldn't think properly, and shouted the first thing that came to her. 'I want to go back!' To be able to do everything over again, and better, this time without making any mistakes, without committing any sins. 'Back?' 'Yes, back!' She kept shouting, even though she hadn't intended to. 'How do I get back?!'

'Why do you want to go back?'

She had to stand still to catch her breath. Her face was drenched, the dress soaked through – you never saw heroines looking like this.

'You have a fiancé in New Zealand, right?'

The ground beneath the soles of her feet was scorching hot. The only thing she could do was keep hopping, from one foot to the other. He came closer, and gave her a searching look. 'What about that?'

It was a mistake, she wanted to say. Stupid. I didn't know so much would be at stake, that time in the grass. I'm just eighteen, can I do it all over again? I would still comfort him, the drowning man, but in a different way, one that had fewer consequences.

'Ada, what about that?'

He took her burning face in his hands. She sniffed, and quickly wiped her running nose. He didn't seem to see it; he was looking for an answer in her eyes. It's too awful to say out loud, she said wordlessly.

The kissing just started, passionate and intense, exactly like it was supposed to be, he wrapped his arms around her, and she wrapped herself in them. 'Oh, sweetheart,' he said every time and then they continued. Sweetheart, sweetheart. Their sweat, their saliva, everything blended together, smelled and tasted incredibly nice. She felt a hand on her breast, on her hips, on her bottom. When her feet were about to catch fire, she stood on his shoes. Now I can reach you better. I'll stay here for now. Someone murmured appreciatively, he did or she did, and the sound surrounded them like the walls of a cosy room. It's awfully nice here. See you later.

*

There was applause. Slowly but surely, the spectators had followed them. Ada jumped back with a start, and the tiny room shattered into a million

77

pieces. She danced around on the blazing earth. Frank looked at her feet, with the stockings that were torn to shreds.

'Hot! Hot!'

He laughed. 'Come here, you madwoman.' He swept her off her feet all at once, and turned towards the crowd, his arms filled with cream-coloured satin – she saw something triumphant in the set of his jaw, the profile of a victor. The hero carries his bride to the hangar. He was breathing heavily. I've put on eight pounds. The people moved back to let him pass, clapping in delight – a wonderful Dutch romance. He laughed, and lugged her up inelegantly, all right, that's better. She threw her arms around his neck, the dress now so tight around her waist she was finding it almost impossible to breathe. She had to think things over for a moment. Just for a moment.

'Ada van Holland,' he said, with a voice that would have been enough in itself, and kept saying her name. He walked through the dark hangar towards the open front, nodded left and right, made a real show of it as long as they were at it. She saw his eyes light up with pleasure. He stepped out into the open air, where a low golden sun was dramatically illuminating the red earth apron, and where on the horizon their aeroplane waited with the propellers turning.

'Just put me down,' she whispered, her voice hoarse with misery.

He couldn't hear her over the roar of the engines. The plane had been refuelled and the hoses disconnected, and ten pairs of hands had wound the massive lengths of corrugated hose back onto the Shell refuelling truck. The steward was standing impatiently at the top of the stairs looking for the escaped passengers; he beckoned when he spotted them: come, quick!

'I'll never let you go again. Will you stay with me?'

'Put me down,' she said, still not loudly enough.

'Feel free to think it over. But first say yes.'

They kissed again, oh, darling, darling, as if they were magnetic. The spectators in the hangar cheered and clapped. She came up for air, rubbed her nose over the stubble of forty hours in a plane without a shave, all the way up to his ear, and told him bluntly she was married.

'I'm married.'

'How's that?' he said a bit densely. She didn't dare look at him, and wrenched herself out of his arms. 'How's that?'

'Married,' she repeated, and started hopping again. 'Married, married, married,' she sang, like an obstinate child.

He stared at her incredulously, a deep furrow creasing his brow. 'The dress…'

'Isn't mine.'

The steward made large impatient gestures, tapped his watch – they were losing precious minutes. They looked at the plane, but neither of them made any attempt to move towards it.

'You're not wearing a ring.'

'He's got it, there. I was married by proxy, someone stood in for him. He's got the rings, there. For the ceremony… there… there'll also be some kind of… ceremony. In the church.'

He shook his head, as if trying to wake up from a bad dream. The salt stung her eyes; she blinked to clear her vision. What must he think of me?

'By proxy…'

She nodded, yes, by proxy, we should go. But he put his hands on her upper arms and pulled her onto his shoes. 'Why by proxy?'

She still knew the answer to that one. 'He'd already left,' she said unhappily, 'and I'm a minor. Otherwise I wouldn't have been allowed to join him… To join Derk,' she added, as if there might have been a misunderstanding about that.

She gave a cowardly nod in the direction of the agitated steward, come along! But he pulled her closer and kept searching her eyes for an answer. 'Do you love him?'

Love will come, her mother had said. It has to grow.

'That kiss just now, what did it mean?'

That stupid silence of hers was driving him mad, and he shook her gently.

'Do you love him?'

Derk had tasted like a postage stamp, her mouth had filled with his saliva, so much so that she'd been forced to swallow it. His tongue had swum around that saliva in panic. A great deal of prayer, the church, and children, that's what she needed. 'I don't know him all that well,' she said, half sobbing. Here it comes.

'Why didn't you wait then?'

She stared at him. Just let me stay for a bit longer in the cool of my room at home.

'Couldn't you wait?'

'No,' she whispered.

He stood perfectly still, engrossed in her with an almost scientific curiosity. The crowd in the hangar, sheltering from the blazing sun, followed the scene with interest. The film was going on for too long, and that's never a good thing.

'Why not?'

Although her sin was branded on to her forehead, she couldn't say the words. Help me, she signalled, I've been struck dumb.

She felt his grasp relax. Saw his pupils widen, as if he'd been put into the dark. 'You're pregnant.'

There had been no need for him to say the words out loud like that. She stepped back, off his shoes and onto the hot ground, hopped inanely with her head bowed, didn't deny it.

'Right...' he said. 'Right...' His arms hung limp at his side.

The steward had consulted the captain, they couldn't wait any longer, would have to intervene. He came down the steps as calmly as he could – our country's honour is at stake, all eyes are upon us – and walked rapidly towards the deserters.

'Come,' said Frank. 'We have to go.'

They walked to the plane without speaking, separated by a short distance. Ada was doing her crazy little skips and felt herself getting angry. It hadn't happened just like that... He shouldn't think... She was no...

'He's from Oude Tonge!'

He didn't respond.

'He lost everyone! All of them drowned!'

'Come,' he repeated, which made her furious. She pulled hard on his sleeve. He stopped and turned towards her. She saw dark pain in his eyes. Leave it, she read, but she couldn't leave it, and her fury exploded straight at him. 'He showed me the place where his house had been and then he started to cry. I was horrified! I didn't know what to do!' Hold me close, the flames are licking at my feet. 'What could I do?' He nodded.

'Comfort him.'

They walked on quickly, their heads lowered, two lost lambs on their way back to the ark. The steward discreetly checked his advance, turned on his heels, and ran to the stairs. He waved to the stewardess – everything's going to be all right, inform the cockpit, we can take off.

Ash came out of Ada's mouth. Words filled with ashes.

'It happened. It shouldn't have happened, but it did. Behind the dyke. I will be punished directly or through my children.'

He stopped, gave her an astonished look.

'What makes you think that?'

'It's a mortal sin. It's very serious.'

He took her face in both of his hands. 'It's very beautiful,' he said softly, 'very sweet.' Then he let go of her.

The metal steps were red hot, and they climbed them quickly. 'Nineteen minutes, block to block.' The steward looked at his watch. 'Not bad. Come quickly, please.' He could tell he should leave these young people in peace for a bit. 'That nasty front gave us all a bit of a fright.'

Frank let Ada enter the cabin first. The storm had been a warning, she'd still wanted to tell him that, but she was too tired. Behind them, the stairs were rolled back and the steward waved professionally at the crowd. In spite of everything, it had been a lovely spectacle.

6

MARJORIE WAS SITTING IN FRANK'S seat. Ada had used noncommittal answers to fend off her whispered questions about what had taken place on the apron. She was too numb to feel guilty about this. Yes, I was a little frightened. Yes, he reassured me. No, nothing else happened. She hoped he wouldn't overhear, and didn't dare look back. After take-off, she was finally able to free herself from the confines of the wedding dress, teetering unsteadily in the 'ladies' lounge', as Esther referred to the humble cloakroom, among the racks where the jackets hung in neat rows, as if they hadn't just passed through a raging storm. Esther undid the buttons and asked no questions, to Ada's relief. She didn't seem to be bothered by the stains and tears in the satin. They showed each other the bruises they'd got when they fell. Ada's feet looked worst of all, covered with bloody scrapes, and open blisters on the soles. They must have been stepped on during the storm, but she hadn't noticed. Now they were becoming horribly swollen and turning purple. Esther moistened a colourful scarf in the lavatory sink and carefully dabbed them clean. 'You win,' she said with a wink. Then she gave her a new pair of stockings, the finest Ada had ever had.

*

As far as she could tell, Australia was made up of monotonous brown plains. It was dark before long. They continued to fly along the northern coast, their course determined by the warning issued by the British government to all those taking part in the race: that night they were going to test a new atomic weapon in the Woomera desert, and would detonate a bomb if the wind was coming from the right direction. For safety's sake, it would be better to fly around this area because of the radioactive clouds. Ada imagined a luminous cloud surrounded by shafts of light, like one of the illustrations in her children's Bible. It was nothing new for her.

Marjorie sat next to her in the half-light and read from the special air-race bulletin. 'Only the outermost edge of Australia is populated,' she said ominously. 'That's where people live and work. In the interior there's just jungle, jungle, and more jungle, inhospitable and always burning – some of the fires burn for ever because it's impossible to put them out.'

Ada turned around heavily and looked between the seats towards the back of the plane, where Esther and Frank were playing cards with the journalists. She saw his fingers around his cigarette and the way he inhaled deeply, the way the tip began to glow like a tiny light that went on and out and then on again at once. It seemed like Morse code. 'In Australia they eat better than anywhere else in the world,' Marjorie read with envy. 'An average of three thousand calories a day.' Even though it had been eight years since the terrible hungry winter towards the end of the war, having plenty of food was still an appealing prospect. The tip of his cigarette glowed on again and their eyes met. She quickly turned back around. Everything hurt when she moved.

*

They all tossed and moaned and tried to find a position in which they would at least have a chance of falling asleep. Even though it felt like morning to them, they were weary enough to embrace the night with open arms. Ada was lucky – she had two seats to herself and was actually able to lie down for the first time, her arm curled beneath her head, her legs bent and scrupulously covered by the floral print. She lay with her eyes closed and tried to ignore the twinges of pain in her feet. Behind her, Marjorie was asleep in the same position. The back of the plane had turned into a dimly lit nightclub. People sat in the aisle playing cards, and their subdued laughter and clouds of cigarette smoke drifted forward into the rest of the cabin.

Something moved in her belly, a soft tickling sensation, hardly noticeable and yet impossible to miss, different from anything she'd ever felt there before. Then it was gone again. Hello, she said silently. She waited patiently, but it didn't return. It was their first meeting, and she was glad there was no-one else around. Hello, there. I'm sorry I've ignored you till now, there was no special reason for it, and while it's certainly possible I'll grow to love you very much, it was just too soon, do you see? There I stood holding those silly little vests, but at the time you were nothing more than my fall from grace, something that had set things in motion at a terrifying pace. And all along I felt my mother watching me and didn't know what she wanted to see, repentance or tenderness. So I tried to fold those little flannel things neatly and put them in the crate without looking at them, like I used to swallow cod liver oil with my mouth open so I wouldn't have to taste it. That's all. It was too soon.

*

Hours later someone knelt down next to her, a large body that had squeezed into the narrow space between the seats and the seat backs. She knew right away that it was Frank. The motion of the plane had lulled her into a light, feverish sleep, painfully interrupted by every involuntary movement of her feet. He placed his hand on her hip and suddenly she was wide awake. She pretended to be asleep, making no movement and hoping he wouldn't notice the pounding of her heart.

'Ada van Holland,' he whispered in her ear, 'listen to me.' He smelled of alcohol and cigarettes. His hand slid softly but surely over her hip to her bottom, emphasizing his words with the gliding of his hand. With him, this seemed normal. 'You can come with me.'

Every cell in her body was alert, but she kept her eyes closed and made sure she continued to breathe deeply, slowly.

'The choice is yours, but I'd like it very much. I'll take care of you and the child.' He changed position, and the hand disappeared for a moment. Then the skirt of her dress was lifted. This couldn't be happening. But it *was* happening, and he put his hand on her hip, underneath her skirt, and with good-natured determination, resolutely set out to touch her bare flesh, that area of skin between her panties and the top of her stocking.

'I'll love you both. We'll have more children.' For a moment she felt his stubbly cheek against hers. 'Think about it. Please. Don't leave me. We can do this. If you want it, too.'

Then silence. She wondered if he was looking at her and what he saw.

'You only live once, Ada, don't throw it all away.' His hand didn't move, and the imprint it made seared her skin. Once in a while she felt a slight pressure, then a tiny shift, like an entirely unhurried, almost absent-minded, examination. Hand on top of thigh, tip of finger at edge of panties, tip of finger just inside panties. Her body sizzled with excitement, she was afraid she would cry out and clenched her teeth because she didn't want it to end. He was breathing heavily.

'This might be our only chance,' he murmured.

Then he stood up and walked away. It was quite some time before she dared to open her eyes. Everything was clear, and actually quite simple. She only had to say yes.

A couple of hours later the lights came on; outside it was still night. After flying for six hours, they started the descent to Brisbane, the last stop before their final destination. To their surprise they were going to be allowed off the plane, because they'd done so well after the storm and hadn't complained. During this leg they'd come in much earlier than their estimated time of arrival. The Viscount – which had taken off from Melbourne just as they were landing in Darwin – would be arriving in Christchurch around now, but even so had lost by a wide margin. A short break wouldn't hurt.

85

'Have a look at that,' said Marjorie, who turned out to be sitting next to her when she woke up. She pointed to the back, where Esther and Frank were leaning against each other, fast asleep, and made a sign that stood for drinking, and ooh la la.

*

As the only participant in the air race to land in Brisbane, the Liftmaster received a wildly enthusiastic reception. Hundreds, maybe even thousands, of Dutch immigrants had assembled in the dark in front of the illuminated hall hung with banners and the Dutch flag. Some of them had travelled for days for their chance to see *The Flying Dutchman*. Mothers were holding small children in pyjamas. When they saw the chosen ones stumble down the steps on their swollen feet, they burst into an emotional rendition of the Wilhelmus. Immediately afterwards someone launched into a popular song: 'Smashing chaps like us are just beyond compare…'

'Oh, no,' said Esther.

'That's why you'll find us… everywhere!'

Ada had spent the entire descent trying to get her shoes on. She hadn't been able to fasten the straps, and they flopped back and forth. Holding tightly to both handrails, she followed behind Marjorie, who was singing along in a sleepy voice. 'Everywhere, everywhere, where the ladies are, where the ladies are…' The girls waved at the fluttering miniature Dutch flags and smiled politely, and once they were on the ground they were served ice-cold Coca-Cola, a drink from America that made you burp.

'Where the ladies are… you'll find us there!'

It wasn't as hot here, and there weren't any stars. 'It's cloudy!' said Marjorie indignantly. Ada saw Frank and Esther standing with the journalists a little further along, listening to the live radio report for the people back home. The latest newspapers were handed out, evening papers with reports of the race. One Australian paper referred to the Liftmaster as the 'Dutch bride plane'.

Together with Marjorie and the other brides, she allowed herself to be led towards the cheering crowd behind the ropes. She was at a loss as to how to act during this stopover, and every step she took was more painful than the last. The euphoria grew, the ropes were let down, emigrants rushed forward and greeted emigrants. They were hugged, kissed, and squeezed. 'This is the most wonderful thing that's happened to me in years,' sobbed one man, pointing to their plane. 'This is pure Dutch daring!' Names of cities and regions were called out, as people looked for others from the places they'd left behind. 'Rotterdam!' 'Eindhoven!' 'Tilburg!' Flashbulbs went off non-stop. Next to her, Marjorie shook hands like a film star who had a touch of the flu during a premiere, smiling bravely but too weak for the required enthusiasm. She paused near an older woman. 'How long have you been here now?' Forty-five years, the woman replied. Marjorie's hand shot up to her mouth, as if something had just now dawned on her.

As soon as she could, Ada slipped away from the teeming crowd near the ropes and went looking for Frank. She made out his outline in the dark, behind the refuelling truck, and her heart leapt. He was talking to a technician from the ground crew, away from all the commotion. She waited and looked at his back, taking in every move he made, the way he changed position as he listened, the way he nodded with interest, his unconscious gestures when he asked a question, his concentration, his earnestness, the sound of his voice, his low, restrained laugh, all those things that already now would enable her to pick him out of a crowd of thousands and all those things she couldn't see but knew were there, how the colour of his eyes could get deeper when he looked at her, how he looked at her, all of those things.

What their life would be like.

She was apprehensive and stayed where she was, until he saw her and walked over. He took her hand and led her around the side of the plane. I have to be strong now, she thought, but as soon as they were in the dark the kissing started again and she couldn't keep it from happening, as if the ground beneath her feet had crumbled away and she had allowed herself to slip down into the depths of a river until her need to breathe forced her to surface. Her body took shape beneath his hands. A beautiful shape, strong and soft at the same time. He moaned blissfully. 'Will you come with me?'

Say it, she thought. Say it now. Now.

'Do you want to come with me?'

'I can't.'

'Do you want to?'

'It's wrong.'

'But do you want to?'

'No.'

'Liar.'

She bit his lower lip and silenced him with a kiss, a kiss that went on and on because they were living their entire life together in that kiss. And for minutes afterwards, they stood perfectly still with their arms around each other, so close together that they began to breathe in the same slow, steady rhythm, minutes in which she saw how it could be, a happy love, a free life. The broad way.

*

He continued to whisper that she could do it if she wanted to, but suddenly the words were vanishing straight into the darkness, and she let them. She couldn't do it. What therefore God hath joined together, let not man put asunder, people aren't up to that task. To violate a sacred vow. And with a heathen at that. For the Lord knoweth the way of the righteous: but the way of the ungodly shall perish. Oh Lord, save my soul from the false tongue. False tongue, she thought, as he whispered her name in her ear.

She hardened her heart and broke away from him, even though the loss had settled into every cell of her body. I'm doing the right thing, she thought desperately, I'm not going to make another big mistake, I'm finally doing the right thing, so this is what it feels like. She stifled his protests. She heard the dry sound of her own voice and made cowardly use of the fact that their brief stop had come to an end and that they had to get back on the plane.

*

No-one slept now – the last leg of the race, think of it, only around six hours to go. Their spirits soared by the minute. 'You're a remarkable group,' said the steward. 'That front was a real baptism of fire, but you don't seem to be the slightest bit afraid. Although we might never meet again, you can be sure our company will miss you.'

After take-off they were served their last meal: tea, coffee, and currant bread. It was night, but the plane vibrated enthusiastically as it flew in the direction of daybreak at a speed of five hundred kilometres an hour – their fastest speed yet. Ada stared into the darkness at the black water below and waited in vain for the feeling of satisfaction she was entitled to. 'The Tasman Sea,' said Marjorie with her mouth full, 'named after our very own Abel Tasman.' She hadn't given up her seat this time. 'Give me your address,' she said. 'Then we can stay in touch.' Ada copied out the address on the back of Derk's letter. Marjorie only had temporary lodgings in a boarding house, because Hans hadn't yet been able to find a suitable place for them to live. She looked curiously at the street name in Greymouth. 'What kind of house is it?' she asked.

'A bungalow,' said Ada softly, so that Frank wouldn't be able to hear from where he sat. In the letter it said 'bunker'. Bunker – she'd read it at least a hundred times because she just couldn't believe it, you couldn't live in a bunker, that wasn't a house, but every time she looked, there it was. The next day her brothers had asked their teacher and according to him there was no such thing, there were no bunkers in New Zealand. They hadn't been at war, it must be a bungalow, and he'd spelt out the word: b-u-n-g-a-l-o-w, that was a modern kind of house, everything on one floor and with big windows that let in the light from all sides. So she tried to see if she could make 'bungalow' out of the scrawl, and sure enough,

89

if she tried hard enough she could, and she laughed in relief at her imaginings.

'A bungalow,' Marjorie repeated, 'you lucky thing.'

During the final hours, all activity was directed towards a glorious arrival in Christchurch. Boredom was now a thing of the past. From the cockpit came the request to leave the plane as clean as they could, because as soon as they got off, the press and other interested parties would be coming to have a look around. The Dutch had a reputation for being clean and tidy, and they would do their best to uphold this. Row by row, they had to remove all remnants of the trip, from on and underneath the seats, the seat backs, and the luggage nets; the cabin crew went around collecting the rubbish. Ada performed her task with meticulous precision, picking up every crumb, every scrap of paper, and every strand of yarn from beneath her seat, stooping over as much as possible to avoid Frank's eyes.

After about an hour all the ashtrays were empty and the litter had been removed from the blue carpeting in the aisle. Then they were given time to freshen up. The men could have a shave. One by one, the passengers were allowed to make use of the washbasin in the lavatory, keep it as short as possible, please, out of consideration for the others. Before their departure, the girls had been asked to bring along a white blouse and a black skirt so that upon their arrival their group would make a good impression. The men, of course, had the KLM tie. When they arrived, they could leave their coats and luggage in the plane, and they would be brought to customs for them.

'You'll arrive more refreshed,' the steward said.

Ada herself was feeling anything but refreshed as she stood in line in the midst of so many chattering brides, with everyone around her increasingly nervous about seeing their fiancés again. 'If he's not there,' said Marjorie, 'I'll be completely lost.' Ada shifted her weight from one foot to the other to help ease the burning, and wondered what she would do if Derk wasn't there. Anything could have happened.

He might even have died.

Esther took her time, unhampered by a sense of consideration for the others. Only when people started to grumble out loud did she squeeze out of the ladies' lounge in one of her own creations, ta-ta-ta-taaa. How did she do it, thought Ada (who'd been sent off with her aunt's old white blouse and a skirt her mother wore to funerals), how did she do it? She'd done what had been asked of her, but had deviated from it entirely. Esther wore a tight black calf-length dress, and over her shoulders had draped an enormous detached collar made from white pleated fabric, actually a kind of stole, which swayed as she moved. Although everyone in line applauded, Ada could see that some of the girls thought she was showing off. They're jealous, she thought, and looked in fascination at the perfectly pencilled eyebrows and her painted lips. 'Red lipstick is messy,' Marjorie whispered in her ear. 'How is she going to manage that? I feel sorry for the poor fellow who tries to kiss her…' Ada wasn't listening – she was watching Esther and saw how cool she remained with all those eyes upon her as she sashayed back to her seat on her sky-high heels. A girl like that isn't afraid of anything.

Frank said something nice to Esther – a compliment or a funny remark – and in response came that deep, throaty laugh. Now it was Ada's turn to feel jealous. Then Marjorie pushed her into the cubicle. The soap, toothbrush, and comb kept vibrating off the washbasin, but she freshened up as best she could to meet her husband.

*

At around six o'clock it was time. 'In a moment we'll start our descent,' announced the steward, 'and it looks like we'll be able to see New Zealand once we've passed through this layer of clouds.' The sun had risen blood red up in their sky world, and in all the excitement they hadn't noticed that the bottom of this world was formed by a solid sheet of clouds.

'Clouds?' cried Marjorie. 'But I thought the weather here was always fine!'

'You can take the same plane back,' said Esther.

'I'm never going to fly again.'

At the first jolts Ada was seized with a familiar fear, and she gripped the armrests. They bumped and bounced as they descended into a grey blanket. She closed her eyes, chewed furiously on the gum that had been handed out for the final time, and started to say a prayer even though she didn't expect it to have much of an effect. And sure enough, the plane kept dropping rapidly, down through the thick fog.

Suddenly, Frank was standing there in the aisle. He unceremoniously directed Marjorie back to where he'd been sitting and slipped in next to Ada, looking at her hands with their knuckles white from squeezing.

In spite of it all, this seemed to amuse him.

'Hold on tight, all right?'

She smiled apologetically. Again the plane dropped dramatically, and someone cried out.

'What did I just tell you?'

He makes everything seem lighter, she thought. How he did this was a mystery to her, as if he didn't take life so seriously. Still, he didn't seem to be the kind of person her father referred to as wild.

'On the other hand,' he said, 'we do have to land.'

She resolved to become like him, and forced herself to unclench her hands and place them in her lap, and she managed to keep them there even though the plane plunged sharply and made her stomach feel hollow.

Then they descended through the last of the clouds into a grey morning where the sun couldn't reach. 'Look,' said Frank, and they both leaned towards the window. 'New Zealand!' someone cried. A cry that was taken up by several voices. There was clapping, cheering, and singing. Behind them Marjorie broke into the football song, a soprano rendition of 'Go, Holland, go…' Everyone tried to see as much as they could of the country that had been the reason for their journey.

Ada sighed. At the bottom of an immense valley surrounded by high mountains, a river wove a tapestry in fanciful patterns. 'The Southern

Alps,' Frank said. 'Beautiful, aren't they.' She saw snow-covered peaks, something she'd only ever seen in photographs, and found herself getting caught up in something of the general exuberance. No matter what happened, it would be a new and exciting life. His face was so close to hers that she had to restrain herself to keep from kissing him. A free life in which anything was possible.

'See that?' he asked. 'This is it. This is where we were headed for. You had a plan. So did I. But where's the flat land I need for my farm?' In an unguarded moment, he took her hand, and became serious. 'This is where we'll go on with our lives.'

'Yes,' she whispered, and when she was sure no-one was watching, she kissed him anyway, a soft, quick kiss next to his mouth and leaned against him as she continued to watch the way the landscape slowly changed, how the mountains turned to hills, how the hills levelled off into grasslands that had been divided into large parcels of land in which they could see small white dots that must have been sheep. 'There's your flat land,' she said.

'The Canterbury Plains,' he said. 'It doesn't look like they saved any for me.'

An odd hush fell over the cabin. This is why they'd left everything behind and allowed themselves to be shut up inside an aeroplane for fifty hours, to come to this country where there was plenty of work, no poverty, and good public services, with the lowest infant mortality rate in the world. 'This is where your baby will be born before long,' he said. She started and put her finger to her lips, *shhh*.

Slowly but surely, the plane dropped closer to their new country. She saw orchards flash by beneath her, and sheep, everywhere were sheep in huge pastures of savannah bordered by trees, and a railway line that came straight out of the mountains and seemed to be following them. Lost in all this vastness occasionally a barn, a farm, a solitary group of wooden houses, sometimes a church. A road that disappeared between gently rolling hills, empty of traffic at this early hour. They came closer and

93

closer to the ground, until they were right over a vast, empty plain where the Viscount and the Canberras stood alongside each other on a runway, just like in London, but without the Hastings. We're here, she thought with a sharp twinge of regret, and moved even closer to him.

Huge numbers of cars were parked on one side of the airfield. Hordes of people were waiting for them to arrive at Harewood.

'Ada,' he said. The tone of his voice made her sit up.

'What is it?'

'If you jump, I'll catch you.'

As always, she started at the thump of the landing gear being let down. The engines howled as they gained speed for the final few yards. They sped over the chalk line between the finish pylon and the control tower at an altitude of two hundred feet.

'This might be our only chance,' he repeated.

Then the tyres hit the runway and burned along the asphalt with a deafening sound. It was Sunday morning 6.27 a.m. local time. Although they were the last to arrive, they'd won the race.

There was an explosion of cheers and applause. *Their* Holland was the champion, *their* KLM the best, *their* captain a hero. The jubilant cries were drowned out by the noise produced by the roar of powerful engines braking at full throttle, the engine room of Hell. It's still possible, she thought. And then: It's what I want, too. Plain and clear. Hand in hand, they braced themselves.

Before long the plane slowed and the noise diminished. The captain taxied the plane towards the airport terminal, and shut down the four engines. Mission accomplished. The crossing completed, the ship in the harbour. Pushed to the limit, but unscathed. It had taken them 49 hours, 57 minutes, and 13 seconds to reach the finish, ahead of their own flight plan by 14 hours and 41 minutes, breaking the 1946 England-to-New Zealand record by ten hours. There was every reason for wild rejoicing.

'I won't let you fall.'

Slowly, reluctantly, she took her hand from his.

Everyone shouted at once, their voices hoarse with emotion. Never before had ordinary passengers been turned into antipodeans in less than fifty hours. People had never emigrated faster. Seat belts were unbuckled impatiently, and the chosen ones danced on their seats. 'Please remain seated,' the steward cried. 'Let's restrain ourselves and make a good impression.' Here as well, a white jacket slipped in and they had to submit to the procedure with the Flit gun. There were fifteen thousand people outside, the man said, almost all of them Dutchies, some of them had spent the night in their cars. And while the emigrants almost choked from excitement as they covered their noses and mouths, the steward broke the news that the plan for a colour-coordinated entrance would have to be abandoned, because they'd just been informed the weather was cold, rainy, and raw. They would have to put on their coats.

7

THE CAPTAIN OPENED THE DOOR of the Liftmaster and allowed his chosen ones to go down the stairs, bon voyage cases in hand. With pale, expectant faces they stepped onto the soil of the country that would be their new home. When they weren't being blinded by flashbulbs they could see a host of their fellow countrymen and women waiting behind barriers a bit further along next to the modest airport terminal, a sea of bobbing heads, shouting, singing mouths, and arms waving red-white-and-blue Dutch flags, and signs being held aloft: 'Welcome to the bird from home!'

Here too the crowd broke into the Wilhelmus, off-key and out of tempo, the voices hoarse and choked with emotion.

Ada suddenly realized that the aeroplane's curved walls had provided security, a manageable world and an orderly life, close to the man who'd won her heart. All of that was over now, and before her lay a place that was overwhelming and unfamiliar and that she would have to explore all on her own on swollen, painful feet. For the time being, the sandy-haired boy who was waiting for her out there could do nothing to diminish this. She shivered, and gathered the collar of her coat closer to her throat. She couldn't make out Derk, it was a bit too far away and there were too many people. None of the brides were able to spot their fiancés – they stood on tiptoe and scanned the crowd. A few of them started to complain, but there was nothing to be done: they were separated from their sweethearts by radio reporters, cameramen, photographers, dignitaries, and an extensive programme. Maoris, who had braved the wind and rain for hours in their bare feet and traditional attire, brandished spears and shouted, danced, and sang, right through the Wilhelmus, from their position beyond the barriers, grimacing fiercely and sticking out their tongues as far as they could.

This gave some of the girls a slight case of the giggles. 'So those are Maoris,' said Marjorie. 'I've heard of them, of course, but I didn't know they looked like that...' Ada looked at the men's brown thighs, saw how they emerged from between the strands of their skirts every time they flexed their knees, their bare chests covered loosely by white capes. In *An Account of the Country and Its People for Emigrants* she'd read that they were brave, fierce, and intelligent. The government wanted to put their natural ability for working with tools to use in service of the entire population of New Zealand. I have to pay close attention, she thought, my new life starts here. But she couldn't. It was as if she wasn't actually standing where she stood. The singing and shouts of the Maoris got mixed up inside her head with snatches of the Wilhelmus and the cheers and formed one bewildering mess. The only thing that actually sank in was that Frank had his arm protectively around her back, and that she could decide to leave that arm right where it was.

*

A path had been set out through the middle of the crowd, fenced off on both sides by barriers. It led to a simple building with a round roof, the Christchurch airport. The captain rubbed his nose against the nose of the head of the Maoris, the ambassador welcomed the champions, and at last they were free to go. Marjorie was the first to break away – she cried out and ran forward. Running was out of the question for Ada, because by now it felt like she had razor blades in her shoes. I'm like the little mermaid, she thought, every step hurts. She was the last to reach the path. Walking between rows of outstretched arms and accompanied by cheers, she had to let people look at her, just like all the other girls, the spectators were entitled to this. Someone called out to her in Dutch, that she was a beauty from the homeland, the prettiest bride on the plane. All sorts of things were being shouted at the women. Somewhere towards the front Esther let people look her over, not the least bit embarrassed. Ada did her best to walk normally and not stumble. There was no way to escape those looks. 'Hey, blondie, are you already married or do I still stand a chance?' Whoops of laughter. Frank turned around, walked over to her, and put his arm around her shoulders demonstratively. 'This one's married.'

'Lucky devil!' Someone else shouted, 'You're not going to let her walk all by herself, are you?'

He kept his arm around her, and the number of remarks diminished considerably. 'Ada's poor feet,' he said. 'If they come with me, I'll anoint them with balsam, wrap them with cool bandages, and sing them sweet songs. Although,' he said, 'that last one might actually make the pain worse.' She moved away from him once they reached the door, where they all had to wait until they were officially allowed to enter the country.

'It's like a barracks,' Marjorie said. 'What a miserable place – they call this an airport?'

*

The small building was a hive of activity, filled with cheerful chattering. One by one, they impatiently underwent a short procedure at the customs department. They had to show their passports and health certificates and pay the required fee of ten pounds. A customs official at a typewriter recorded the necessary information: date of birth, colour of hair, colour of eyes, build, temporary address. Then they had to sign the form. *Certificate of Registration of Alien* was printed at the top in fat letters, with a number in the upper right-hand corner. Keep this with you at all times, cautioned the official, it contains your personal information; you must report every change of address and enter this on the back of the certificate. Welcome to New Zealand.

She hadn't understood a word. In mounting panic – her ears were ringing – she stared at the official. He tried to use sign language to explain to her what it was he wanted to know and in the end he took her passport from her and filled in what he saw in front of him. Further on, another department handed out letters with jobs for the scheme emigrants. They were then allowed to go and find their fiancés. Over all the heads she could see that Frank was watching her with concern. She was afraid that Derk had already spotted her, and signalled to him: let it be, it's all right. But it wasn't all right, and it would never be all right again. The customs official motioned that she could go, and gave her a sympathetic look as she walked away. I'm worthless as an emigrant, she thought as she wandered among the couples with her certificate in her hand. Everywhere she looked people were either kissing or standing awkwardly facing each other, ill at ease. She searched and searched, but didn't really know who she was looking for.

'How was I supposed to know!' laughed the young man standing next to Marjorie, the Hans in the plus fours from the photo. 'Turns out that men here never bring flowers, so they could see straight off I was Dutch and that I was waiting for my bride. I've already given three interviews!' He had a friendly, open face, just like in the picture. They were surrounded by photographers shouting 'Kiss, kiss,' and every time, Hans would hold out his flowers again and embrace his girl, and every time, Marjorie would gently fend him off. He has to give her time, thought Ada. She moved on, squeezing her way through the sea of men and girls, between hands touching hips and cries of oh, I missed you so much. She was looking, but also not looking, or wasn't looking for the person she should have been trying to find. Opposite Esther stood a young man with black hair. They were standing close together in the crush, but Ada could see the distance between them. He was a head shorter than Esther, and seemed to be startled by her. 'I'd forgotten...' she heard him say, 'did you used to be... did you get taller?' A soft, nasal voice. Esther didn't reply, and impulsively took off her high heels. Now she was only half a head taller, but it didn't seem to help matters much. Ada continued to squeeze between the backs of those around her with the howl of the engines still in her head, to the left and to the right, with no idea where she was headed. Sorry, she said silently when she bumped into someone, I'm not paying attention, where is he, anyway – and who is he?

At that moment she felt a hand on her shoulder, and a voice she recognized from its South Holland accent said: 'Pastor…'

She turned around with a start and came face to face with her husband. In that very instant she realized with devastating certainty that she would never love him and that there was nothing he could do about it. He wasn't bad-looking, and she was touched to see how he'd spruced himself up for the occasion – a nice suit, his sandy hair combed into a wet part. But he didn't dare look directly at her. She felt a powerful wave of shame arise and knew this would blight her life.

'Pastor, this is Ada,' he said shyly to the man with grey hair and glasses next to him.

'Ada, this is Pastor Houtsma.'

She mechanically held out her hand. Behind his eyeglasses she saw confusion, and hesitation. He knows about it and finds me contemptible. Derk leaned towards her. She thought he wanted to kiss her and obligingly offered him her cheek, but instead he whispered something into her ear. Your buttons. She looked down and saw that the buttons of her white blouse had come undone near her swollen breasts. Don't, don't, said a deep voice inside her head, while her fingers struggled nervously to get the buttons closed.

The pastor was relieved with the outcome; he regained his composure and held out his hand.

'Welcome, daughter,' he said, 'to our small congregation.'

'We've got our own congregation now,' Derk explained, 'the first in Greymouth. We don't have a building yet, we hold the services in a pub, you'll see this afternoon, we have to mop up the beer first… but at least it's ours.'

She suddenly realized it was Sunday, the Lord's Day, she'd completely forgotten. All the while, her eyes were searching the hall, looking among all the heads, shoulders, and backs. 'We're not happy with the Presbyterian church,' said Derk, 'no inspiration, and they sing in English.' She nodded as sympathetically as she could. Then a bashful silence fell between man and wife. He stole a glance at her and she could tell he liked what he saw. I'm his wife. He's been thinking about me at night, he expects everything you might expect of marriage. They kissed each other on the mouth. The pasty smell of postage stamps. He took her hand; his own was cold and clammy. But he seemed genuinely glad to see her.

'How are you?'

'Fine.'

'Did you enjoy it?'

'Oh, yes!'

He took her suitcase from her in an awkwardly gallant gesture. 'If we drive straight through, the service can start on time. Shall we go?'

No, she wanted to shout, we won't be going for quite some time yet, people are going to make speeches, the ambassador and a government minister, we won, you know, they're going to give our captain a cheque for a hundred thousand pounds, it's all going to charity, isn't that nice, and then we're all going to get onto a bus, there's a bus waiting for us, we've spent fifty hours together, weathered storms, at the very least I want to say goodbye to everyone, I can't leave just like that. And what's more, I'm going with Frank because I love him, because my body comes to life when he touches me, because when he speaks my soul shakes itself off like a puppy does after a swim, refreshed, almost like there's nothing for me to be ashamed of, and that's what this is supposed to be all about, isn't it, that we're all going to be happier? Well, then.

But she said nothing, because she was already part of a small congregation, and she followed the two men to the exit. While Derk enthusiastically explained how he'd been able to get a real bargain on a used truck, she kept turning around and looking for Frank, and even for

Marjorie and Esther; when she was surrounded by those three faces, a better future had seemed possible. But she couldn't spot any of them in the whole cheerful mob.

'They make them out of an ordinary car, you know how? They cut off the back and build the truck bed out of wood, that's how.' He pulled her through the crowd; she bumped and stumbled, and the pain in her feet radiated upwards. 'They like to make things themselves here.'

The pastor held open the door for them.

She wanted to say everything now that she still had the chance, but all that came out of her mouth were moans, little sounds that evaporated into the hall, where they didn't stand a chance amidst the laughter and joyful reunions.

*

He was proud of his truck, and his eyes shone as he showed her the ancient Ford, where sure enough, a makeshift wooden truck bed had been mounted onto the back. He helped her climb in, and must have apologized four or five times: he hated to do it, but the pastor was driving back with them after a visit to Christchurch, the pastor didn't know how to drive and they couldn't let him ride in the back, they just couldn't. And she'd waved aside his apologies, because of course they couldn't. She settled meekly into the back of the truck, shivering and yawning. He looked concerned and pointed to a pile of blankets, suggesting she might sleep for a bit.

How long will it take then? she asked, suddenly uneasy.

Five or six hours, he said, if they didn't have any problems on the way and if the weather cooperated at Arthur's Pass, something you could never be sure of, because it could get bad up there. She wrapped the blanket around her like an Indian robe. He patted her leg clumsily, hesitated, and pointed to her belly. Asked softly how she was feeling. We're going to have a baby together, she thought, and nodded reassuringly, everything is fine. Relieved, he got behind the wheel in the small cab, next to the grey-

102

haired man who sat waiting. When he accelerated, she fell over for the first time.

She manoeuvred herself into a corner with her back up against the cab and tried to keep her balance while the truck rattled westward through a vast, deserted landscape. A landscape to feel lost in, without a single point of reference. She held on to the rough wooden side with both hands. Her blue bon voyage case slid back and forth over the bottom of the truck bed.

They'd been on the road for less than twenty minutes when she saw a bus approaching in the distance from the direction of the airport, and she hoped it wasn't the one with the passengers from their plane, because she didn't want Frank to see her like this without being able to explain. It couldn't be them, because they would still be listening to the speeches. The bus was travelling much faster than the old Ford, and when the driver started to overtake them, she saw she'd been mistaken, that her fellow travellers hadn't waited for the ceremony, either, and that the bus was full of exuberant young people, the emigrants, the chosen ones, *her* companions, *her* group. Esther saw her first. The pencilled eyebrows shot up, the red mouth fell open. Ada tried to give them a light-hearted wave, but just then the truck hit a pothole, and she had to grab on quickly with both hands. She laughed as she regained her balance. Esther walked to the back of the bus. Marjorie just kept waving, as if by waving she could offer comfort, or encourage her somehow.

He was sitting on the seat at the back. Esther leaned towards him. He swivelled sharply and looked out the window. Here I am, she thought, and something broke deep down inside, because in his eyes she saw herself drowning, and she couldn't explain it to him.

The bus overtook the truck and she followed it with her body as it passed, clutching on to the side of the truck, her eyes in his. How could she have explained that he should stop thinking about it, because this was the only way open to her – submission to a cruel God she sometimes hated for his cruelty – because the alternative, choosing *for* him, would be to go against God, against the Church, against her parents, against everything she'd ever been taught and in which she believed. That she didn't have the courage to call down the terrible wrath of God upon herself and be cast out. She could explain none of this, so instead she just kept watching him as long as she could. And when she could no longer make him out, she kept watching the bus, which seemed to be moving away from the truck faster and faster. At a fork in the road where the bus went straight, the truck turned right. She leaned up against the back of the cab and watched until the bus was only a tiny speck that was then swallowed up by the vast, overwhelming landscape.

*

The truck drove through the countryside she'd seen from the plane, only now in the opposite direction. They were going back west. The orchards, the enclosed pastures, the outbuildings, the groups of houses, the wooden churches. Still no sign of life, making it seem like they were driving away from the civilized world. Funny sheep they have here, she thought. The mountains came into view. To the left, the train tracks, the railway line. The mountains with their snow-capped peaks came closer, huge, high mountains. The road crossed the tracks, which now followed along on the right. But where to? She saw how foreign the landscape was. The mountains stretched from left to right. The first ridge loomed up next to her. Coal-black cows, a bit on the small side. The ridge thrust itself upon her and came closer and closer. Horses, one white and one brown. Are these mountains called the Alps, she thought, just like the Alps in Europe, is that what he said? The road curved to the right. Suddenly she was surrounded by mountains. The curves became sharper and the road more steep. They were climbing. To the left a narrow stream appeared, which quickly became wider and deeper. Yes, we're in the mountains, then. Shimmering tufts of golden brown grass that waved in the wind. A momentary awareness of beauty. You could lose yourself in country like this. Stay here, not as a human but as a river. The wind pulled at the car. Fog appeared between the mountain tops, the cold became more intense. Nature can turn against you, and then shelter becomes important. She took another blanket but didn't manage to wrap herself in it, because the road was now unpaved and the truck jolted through the numerous potholes. The cold didn't really bother her. What big ferns they have here, like palm trees. The truck kept climbing. The road got narrower and turned into a track. It started to rain. She saw the river, at the bottom of the ravine. Yes, she thought, you can say 'I won't let you fall', but if I jump we'll both fall, and it's a long way down. Then she lay flat on her back and stared into the fog. Her feet were numb. She slid back and forth over the rough wood like a doll. I've lost something, she thought, but I don't know what. I'm the shell that surrounds my child, so it can grow properly. I let myself be driven from A to B. Somewhere, once, I must have had my own will, my own desires and direction, but where, and when? She couldn't remember. She was too tired. She would rather not think about anything any more.

'Whatever the future may bring, the hand of the Lord will guide me.'

8

BOB PARKS THE CAR BENEATH the sign welcoming them to the estate. They walk over the grounds between huge silver fermentation tanks that mirror back the blazing sun and make them blink. 'Unbelievable,' says Marjorie. The vineyard she remembers is gone. She doesn't recognize a thing except for the rows of grapevines on either side of the drive, which are all exactly the same except that there are thousands of them, as though someone has played a clever trick with mirrors.

'Can you still remember what it used to be like?'

'No, not really.'

He looks at his watch; he has to go back to Wellington soon, to the airport, to pick up his daughter, who's flying in from Sydney. 'What I wonder,' he says, 'is how they pronounce Druivebloed here.'

From the fields comes the dry crack of a gunshot. Bird shooting, Marjorie thinks, and in her mind's eye she sees an open jeep, muscular arms at the wheel, a lock of brown hair blows back, and next to the driver sits a little boy. His small hands proudly grip the butt of a gun – much too large for him – that stands upright between his legs: bird shooting. A troubling sense of guilt, a familiar stomach ache. She looks around nervously.

'This is really impressive,' says Bob as they walk on. Elevated walkways have been built alongside the gigantic tanks so they can be opened from the top. Large, simple outbuildings stand near the tanks; they have an

106

industrial look to them inside, with metal presses and fermentation vats. In another outbuilding they see the smaller, more familiar oak casks and countless stacks of crates with bottles of wine. Long lorries are parked next to the buildings, and also various kinds of agricultural implements. They keep walking until they arrive at an elegant restaurant with a large patio. Opposite this a shop, with a tasting room next door. Further along, at the edge of the fields, a small number of pretty, one-storey houses that look like they might be guest cottages. Next to the tasting room, an attractive modern office with a greenhouse behind it, and an imposing three-storey brick building with DRUIVEBLOED VITICULTURE COLLEGE in large letters above the entrance. Everywhere they look they see the Druivebloed crest. Everything has been done tastefully; there is a lush abundance of subtropical plants in the green spaces between the buildings, tall lavender plants spread their perfume along the footpaths, and fountains in courtyards produce pleasant splashing sounds. Beyond the buildings, where the hills begin in the distance, you can see the white country house from the brochures.

Impressive indeed.

But not a living soul in sight. An oppressive silence hangs over the grounds. The lorries stand in the sun, driverless and out of work. Inside there is no-one at the restaurant's immaculate tables, which have already been laid. Outside on the patio, oversized canvas umbrellas above the wooden tables keep the sun off guests who aren't there. A fountain splashes in vain, and a wide pergola grown over with grapevines provides shade for no-one. Marjorie points: a flag hangs at half-mast. The wind slaps the rope against the aluminium pole with a tinkling sound. Bob nods and looks at his watch. 'Mama,' he says, 'I've got to go, otherwise I'll be late. Will you be all right here by yourself?' He kisses her on the cheek. 'Where is everyone?'

She's suddenly terrified, not of the silence, but of the person who would break that silence. She chatters cheerfully as she walks him back to the car park. The sling pulls at her neck. Underneath the cast, her skin itches. The black suit is too warm – Hans died in November. She makes up her mind to go and sit on the patio at one of those wooden tables, under an umbrella, until everything starts.

'Do you think you'll make it back on time?'

'If her plane isn't delayed.'

She can see he's excited – he hasn't seen his youngest child for months. The whole family had gone to Schiphol Airport, and there were also a couple of girlfriends from school with skimpy crop tops, and an adorable boyfriend wearing a pair of jeans with the crotch hanging down between his knees. All of them there at six in the morning to see Hannah off. Toodle-oo, she said cheerfully, as if she were going off for a day at the beach and not backpacking on her own through Australia for a whole year. Marjorie can still see the slight figure in the suede jacket disappearing behind passport control with her head held high. The long dark curls, with a hat like the ones you often see young people wearing these days. Still a child, nineteen years old, so young. And far too pretty. Vera cried of course, the whole way back and while they had their coffee. Marjorie had looked at her daughter-in-law and thought about her own parents, back then.

We were just as young. We never came back.

She watches as her son backs up the car, and waves at him with her good left arm. Don't forget the liquorice, she wants to call out, but he accelerates and drives out of the car park onto the road that leads to the exit.

As soon as Bob is out of sight, her agitation returns in all its intensity. In the distance she can see a taxi approaching. She turns around abruptly and starts to walk. I have to get a cup of coffee and something to go along with it, scones, or a muffin, something that helps. Gravel crunches beneath her shoes as she walks back to the restaurant, in the hope that someone from the restaurant will now be there, wearing an apron, notepad in hand to take her order. She tries to imagine she's on holiday and that she and Hans are driving the wine trail. At lunch they drink an entire bottle of pinot blanc and eat fresh trout, and later on they drive back to the hotel for a nice nap. In their deliciously comfortable hotel bed they hold hands and say, remember this? remember that?

Her eyes fill up with angry tears. Where are you anyway? she asks out loud. She's been asking this question for four years now, but never gets an answer. Death is an invisible perspex wall and she keeps walking into it. She can't picture 'not existing'. At nursery school, the teacher had held a bunch of pencils out to her, saying: go ahead and take zero pencils... no, that's three... no, that's five... no, that's eleven. She couldn't do it, and had stamped her feet in frustration. She never again forgot what zero meant. She can't forget what death means either. She'd always laughed at Hans's jokes – if not always entirely wholeheartedly, then out of love – but this last joke just isn't funny at all. She lowers herself onto the wooden bench, takes her arm with the cast out of its sling, and rests it on the table in front of her. It's not as hot under the umbrella.

'Hello...' she calls out. Her voice vanishes in the wind.

Somewhere behind the buildings she hears the taxi pull out of the car park. Someone must have finally arrived. If only her heart wouldn't beat so fast.

*

Ada is still sitting on the bench at the bus stop gathering courage to go into the estate. Her new black patent leather shoes are covered with dust. Your shoes were always dirty by the time you reached the bunker.

She stood shivering at the bottom of the hill. Derk pointed up. She couldn't believe her eyes. 'A bunker?' He pulled her triumphantly behind him through the wet, sandy earth. Her shoes sank down into the mud. 'They were afraid the Japs were going to invade,' he explained. Both of them were out of breath when they reached the top. It was nothing more than a rectangular concrete box. A single door, with a spyhole next to it that had been hacked out and made into a window. A tap on the outside wall with a basin beneath it. On top of the hill stood a solitary tree that had been severely pruned, all the way back to the trunk. Sand and mud everywhere. Derk didn't seem to see it. He turned her around with her back to the bunker and showed her the view. Her teeth were chattering from cold and dismay. Even so, she was also able to see the beauty. The village below, the wide street that went straight down to the river, the river that flowed into the sea. Tall black cranes in the distance, in the harbour, dramatic silhouettes against the purple sky. It hadn't stopped raining since Arthur's Pass. She looked longingly at the ordinary houses in the village below.

'The local council owns the land,' said Derk, 'but the bunker is ours.'

And the sea can't reach it, she thought, because she was trying to understand, but when she said this out loud his face grew dark. He shivered and hugged his thin body as if to protect himself from her arrogant notion. 'If God wants to punish the sinners, He will send His seas wherever He likes.' The child that had been conceived in sin moved inside her belly.

It was dark and chilly inside the bunker. He pointed to a rough opening in the wall surrounded by large chunks of concrete. That's where the fireplace would be. But he hadn't had time to finish it, because he worked long hours at the railway. She stood shivering in the middle of the bare room and looked at the grim young man who was her husband, how he tugged at the pieces of cement. 'The people here,' he said, 'they'll take you for a ride. You have to join the union, and I won't. If they teach you words, it turns out later they're filthy ones. They may say they believe in God, but you wouldn't know it from how they act.'

Run, now, said someone somewhere far away, turn around, now, jump, now.

A table, two chairs, a concrete floor. In the corner he'd made a start at building a wooden wall and floor so the damp wouldn't bother them as much. He'd made a start at everything. Only the bed was finished. He'd got the mattress for a song, he said. Used to belong to an old widower who'd recently died. It was a good mattress. She pushed back her tears and said his name. 'Derk?' He finally looked right into her eyes. She took his hand. 'You've done a good job,' she whispered. His features softened.

110

The taxi that had turned into the access road is leaving, without the passenger. Well, Ada thinks, if I sit here much longer I might just as well take
the bus back to the hotel. She stands up and crosses the road. Her knees
hurt dreadfully. In spite of this, she is still filled with a peculiar, rather
pleasant kind of excitement. She enters through the wrought-iron arch
and starts her long walk between the grapevines. There you are, says a
deep voice.

*

In the car park, Esther takes her compact from her handbag, opens out
the mirror, and touches up her face. In the sunlight you can see all the
growth rings on her skin – oh, well, there was nothing she could do about
them. She applies lipstick and checks to see if she has any hairs on her chin
like Grandma Berthi used to have, but there aren't any, or her eyes aren't
good enough to see them. It makes no difference to her. What you can't
see doesn't exist. She once again wonders if Marjorie is here, whether she
had been able to summon up the courage to come. She puts on her sunglasses – she's had them since the end of the sixties and according to her
they're terribly hip again – and looks around. He must have worked so
hard. She hears the sound of an engine. One of those luxurious modern
jeeps is approaching the car park through the field from the direction of
the country house. Esther waits. Behind the wheel is a boy who seems
vaguely familiar. He drives the vehicle over to where she's standing, turns
off the engine, and greets her politely, good morning. He gets out, shakes
her hand, and introduces himself as Kris. 'Are you here for the funeral?'
She nods. 'Sweet,' he says. It sounds like an 'okay'. Through his eyes she
once again sees how old she is, sees herself suspended somewhere out in
space, light years away.

We're all in the big house, he says, I've come to get you. He's wearing
a black shirt with Maori words in white letters. Brown muscular arms

emerge from the short sleeves. A greenstone hangs around his neck on a leather thong. His oval face is handsome, with olive skin and a small dark goatee. Intelligent brown eyes that look out onto the world with an open gaze – you can see he's been raised with love and security and that he doesn't know how special this is. She could fall in love with him on the spot, and continues to find it sad that no-one expects anything more from her in that area. Kris opens the door for her. Like a film star on her way to a gala, she places her hand in his with an excessively elegant flourish to keep the scene from seeming too much like one in which an ailing elderly woman is being helped into a car by a carer. Unfortunately, she doesn't manage to fasten the seat belt on her own, and he obligingly buckles her in. 'We're all very sad,' he says. They zoom out of the car park. The vehicle's suspension is wonderfully smooth, and Esther thinks back to the old jeep. She looks around at the vast expanse of fields and the mountains behind them. For a moment she sees Frank running through a field and dropping down on his knees in despair. We were so much alike, why couldn't we help each other? She shakes her head, don't do this. She notices that Kris isn't driving towards the house. Instead, he turns into the grounds of the estate. We saw another car drive in, he explains, there must be someone else as well.

9

THEY WERE NO LONGER AFRAID to be seen. Six years after the end of the war, when she'd just graduated from the fashion academy, Esther met Leon again. In the overcrowded jazz club on Amsterdam's Leidseplein – a smoky, dark cavern – they recognized one another immediately, if only by the way that enjoyment was tainted for both of them. Hey, hello, how are you? No-one from either of their families had come back from the concentration camps. But this wasn't the time or place.

Loss, fear, grief, and agonizing questions for which there were no answers: these were the wild beasts that had lain in wait in the corner of her cage for years now, waiting for a moment of diminished vigilance. Dressed in the flamboyant attire of an animal tamer, she kept them at bay with an iron will. Now she gladly made use of the loud jazz and cosmopolitan setting. She and Leon reminisced about innocuous memories from their early days with the Rep family, where they'd spent three years in the attic during the war: he, a pale, serious boy of twelve pining for his mother, and she, three years his senior, a sarcastic adolescent with angry eyes who kept herself entertained with her sewing basket and refused to bother with the tearful little boy. Why don't you be a little nicer to him, said the rotund Mrs Rep (who they had to call Aunt Nel), shaking her head. But she just gave a disparaging hiss, the way teenage girls do. Remember?

'You used to hiss,' Leon shouted so he could be heard above the music. 'Do you still do that?'

'If you'd like,' she said flirtatiously. 'Did you miss it?'

He wasn't bad-looking, a young man in his twenties, slender, with dimples in his cheeks and thick black hair he wore combed back. He worked in the bookkeeping department of the transport company Van Gend & Loos and had managed to finish secondary school by taking evening classes. A clever boy. As for herself, once the war was over she hadn't been able to put her mind to finishing grammar school. Although he was smaller than she was, they danced well together. Later that evening they wandered along the Lijnbaansgracht and imitated the Reps' regional accent. Gaden, instead of garden. 'I should be getting hum,' she cried, choking with laughter. 'We owe our lives to those people,' he said, suddenly serious. 'I kno-oow,' she sang, 'what if we hadn't been able to go into hadding there!' And collapsed again in shrieks of laughter. They lingered in the street where she rented a room above a garage. He told her about how he would be emigrating to New Zealand soon. I've got to get out of here, he said, and she knew exactly what he meant. In the end they kissed, which felt strangely incestuous but not unpleasant. Write to me, she said, full of promise. She couldn't sleep, and later that night was so terribly sick she didn't think she would ever be able to touch another drop of gin.

*

He kept his word, and the letters arrived at fairly regular intervals, telling of a relaxed and friendly country with a great deal of future and not much past. In the meantime, she continued to flirt and go out. People always noticed her, not because she was either beautiful or ugly (she was neither) but because the way she moved called attention to who she was. She put off going to bed, because she slept badly. During the day she trained at a celebrated fashion house, which in practice meant that she did the worst jobs for a pittance. She always seemed to be at odds with her boss because she would give her opinion in front of clients. I'm ready for my own shop, she thought. But to set up a business in Holland you had to have capital, and a mountain of documents that were difficult to obtain. She didn't want to wait endlessly for permits. She didn't want to wait endlessly for anything any more.

In addition, Amsterdam itself made it hard for her to forget. She avoided entire neighbourhoods because every stone called forth questions. In the middle of a winter's night, as she lay naked on the bed beneath the open window in order to feel the cold, she heard the wild beasts clawing at the floor and suddenly realized she would never be able to sleep again if she stayed in Europe. So, when after corresponding for a year Leon wrote to say he could envision the two of them building a future together, she didn't hesitate for long. For an emigrant, New Zealand was as far away as you could get; if you went any further, the distance got smaller again. It did bother her that he mentioned the Jewish community in Christchurch with increasing frequency. Well, I'll hiss that out of him, she thought.

*

We'll see how things go, he wrote, and chivalrously offered to pay for her trip back if she didn't like it. Even though he hadn't exactly proposed to her, she started to dream about a wedding gown. In the evenings she would sit with her sketchbook and design one dress after another, with the bells of the Westertoren chiming in the background. She took her inspiration from Dior's New Look and drew a spectacular dress with a broad shoulder line, a fitted bodice, and a full, flowing calf-length skirt. Ballerina length. The skirt should be an explosion of fabric, no scrimping here. At last, fabric was no longer being rationed, and she used her savings to buy yards of heavy cream-coloured satin, an insane outlay of cash. For weeks, when she came home from work she would let the fabric slide pleasurably through her fingers, spreading it out on her bed, folding and draping it around her tall figure in various ways so she could see what the material did. To try out the design, she made a toile from her threadbare cotton sheets and used this to make adjustments to the pattern. She used tailor's chalk to draw the pattern pieces onto the material, sighing deeply as she worked with rapt attention. When she couldn't put off cutting the fabric any longer, she surreptitiously took the atelier's large fabric shears home with her one evening and concentrated intently as she allowed them to glide through the satin, an almost sacred experience. Using the old hand-operated Singer sewing machine Aunt Nel had given her, she would work on the gown until the early hours. I can do this, she thought, bending over the tiny buttonholes she was finishing entirely by hand, I can do this, I have it in me, it will be wonderful. And by this she was not referring to marriage. For the last time she cycled out to Landsmeer and asked Aunt Nel and Uncle Jan to accompany her to the airport. The big farmer and his fat wife lumbered along beside her, awed by the official ceremony. I'm for ever in your debt, Esther said hoarsely, even if I never write. See how you get on, they nodded good-naturedly, and say hello to Leon. Just then, out of the corner of her eye she saw a young man stroll by, the kind of person who's at ease no matter where he is because he carries the world inside him, and answered: 'If I see him.' She regretted it immediately when she saw the shocked looks on their old faces. 'He's coming to meet you, isn't he?' Aunt Nel asked with concern.

'Just kidding,' she winked, but as she sashayed to the plane she could feel them shaking their heads as they watched her walk away – they'd never really been able to understand her jokes and, to be honest, she didn't always understand them herself.

*

All those chattering girls on the plane. She wasn't the least bit interested in that bride business. In London, she and three of the journalists travelling with them had gone to a club and stayed till it closed. They wanted to know how she saw her future in her new country. 'I'm destined to become a fashion designer, no matter where I end up,' she answered haughtily, with a flair for the dramatic. 'I'm not taking anything along, just myself, my sewing machine, and my talent.' The men were an appreciative audience. She said nothing about what she was leaving behind. Afterwards, they lost themselves in the streets of the city, with Esther as the ice queen surrounded by her retinue. She enjoyed it immensely – they kept offering her cigarettes and would then light them for her, and they bent over backwards to make her laugh. They sang Cole Porter songs as they sat on a bench at the edge of a large park. It was so late when they got back to the hotel that they had to ring the bell. She only met her room-mate the following day, right before they left, at the bottom of the steps that led up to the plane. Her name was Ada, still a child, but so lovely it was unsettling. The handsome man of the world, whose smile awakens a painful longing to have it all to yourself, was called Frank de Rooy. With that smile on a Persian carpet, well, you wouldn't hear another peep out of me. As she always did, she sized up what he was wearing, the light coat and the suit beneath it: elegant but outdated, expensive but worn, from a good family, but poor like the rest of us. She'd wanted to flirt with him, and sat down right behind him in the cabin with this in mind, but he only had eyes for Ada – blonde Ada who was blessed with a voluptuous body and a stunning face but didn't have the slightest notion of what you could do with it. Without a doubt the worst-dressed girl on the plane, in a tired cotton dress from before the war.

*

The flight itself soon became tiresome, and she had Ada try on the cream-coloured dress partly to alleviate the boredom and partly because she found it thrilling to see all of that unconscious beauty emerge in something she created. This sensation came not from what the dress represented, but from the dress itself. She really did want to wear it herself, but even more than that she wanted to make the dress and see if she'd been right. See what cutting the fabric on the bias did for a hip line, what pleated organza did for the bust. See what happened in the eyes of the girl when she looked at herself. I can do this, she thought again triumphantly, I have it in me.

Seen in this light, the rips in the satin after the storm were insignificant.

She also felt sorry for the sweet child. Right before her very eyes, she saw something blossoming between the girl and Frank, something that clearly had not been meant to happen. Her neighbour Marjorie – conservative, boxy suit from the war years – saw it, too. Esther didn't allow herself to be drawn into whispered gossip. So Esther was silent for long periods at a time; she stared out of the window, smoked, and had ecstatic visions of a catwalk with models wearing her gowns in a gorgeous array of colours. Her parents and Sallie were in the audience. When she wasn't silently dreaming her dreams, she was playing cards with the journalists. Frank joined her there on the last night, making her laugh with the kamikaze jokes of someone who has just been rejected. They enjoyed each other's company.

*

A fresh start. Her throat was raw from all the cigarettes as she stood at the bottom of the aeroplane steps, squinting her eyes against the flashbulbs and the watery light. Everything smiled upon her. So this was it, then, New Zealand, not a bit swampy, just a fresh, young country, ta-ta-ta-taaa. The brisk wind and dark clouds didn't dampen her spirits, for blue skies played no essential role in her dreams for the future. The unpolished and rather amateurish performance by the chilly group of dancers and the barrack-like airport terminal didn't bother her in the slightest. She could feel firm, clean ground beneath her heels. She said a warm goodbye to the journalists, shook the hands of the Dutch people behind the barricades, and let people look her over. Here I am, this is me.

Marjorie was brandishing her alien certificate. 'It's as if we came from the moon!' she cried indignantly. Esther made no comment as she slipped her own certificate deep into her pocket. Just a little while longer. She intended to apply for citizenship as soon as she could: here's my old passport, I'd like to trade it in for a new model. I'd like to trade in my language too, please, *hopla*. She wanted to speak in English, think in English, dream in English, breathe in English. She wasn't worried about homesickness. For ten years now, she'd kept the sickening, stomach-churning loss at bay, one of the wild beasts. It remained to be seen whether it had dared to come along with her. Even seeing Leon again hadn't been a disappointment, and he looked stronger and healthier than she remembered. That *he* was shocked by how *she* looked hadn't been a disappointment either.

The streets they could see from the bus were lacklustre and quiet, with wooden bungalows and neat lawns, something she found encouraging. She didn't want to be impressed, she wanted to make an impression. Yes, sleep on, sluggish citizens, she thought, I'll shake you wide awake. I'll shake this town to its very foundations when my designs hit the street. In spite of her headache, she would have liked to have started right away.

In the centre of Christchurch the lawns disappeared and the houses were made of brick and stone, the blocks of flats higher. What remained was the quiet. 'Lively,' she joked as she inspected the deserted Cathedral Square after getting off the bus. Leon, who had no way of knowing she liked it, felt called upon to defend the town where he'd lived for almost two years. 'It's half past seven on a Sunday morning,' he said. 'Normally it's a pleasant town, nice people. There's no anti-Semitism here.'

'No,' she teased, 'there's absolutely nothing here.'

Marjorie's fiancé backed her up.

'You know what they say? "Christchurch is half as big as the cemetery of New York, and twice as dead!"' He laughed heartily at his own joke.

Nice fellow, she thought. Grey flannel. Honest through and through. Not my type.

And then, on the wet cobblestones of that sleepy square, she was suddenly overcome with an inexplicable feeling of happiness that nearly made her weep because it had been so long since she felt like this. For a moment she didn't know what to do and simply stood there, happy as could be, on this random spot on the face of the earth that now happened to be her spot as well.

You could sense the disappointment among the other passengers from the Liftmaster. They were a dishevelled lot, pale, tired, and cold. Unused to the new situation – suddenly finding themselves with no schedule and no captain – everyone lingered on the square in front of the sandstone cathedral.

Marjorie leaned towards her.

'Pa will just have to send some money,' she whispered. 'I'm going back.'

Esther awoke from her reverie, turned on her heels, and set out for the other side of the street to examine the displays in the shop windows. She sashayed across the street with Leon in her wake, pointing derisively at the posts on the pavement that held up the canopies in front of the shops, just like in the Wild West. 'This must be where they tie up the horses.'

'Esther, stop for a moment.'

She pulled him past shop windows that confirmed her hopes. Fashion from at least ten years back, and everything displayed without the slightest sense of flair. Suits you wouldn't even want to be caught dead in. Sad dresses in sweet English pastels. Dowdy knitted cardigans. '*All wool, distinctive design, nothing better.*' Distinctive design, my eye.

This country needs me.

She ran a triumphant little lap around the pavement and raised her arms. Trumpeted around the ring. 'Ta-ta-ta-taaa… from the simplest dress to the most divine creation, they won't believe their eyes. Here I am, ready to bring all of my talent to this wasteland.'

Leon looked on doubtfully. He'd already said something about her figure-hugging black dress with the white pleats. A virtually geometrical tulip silhouette, so tight around the knees that they rubbed against each other when she walked. It was one of the designs the fashion house had allowed her to try after a great deal of wheedling, but no-one had bought it, too radical for their clients. They'd given it to her as a goodbye gift.

'Esther, stop for a moment.'

She stopped reluctantly, pulling the thin pleated fabric around her in the October chill. After the wedding dress there hadn't been any money left for fabric to make a coat, and she'd rather die than start her new life in her old one. She looked for Frank, and saw him standing in front of the cathedral next to Hans, who was explaining things and pointing to the left and to the right. From his manner she could tell Frank wasn't listening, and she wondered if he was thinking about Ada. Ada in the back of that pickup. Carried off in the back of a truck.

She shook back some of her curls and straightened up. Over by the men, Marjorie had dropped down onto her suitcase, the picture of despair.

'If we...' Leon began hesitantly. 'I've arranged for us to...'

She could have a room with a family he'd got to know through the Jewish community, and that was quite an achievement, because it turned out it wasn't as easy to find somewhere to live as they'd thought back in Holland. Even this didn't disappoint her. Nothing could spoil her good mood. It was just that the prospect of the family didn't appeal to her. He pointed to the geometric silhouette.

'Do you have something else with you? Less... I don't know if they...'

'Who?' she asked innocently, as if she hadn't heard anything he'd told her in the bus.

He remained patient.

'Mr and Mrs Jottkowitz.'

'Jottkowitz...' she mused, and felt deeply weary.

'From the room. They're related to the rabbi.'

'I'll have to see.'

'It would be nice if you could wear something else. Because I don't know...'

Frank saw her looking at him and waved. Impulsively she started to cross the street, back to the square. The first car of this Sunday morning, a taxi, narrowly missed her and honked furiously. She let out a cry and jumped back onto the pavement.

'Yes,' said Leon, 'they drive on the left here, you have to get used to it.'

He offered her his arm, saying drily, 'All that talent of yours just about ended up under a car.'

Esther recognized the dimples in his cheeks. Arm in arm, they crossed to the square where Hans and Marjorie were hailing the taxi.

'We can walk,' said Leon. 'It's not far. They'll give you breakfast. They made challah for you. And this afternoon we'll get you registered.'

The smell of challah baking in the oven.

She pulled away. 'Register? Where?'

'With the Jewish community.' So patient. He'd already explained all of this. The Jewish community in Christchurch wasn't large, around a hundred people; they'd looked after the refugees and now they were looking after the immigrants. They helped you out, but you had to register on your own. There was also a synagogue, with a stained-glass window. But her thoughts were elsewhere, don't mind me.

'Esther...' Disheartened, he stood there in the middle of the square.

'Where was it you're going again?' she asked Frank innocently. She already knew the answer to this as well. She didn't mean anything by it, she just wanted to gain some time, because along with her newly won happiness – which had to do with freedom – came the need to consider all of the available options. Frank had to get to the harbour in Lyttelton, an hour by train, and he would spend the night there in a camp for immigrants before taking the boat tomorrow night to Wellington on the North Island; from there he would go by train to Masterton, where he was expected on a farm. He held up his hand to flag down a taxi. He didn't feel like going to the camp.

'I'm staying here tonight, I'm going to find a hotel,' he said. 'What about you?'

Leon tapped her lightly on the back. The challah was warm and fragrant beneath a white napkin, a family napkin.

'Esther...'

She wished she could turn towards him.

'I'm going to a hotel, I'm sorry. I'm too tired. I have to get some sleep. You can understand that, can't you?'

He did his best. She could feel herself becoming terribly annoyed, hadn't asked for any of this, not for challah either. 'I'm completely shattered.'

Come on, will you, tomorrow's another day. For God's sake, she'd just flown for fifty hours with nowhere to put her knees, had been flung from one continent to another, and in spite of her solemn vow never to drink gin again she'd done so anyway, because there wasn't anything else left at the end, which is why she now had a headache and was feeling the worse for wear, just look at my eyes. So now was not the time – he had to understand this – to sit up and beg for the Jottkowitzes, offering them her little Jewish paw. Nor was she going to register anywhere today.

Did he understand? He understood.

With a surprising surge of energy, she kissed him on the forehead, folded herself into the back of the Morris, and waved at Leon, who was left behind on the square all by himself, because by now all the brides had gone off to their new lives.

*

If she hadn't slept the day away, she could have seen how Christchurch came to life on Sunday. Families walked sleepily to church and returned home uplifted. The smells of the Sunday roast wafted out through the open kitchen windows and were carried off on the October wind. Cars headed out of town for a drive, old models, because they didn't make cars in New Zealand and everything had to be imported. And on the left-hand side of the road as if it were the most normal thing in the world. Buses operated according to the weekend timetable. Electric trams. Cyclists, here on the other side of the world as well. Christchurch was one of the few flat places in New Zealand and was known as 'the city of bicycles'. Men and women, pedalling briskly, on their way to their old mother or the cricket club. If Esther had been awake, she would have been able to see hats and dark plaid skirts, countless cardigans in muted colours and concealing styles. But she saw none of this, because she was asleep in a narrow hotel bed and in her dream she was walking around a house, a large house with many windows. In one of the rooms they were sitting around the piano singing happy songs, her parents and little Sal, and when she walked into the kitchen they were there eating challah. They were sitting in all of the rooms, and even though they smiled good-naturedly, they wouldn't show her where the door was. She awkwardly pulled herself into a sitting position and for a few anxious seconds she didn't know where she was, until in the half-light she made out the striped wallpaper and knew she was safe in her hotel room. She started to cry like a little child, her body racked with sobs. She didn't know where all those tears were coming from, because she couldn't remember her dream. Only that it was awful, just awful.

Over and done with. A fresh start.

She threw off the blanket, stepped onto the carpet, switched on the light, and cracked her whip until all of the wild beasts retreated meekly into the corner. God dammit. That's that.

But she didn't dare go back to bed. She took her wide trousers – the ones with the deep cutaway pockets that were set in so that the pattern of the fabric matched perfectly – out of her suitcase, wrinkles and all, and put her high heels back on, even though her feet said no. Make-up refused to conceal the dark circles under her eyes. Then this would just have to do.

They were both famished, and she and Frank attacked the remains of that afternoon's lamb. They were the only guests in the dimly lit dining room. The owner, a woman whose ample bosom sloped downhill like a broad ski jump, joined them at their table and interrogated them about the air race. She already knew everything about Holland. It must be hard for you to wear regular shoes after those wooden ones, she said.

By the time they went out, the city was closed again. And closed meant that you could walk down Colombo Street as far as you liked and you wouldn't find a jazz club, a cinema, or even a pub anywhere that was open on Sunday night.

So they followed the course of the Avon, which meandered through the city. They didn't say much, because they didn't know each other very well and because those few hours of sleep had robbed them of what was left of their sense of time and direction and their usual routines. Carrying on an ordinary conversation seemed like an impossible task. As did making a problem of this. Occasionally one of them would point to a building: look, there's a classic example of English Gothic Revival, and then the other would nod and they'd walk on in groggy contentment. Sunday evening in Christchurch. The place was utterly dead.

He asked about her and Leon, short and to the point. She told him the way things were, short and to the point. She was an expert in short and to the point. Were they going to get engaged? That was the idea. He didn't ask any more questions and they walked on in silence.

She asked him about Ada. He ran his hand shyly through his brown hair. Nothing like this had ever happened to him before, he said, and shook his head as though he found it hard to believe. 'Tomorrow I'll probably think it was all a dream.' But right now it was making him miserable. Such a sweet girl, who allowed herself to be guided by a higher power. Esther said she wasn't so fond of fatalism, but that she couldn't help but be more forgiving towards someone so beautiful.

They walked on in silence for quite some time, thinking about all of these things and with no idea of where they were, but as long as they followed the river they could go back the same way. The river eventually ran through a botanical garden, with a profusion of dark tropical plants and trees. Frank lit a cigarette and looked around. 'Indeed,' he said as he blew out the smoke, with reference to nothing in particular. Esther ran her hand through a tall lavender plant, and a heavy perfume floated up – Grandma Berthi pulling yards of black Polish lace out of the walnut linen cupboard for her, here you are, Bubeleh, so that she could be the wicked stepmother, or the bad fairy who turns little Sal into a hawk with her magic spells.

She flopped down onto the grass on the sloping riverbank between the big weeping willows, pulled off her shoes and stockings and put her feet into the water – something that was heavenly for a brief moment but which quickly became too cold. This country, where everything happened the other way round, had only just emerged from winter. In spite of this she left them in, as long as possible and then some, until she was gasping for breath. He dropped down next to her, wrapped his arms around his knees, and watched her. She rolled up her wet trousers so he could see her long legs. Somewhere a dog barked. Long legs, shapely calves.

'Do you ever sleep?' he asked.

The hair on her neck stood on end, as if she were a thief who had imagined herself to be safe in the darkness but who suddenly found herself surrounded by searchlights. Outwardly unaffected, she splashed water gracefully into the air and said nothing.

'I mean like normal people do.'

'I'm not very good at it,' she admitted bluntly as she carefully dried her feet with the neatly folded handkerchief he'd offered her. She really had no idea what she should tell him. He seemed to understand just the same, because he didn't press the matter and took refuge in a playful poke.

'And it's so easy.'

'Oh, is it now?' she teased back, slipping safely into flirtation. 'Teach me then.'

Without hesitating, he placed two fingers on her breastbone and pushed her back onto the grass, so unexpectedly that she burst out laughing. He leaned over her, his face close to her own, his gaze penetrating deep inside. Casanova, she thought.

'This is how you start,' he said with that voice, 'and then you close your eyes.'

She couldn't quite gauge where he was going with this. She who was so accomplished at flirting was at a loss. There was seduction in the air and many other things as well, which made the whole situation quite unfathomable.

'Show me how,' she retorted, trying to gain time.

He closed his eyes to demonstrate, positioning his face just above her own, offering her the ideal opportunity to study his features in the moonlight, and even to admire them if she chose. He was a beautiful man, a

126

person anyone could fall in love with. He used his looks casually, as if they didn't interest him and that just thinking about them made him tired. But he did use them all the same. Perhaps this made it easier to conceal whatever lay behind them.

'See? Anyone can do it.'

Suddenly she knew. Back at the hotel she'd pounded on the door of his room; he'd appeared in the doorway looking rumpled and with alcohol on his breath but his well-bred manners were intact and he was immediately up for a night-time stroll.

'Except for you and me,' she said evenly.

It was silent. He opened his eyes. All the flirtatiousness had vanished, but he didn't avoid her gaze.

'Were you and your family still in the East Indies when the Japs came?' she asked.

He bit his lip and said nothing; he rolled off her onto his back, and lay alongside her on the grass, folding his arms behind his head.

'Yes.'

She did the same. In between the tall trees she saw that the night sky above Christchurch was filled with an overwhelming, cloudless sweep of stars.

They lay next to each other for a long time, listening to the lapping of the water of the river, to a duck that flew up quacking, to the soft rustling of the wind in the trees above their heads, to the sounds of the night. They shared their last cigarette from Holland. She gestured slowly towards the stars with her long, slender arm. Her other hand looked for his.

'It will be a clear day tomorrow,' she said.

*

Because they would probably never see each other again, that night in his cramped bed she vowed to see him off, but when he knocked on her door in the morning she'd actually just fallen asleep. Blindly, she pencilled in her eyebrows. In the dining room her head bobbed sleepily over her bacon and eggs, the baked beans in tomato sauce with greasy sausages, which she left untouched. I ordered tea, she grumbled, pointing to the bitter, milky liquid in the cup. That's how we drink it here, said the owner with the ski-jump bosom, and Esther could tell she'd made her first enemy. Frank, whose face was clean-shaven but lined with fatigue, ate with relish and complimented the woman amiably. Sycophant, said Esther in Dutch as she slid her plate in his direction.

Outside they put on their dark glasses to shade their eyes from the morning sun, which skimmed in at a low angle and made the streets unexpectedly alluring. It was warm. The excitement – that she was really here and that everything was different and had actually, irreversibly begun – woke her up with a start. Onward and upward. The city began to stir. There were men, most of them wearing Harris tweed sports coats, grey flannel trousers, and felt hats. Good God, she thought, what year is this, anyway. The women walked around like they were cold, or didn't know what to do with themselves, with their arms crossed in front of them and their shoulders hunched forward. Here and there a Polynesian face.

Esther, in her wide trousers and high heels, saw herself reflected in the eyes of the New Zealanders in the way she was accustomed to, which she found reassuring. People noticed her. Not one of the women here was wearing trousers, or swinging her hips quite so dramatically. This didn't seem to bother Frank, who strolled alongside her with his travelling bag. It made most fellows uncomfortable and after a while they would ask her if she could rein herself in a bit. This usually put an end to the courtship before it had ever really begun. I like him, she thought, and was sorry they would have to go their separate ways.

In a cluttered shop they asked for cigarettes and a *Christchurch Press*. The shopkeeper in the threadbare pullover spoke with such a strong accent that they had to ask him to repeat himself three times before they were able to understand his reply. Might they be Dutch? When they nodded in the affirmative, he clapped his hands, his mother would love this, today he'd met real Dutchies! Which brand of cigarettes would they like? Most of the brands were unfamiliar to them. She pointed to an advertisement in which a superior-looking, immaculately dressed man was smoking a cigarette, with above him a caption: *Peter Jackson: Notice the people who smoke them*. That one, of course.

Good choice, said the man doubtfully.

'Look,' said Frank. They sat on the bench at the bus stop, waiting for his bus to the train station. 'All these jobs, have a look, whole columns of them, whatever you like, foreman, boilermaker, electrician, carpenter, welder, painter, baker, butcher.' Esther tasted her bitter cigarette and watched him turn the page. He had to go God knows where, somewhere way up north to a sheep farm, but he didn't seem to be the least bit concerned about the long journey or all the unknowns that awaited him there, and sat quietly reading his first newspaper in his new life, occasionally brushing the hair off his forehead with an unconscious gesture. She had Leon to show her the ropes, but he had no-one. He doesn't need anyone, she thought, this man doesn't need anyone. She had no idea why this made her feel so sad.

'Look,' he repeated, and pointed to an advertisement for a shoe shop. *It's air race week at Hannahs*, it said above the drawings of different styles of shoes with names like *Joystepper* and *Jeanette* and in the middle of the shoes, *Winners all!* The air race had caused quite a bit of excitement in the city, that much was clear, and the shop windows were filled with references to this. There had even been a Queen of the Air Race pageant, and this week there was to be a programme of events with all the participants in the race. But they, the cargo from the Dutch ark, were not involved in any of this, having been set free and sent off.

A chattering group of schoolchildren in uniforms walked by. Blazers, striped ties, shorts, pinafores, and knee socks. They watched the group wordlessly until all of the children had rounded the corner.

'So young,' he said, 'and they all speak perfect English.'

The bus took them by surprise, because once more they'd forgotten it would come from the right.

129

'Just you wait,' said Esther. 'Next time we meet, we'll speak it just as well as they do.'

'Even better.'

The door thumped open. They stood there, momentarily shy. It suddenly occurred to her she could go with him. Why not? She was free to do as she liked.

'May you succeed in everything you do,' he said.

'You, too.'

He tousled her curls and hugged her affectionately. As the bus drove off, they waved to each other, and Esther placed her hand upon her heart. He did the same, and smiled the broad, friendly smile of a man drawing back the bed sheets. Her throat squeezed shut with sadness, just like that, with no warning. Nonsense, she thought, this is getting ridiculous. They were going their own ways and sentiments like that were all she needed.

And that was that. Over and done with. A fresh start.

But when the bus had disappeared from sight, she still hadn't moved.

10

THE LABOUR DEPARTMENT SENT HER to Lane, Walker & Rudkin, a large, modern clothing factory, one of many located throughout the country. 'My word, look at you,' said the supervisor as he took her in from head to toe. 'I'm Ray.' She introduced herself coolly as Miss Cahn. 'We all use first names here,' he replied, 'no matter what your position, because we're democratic,' and waited in vain for her to blush.

She went to work in the morning on the bicycle Leon had bought for her. Stay on the left, stay on the left, she would say to herself, and again on her way home at night: stay on the left, stay on the left. In between she would sit at a sewing machine in a large hall together with hundreds of other women. Among the six hundred employees who worked in this branch were thirty Dutch, all of whom had been in the country much longer than she had. She sat between a Bep, a Truus, a Gerda, and an Ietje, and sewed swimsuits. The work was nothing near what she was capable of doing, and the racket from the machines and the loud music meant to drown it out was enough to drive you mad. It doesn't matter, she reassured Leon, it's only temporary. He nodded hesitantly. He probably thought she was referring to their getting married, which would bring her life as a working woman to an end, and he still found the thought of this unnerving. She saw clouds of confusion pass through his eyes and left it at that. She meant something else. She would become a leading designer in this country and have her own celebrated salon; working in the factory was only the first step in this direction. It paid well and that's why she did it. She worked at a furious pace and sewed and smocked her way into the future. 'Take it easy,' said Ray, looking at her breasts in her revealing blouse. 'You Dutchies work too hard, can't you see we don't appreciate that? People are complaining about you, I just wanted to mention it. We like to keep things pleasant at work.' She gave a derisive little laugh, left her breasts as they were, worked even faster, and otherwise ignored him. He knew he'd been rebuffed and walked away shrugging his shoulders. There's another preconception confirmed, she thought in amusement. She kept her distance in the canteen, where twice a day the employees had a ten-minute tea break and at lunch could get a two-course meal for one and six. The Ietjes and Gerdas tried to draw her into their group of Dutch immigrant girls, but she wasn't interested. She didn't like cliques. Although her Kiwi co-workers were polite, they were somewhat reserved. She'd been so proud of her English, but now she often found it was inadequate. That New Zealand accent was hard to understand, her ears were often too tired, and her tongue inexperienced. Shades of meaning escaped her. They couldn't understand each other's jokes, which led to misunderstandings. She was eager to learn, as she didn't want to have any miscommunications with her own clientele. 'What do you mean by "a cuppa"?' she asked. Would she like to join them for something to drink? No, but thanks all the same, and she diligently recorded another expression in her notebook. She didn't want to waste any time. When the ship with her crate arrived in November, she would get her sewing machine back. The only thing I'll need then is a client and a length of fabric. Until then she wanted to earn money. Because overtime paid well, she worked on into the evenings. Moreover, this provided her with a free hot meal. Saturday was normally a day off (something that was unheard of in Holland) and on that one day she could earn four pounds and five shillings – nearly forty-five guilders – and she would cheerfully accept the small brown envelope that contained the money.

She waded through her new life as if making her way to shore through a heavy surf, moving ahead as fast as she could, as far as she could, all the while remembering to enjoy the sun on her face, the warm wind that lifted up her hair, and the vast space she finally found herself in. Wading, wading, her eyes focused on a point in the distance that seemed to be out of sight for others, but not for her. The piles of swimsuits grew left and right, and beyond them the suspicious looks of her co-workers: what was that Dutchie up to, what is she after, why does she push herself so hard that she won't even join us for a drink, why does she wear high heels? Although she did actually notice all the signals that came her way, the most she could manage was a friendly nod. Sorry girls, she would think indifferently. She had to keep going.

*

But she did realize she had to be careful not to push Leon aside as she waded. On Sundays they would go on outings. He worked as a mechanic in a garage and had been able to buy a '38 Ford. They had self-conscious conversations as they headed out of town to explore the open countryside around Christchurch, and if the weather was fine they drove to Sumner Beach, where families sat having their copious picnic lunches. Esther loved the beach, loved the gorgeous skies above the sea, loved the wind around her ears. It was a marvellous country, and time and again she would be overcome with a childlike sense of joy and appreciation for being allowed to live her life here from now on. She ate her first fish and chips sitting on the sand, while her hair blew into her face and the greasy snack on the newspaper quickly grew gritty. In high spirits, she fed the rest to the seagulls. 'Don't do that,' Leon said. 'Then they'll never leave.' He was right, of course, but she didn't care, because she was now watching a bridal couple having their pictures taken down at the water's edge and commenting loudly in Dutch on the bride's dress. 'Well, if you think you can pull it off, then by all means wear it.'

She was in seventh heaven. Even so it felt unreal, as if she were acting. Oh sure, everything was new and wonderful, but she couldn't spend too much time thinking about it.

*

Sometimes Leon took her out to dinner on Saturday night. There were no restaurants, and if you wanted to eat out, you went to a hotel. The food was mediocre and the interiors uninviting, but she made the most of it and went on wading. Sometimes they went to the cinema, impressive buildings with names like Majestic and Regent, and he would buy her ice cream during the intermission. She drank her first milkshake in a milk bar. Almost none of the establishments served spirits, the pubs closed at six o'clock and from five to six were filled with men who drank as much as they could hold as quickly as they could. Women weren't allowed in. On one occasion she boldly managed to worm her way inside but was politely but firmly asked to leave the premises, and to be honest, the sight of all those beer-swilling men was too much even for her.

The first time she entered a dance hall she was seized by an intense longing for Amsterdam's boisterous Leidseplein. In a cheerless room with chairs lining the walls on both sides, old-fashioned ballroom dances were the norm, quick-quick-slow, pink and yellow hats wobbling atop the ladies' chiselled hairdos. Leon sat down on one side and she plopped down next to him. All heads turned in their direction. 'You have to go over there,' Leon said, but she didn't understand, or didn't want to understand, and stayed put. Then the music stopped and the dancers hurried back to the chairs, women on one side and men on the other. Spluttering in amusement, she stood up and sashayed over to the other side. He came to get her for the next number, which was how it was done. She regally offered him her arm. 'Just act normal,' he said. Dancing together was sublime. The two-step, the cha-cha-cha, the dimples in his cheeks. He could lead wonderfully, and she responded to the slightest signal from the finger he held inside the hollow of her back. Had he not been far too proper and respect-

134

ful for that, he could have used the light pressure of that finger to dance her straight into bed. Or marriage. During the Latin dances they moved their hips together in the same rhythm, and the fact that he was shorter and more slightly built became unimportant. If he asks me now, I'll say yes. But he concentrated on his dancing and didn't speak; over his shoulder she couldn't resist looking provocatively into the eyes of other men.

*

She tried to imagine they were married. He's too small for me, she thought, I'll crush him. There was something unreal about the whole thing. Even so, they were very fond of each other and did their best to act like sweethearts, nuzzling up to each other and stroking each other's backs. We belong together, he said, as the ultimate declaration of his love. She wasn't all that pleased by what he meant with this. Usually he would then want to know when she was finally going to register with the Jewish community.

I'm glad you mentioned it, she'd answer sweetly, tomorrow.

Deep in her heart she considered the existence of a Jewish community to be absurd. The old differences between Jews and non-Jews didn't exist here in this country of settlers where everyone was a newcomer. Why in God's name would you then want to go and create this yourself?

The room at the Jottkowitzes' came to nothing. She kept putting off visiting the family: one time they'd made apple pudding for her, another time it was blintzes, but every time she decided not to go after all, and one day Leon told her reproachfully that they were going to give the room to a niece from Israel if she didn't come tomorrow.

'Oh, what a terrible pity,' she cried. 'But a niece has more right to the room than I do – family comes first. You know what? Tell them to give it to their niece – I'll find another room.'

Which turned out to be easier said than done. She finally admitted that being a private boarder with a family, as Leon was, didn't appeal to her. She wouldn't have enough privacy. Renting a room in a boarding house seemed like a better option. Although she scoured all of the newspapers, she couldn't find a thing. Staying on in the hotel wasn't a good idea, as it cost too much money. Her room wasn't much bigger than a closet and just as dark. She hated it, couldn't cope with the nights, and wasn't able to rid herself of the notion that the beams were gradually subsiding. The greasy breakfast smells were also starting to bother her. And the coffee almost made her throw up, which she found embarrassing. Tea – the pale, bitter brew they called tea here – was the national beverage, but she continued to yearn for coffee and in the end the ski jump was willing to make it for her, she was no slouch. Every morning from then on, she would place an open saucepan on the burner and boil coffee. And to prove her good intentions to the Dutchie, the woman would add a bit of mustard for flavour.

*

Spring arrived at the start of November. One Sunday Esther squeezed her long body into the swimsuit she'd bought at the factory and dived into the deliciously cold ocean. As she waded back through the surf she heard a woman's voice ring out, calling her name from the beach. 'Esther!' To her own amazement a wave of joy washed over her, as if the flight had made them into some kind of a family.

By the end of the day she was carrying her two suitcases behind Marjorie down a path that ran alongside a light blue wooden house in a hilly neighbourhood on the outskirts of town.

'You go around to the back door,' said Marjorie, who knew all about everything. 'If you go to the front door, they think you're putting on airs.'

I don't care if I have to climb over the roof, Esther thought.

The room was spacious and sunny and even had a balcony from where you could look out over the city. Esther was given the divan. 'Fantastic,' she said, and kept telling Marjorie how happy she was they'd run into each other. Marjorie felt the same way, and was glowing. 'I enjoy helping people out,' she said modestly, 'and I won't have to pay as much rent.'

A short time later she took Esther down to the large kitchen, where a middle-aged man was washing dishes, and she introduced him as Gordon, the landlord. The man, wearing a baggy sweater that was full of holes, apologized for his soapy hands.

'Did your wife die?' Esther asked sympathetically.

'Good Lord, no,' he laughed. 'Why?'

She stammered something but didn't know how to finish her sentence. Marjorie explained things to her on their way to the big living room to look for Peggy. In this country it was considered normal for men to help with the household chores. They both had to laugh: the poor things.

'And the way he looks,' said Esther. 'Like a dustman.'

He was a lawyer. His wife, whose attractive features had been blurred by a downy layer of maternal softness, was neatly dressed, so respectable, so proper, thought Esther, so English, and decided that she would be her first client. They were warm, friendly people, and they hoped she would enjoy living under their roof. They celebrated her arrival with tea and homemade rolls, and the whole time she felt a spring breeze wafting through the house. It seemed like the kind of place where you'd never need to close a door. Later, watching the setting sun bathe the city in an orange-red glow, she became almost sentimental, capable of believing that everything that had happened could be set right. There was no room for wild beasts here. They had no place among the tea roses on the mint green carpet.

*

For the first time since her arrival in New Zealand, Esther unpacked her bags. She pinned sketches onto the wallpaper above the divan, the ones she'd made late at night in her hotel room. Female forms in bold, defiant lines with dazzling evening gowns that flew off the paper.

'Nice,' said Marjorie. 'Different. Not my taste, but quite nice for a while.'

Hanging neatly above her own bed was an old Dutch fringed wall hanging. 'I nicked it, from my parents' house,' she beamed. 'I would have loved to have seen the look on Pa's face!' Then she plopped down on her bed and watched her new roommate hang up her sketches. She chattered the whole time about how tired she'd been after the flight and how she'd hated everything, just everything. If it had been up to her, the whole of New Zealand could have gone up in smoke. And Hans along with it. She had to laugh at the memory.

'You know what bothered me the most?'

No, Esther didn't know.

'His hands. Mad, isn't it?' How she'd longed for those hands, those big, sweet hands of his that he always used to put around her waist, those hands, she'd been dreaming about them for two years and when she got to that stupid airport, when everything had been such a disappointment, he'd been a disappointment, too, and on the bus she kept staring at his hands and didn't hear a word he said, just kept thinking, what happened?, something's not right. His hands were rough and calloused.

He brought her to this room, and although of course she could see how nice it was, how well he'd arranged everything for her, he looked at her so expectantly that she couldn't bring herself to show her appreciation, and only managed to pick at the lapel of his jacket; what she'd really wanted to do was to cry her eyes out. Have a good sleep, he said, the sweetheart, and I'll come and pick you up tomorrow.

'I wasn't able to cuddle with him right away, even though I'd been so looking forward to it.'

Esther wondered what she meant by cuddling, but said nothing and took the satin wedding dress out of her suitcase, crumpled and torn. 'Oh, my,' exclaimed Marjorie. 'I hope that can be fixed.' And immediately rattled on about how everything had changed when after sleeping for twenty-four hours she'd opened the curtains and looked out into a clear blue sky.

'You sleep really soundly here,' she sighed. 'You'll see.'

You know, it turned out it wasn't so bad after all. Hans, his hands, and this country. He came and picked her up on his motorcycle and they rode out of town, into the hills, and it was all so beautiful she cheered up immediately. And somewhere on a hillside, they rolled on the grass and had a lovely cuddle and the love was back, just like that. 'He's good-looking, isn't he?' You know, life here was a lot of fun, people were nice and they didn't make fun of your English if you made a mistake. Hans shared a house – it was called a 'flat' – with three 'mates'. New Zealanders, colleagues from work. Those fellows also had girlfriends and they had a wonderful time together, no, to be honest, she hadn't had time to miss her family at all. Pa and Ma were overprotective, she knew they meant well, but when she was eighteen she still had to ask permission to go to the cinema, and she had to wait till she turned twenty-one before she could go to New Zealand. So, long live freedom, no-one could tell her what to do any more, she was in charge of her own life.

'And I'm not homesick. Are you? Maybe it's not a very nice thing to say, but that's just how it is. I miss the salt herring, but my family? No. What about you?'

Esther placed the photo of the family that had ceased to exist more than ten years earlier on top of the chest of drawers. Don't look at it too long. Marjorie tucked the flowered pillow under her head. 'Who are they?'

'My parents, my little brother, and me. I was eleven then.'

'Oh, how sweet. What time would it be there now?'

She felt the hook of a wild beast's claw dragging down over her heart. 'They'll be asleep, I think.'

Yes, Marjorie thought so, too.

'I'm going to have my own family now,' she said contentedly. 'I want to have a big family, just like the one I grew up in, it's so cosy. There are six of us. Have you seen what they do with the prams here? They hang them on the tram. I only hope they take the babies out first.'

Esther looked at her. What a wholesome-looking girl. Funny little nose. Skin like a polished apple with just as little mystery beneath it, just core and flesh.

'Do you have a job?'

'Yes, I do,' said Marjorie.

'Where?'

'In the hospital, of course.'

Of course.

It became oddly silent as Esther put the few clothes she had with her on hangers and hung them in the wardrobe, oddly silent. Marjorie moaned as she lay on the bed, twisting and turning like she was on the rack. 'What's wrong?'

But nothing was wrong, no, nothing, no, really nothing, so incredibly nothing that she was ready to burst. Esther looked on with interest, waited as the cheeks went from pink to purple and Marjorie shot up and exploded, simply because she had nowhere inside where she could keep anything to herself. 'I've got my nursing diploma!' she bawled at Esther. 'I'm qualified for obstetrics, I've got all of my qualifications. Paediatrics would have been nice, too, but *this*!'

It was so humiliating. With all her qualifications, she'd been sent to work in the laundry room and spent the whole wretched day stoking boilers. Esther tried not to laugh. 'What are you going to do about it?'

'Get married and get out, what do you think. As soon as Hans finds us a place to live. How dare they!'

That's why I'm here, thought Esther, she'll be leaving anyway.

*

She kept on wading from the mint green carpet; she pushed herself through another, more light-hearted chapter – the one about fearless young immigrants enjoying life simply because they happen to be young and want to enjoy themselves. She and Leon, never entirely at ease when it was just the two of them, spent a lot of time with Hans and Marjorie. There was something reassuring about those two, as if just following in their wake would entitle you to a carefree existence. This was mostly thanks to Hans, his plus fours, and the stout-hearted way he scanned the horizon. He was a tall, muscular young man, strong and tanned, with hints of future baldness showing through his brown hair, and his enjoyment of New Zealand was so contagious that no-one was immune. He laughed readily and talked easily; he put his arms around Esther and Leon and pulled them gently into the society of silliness. He could tell a string of immigrant stories, the kind Esther could listen to for hours because she liked how they sounded and because it didn't matter to her what they were about, as if the room was filling up with light, breezy music.

'I said, Geoff, I was in the army and I've heard it all before. So it was bloody this and bloody that… and there we are, rowing the bloody boat back to that bloody spot where we'd put out the nets… and let me tell you, you feel pretty insignificant out on the water like that, between those huge hills… and what do you think? Twenty-one butterfish… a couple of enormous mokis… a couple of kawhai… and a small shark! And Geoff cleaned all those bloody fish… he wouldn't let me help… didn't think a Dutchie could do it… well, then I wasn't about to burst his bubble!' Then he would laugh and slap his knees and pour them all generous quantities of beer. He'd already gone skiing on Mount Cook and skating on Lake Ida, gone deer hunting at Lewis Pass and fishing in Lyttelton harbour, and they'd do all of these things, too, mark my words.

Although he'd studied architectural history back in Holland, here he'd been working as a carpenter for two years now, from north to south, on construction sites and farms. He proudly showed off his nicked and calloused hands and used them to tease his middle-class sweetheart: 'Not what you expected, eh? You've hooked yourself a working man.' He adored Marjorie. When he was talking he would sometimes suddenly fall silent and place his hands around her waist with a look of childlike amazement, exclaiming, 'How is this possible!'

Esther could see how the two of them operated. Marjorie pirouetted like a princess on a pedestal and he danced lovingly around her in his high-spirited way, and if she suddenly happened to sigh and fall backwards, he was right there to catch her and help her back on her feet with the next joke.

Those two were so in love that she and Leon had to keep up and before long they were acting just the same, so that the four of them formed two happy, harmonious couples, four young friends who flung open the windows in the girls' room, smoked cigarettes, drank beer, and told one joke after another with Radio Netherlands in the background reporting on the arrival of good Saint Nicholas in Holland while outside the blossoms swayed in the breeze and perfumed the air with their sweet fragrance.

On their Sundays off, the four of them went swimming or out for a drive. Hans's Kiwi friends often came along as well. They taught them how to have a picnic New Zealand-style, with sandwiches, scones, pudding, cake, everything homemade, there were even pots of tea made over campfires. This is the kind of life they led, and although each night Esther still battled her demons in the dark, she enjoyed the days. She even talked Hans into teaching her how to ride his motorcycle on the gravel roads in the hills. 'It's not that I'm afraid,' said Marjorie that night as she plucked Esther's blouse irritably from the chair they shared, 'but Hans is dead set against it... he thinks it's far too dangerous... he's so concerned about me!' And followed this up in one suspicious breath with, 'So are you and Leon getting married?'

At night, Esther softened when she heard the soft spluttering of girlish snoring coming from the other bed.

*

In fact, she'd already been proposed to. 'We should get married, then,' said Leon one day as they lay by themselves, kissing in the sunlit dunes; he said it seriously and also a little furtively, looking down in the direction of his bare feet. She nodded; of course, it was to be expected.

'But we don't have to do it right away,' she said to reassure both herself and Leon.

Apart from that, they didn't talk about it much, because neither of them knew what to say on the subject. Getting married meant going to bed together and starting a family. I'm not his type, she thought as they kissed; he's just as hungry for this as I am, but I wonder if we're right for each other. I wonder if we're in love. I wonder if that's essential. 'Do you want to sleep with me?' she asked. They'd been everywhere with their hands. He moaned in reply. 'Now?' she went on. He sat up; she never ceased to amaze him. 'Once we're married,' he said. 'I thought that's what you wanted, too.' He probably thought she was a virgin. He'd never asked. She looked at his lips, he had sensual lips, and nodded virtuously, yes, we'll wait, relieved almost, a kind of relief she found baffling. Neither could she understand why those sensual lips had so little effect on her. The kissing, the touching, it was all delicious, but the next level, where the boundary between his skin and hers would dissolve, was a place they couldn't reach. They were stuck somewhere in between, and though they did their best, they didn't get much higher. Even so, her body was filled with irrepressible desire. Promenading over the beach in her tight capris excited her, because she knew her bottom looked good in them. Then she would swing her hips out so far she'd almost fall over. The men's burning looks warmed her behind. She was disdainful of the men themselves and ignored them, just as she ignored Ray at the factory, all the while enjoying their amorous stares. When Marjorie went to mass with Hans at Saint Mary's on Sunday mornings and she had the room all to herself, she would throw back the sheet and look at her naked body from every possible angle in the mirror on the wardrobe door. Look at herself through the eyes of a man, something she found so arousing that at first she would put the strangest things between her legs and slide them inside – the most strange of all being the wooden handle on the drill in Hans's toolbox – and then she would masturbate. Afterwards she would drift off for a few delicious hours of dreamless, fearless sleep. The eyes of the man through which she looked at herself were never Leon's. But there had indeed been talk of marriage, and lately she'd noticed this was taking on a more definite form inside his head. For example, he started talking more and more about the synagogue's stained-glass window and what it was like when the sun shone through it, how it gave a beautiful glow to any number of ceremonies. Would she like to come and have a look? When? Or he would suggest she think about taking Friday afternoon off so she could cook a Shabbas meal for the two of them, something that would happen more frequently in future. Oh, of course, she'd certainly think about that.

*

Nonetheless, these kinds of promises faded quickly, because she needed to concentrate on a new design, for instance – an evening gown with a reinforced hip section – and was putting a lot of thought into the many intricate details. Late at night, once she'd given up any hope of falling asleep, she would sketch the designs for her own collection, dresses, suits, evening dresses. During the day, while she yawned and blindly sewed swimsuits, she would work out the patterns inside her head. She was obsessed, counting off the days not till her wedding but till she would get her sewing machine back. To stay abreast of things in this unstylish country, she took out a subscription to *Vogue*, even though it cost a fortune. She would have begged for it if she'd had to.

At the end of November they finally got word of their belongings, and a short time later the ship with their crates arrived in Lyttelton harbour. That Sunday Hans and Leon borrowed a small lorry from the garage to pick up the two crates and carried them companionably inside: Esther's was a battered trunk bought for a song at the Waterlooplein in Amsterdam, Marjorie's large and heavy and reinforced by her father with so many fittings that it would last for ever. They squealed like sentimental schoolgirls when the lids were removed and the great unpacking could begin. Marjorie was jubilant as she systematically removed a complete collection of solid, well-made household items from the wood shavings. An entire set of dishes neatly edged in blue. Cutlery, sheets, pillowcases, towels, everything of high quality, it was almost embarrassing, as if their entire married life was being set out before you. She'd rehearsed, thought Esther. With every cup and saucer she'd packed into the crate she'd played house, poured his tea at the breakfast table wearing a housecoat while he sat with the newspaper opened out in front of him. She couldn't wait. She can't wait.

'I can see you two are ready,' said Leon.

Marjorie and Hans looked at each other. Yes, they were ready.

'As soon as I can find us a flat,' said Hans.

Marjorie held up a set of pots and pans, a tower of marbled grey enamel. She looked for a spot somewhere among her display of trophies. 'There's not much room for my things, Es, what with the two of us,' she cried, 'but I'm not the kind of person who would put someone out onto the street!'

Esther inclined her head gratefully, as was expected of her. She would have stood on her head if she had to, because it was a perfect Sunday afternoon – with the balcony doors open wide, and the two open crates with the customs stamps in the middle of the mint green with the tea roses, Maori songs on the radio, their two good men, plenty of cigarettes, all of Marjorie's idiotic remarks she wasn't allowed to laugh at. And the afternoon was on its way to becoming a lovely summer evening, and her throat was squeezed shut with emotion at seeing her sewing basket, patterns, rolls of paper, drawing things, and piles of charcoal sketches, and even more so when her Singer emerged unscathed from the bottom of the crate.

She could feel Leon's eyes upon her the whole time.

Even as he laughed, smoked, and drank along with the rest of them, he was watching her. She knew that in amongst all the objects she was taking from her treasure chest with such cries of delight he was hoping to find something that had to do not only with her, but with both of them. Which is why she left the menorah wrapped up in the worn-out slip and casually placed the whole thing at the back of her wardrobe. If he hadn't had that tortured diaspora look in his eyes, she would have unwrapped the menorah and put it on the windowsill, but she refused to give it the required extra layer of meaning, even though it was the only thing she'd been able to retrieve from her family's home in Amsterdam after the war. *What do you think you're doing here, love? the hag had asked. It's been hard for all of us.*

Don't think about it.

And because he kept staring and because the desert sand in his eyes kept getting darker, she hoisted her sewing machine high up in the air – ta-ta-ta-taaa – and kissed the black metal with the golden curlicues as if it were a sacred object. Or her child.

'Are you back, darling? Come to Mama…'

Her voice high and hysterical. Over the top, she knew, but that's because of the way he's looking at me. She placed the machine on the table ceremoniously, checked to see whether everything was still intact, polished it with a cloth as if it were made from purest gold, put a spool on the pin and guided the thread through the eyes, blew dust from the bobbin and started to wind it. Everything worked fine, which should have made her happy, but because of all of that staring of his she only felt a nagging pain in her belly, because she saw their marriage looming up ahead in all its intensity and knew it would be charged with emotion and top-heavy and not something you could just look forward to. That the rotting breath of beasts would poison the very air they breathed.

In the meantime, Marjorie had reached the bottom of her crate. She lifted up the thick book by Dr Spock and waved it in the direction of Hans, who was sitting on the windowsill with his hands on his knees. 'This is how I'm going to raise our children.' The final item to emerge was a carpet-beater. She defended herself good-naturedly against their hooting, her face bright red. 'That's what I'd heard, that you couldn't get these here.' Hans laughed so hard he nearly fell over backwards. 'Does Dr Spock prescribe them?' Then they all laughed and Leon refilled their glasses. Esther leaned forward, pulled the bobbin from its holder, and bit through the thread.

Talking Peggy into a new jacket didn't take much doing. The only condition was that she shouldn't go overboard. Of course not, Esther said indignantly. Wearing the same expression, she impressed upon her landlady that a slightly flared pleated skirt would have a slimming effect and make a fetching ensemble. Wouldn't a pleated skirt be too complicated? A pleated skirt is the mark of the master, she answered mysteriously, and Peggy's eyes began to glisten dreamily. They agreed on a price and together chose a lovely summer wool at Ferguson Fabrics in a colour they called 'banana' for the sake of convenience. To set off the lapels, cuffs, and bottom of the jacket they chose a paler yellow in the same material. For the skirt one of those modern fabrics, a wrinkle-resistant acetate in a fish pattern on a pearl background, very chic.

'Fish...' said Peggy hesitantly.

'Of course,' said Esther. 'Why not?' She assured her victim that the end result would be stunning, and the envy of all her friends. Peggy giggled. As a rule, she didn't go around stunning people.

Working overtime at the factory was now out of the question for Esther; she needed her evenings for working on the design, talking things over, taking measurements, making the pattern and then the toile, and fittings. Peggy was delighted by it all and didn't object when Esther suggested a cascading flounce instead of the pleats, which would make the skirt much more elegant, nor when Esther emphatically maintained that she should have a blouse with a jabot to complete the ensemble, and that it was already there inside her head.

It worked. She took the bait. Onward and upward.

Although Marjorie complained about the mess, Esther didn't allow herself to be distracted, setting out fabric, paper, ribbon, and buttons on the carpet for inspiration. With her advance, she bought a modern new iron at Ballantynes and left the department store with her purchase cradled lovingly in her arms.

On the evening of the fifth of December, Esther, Leon, Marjorie, and Hans made a valiant attempt to celebrate the Dutch holiday of Saint Nicholas, something that wasn't easy in the heat and without the traditional spice biscuits. They all got the giggles. Hans had written a Saint Nicholas poem for his girl in which he revealed his gift to her: he'd found a basement flat for them in Armagh Street. There were two rooms and a kitchen, they would have to share the bathroom with two other couples and you had to put pennies into a meter to get hot water, but it would be their very first place together.

Would she marry him?

As could be expected, Marjorie shouted with joy and threw her arms around his neck. Pressed her body against his because she was ready for their marriage and everything that went along with it. Esther avoided Leon's eyes and quickly grabbed the next gift.

*

Hans and Marjorie decided to get married just before Christmas. Marjorie gave notice at work with devilish delight. Hans would be the breadwinner and she would be the mother of his children, because that's the way the world worked. From then on, everything revolved around the approaching wedding. The future bride could talk of nothing else. The wedding this, and marriage that, the words were uttered so often within the walls of their room that they seemed to stick to the carpet and the soles of your shoes like melted sugar. Marjorie herself wasn't troubled by this. She roughly shook out her wedding dress from the balcony, as if she were doing the spring cleaning, and it could be considered a miracle that the delicate gown survived. To make matters worse, the *Illustrated Catholic Review* arrived by surface mail and there she was, gracing the cover in her wedding dress, an unexpected reminder of their departure from London. Grumbling that her mother had sent only one copy, she showed the mag-

SUPERBOOKDEALS

5520 Brick Road
South Bend, IN 46628
USA

Tel # 410-964-0026

www.superbookdeals.com

Deliver To:
FRANKLIN A MORSE II
4437 SOUTH INDEPENDENCE DRIVE

SUTTONS BAY
MI
49682
USA

Ordered By:
FRANKLIN A MORSE II
4437 SOUTH INDEPENDENCE DRIVE

SUTTONS BAY
MI
49682
USA

Qty	ISBN	Title	Price	Total
001	9781846271724	BRIDE FLIGHT		

Despatch Summary:		Total Items:	1
Despatch Date:	20/01/2011	Goods Total:	
Delivery Method:	Superbookdeals		
Total Parcels:	1		
Delivery Charges:		Reference:	10048138

PK: 3135

THANK YOU FOR YOUR ORDER.

azine as often as she could to anyone who had the misfortune of being in the vicinity – and that was usually Esther. While Esther tried to concentrate on designing the sleeve crown for the jacket, Marjorie went over the photo with a fine-toothed comb.

She said: 'All those teeth!'

She said: 'That hair!'

She said: 'I don't look like that, do I?'

She said: 'Tell me, what do you think of my dress?' (Esther was cleverly able to sidestep that one.) Marjorie became nervous and insecure. Every night she would take her dress, veil, and gloves out of her wardrobe and inspect them for non-existent flaws and stains. Gabbling on the whole time.

She said: 'Shall I wear my hair up, or down and curly?'

She said: 'Should I starch the skirt more?'

She said: 'You only really become a woman once you're married.'

She'd read that in one of her booklets. Agitated, she leaned up on one elbow in bed and speculated aloud about what was being implied between the lines and what that actually meant, all of this couched in the guarded terms of a Catholic girl. Esther behaved as if she knew nothing. It had become impossible for her to think. She started to feel like her thoughts were becoming trapped inside yards of bridal veil, something she began to find extremely annoying. It made her head swim, and she nearly made a mistake when she was cutting the flounce. One night she woke with a start from a nightmare, gasping for air; she'd been drowning, thrashing about as she tried to get to the surface of the water, but she was trapped at every point by layers of netting. After that, she decided to finish the jacket when Marjorie was asleep. In the dead of night she bent over her work beneath a small lamp, finally able to devote all of her attention to the diagonal welt pockets, which then turned out perfectly.

★

Inspired by Hans and Marjorie, Leon started to become more insistent. One Sunday, he was leaning up against the door jamb and staring gloomily at his future wife, who was sitting at the sewing machine surrounded by fabric, pattern pieces, and colourful sketches and who didn't deign to look at him. This was due not to any aversion on her part but to lack of time, because her client had informed her she wanted to wear her new outfit on Christmas Day. Draped over a chair was her own satin wedding dress, which she'd been intending to repair. She hadn't got around to it.

'If we get married, it will be easier to find a place to live,' he said.

'Let's get used to each other first.'

'When are we supposed to do that? You're always so busy.'

'And that's something *you're* going to have to get used to,' she said evenly, raising the presser foot and pulling on the thread.

'But it won't go on like this, will it?'

She looked at him. 'What do you mean?' Keep things light.

'If we get married, I mean.'

'Have you changed your mind?' Keep things light, act like it's a joke.

He didn't reply. He walked to the window and lit a cigarette. She looked at his back, a nice-looking back, all in all. Even so, she could see warning lights flashing, danger, danger. No idea why. He turned and pointed to the satin that sat slumped in the waiting room.

'Is that... your wedding dress?'

She was instantly aware of her carelessness. The groom isn't supposed to see The Dress. Marjorie had exercised a great deal of self-control and kept Hans from seeing the magazine. She hadn't given it a second thought.

'Such enthusiasm, how delightful...' she said. This exchange wasn't going well. There was a long silence, she didn't dare look up, busied herself with a thread that had got stuck in the bobbin, heard him blow out the smoke and felt his eyes upon her. He was actually so tiresome. He stood there with his silent reproaches. Damn it, if there was anything she detested, if there was anything she found so utterly infuriating.

The silence persisted.

'Esther,' he said at last, sounding so unbearably profound – now *that* she found simply intolerable, such a we-are-the-people-of-Israel tone of voice. 'Esther, what does marriage mean to you?'

She leapt up, saw herself doing it, heard herself shouting. The stool fell over. 'Marriage! Marriage! I never want to hear that word again!' She snatched the cream-coloured gown from the chair, pulled open the door of the wardrobe, and crammed it in all the way to the back. Slammed the door. Now you see it, now you don't. Breathing hard, she turned towards Leon, opened her eyes wide in a portrayal of genuine, palpable indignation. 'Could we maybe talk about something else for a change?' She gave a harsh laugh. A horrible laugh.

He looked at her in bewilderment. He sees a stranger, she thought, one with hard, ugly features and a mouth that makes cynical noises. Something watery and sad welled up in her chest, and she couldn't stop. With arms flailing, she collapsed down onto her stool and motioned that he should just leave for a while, but she needn't have bothered, because when she looked up he was gone.

*

She continued to work towards her goal. There was an old dressmaker in an ugly shop on Cashel Street, and although everyone said she made lovely things, she didn't have much business from the look of it. Esther walked there one day after work, and upon entering, one glance was all she needed to see that the woman wasn't a patch on her. Old-fashioned fabrics, yellowed patterns, everything smelled of stagnation; she still heated her iron with charcoal. Esther nestled sweetly into the chair opposite the grey-haired lady, who looked at her in surprise from behind her thick glasses. 'I've just arrived,' she sighed. 'I'd like to start my own business, but in the meantime could I possibly work for you so I can learn?' She spread her sketches on the table and unfolded her ideas, and after a time the woman, whose name was Rose, said, 'Oh dear, I can see I might as well pack it in with you around.' She groaned as she hauled her old body out of the chair and showed Esther around the rest of the shop. It wasn't much, but everything was there: sewing machines, dress forms, sleeve rolls, pressing hams, pressing mitts, velvet board, clothes brush, everything she would need. Esther showered her with praise. Then Rose suggested that she come and work with her in the shop. Although she wouldn't be able to pay Esther, she could bring in her own clients. If everything went well, she could take over the business. The rent was ridiculously low. Esther protested for form's sake.

*

As the wedding approached and the summer light made the December evenings ever longer, Marjorie came down with a bad case of homesickness, the dreaded emigrant fever. It started with something intended to be humorous, a ban on the word 'herring', and only if there was no way around it, to refer to the fish as 'those salty rascals'. After that, things became progressively less amusing. She ranted about the climate, how it was impossible to celebrate Christmas in the summer heat, and why did those New Zealanders bother putting lights on trees when it never even got dark? Then it made her ill. She sat quietly holding the plaster of Paris shepherd, the figurine she'd stolen from the nativity scene at home. 'To protect me,' she said. 'I would rather have had Baby Jesus, but, well…' Esther watched her become paler by the day, gradually losing something of that boundless energy of hers, as if she herself were turning into a long, limp bridal veil. She felt sorry for her, and helped where she could with the preparations for the wedding. She pressed the dress with her new iron, polished the shoes, and the night before the big day rolled rags into the straight, listless hair, trying not to laugh at the sight of that head on the pillow. She was pleasantly drowsy as she sat sketching under the light, working on a design for a blouse with a jabot and dreaming about the best material for a blouse like that. Peggy had bought olive seersucker, but Esther had her doubts.

The bride shot bolt upright like one of the living dead. She couldn't sleep.

'Am I keeping you awake?'

Marjorie came and sat next to her in her pyjamas, mute and meek, and plucked miserably at the seersucker on the table. Like a little girl, thought Esther. She stood up to get her a cup, poured out some tea, and waited for whatever was going to happen next.

'I used to have wallpaper this colour,' said Marjorie. And then another long pause. Esther picked up her sketchpad and kept working. They drank their tea.

'In my room. I picked it out myself. When I was fourteen.'

Esther nodded.

'Later on I thought it was so ugly. A dirty colour.'

She shoved the fabric away. Sighed, squirmed in her seat. Hung her head. Felt at the rags in her hair. They were still there.

'This is terrible, I should be asleep.'

'Oh, I don't know,' said Esther.

'I'll have dark circles under my eyes tomorrow, at my own wedding.'

Another long silence, the agreeable silence of the night. In the distance, a tower clock struck two. Esther refilled their cups.

'Do you miss that wallpaper?' she asked.

It was like pushing a button. The princess fell from her pedestal and started to cry, high-pitched howling sobs, nearly choking on her sense of loss.

'A bride... should leave... for her wedding... from... her parents'... house!'

Sadness is sadness, no matter what the cause, thought Esther, and put her arms around Marjorie, rubbed her heaving back.

'I... miss... Pa... and... Ma!'

'Yes.'

'Am... I... doing... all right?'

'You're doing just fine.'

153

Minutes passed as Marjorie wept. Esther rubbed her back and suddenly knew that the seersucker wouldn't drape well enough for the kind of blouse she had in mind. She'd have to convince Peggy of this tomorrow. Actually, what would be nicest would be to do the lapel facings in the same fabric as the blouse, like Coco Chanel. Why hadn't she thought of this before?

Marjorie was calmer as she sat up, still sniffling. Esther gave her a handkerchief and looked on as she blew her nose noisily, breathing in deeply through her open mouth and then out again, as if gathering courage for her life as an adult that would start tomorrow.

'Hans is good-looking, isn't he?'

'Very good-looking.'

This opened up the floodgates again.

'I... miss... them... so... much!'

The whole ritual repeated itself and as she rubbed, Esther looked around, relishing the thought of having the room all to herself before long; her eyes moved over the furniture in the dark, as if everything had changed shape at the prospect of this. She didn't need to look at the family portrait on the chest of drawers, which would never change, or at the funny little photo of Sallie next to it, with his ball in his strong little arms and that bold look in his eyes.

*

'Maybe we're making a mistake,' she said to Leon. It took him by surprise. He cleared his throat uncomfortably, sniffed, and indicated she should lower her voice, they were sitting in Saint Mary's surrounded by Catholics, after all. In all her glory, Marjorie was striding majestically (there was no other way to describe it) down the aisle to the front of the church on Gordon's arm. With no father present, he'd agreed to give the bride away and had donned a dated double-breasted suit for the occasion.

'Maybe we're making a mistake,' she repeated, more softly now, as she sat facing the aisle so she could nod reassuringly to Marjorie: it's going just fine, you look gorgeous, this morning you said you were going to call the whole thing off and take the ship back home, but look, down there next to the priest stands your bridegroom, and he loves you.

Leon had been pressuring her. His two years of working under contract were up. He'd applied for a job as a manager in Auckland. The pay was better and accommodation was included. He could start next week. He had to know. She understood.

'And what if it turns out we're not compatible?'

He sighed. Why here? she could see him thinking. Such a response was exactly what she meant. He leaned towards her wearily. 'It wouldn't matter,' he whispered. 'We belong together. There's no-one else. We have no-one else.'

She held her breath in trepidation, unable to understand why her chest was filled with this feeling of dread. From the organ came a monotonous droning; it was enough to drive you mad. She smoothed her nylons and looked round the pews to regain her composure. There weren't many people there, they didn't know many people yet. Gordon and Peggy, some co-workers of Hans and Marjorie, their friends from the beach. Around ten or twelve New Zealanders, all told. She turned back to Leon and took refuge in sarcasm, her voice a little too loud.

'Will we be happy together?'

She saw him looking at her in disbelief, something that happened more and more often these days: the chutzpah to talk about happiness, as if people like them had any claim to happiness. He leaned away from her, gripping the top of the wooden pew in front of him. He's counting to ten, she thought, that's the kind of person he is, someone who knows how to control himself. Even so, when he sat back up his tone was derisive. 'You were the one who started talking about it in your letters. You talked about a safe life, remember? For who, I wonder? Just for you?'

That's what this is all about. Her head seized up. He's talking about children. He wants to become the new patriarch, feels responsible for producing a new generation of Jews, and there's no-one but me to help him bring that off.

The lack of sleep. The droning cadence of the organ. Terrifying bellowing she could no longer escape. The smell of incense, which made her nauseous and gave her a blinding headache. That ridiculous pounding in her chest.

He didn't continue, motioning they should be quiet. They sat stiffly side by side and concentrated on the ritual down at the front. Hans held out his hand to his bride, and Marjorie, radiant once more, put her hand in his. That's how fast things can go. Esther wasn't against marriage. Marriage was a natural part of a young woman's life, followed just as naturally by motherhood. There was nothing wrong with Leon. Nor with what he wanted. She cautiously reached for his hand. He turned towards her in surprise, and dimples appeared in his cheeks. He has soft eyes; I'm getting sentimental because of the way the bride is placing her hand in the hand of the groom. I can't think straight because of that organ. If I'm not careful I'll start to cry. I'll marry him. We won't be happy. I wonder if I'll be able to repair those tears in the satin so that you can't see them.

*

'I need to know now,' he repeated, once they were outside and walking along the Avon, a short distance from the wedding breakfast that was taking place beneath the trees in the park. She nodded. Her high heels sank down into the grass, just like on that first evening with Frank.

'Esther, stop for a moment.'

Here it comes; marriage is contagious. She stopped. He took her hand and valiantly tried to ignore their difference in height. Here it comes. He cleared his throat.

'Esther, you are a daughter of Israel.'

She burst out laughing. 'How wonderfully solemn!' she cried, and knew she was being cowardly and mean. Her hands were trembling. He, the valiant one, the indomitable one, the better of the two, was trembling as well. Just look at us standing here shaking.

'I've given it some thought, and I'd like you to keep a kosher kitchen,' he continued. 'Our children should be raised with our traditions. It's important.'

They'd never talked about children before. The word children had never been mentioned.

'We'll keep Shabbas, celebrate Purim and Hanukkah, everything. It's the only way we can pass on our way of life.' A dirty cloud passed in front of the sun, the day grew dark, the organ droned on inside her head. In panic, she scratched at the back of his hand where dark hair grew, just like on his chest and legs. 'Auckland,' she said.

She heard his voice in the distance. 'You've got so much energy. Put that energy to use for a higher purpose.'

'And what might that be?'

'You know very well what I mean.'

The words spilled out of her mouth, hard and metallic, and as she spoke her fury won out over fear. 'Oh, I get it,' she said shrilly. 'The resurrection of the people of Israel. I'll bear your Jewish sons and daughters and they'll grow up happy and free...'

He let go of her hand and stepped back in horror. 'If you want to put it like that...'

The point of no return. Now he'll never come back. She could see ripples on the sparkling river behind him. But she couldn't stop, and hissed at him, whipped him away from her with her words. '... I'll make the Shabbas meal, you'll lead the prayer, our children's hair will be freshly washed. We'll be one of those warm, close-knit Yiddish families. We'll light candles and sing traditional songs for all of those skeletons rattling away up there on the sideboard. They'll sing along with us. They'll eat with us. One bite for Grandma, another for Grandad, a bite for Sal, six million bites. Gosh, I can hardly wait!'

I'm disgusting, just look at his face. He sees a traitor.

'Was I your emigration ticket?' he asked coldly.

'Yes,' she said. And then to settle things once and for all, she surged forward and shoved him into the river. I'm setting you free, be glad. I'm deciding for the both of us. You'll hate me so much you won't have any doubts, and can go looking for the perfect wife. For your new Jewish earth mother. Get out of my life, because I'm not going to be part of this. Aside from that, you're quite a nice fellow.

She watched his attempts to get to the riverbank, on compassionate grounds. He was a strong swimmer. 'You idiot!' he shouted. Damp strands of curls were plastered to his forehead, which made him look foolish.

'So long,' she called. Without a backward glance, she turned and sashayed back to the party – the mighty animal tamer able to get vicious beasts back into their cages as if they were tiny dogs – to Marjorie, who came running up, tripping on her wedding dress, taking her aside and sharing her indignation, her cheeks flushed scarlet because the Kiwis weren't eating the wedding cake, they didn't eat anything that wasn't homemade, how ridiculous!

*

That night she drowned in a sea of tears. She choked and gasped for air and her eyes burned from the stinging salt. There was no need to hold back, because she had the room to herself now. She tossed and turned, sat up in bed, then fell back down, again and again. That night she said goodbye to her children once and for all. Her children, for whom she had so much love to give. Her children, who would always be Jewish children. To protect her children, to keep them safe, they had to remain unborn.

Dry-eyed and numb, she took her torn wedding dress from the wardrobe in the first light of dawn and ripped open the seams. She pressed the pieces smooth with her modern iron and pinned the pattern for the blouse with the jabot onto the fabric. By the end of that Sunday evening she'd finished the blouse and faced the jacket lapels with the same fabric, which produced just the result she'd envisioned. Peggy giggled with delight as she turned in front of the mirror and counted out the bank notes. Then she poured out two small glasses of gin to celebrate. They toasted. Esther looked out the open balcony doors at the moon. She couldn't stand the smell of the gin.

11

THE STILL HUSH OF DEATH dominates the room where Frank is laid out. The low humming coming from the refrigeration unit under the coffin only serves to magnify the silence. It's dimly lit, the curtains closed. Flowers and candles spread a perfume so heavy it makes your head hurt. The three women stand without speaking next to the coffin, which has been covered with glass, as if the body is in a museum and has to be protected from curious hands. In the corner of the room sits an elderly Maori woman in an armchair. She sits with her legs apart, and her lower arms rest on the plaid blanket spread out over her lap and thighs. We don't leave our dead on their own, she says. Then she falls silent and returns to her own thoughts. We even leave the living on their own, thinks Ada. She doesn't know that Esther and Marjorie are thinking exactly the same thing. None of the three know the woman. No-one dares speak. They're paralysed by the presence of the others. There's so much to say that in the end they say nothing. They look to the dead man to steady themselves. Their eyes dart to and fro trying to gauge the others, but as soon as there's any danger of someone returning their gaze they return quickly to the lifeless body behind glass.

Ada, in the middle, leans forward until her face is just above the coffin. With her left hand, she holds her paua necklace against her chest to keep the hard pieces of shell from hitting against the glass and making noise.

She's unsteady on her feet. The way Frank looks now, so old and with his sharp nose so prominent, his thin white hair combed straight back and his closed lips stern and forbidding, she doesn't recognize him at once. In her memories, he never aged. Neither did she. Now she's face to face with the fact that they've both grown old, and with everything that's gone for good. She hadn't expected this. Nor had she expected that Esther and Marjorie would be standing here next to her. She's also still taking in everything she saw along the way, the beauty of the estate, its prosperity, the obvious yet understated presence of money. First those seemingly endless fields, so that she nearly became sick from the heat and fatigue and the pain in her knees. The extensive grounds, walking between those silver monsters and all the buildings as if she were in a surrealist painting or a dreamed memory in which you're the only person on earth. The fountains, the flower borders. The ride in one of those expensive new jeeps with that nice young Maori named Kris, who reminded her of someone. And then, at the end of the fields, close to the hills, the vehicle rounded a curve and the white country house suddenly came into view. The house from the crest. He'd done what he'd set out to do, and she found it unsettling. It's too much, too beautiful, and too bewildering. In front of the house, to either side of the porch with the white pillars, were more of the beautiful plants that made her think of Indonesia, that she knew from the pictures. He never stopped searching. Everything she saw made her sad. The same thing happened inside the big house, after Kris accompanied her courteously across the porch – she couldn't take it in, and could feel herself looking around like a child, open-mouthed, clutching her handbag to her body, and she was overcome with grief, not because of his death but because of his life. The entrance hall, where a large number of mourners were already assembled, was like that of a five-star hotel: just as grand and just as impersonal. Persian carpets, large paintings, and chesterfields grouped around a huge sandstone fireplace. Antique side tables with shaded lamps on alabaster bases. This was no ordinary house as far as she could tell, or it would have to be one like she'd seen in the glossy magazines at the hairdresser's, *House and Garden* or *Country Life* or whatever their names were. The walls had been painted a tasteful, dark colour she wouldn't have been able to give a name to, one of those colours you'd never come up with on your own. He'd had it decorated, she thought, as she backed down onto an antique chaise longue and fumbled in her bag for a tissue, he had it decorated by a professional, what do they call someone like that again, a stylist, or interior decorator. Why did he do it? It was like he'd withdrawn from everything. She wondered what his life here had been like, where he sat when it got dark, which role he'd cast for himself in this decor. She couldn't find a tissue among all the clutter in her bag, and used her hand to wipe her damp throat and forehead. No matter how hard she looked, she saw nothing she recognized. This was not a house you became attached to. Not an ordinary human house in which the wallpaper was permanently smudged by the sticky hands of children, and someone's hideous favourite chair was allowed to remain because it was familiar and comforting. This is a film set, a country house from a brochure. She nodded as pleasantly as possible to a group of people she didn't know who'd come to sit down around the large, gleaming coffee table nearby. People who had no idea. On the other side of the hall, she could see tall glass-fronted cases made from dark wood in which old hunting rifles were displayed. She narrowed her eyes and tried to isolate a single special gun from the rest, a gun he would have picked up and put down again hundreds of times, a gun that had known him well, but it was too far off and she didn't dare walk over by herself and run the risk that everyone would look at her. Then she tried to imagine him alone in this house. She found it hard to do, couldn't get beyond the image of a man briskly walking the distances between the furniture, the pace of an employee in a hotel, as if he was constantly on the go and would never dream of plopping down somewhere along the way. But this isn't a hotel. This is the house where he lived. Stay calm. She breathed deeply, in and out, and tried to see herself here together with him. That was easier to do. With her there, he does plop down onto one of the chesterfields. They lean against each other and stare into the blazing fire in the sandstone hearth. Nothing has to be said. They sit hand in hand, like they did on the plane. I should never have let go. An old regret surfaced, her constant companion. But for the first time she distrusted this regret, because it was now intermingled with a murky layer she didn't quite know what to do with. The opulence of the estate had eaten away at her. If I hadn't… then I would have… then now I would be… She's confused by these intrusive thoughts, and ashamed.

She knew none of the people in the hall – or living room – and breathed a sigh of relief when Kris came to get her so she could pay her last respects to the deceased. He led the way down a long carpeted corridor. The walls on either side were hung with framed prints, like in a museum. Then Kris knocked softly on a door. And there, in the dense silence of that dusky room – his library, judging by the walls lined with bookcases – stood Esther and Marjorie.

Her breath fogs up the glass and hides Frank's face. She straightens up slightly, leans carefully on the edge of the coffin, and looks at his folded hands. They're still beautiful hands, but they're also old hands, with liver spots, just like her own. The skin sags deeply between the tendons. She tries to make sense of the hands, as if she wants those hands to show her how he brushed a lock of hair from his forehead, how he held the grapevine while grafting, how he put the back of his hand against a woman's hot face, how his hands unbuckled a heavy belt that held the birds he'd shot, how they cocked and aimed a gun, pulled the trigger, how they glided over a woman's breasts and cupped them gently in their palms. But no matter how hard she tries, the only thing she sees is this: how he reached out his hand in vain for help and how he then fell to his death.

*

Esther is the one who knows all of the secrets. She's dying for a cigarette. There's Ada, so deeply moved as she bends over the coffin, and Marjorie, breathing heavily as she picks at her cast – she finds the silence in the

163

room quite unbearable, the air choked with all of the unuttered words that all have to do with the dead man. Our lives draped themselves around his own, she thinks, yet he himself can't be traced in this story. It occurs to her that even during his life he was separated from the world by glass.

⋆

'Mortal remains' – those words keep forcing themselves upon Marjorie. She knows the procedure, knows how a body is tugged this way and that to get it to look so good.

Hans must have died just before she woke up, because he was still warm. If only I'd woken up a little earlier. His heart had given out on him, in spite of four bypasses and a number of angioplasty procedures. The doctor came together with Bob, whose face had the sad, abandoned look of a child, as if he were four years old instead of forty-eight. Shortly after, a phantom-like figure arose straight out of Hades with a case in his hand. The man who'd come to lay out the body. Would everyone proceed to the living room so he could get on with his wonderful work? It was all a ridiculous dream. The idea that she would leave Hans alone with this ghoul. I'm staying with my husband, she said disdainfully. Together they removed Hans's pyjamas. A formidable job, because a dead body is unwieldy, and in any case Hans was far too heavy. She still cooked with butter and cream, that's just how he liked it. She pulled and tugged and pushed and looked at his dear old body and could see he wasn't there. Even so, she was appalled when the emissary from the underworld filled a metal basin with cold water. Hans absolutely detested cold water. 'Your husband can't feel it any more.' Nothing had any real meaning, it all went too fast. She washed the beloved body with soap and a flannel, just like she used to wash patients during her years as a nurse. Lifted the heavy arm and washed his armpit. Between his fingers. Behind his knees. Underneath his testicles. Oh, my poor darling, she kept repeating in a paper-thin voice. She helped the man pull the soiled sheet out from under her husband and put a clean towel in its place. He lisped at her the entire time, standard phrases that slid right off her. She only listened when he asked her

164

what she would like her husband to wear. She briefly considered pyjamas, because she couldn't face the amount of work a suit and shirt would entail, couldn't face any more tugging on the heavy body. But in the end she took his new suit out of the wardrobe, a tasteful dark blue suit he'd allowed her to talk him into, as usual. He would be wearing it for the first time. She panted, groaned, pushed, and pulled, and once again her hands understood that Hans was gone, that his body had become matter, a body that had served him well but meant nothing without him. Mortal remains. She tied the striped silk tie as best she could and buttoned his jacket. Then the man produced a can of dry shampoo from his case. How old-fashioned, she thought, dry shampoo. The problem is, he said, if you wash a dead person's hair with water, it will never get dry. She would remember that sentence. White clouds of dry shampoo around Hans's face and there she was, afraid he might breathe it in. The man lifted the head and she carefully combed the thin hair. Oh, my darling. Next, the man brushed off all of the powder, and went on to the manicure and removing the nose hair. It might have been the other way around. He started to explain something about the mouth. These days there were a number of options, and each of the options had their own advantages and disadvantages. As the widow it was up to her, of course, but he strongly recommended sewing the lips together invisibly, so her husband could look his best: his mouth wouldn't drop open, nor would it be necessary to tie a band around his chin, which would be unsightly. It was common practice, he assured her, it looked so much nicer. But she should ask herself whether or not she wanted to stay in the room. He took a needle and thread from his case as he spoke. I used to be a nurse, I'm used to such things she wanted to say, but instead fled into the hallway where she leaned back heavily against the wall next to the door and waited for him to open it and let her back in. She didn't dare look at Hans's mouth, and was sorry she'd allowed it. That a needle had been stuck into his dead body, into the soft interior of his lips, and that those stitches would be there for eternity. The man announced he was going to slide small rounded discs under the eyelids because otherwise the eyes would collapse, which would be unpleasant for those viewing the body.

She – who shrank from nothing – went back into the hallway, slumped her head against the wall and listened to the subdued voices of Bob and Vera in the living room so she wouldn't slip away. Then Hans was ready to be viewed. Finally, they straightened the sheet and folded his hands over his stomach. His hands were cold and unresponsive, which felt like a rejection. And while the man went to the living room to tell the others they could come in, she sat next to her husband's mortal remains in a dreamlike state. Once this business was behind them, they could get on with their lives. He needed to have a haircut, and they would finally get round to going to the Mauritshuis in The Hague, see the paintings. Moreover, they were in the middle of talking about something important and weren't finished with this yet. They had to make a difficult decision. He couldn't expect her to do it on her own. And that was that.

The man shut his case, expressed his condolences, and disappeared as silently as he had come. She was grateful to him in a way. An hour later she tried to recall what he looked like, but he'd vanished without a trace, as if he'd never been there at all.

12

MARJORIE WAS BORN IN HER parents' bed in the eastern town of Enschede, the frolicsome afterthought in a family with five children. Her real name was Margot. She had her father's energetic disposition and like him she was hungry for praise. As soon as she learned to walk she developed the same spring in her step that he had, almost a bounce. Her thin body was wiry and strong, with boyish muscles. On rainy Sundays she would drag the coffee table to the middle of the room and force the entire family to watch her leap higher and higher on the gleaming surface; she called them 'Russian' jumps. Although as a rule her father was not a paragon of patience, he was the one who would watch the longest – an adoring fan enjoying the show from his Morris chair – because this bouncy little girl was the apple of his eye, his favourite, his princess. She could wrap that man around her finger like no-one else. 'When you laugh,' he would say, 'the sun comes up.' As he spoke he would tap her on the nose, which he affectionately referred to as saucy. In turn, little Margot was extraordinarily proud of her father, an important commercial traveller for a renowned textile manufacturer, and her nose grew in the direction of his finger.

★

He prided himself on his ability to speak foreign languages, that this was why the firm sent him all over the world to establish new business relationships. He would come back from his trips bearing wonderful stories and exotic gifts, things like shadow puppets and kris daggers and kimonos. He gave his little girl a toy pram from Paris and would bring back new dolls, including small nuns and sailors, from everywhere he went. The fact that, in the end, the company no longer needed him was not his fault, but the fault of the depression and the threat of war. Even so, it hurt. Insulted, he turned his back on Enschede and moved his family west, into a large, dark house in Zaandam.

Helped by his business connections, he set up his own import company in English porcelain and Swedish crystal, and although he threw himself into the venture, his belief in himself had been badly bruised. His sense of fun and playful whims turned into unpredictable fits of rage. When she heard his key in the door, little Margot would dash into the toilet so she could hear what kind of mood he was in as he hung up his coat in the hall. If he was in a good mood, he was the most wonderful father in the world, and would play chopsticks for her on the piano, his fingers gliding down over the keys again and again, or he would put on her favourite record, the one with the dentist sounds, with a moaning child and gargling noises and a whining drill, so she could enjoy being thoroughly horrified. On good days he was entertaining and charming, a handsome man 'who'd been around the world three times'. He liked a glass or two, cabaret, garden parties, and elegant table manners. Every Friday he treated the family to salt herring. But you were never completely safe. If the wind was blowing from the wrong direction he would pick a fight with their sweet, round mother, who didn't know how to defend herself. At times like that no-one was good enough, all of them ne'er-do-wells who were hugely disappointing to him. The only one able to divert his attention was Margot, with her saucy little nose and cheerful childish bouncing. The sun came up when she laughed, so she laughed quite a lot. And once the sun was up, she had to go on laughing to keep it there. And when Father was finally sitting in his chair reading his newspaper, she would slip out the front door and try to get the neighbourhood children to play one street over, because she knew the sound of their voices bothered him.

Occasionally even she would be in for it.

One Sunday morning at the beginning of December, she found a pair of real scissors in her shoe, with blades that formed the beak of a stork. It was a gift from Saint Nicholas and, as was the custom, he'd left it there for her because she'd been a good girl. She was over the moon. To try out her scissors, she climbed up on the table and snipped a sizeable chunk out of the fringe that hung from the lampshade. 'Don't! Don't!' cried her older sister fearfully, but the deed was done. She crept hesitantly back to bed. A short time later her father burst in. He stationed himself next to her bed, crossed his arms in front of his chest, and looked down at her in silence. This went on for a long time. It made her cry. Then, without so much as a word, he tore her favourite book to pieces, the one with the beautiful red and green letters.

Mama, don't give me too much, she would plead if she smelled Belgian endive cooking in the kitchen. Her mother would then try to give her a small helping as inconspicuously as she could, because if her father noticed he would personally dish her out a double portion. 'I'm doing this to build your character.' He means well, her mother's eyes said. He was of the opinion that his children had to become hardened to be able to hold their own in the world later on. He was concerned and wanted only the best for them. The boys had to attend a good secondary school. 'It will give you an edge when you're out in the world.' Marks were compared at the dinner table and the child with the lowest scores would be humiliated in the presence of all the others. To his daughters he said, 'As long as you don't become a factory girl.' Little Margot worked herself ragged, and got reasonable marks all through primary school.

*

Then the war broke out and the market for tableware collapsed. No-one was spending money on porcelain and crystal, unnecessary luxuries, people used what they had and that was that. Their house was filled to the

169

rafters with unsaleable Wedgwood plates and covered serving dishes. He'd set aside money during the good years, and with a great deal of diligence and thrift managed to get his family through the difficult times, something he could have been justly proud of, but he saw only his failures, and saw just as many failures looming up ahead of his children, and all of these things made him bitter and short-tempered. Margot, who had always done her best at school, went on to advanced primary school, it was the best she could hope for. Two years after the war, when she was fifteen years old, she barely passed her final exams. She beamed at the graduation ceremony with her nose lifted towards him, waiting for him to offer his congratulations. He gave her a long embrace, so that she nearly suffocated in his worsted wool lapel. 'A capable husband,' was all he said, over and over, 'a capable husband,' as if she had a life-threatening disease and this was the only cure.

After this he insisted she attend the Catholic domestic science school for two years to prepare her for her life as the housewife of that capable husband. It wasn't much of a success, she was wilful during class, had no aptitude for baking and cooking, outright refused to do any sewing, mending, or fancywork (she was just as stubborn as he was) and as a result received no mark for this on her school report. She did enjoy child care – messing about with baby-sized dolls – and child-rearing. And laughing with the girls in her class. She wasn't interested in boys. The nuns warned the girls never to take the street that went past the boys' school. The fact that she never did was due only to indifference.

In the post-war years as well, there was little demand for tableware. Holland was struggling to get back on its feet, and there was a lack of the most basic items. No-one was buying new dessert plates or cognac glasses. There wasn't much to laugh about at home any more, but Margot did everything in her power to get the sun to come up. If Father announced he wanted to take his youngest to the cabaret – 'for your cultural enrichment' – she would borrow a dress from her older sister and allow herself to be escorted to the theatre like a perfect lady, his arm around her waist.

170

He tapped her on her bottom to steer her through the revolving door, something she wasn't sure if she liked. She endured the cabaret, sighing inwardly. By now she was seventeen.

As long as she could remember she'd wanted to become a nurse, especially in paediatrics, because she just loved children. But she was too young to be taken on anywhere as a trainee nurse. He talked her into studying to become a chemist's assistant. She was good at making pills, weighing out milligrams, and folding powders into translucent pieces of paper, but not at identifying plants. As soon as the teacher changed the sequence, she was lost. She didn't want to fail, and pushed on with grim determination. She would study the Latin names until late at night. 'Acidum acetylo salicylicum…' she murmured, her head nodding above her books. In the meantime, she secretly wrote to all the hospitals. Even before taking the exam she probably wasn't going to pass, she received an answer from Saint Joseph Hospital in Eindhoven. The nuns there had no qualms with her age, and she could come and work as a nursing assistant, and would be given a room in the nurses' residence.

She whispered to her mother in the kitchen and managed to persuade her to take her side. As she waited in her bedroom for the conversation between her parents to take place, she didn't dare move a muscle. She trembled as she endured the tirades that followed, and the subsequent icy silences.

She, the youngest child, his favourite, was going to leave home first. He was so hurt he didn't want to see her off. Moreover, he wouldn't allow Mother to give her any extra clothes so she arrived with a single outfit, and keeping it clean quickly became problematic. This didn't diminish her happiness in the slightest. She was enjoying herself.

The title 'nursing assistant' sounded wonderful to her ears, sounded real, and it didn't matter to her that in practice it didn't amount to much more than washing patients, applying plasters, changing beds, and putting flowers in vases, all at a feverish pace. She was also allowed to wash, weigh, feed, and hold the children. In the morning, she would sit in her small room in the nurses' residence and look around in a state of bliss because yet another day as a nursing assistant awaited her.

Her wages were just enough to live on, but she needed nothing, and had her meals at the hospital. She seldom went home. In her free time, she and the other nursing assistants would cycle to the countryside in high spirits, and in the winter they skated. She would make figures of eight and glide over the frozen canals as part of a chain of girls, screaming with laughter. Mother Superior summoned her when she signed up for dancing lessons in town. 'I forbid it,' said the elderly nun. 'It will be too much of a distraction. Nursing is a serious profession.' Margot was too insulted to reply. If anyone was a good nurse, she was. She knew there was no rule against this and did it anyway. Unencumbered by any sense of rhythm, she galumphed through the ballroom in the arms of sweaty office clerks and thought she'd done splendidly.

*

No-one could doubt that she took nursing seriously. After a year, she applied at Our Lady Hospital in Amsterdam and was taken on as a trainee nurse, also residential. She could start her training at last. She had to pay for her uniform herself, because nursing was seen as a privileged profession for girls from good families and nothing was handed to you. Although she could have asked her father for money, she had her pride. Here too, she worked her fingers to the bone for a pittance, sat all the way down in front during the lessons the doctors gave, studied until late at night, was up and running through the wards again at the crack of dawn – and enjoyed every minute of it. It didn't bother her that the nuns who ran the hospital were shrews who made life miserable for everyone. My patients' gratitude is the best reward, she would say to herself in the mirror, something that would make her insides feel all warm and melting. The uniform looked good on her.

Things were also going better at home, business was gradually picking up, her father was treating the family to herring again, and after all was said and done, she was still his favourite. So she started going there more often on her day off, taking the train to Zaandam, and would stay until after the evening meal, cheerfully chattering about hospital life. Two of her older sisters had got married in the meantime, but because of the housing shortage they were still living in their parents' home with their husbands and babies; she was glad she had nothing to do with the resulting tension. After dinner she would wave brightly, bye, Pa, see you next time. Once in a while he would tap her on the nose like he used to. Did his little girl already have her eye on a handsome surgeon?

*

She was required to work on all the wards as part of her training, including the isolation ward for tuberculosis, which was housed in a separate building because of the serious risk of infection. She had to wear a face mask and wash her hands frequently, and when she dressed wounds, she would tie a heavier apron over her own to stop the tuberculosis bacteria. A strong solution of Lysol was used to clean the spittoons. Some of the patients on the ward were very ill, others were recuperating slowly, and the really unlucky ones died. Those whose tuberculosis was no longer 'open' shared a room. It could take years for them to recover, and recovery meant rest, because a body at rest was better able to fight the bacteria. If things didn't go well – damaged vertebrae, a risk of paralysis – a patient would have to lie flat on their back for six or seven years on a narrow board fastened to a high iron bed with no sides, which meant that the person would fall out of bed if they moved. To keep all that rest from driving them mad, the patients were given occupational therapy, weaving baskets and belts and stringing little beaded bags.

All except one.

For three years now, Hans Doorman had been studying as he lay in bed in the room he shared with five other young fellows. He'd been lucky: only his lungs had been affected, and he was almost fully recovered. He'd got his secondary school diploma while lying down, holding his books up over his head. He was now able to sit up, and had started studying architectural history. Every time Margot came in, he would look up and watch her as she worked. If she leaned towards him to put drops into an infected ear, he would tease her with a pencil held between his fingers, moving it back and forth in front of her face.

'Keep that pencil still, would you?'

'Is it bothering you, nurse?'

'Yes, it is.'

He kept taunting her and she stamped her feet. 'Don't do that!' she cried, and tried to take it away from him. It was a ritual, and the young men in the other beds looked on with interest. Every day when she came to give him the eardrops, he would tease her and she would stamp her feet. An unfamiliar feeling crept up on her, and she started to invent excuses to be around him more often.

Hope reigned in that room, the six young men would play pranks and horse around; they were feeling better and also bored. The closer patients got to being cured, the harder it was to lie still. They were bursting with energy and the presence of pretty nurses drove them to do the craziest things (which of course had to be hidden from the nuns). Most popular was a game of handball between the life-sized Sacred Heart statue near the entrance and the aquarium opposite, and they would throw the ball as hard as they could. The more the nurses screamed, the faster the balls would fly. Sometimes they would wear disinfected spittoons on their heads and sing mangled versions of church hymns as members of the Iron Choir. Margot – who, although Catholic, hadn't been raised to have a very high opinion of priests and nuns – nearly wet her pants laughing. Even when she no longer worked on their ward, she would wander through the hospital in her free time and to her own amazement would always end up with 'her' boys. As soon as he saw her come in, Hans would set aside his books, pretend he was making a belt, and measure her waist – her little middle, as he called it. He could get his hands all the way round that middle, something that never ceased to amaze him. It made her feel all warm inside, and quivery – as far as she was concerned, those hands could stay there for hours, or slide down along her hips, or up under her arms to, to. Well. Anyway. It confused her. She didn't mention it to anyone, because she didn't know what to say. On one of her nights off, she accompanied her father to the cabaret. He put his arm around her waist, as he always did on these occasions. She was startled to find she recognized the feeling; she arched her back and slipped out of his arm, distracting him with a funny anecdote.

*

Spring came. Behind the isolation ward was an open area where cast-off items were dumped, dirty brown carpets, a discarded iron bed. They started to meet there during the few hours when she wasn't working. To avoid running into the nurse in charge of the ward – a heavyset, bad-tempered nun by the name of Sister Cherubine, although the patients called her Sister Toad – Hans climbed out through the window while the other boys stood watch. Then they would sit side by side on the iron bed, warmed by the weak sunlight and the other's presence. They would have long conversations that became increasingly serious and more personal. He was twenty-four, from a large, poor family, his father worked in the harbour in the northern part of Amsterdam and the priest had talked his oldest brother into entering the seminary. After finishing advanced primary school Hans got a job as junior clerk in an insurance company; his wages went to his family. Although some people might be well-suited to office life, he – who'd roamed the harbours of Amsterdam as a child – thought it was awful: he couldn't get used to the lack of daylight or the oversleeves on the shirts, and the hours crept by as if his life had come to a premature standstill. Towards the end of the war he'd had to go into hiding, at the home of his deaf great-uncle in the Groningen countryside, so the Krauts couldn't send him to work in Germany. That wasn't much of an improvement. So he'd been thrilled when he had to enter military service after liberation – at last his life was moving forward, and the air force at that, just what he'd wanted. Going back to the barracks at the end of a weekend furlough, the man across from him in the tram had been coughing. A short time later, Hans came down with a fever. The diagnosis had been a real blow, a verdict with an uncertain outcome. In the best case, years at a standstill. Another standstill.

It was all so unfair, so terribly cruel, that he promised himself not to waste a single minute of his life, even if that life might not last so long now and he would spend what was left of it in a hospital bed. The only thing he could do was read and study. Well, that's what he was going to do, then. 'And do you know what?' he said. 'I like it.' In spite of his troubles, he was full of self-confidence. That's just how he was.

Margot would then tell him about her family. She bragged about her father. Hans listened patiently, and she felt completely safe with him; behind all the crazy joking was a gentle heart and an optimistic spirit. Because of this, she also had the courage to tell him about the things that were less than pleasant, the angry outbursts and the tensions, and she could tell from his reactions how terrible things had often been. Then she would quickly come to her father's defence, although she didn't understand why she was defending him. Neither did he, but he welcomed her words warmly as they surged towards him, and channelled them into a wide riverbed.

They grew closer, and more intimate with each other. Strange how I never noticed how good-looking he is, she thought. Neither of them dared call it love. Or dared to kiss the other, although their longing was becoming almost impossible to suppress. Without the pretext of taking her waist measurement his hands had no business being there and lay idly on his thighs. She stared at them, large hands that looked as though they should be strong but had instead grown thin and weak, hands she loved more each time, until it became almost unbearable. In the meantime their mouths just kept churning out words, because that's all they were allowed to do. The word tuberculosis droned along in the background, unspoken. As in every hospital, in Our Lady Hospital the first-class patients got more and better food than those who were less well-off. But often the rich patients didn't have much of an appetite either, and when that happened there would be good food left over. The nuns wouldn't allow this food to go to the poorer wards. Margot thought this was wrong. 'Her' boys – young fellows, almost fully recovered – regularly complained that they were hungry. 'If there's one thing I can't stand, it's injustice!' she declared to Hans, her cheeks flushed with indignation. He smiled. She started to steal slices of bread that had been sent back to the hospital's main kitchen, something she was amazed to find she enjoyed enormously. I have a talent for crime, she would think to herself, glowing with pride. In the boys' room, she accepted their expressions of gratitude with good grace. Buttered bread was something they never got otherwise.

Summer came, and her thieving had still gone undetected. One afternoon, she was sitting outside with Hans on the iron bed, and had just enjoyed watching him polish off the pieces of bread. She stuffed the napkin into her apron pocket.

'You're going to get caught one of these days,' he said.

'I couldn't care less... greedy nuns.'

'You rascal.'

He looked at her so tenderly she couldn't hold back. 'Do you love that rascal?' she asked, her voice higher than usual. His face clouded over. 'Yes,' he blurted out in a voice that was harsh, almost angry. They immediately gave each other a long kiss on the mouth. She remained aware of the risk of infection, which added something noble to this exquisite, overpowering kissing. They let the kiss go on as long as they could, uncertain if there would ever be another. They only stopped when he ran out of breath. From that point on, they couldn't ignore their love – or the obstacles. She saw him turn gloomy, and the cheerful clown vanished before her very eyes. 'I'm just a lousy TB patient without a cent to my name,' he said, shaking his head. 'I've got nothing to offer you.'

'Love,' she said.

She meant it and this surprised her, because she'd always imagined she'd have a rich and influential husband. Well, so this was what love did to you. Magnanimity flowed through her like a river from head to toe, and she tried to kiss Hans again. But he said they should forget about each other, that there was no way of knowing whether the TB bacteria would remain dormant. 'Have a good look,' he said, and knocked on his breastbone as if it were a wooden door. 'Thin as a rail... flat broke... the future uncertain.' She knew he was right, but she also knew she had to be with him. 'Isn't that what every girl wants?' she asked, in a desperate attempt at a joke. Then they kissed each other again, nothing could stop them now. During that second kiss, she thought of her father in alarm.

*

Every day Sister Toad would slip through the halls, leaving a trail of slime behind her and hoping to catch someone in an ungodly act. She knew she'd made a good catch when she saw Margot come out of the main kitchen – somewhere she had no business being – with napkins filled with generously buttered slices of bread. Sweating profusely and licking her lips, she informed Mother Superior. In the dark brown room with the stained-glass windows, where the smell of furniture wax was always so overpowering it made your eyes water, Sister Benedictine delivered her verdict without delay. Margot had committed two offences: associating with boys from the isolation ward, and stealing food that belonged to the first-class patients. Such wanton behaviour would not be tolerated here. She was dismissed on the spot and was to vacate her room at once. Then Mother Superior returned to her paperwork. Anger made Margot's voice shrill and bold, which surprised her.

'You're going to give me my certificate, aren't you?'

Minutes passed as the nun behind the heavy desk stared at her, eyebrows arched and eyes open wide, eyes that had seen so much sinning they'd taken on the colour of dishwater.

'Remarkable,' she said at last in a soft voice.

Nor was there any chance she would be allowed to visit the isolation ward. 'I would like to see the young man find a more respectable girl,' Sister Benedictine said in conclusion.

Margot asked a trainee nurse she was friendly with to let him know what had happened. Numbed by a general hatred of nuns, she left the hospital and took the train to Zaandam. She stared blindly out of the window at the fields. Until now she'd successfully completed all of the various parts of her training. With no certificate, she'd have to start all over again. But no-one would take her on.

*

At home, she gave a detailed account of the injustice. She sensibly made no mention of Hans. Her father responded in exactly the right way. It was marvellous, he was at his best if it had to do with those despicable, treacherous, underhanded, bitter (along with a great many more adjectives) nuns. He telephoned, demanded an appointment, and early the next morning departed for Amsterdam on his high horse. That's when she started to worry.

He was back with her certificate in time for morning coffee, and flung it onto the table in triumph, ha! those witches had been no match for his indignation. Out of pure spite they'd then tried to catch him off guard by making insinuations about his daughter and a TB patient.

'You were supposedly seeing one of those fellows.' He looked straight at her, his eyes hard. Margot scarcely dared breathe. Then he shook his head. 'They're dragons.'

He turned away sharply, walked regally over to his armchair, opened the newspaper to show that the matter had been settled, and proceeded to ignore her. A thousand needles pricked her neck. In the silence that followed, she listened to the sounds from the kitchen where Mother was making his coffee, tinkled on the piano keys, wiped some dust off the lamp, and inched her way over to the sunroom until she was standing next to the wooden armrest of the low-slung chair.

'Pa?'

'Margie.'

He turned a page and studied the stock-market report.

'Say that something like that had happened.'

Silence. He was reading.

'That I'd fallen in love with a TB patient.'

He didn't look up, murmured solicitously, go on, as if they were having a casual discussion about some perfectly ordinary hypothetical question. She took courage, why shouldn't she.

'And say we should want to get married.'

'Hmm…'

'What would you do?'

He turned to the sports page and tapped it smooth. 'Forbid it, of course,' he said matter-of-factly. 'You're a minor. I would forbid you to see each other until the infatuation passed. Just imagine, a tubercular man… fellows like that are weaklings. Any father would do the same. Oh, you'd be furious with me, but deep in your heart you'd know it was for your own good. And later on you'd thank me for it.'

She stood there next to his chair, rooted to the spot. He continued reading his paper. Only when her mother came in with his coffee was she able to get her frozen body to move.

At her wits' end, her head filled with an agitated clamour of formless defiance, she lay on the bed in her old room and stared through the olive wallpaper at the tall, thin youth. He was also lying in bed and gave her such a miserable look it made her shiver. I've seen with my own eyes how you're the one who always throws the ball the hardest, she told him. You're no weakling, I've seen how strong you are, you only have to look at you. You've got so many plans, you're getting an education, you're always laughing.

But he wasn't laughing now.

Yes, I know, she said, there's a chance you might never get out of that bed again. But I don't believe that's going to happen. You might be weak. But I don't believe it. After all, I know what I see, I know what I feel. You might die. But that strikes me as ridiculous. I think it's more likely you're going to take good care of me. I'm going to take very good care of you, too. Those lungs of yours need lots of fat. Bacon fat, that's what you need. It's gone on long enough.

Then she saw the children: they were strong and wiry and athletic, with twinkling eyes just like his; she wanted them so badly and couldn't imagine that these children might not be born, or that they could ever be anyone else's. Once this was clear to her, she was almost there. She couldn't bear looking at Han's sad face a minute longer, so she got up and went down to the living room, said something about going to visit a friend, took the train to Amsterdam, the tram to the Oosterpark, climbed onto the postbox and over the spiky iron fence, and knocked on the window of his room. She had a plan.

Although she was very upset, she was also determined.

*

At home, she didn't bring up the subject again for two years, nor did her father ever mention it. She finished her training in the regional hospital and got her nursing diploma. She lived in her parents' house the whole time, and took great pains to make sure the sun kept shining. If he wanted to go to the cabaret, she would accompany him cheerfully, her arm firmly linked in his so it wouldn't end up around her waist. If she wanted to go to the cinema with a girlfriend, she dutifully asked for permission. And this was always granted, as long as she was home on time. Hans sent his letters through the same friend. He was recovering well, and would soon be allowed to go for a walk. Then they would meet in the Oosterpark, he in a suit that was too short for him, which had belonged to a boy who hadn't pulled through. A few months later he was pronounced fully recovered. According to her plan, he immediately applied for emigration. During the months before his departure he lived in the small house with his parents, brothers, and sisters, whom she'd got to know during the evenings she was supposedly working the late shift. She got along particularly well with his father, a gentle man with hands of concrete. Together with her future in-laws, she accompanied Hans to the ship. She squeezed him tightly as they said goodbye, and could feel he was putting on weight, that his muscles were developing. And when he put his hands around her waist for the last time, she noticed they were strong again. Their imprint smouldered the whole year long.

*

Father encouraged her English lessons. She took an almost perverse pleasure in allowing him to test her vocabulary. When he asked her once what she intended to do with it, she declared flatly that she was thinking about becoming a missionary. Later on she felt awful. But not for long.

She would cycle over to her girlfriend's house at regular intervals to read the latest letters from Hans. Every sentence contained accounts of pleasure and progress. He wrote that he was feeling very fit from all the hard work in the fresh air, that he'd gained several pounds, and had become strong as an ox. And also, sweetheart, oh sweetheart, how I yearn for you. It won't be long now, she wrote back, just a little while longer.

*

On the morning of her twenty-first birthday, she went to The Hague and submitted her own application for emigration. That evening at her birthday dinner, amidst the sparkling crystal and their best dishes, she stood trembling as she revealed her deceit, concluding with the announcement that she would be flying in an international air race.

'And by the way,' she said in English, 'from now on my name is Marjorie.'

*

Father pulled out all the stops: he shouted, threatened, pleaded, smashed dishes (they had plenty), coaxed, cajoled, flattered, fell silent, ignored her, paced back and forth in the hallway, his lips stretched back over his teeth

– she took it all in and remained civil, because it left her cold: she was her own boss, and no-one was going to tell her what she could and couldn't do. And when he finally figured this out he came round, and started to organize the contents of her crate, filling it from bottom to top with a fine selection of dishes, because he would not have his daughter living like a pauper, and even pounded in the metal fittings himself.

And as for his tubercular future son-in-law, he simply never mentioned him.

At Schiphol Airport she saw dark tears in his eyes, for the first time in her life, and was taken aback. He tapped her nose so hard it hurt. 'Remember,' he said, 'there will always be money waiting for your trip back home.' For a time she was touched, but at the windy airport in London, as she posed for the photographers in her wedding dress – just her! – she recalled his words and was suddenly furious. He doesn't think it will work out. She kept on waving, her arm moving furiously, her mouth open wide in a triumphant, silent shout, as if he were still standing there and she wanted to convince him he was wrong, that he was totally, utterly wrong. He thinks it will come to nothing. That I'll come crawling back. That's what he's hoping for; it would prove him right. But she would do everything in her power to make sure this never happened, that her life with Hans and the children would be a wonderful life, in a country where the sun would always shine without requiring any effort on her part. And as the cold October wind sent her veil fluttering out in front of her face, she felt her cheeks becoming hotter and more flushed.

13

FOUR MONTHS AFTER THEIR WEDDING, Marjorie and Hans still hadn't managed to consummate their marriage. After the first night in particular, she'd barely been able to hide her disappointment, because it hadn't gone like she'd imagined it would. It hurt too much. 'You have no idea, this can't be normal,' she said when Hans carefully suggested that perhaps they shouldn't give up quite yet. She really wasn't exaggerating how much it hurt, no-one in her family did that, you wouldn't dare.

They'd had to confine themselves to caressing, kissing, touching, the things they'd been doing already. But whereas that had once been thrilling – the thrill of that which was secret and illicit – it now seemed like a consolation prize.

The first few nights they kept trying. With the rain beating against the windows of the hotel, Hans would slide up his wife's nightie and admire her strong, healthy body. The firm young breasts, the broad hips. The pinnacle of health and vigour, those hips. He was aroused by this and so was she, she was more than willing to let him in, determined to, actually, but this was gradually being obscured by another feeling, one she'd never felt before, the feeling of panic. What were they doing wrong? This can't be happening, she thought, I have to be able to do this. But time after time he didn't make it beyond the gate, that firmly closed hymen of hers.

Their love was real and strong, it had easily survived two years of letter-writing and would survive this as well, but it had lost something of the lustre with which Marjorie had entered into her new life as a married woman. It didn't make sense. This wasn't how a honeymoon was supposed to be. She found the West Coast disappointing as well. When the rain didn't let up, they decided to go back early. There in the basement flat, every night they would open out the bed full of hope, and every morning they would close it up again, trying to hide their disappointment from each other.

Morning, darling, did you sleep well?

It started to get ridiculous. Hans dug out the book by Huddleston Slater he'd brought with him from Holland to prepare for their life as a married couple. He learned that it might have something to do with the position, but when he tactfully attempted to explain to Marjorie what other position they could try, she wouldn't hear of it. They weren't animals.

*

A few weeks later the bleeding started. From time to time, Marjorie found small bloodstains in her panties. I'm not normal, she thought, and every day it was becoming more and more of an effort to keep the blissful smile of the newlywed on her face. She had so looked forward to that smile, had even practised it, but now it seemed like a gruelling task that wore her out and made her jaws ache. She was glad she was so far away from her parents, and over time her letters home became more and more euphoric. 'Now I know it's true: a girl only truly becomes a woman once she's married,' she wrote.

*

'Please stop.'

Hans rolled off her and a short time later they lay alongside each other looking up at the flaking paint on the ceiling. Not again, she thought, and said it out loud as well. 'Not again.'

He didn't know what he should say and this made her furious. 'Do you think I'm abnormal?' He turned towards her and stroked her face, of course she was normal. 'You know it might be the position after all,' he said. She thought about it for the first time.

'What did the priest say, anyway?'

Before their wedding, he'd had a talk with the priest to prepare him for his duties as a husband. He was outside again before he knew it.

'He said, If you avail yourself of your wife, make sure you don't spill your seed.'

It was quiet for a moment, then they started to snigger. 'Did he really say that?'

It had seemed idiotic to him as well, but you can't say it, after all, it's the priest we're talking about. Feeling relieved, they slipped into each other's arms. Marjorie smothered her husband's face with a shower of noisy kisses.

'Come on, then, let's give that other position a try.'

He waited, was surprised. She got out of bed, took the book off the shelf, and handed it to him. When he found the part he was looking for, he gave her the book and waited patiently till she'd finished reading. Noticed the look of mild surprise.

'It's all right. We're husband and wife.'

This is bad, this is very bad, she thought, but even so got down on her hands and knees with her back to Hans. He took up his position behind her and she tried not to think about what he could see. Keep at it now, it's clear enough why it's important. She wasn't entirely able to keep her embarrassment to herself. 'It's like I'm a pig,' she said lightly, her voice a little too high.

He tried to enter her very gently, but there was the pain again straight away. She moaned, but didn't want to give up. 'Try it like this...' She arched her back, he tried and tried.

'That's enough.'

Her words didn't seem to register with him, and all at once he grabbed her by the hips and pulled her towards him sharply. A nauseating, searing stab of pain, she cried out, turned around, and kicked him off her. She didn't care that the other tenants might hear. She was beside herself with fury, and punched him in the stomach.

'I said that's enough!'

They sat opposite each other on their battleground, gasping for breath, two naked warriors with blood on the sheets, but she knew no-one had won and that the blood wasn't the right kind of blood. It can't go on like this, something's wrong, something has to be done, who would have thought this could happen, help me, what should I do?

Hans kept apologizing, sorry, darling, sorry, I thought... But she could tell by the way he lay alongside her that he was despondent.

They stopped trying for a few days. The bleeding continued. She probably *was* abnormal. But because she still found this hard to believe, something akin to blame crept into the way she looked at her husband. A terrible thought came into her head: was he just inept and had she somehow failed to see this?

*

'It's driving me mad,' she said to the doctor irritably. What kind of country was this, anyway, where doctors went around looking like tramps? Here she'd finally decided to consult a doctor and came walking up to the wooden house – that's another thing, all these flimsy-looking wooden houses, she just couldn't get used to them – and there was a painter standing on a ladder painting the windows (which was quite something in itself, because most of the houses here could stand a fresh coat of paint, it's like the only thing these Kiwis were interested in was playing cricket and rugby); she asked the painter if the doctor was at home and where she could find him, turns out he's the doctor. Says it with a big grin on his face, like *she* was the one who looked silly. Lucky for her he put on a white jacket over his dirty clothes before he examined her. At least in Holland you could tell the difference between a doctor and a house painter.

'It's driving me mad, I just keep bleeding, a little bit at a time, then it stops, then it starts again. Could it be the air here?'

She'd been disappointed in the weather as well.

'I'm always so tired. That's not how I am. You don't know me, but that's not what I'm like. I'm never sick, never.'

Those aren't real houses, the ones made of wood. The doctor (or the painter) washed his hands, well, what do you know, that's something at least.

'And now... all this bleeding, the constant stomach ache. What's causing it?'

'Well, I can't say just like that,' he said pleasantly.

Of course she knew she was being unreasonable, but it's hard to stay cheerful at times like this. So many things had been going wrong lately, she tried to figure out how to talk with him about this, too, but didn't know how to express this in English. Which words you had to use. 'We are not... living together.'

He looked at her, mystified. Dry your hands, will you.

'My husband and I.'

Cohabitation, she'd meant to say, sexual intercourse, something's wrong there. She turned bright red, felt her cheeks explode again. Living together in the sense of coitus, man, she thought, but didn't know how to say this. Never mind, she gestured. It was exhausting, all these problems with the language. Sometimes she and Hans would try speaking English at home and occasionally they managed, but it usually sounded forced, and they never kept at it for long. His English was better than hers, which was logical, since he'd already been here for two years. She was crazy about him, could feel the tears burning behind her eyes, what were they supposed to do now?

'What do you mean?'

Never mind, she motioned again, but at the same moment she decided to give it one last try, this time with a great deal of emphasis and reproach in her voice. 'We cannot... be... together.'

now, well…

d this office visit, this man, this country. To hide her
red down at the floor, which was covered by one of
d English carpets. No taste, these Kiwis. Just look at
flat, those massive dark oak chairs, with upholstered
ancient you'd swear Queen Victoria herself had once

*

better to do, a short time later she lay staring at the
apart. Let's be honest now, she *didn't* have anything
e'd quit her job to have children and look after her
he hadn't done much more than prepare lavish meals
mpletely convinced his lungs wouldn't act up – he
plenty of food and lots of fat, well, she was certainly
gh she wasn't a born cook, she'd become one by con-
matter of time and she'd be able to make a Sunday
he rest of them here. It was also her job to feed the
, to heat the water so she could do the laundry. They
y for a washing machine. And that was the extent of
ight just as well look for a job. Nor was it much
who would either be sitting at her sewing machine
face blotchy and grim, or she'd be in bed with a
n't want to receive her. Some friend. And after having
times, well, she'd had enough of that. Once she'd
bour Department in a defiant mood, but when they
et a factory job spreading cream on biscuits, she'd
ke sure you never become a factory girl. Which didn't
She should go and see a doctor. Wonder what you'll
id that morning. Like it had already been established

usually regular?' asked the man down below.

'You don't know me,' she snapped. 'In my family we're all regular. It must be the air here. Or the food. Everything is different.'

This morning a letter had arrived from Holland. Although Ma hadn't dared put the question directly, she could read it there between the lines: she should have been pregnant long ago. Not a word from Pa. If only that doctor would stop gawking at her insides. If only she wasn't so tired.

*

She got dressed and sat down opposite him. 'You're still a virgin,' he said. 'Technically speaking.'

All she could see was his mouth moving up and down; the English words eluded her at times. He'd noticed this and was making an effort. He explained again, speaking slowly and enunciating his words. 'The hymen is still intact.'

I'm not deaf, she thought to herself. She knew the word 'hymen' from her training. He thought she still couldn't understand him, started talking to her as if she'd escaped from a mental institution, contorting his mouth as he spoke. 'Virgin… You're still a virgin… Hymen… Not broken…'

She must have looked like an idiot.

'Sometimes,' and now he was almost shouting, 'hymen so strong… won't break… husband can't get through.'

'I understand perfectly well,' she said haughtily, in an attempt to keep something of her pride intact. He laughed, a pleasant laugh. 'That's why you're having problems with sexual intercourse. It's a minor procedure, we'll make an appointment with the gynaecologist.' He dug into a tray of papers. Suddenly she realized what this meant. It's going to be all right, cried a jubilant voice inside her, just a minor procedure and then everything will be all right. A huge weight slipped from her shoulders, a weight she hadn't been aware of, but that had made her feel sluggish and tired. As if a curtain had been opened. She could have kissed the man. What a lovely house this was, so light and sunny.

'Now I understand,' she cried. 'That's why I'm not pregnant yet!'

ought of this herself, a strong hymen, she was strong
er family was. Hilarious. Hans would slap his knees.
able to make love like ordinary people.

d have been pregnant long ago! We're so fertile, you
to look at us, my eldest sister is expecting her third,
s four already.' Right, said the doctor. If everything
ild could be born this year yet. 'And you'll see,' he
hook her hand, 'that happens here just like it does
had the vague impression he was making fun of her,
because he was such a good doctor.

*

Women's Hospital in Colombo Street – a modern
toreys high with a round garden in the centre of the
front (they'd found themselves walking round this a
rking up the courage to go in through the glass
n was surgically opened. She was given a mild anaes-
ay overnight, and was sent home the following
old that for reasons of hygiene, she and her husband
aving sexual intercourse for two months.

always, said that it only made him want her more,
easts, something he could never get enough of.
or you women they're so ordinary, for us they're the
else has a husband who says such sweet things, she
ove. They would manage to get through those two
hat wasn't the problem. What was slowly driving her
hat she still didn't feel well. Sick, weak, and tired. She
od. It's because of the operation, she thought. She
ch and had to vomit, even before breakfast. It's from
times she crawled back in bed after Hans left for the
tting up miles of wooden fencing for a sheep farmer.
eration, it makes you tired and irritable. But after

three weeks she had to face the facts: there was something terribly wrong with her. And the hills of Zion were swollen and painfully taut.

*

Two weeks later during her check-up with the gynaecologist she burst into tears, and the man looked up with a start. 'I'm so nauseous every morning,' she sobbed, 'it's like I'm pregnant.' He straightened up and pulled off his gloves. 'Wishing won't make it so,' he said pontifically. To convince her of this, he had her urine tested. A week later, he gestured her irritably towards the chair opposite his desk. 'You're pregnant,' he said, 'around two and a half months now. Congratulations.'

For a moment she thought an archangel must have had something to do with it. He explained. Strong sperm can always find their way in. Sometime during their honeymoon, a strong, smart sperm cell had persevered. Congratulations, he repeated. She just kept staring at him, it was hard to believe. What about the bleeding? That happened sometimes, he explained, small amounts, during the first few months, it was completely normal. The stomach ache and fatigue as well. He looked at his watch, pushed back his chair, and stood up.

Everything that was heavy and of this world left her body. She floated three feet off the ground as she followed the doctor to the door, shook his outstretched hand with extra warmth because she wanted to express her appreciation and because she didn't want it to seem like she was rubbing his nose in his mistake. She felt herself to be wonderfully magnanimous and had a fertile spring in her step as she strode through the halls to the exit. She stepped pregnant into the daylight and noticed the streets were filled with other pregnant women, as if it had been planned that way, an organization. She had to suppress the urge to say hello to them. It trumpeted at the back of her mind, you see? you see? I'm normal. In six months I'll have my first child, my eldest. This is my eldest child, you say, and then comes a row of little heads, descending at an angle according to height, and then you point into the pram and say, this is the baby of the family.

the child, her child, how her baby would smell, didn't

six more months; she wanted to be able to brush its

hair on that wobbly little head with one of those soft

ear the tiny hiccupping sounds and touch the help-

moved in time with the sounds, my baby, my first

have lots of them, in the kind of house that always

d cake, she wanted to call out to the passers-by, she

ough the streets, had to suppress an urge to make

pushed her belly out in anticipation. Strong sperm

way in. Pa and his 'weakling'. Actually, she thought

ad she truly saved Hans's life. Her love had given

her plan had brought him to a healthy climate, her

acteria at bay, her child gave him a link to eternity.

ical when you're pregnant. Euphoria breezed in and

n so, in the midst of this there was an uneasiness, an

have gone differently, that it had somehow run off

st control.

*

y in March, the woman who could conceive through

he man with the strong sperm walked over the

nt with their arms around each other, on their way

k out a pram. With every step they took, flowers

ing stones, so that in their wake the barren city was

brightly coloured garden. At the sight of so much

mazement stole over the faces of those they passed.

t us, thought Marjorie, and took pleasure in pres-

oser to the father of her children, so that they

ng, the Perfect Couple, with two heads, four legs, and

t, three souls. As they walked, they talked dreamily

ers, because they could both see the importance of

'I can rent a big caravan,' Hans said. 'It's just outside town, in kind of a park.'

Their dreaming had started at once, as soon as she told him her sweet news that night in the flat. He stammered out professions of love and put his hands around her waist, whispering hoarsely that already now they didn't touch, because her waist had expanded with his child. She saw him swallow hard to keep from crying, something that would naturally never do for The Man with the Indomitable Sperm, and less than an hour later, as she was looking for the best way to begin a triumphant letter home, he unfolded large sheets of drawing paper on the oak table and started to design a house for his family, a two-storey house with at least four extra rooms for the children, or six if she wanted, a house he would build himself when they'd saved enough money to buy land and materials. They still had a long way to go, he first had to repay a large part of the subsidy he'd received for his passage to New Zealand. But dreaming didn't cost a thing, and there was no doubt in their minds he would one day build this house. And now they were ready to get out of that dark flat with the shared bathroom and the heavy furniture. It was time they had their own furniture, Swedish, modern, light. It was time to find another place to live. A caravan wasn't exactly what she'd had in mind. 'A caravan…'

'It would be our own "mobile home",' he said, as he helped his pregnant sweetheart carefully up the department-store steps. He held doors open for her, would like to have bridged rivers and levelled mountains for her. 'No shared walls, and it's out in the country. You can rent one for one pound, seven shillings, and six pence a week.' It was worth thinking about, she nodded. Funny how mild she'd become as a result of the life inside her. Mild, soft, round and warm. A bit of a stomach ache now and then, a little blood, what did that matter.

It was all part of it.

At the children's department she led him straight over to a sturdy pram displayed prominently on a platform. *Pedigree Cane Pram 9/13/4.* She

tform to see how wonderfully real it would feel to
t in her hands, and tested the suspension by roughly
k and forth. The saleswoman looked on in alarm, but
tried to divert the attention of the reckless Dutchie
ther models further on. 'We've got them in three dif-
studied the prices, which ranged all the way up to
orie saw his worried expression and had to laugh. In
her, filled with awe. 'Incredible,' he said, running his
, 'incredible,' and she had to agree with him that it
nent, that the two of them made an exceptional
that their child would be someone special as well.
ait six and a half months, but the child was there. It
l.

she called out from her platform, and at that same
e had the rocking pram under control again, she felt
deep inside and knew something was wrong because
nd the next moment her teeth started to chatter and
elly took her breath away and then she collapsed
ll's legs gave way and in front of Hans and the sales-
off the platform and into the dark, or rather, onto
floor. This was so out of the ordinary that at first the
re whether she should go to the Dutch woman and
l, or run and get her supervisor. But Marjorie didn't

*

e and more like she was lying on a trolley, in a room
osed it was in a hospital because she could smell
r back, and someone in the blue uniform they let
ountry was holding one of her hands and Hans was
e could clearly feel the difference between the two.
m, dry, and pleasant, like a little cave to take refuge

in. The nurse's had fingers like twigs. An unfamiliar man in a doctor's coat was bending over her. So it could also have been a house painter. He gave her a penetrating look, and she got the feeling she hadn't been paying attention for some time now, and that she should have been. She tried her best to sit up, but couldn't. She discovered this was because the man was holding her down. How bizarre. What's more, he was talking to her, she could see his mouth move, heard the English sounds and the Kiwi accent, but had no idea what the words meant. 'You're not supposed to move,' said Hans. Ah, he really *was* sitting there, and here she thought she'd just dreamt him. So what if she wasn't allowed to move, that was fine by her, she was very comfortable and so incredibly tired. As far as she was concerned, they should leave her in peace. She didn't have the energy to ask if that could possibly be arranged, but with a great deal of effort she managed to turn her head to the side where Hans's voice had come from in the hope she could make clear to him that he should take care of this. He really *was* there. She smiled at him. He didn't smile back. Actually, she wasn't sure if she'd really smiled.

'They've called the surgeon,' he said in Dutch. 'He's on his way.'

*

After a long time, his face appeared again out of the darkness. This time he was standing where the house painter had been and gave her a searching look. Hey, sweetheart, she'd wanted to call out, but decided to wait, because she wasn't quite sure of the order in which she would need to do things to make that happen.

'I went ahead and rented the caravan,' he said. His voice sounded strange. Esther's face appeared next to his, would you believe. Marjorie had no idea what she was doing here.

'He came down a bit on the rent.'

Her eyelids closed of their own accord. It wasn't unpleasant.

*

d inside the ray of sunlight that entered the room
tains. She was looking at this when the surgeon came
e following day, sitting on a stool next to her bed.
asthma. She could recognize many of the words, like
others not at all. Hans, who stood at the end of the
h a worried expression, translated for her. The fetus
e uterus, had nearly gone through the wall of the
ad gone on much longer she would have died. He'd
n tube. Full of adhesions – scar tissue. That's why the
he uterus. Her other Fallopian tube was also blocked.
much tissue as they could, but it might grow back. It
heory, she could still get pregnant, but the chance of
lim. Marjorie observed how the dust motes danced
stened to the sucking sound made by the crepe soles
he into the room bringing tea. It's all going too fast,
e's going faster than I am, somewhere I fell behind.
here,' the surgeon wheezed. 'The chance of this hap-
Hans translated. She'd understood just fine. She just
a stood up, had to get on with his rounds.
chance,' he said.
. The doctor took his files from the bed and shooed
Try to find a new purpose in life,' he said. 'There are
han to find fulfilment.' Then he nodded briskly and
ticed that Hans had stopped translating. She didn't
her. The words had no meaning anyway, and swirled
as dust. I handled that well, she thought. Somewhere
ague notion of the implications this might have at
he moment, as far as she was concerned, she wouldn't
talk a couple of times. 'Did you understand?' Hans
ce did that make. She shrugged her shoulders, very
the sharp pain in her belly. Just leave me be. 'Shall I
slowly?' She closed her eyes, no, I'd rather you didn't.

The sucking sound of the nurse's footsteps moved to the curtains. The ray of sunlight disappeared. Darkness fell.

*

Look, there goes the mother pushing her modern new pram. It's the best money could buy, of course. The handle is pleasantly cool to the touch. The scenery is stunning, a coastline with limestone cliffs. High above the ocean, she walks over the grass, pushing the pram proudly out in front of her. Naturally, the sun is shining. What a day. The pram's wheels turn as if of their own accord over the rough terrain, and have sturdy new tyres. What a woman. What happiness. She has so much energy, and roams through the landscape at a pace that could put a smile on your face. Even so, she doesn't have to make the slightest effort – it's like the pram is pushing itself. That's what these modern things are like. Nor does she need to look into the pram to know her child is in there. All she has to do is touch the handle with her fingertips and walk on with her head held high. The wheels will keep on turning. The wheels start to turn faster and faster, like the pram has a destination in mind, has to get somewhere. She doesn't know if it will still do her bidding, has to go faster to keep up with it, but without any warning her legs become tangled and adhere to each other in a knotted clump and she has to let go of the handle and watch while the pram with her baby rolls towards the edge of the cliff. She stands rooted to the spot, can't do a thing, can't even scream. Watches while the pram disappears over the edge.

*

In the middle of the night she woke up shrieking. She couldn't see, was drenched in sweat. Help me, she sobbed, but only raw bursts of sound came from her chest. The nurse rushed in from the hall, made soothing noises, carefully helped her sit up. A fiery pain in her belly and she couldn't sit up properly, as if the muscles had been severed. Hold on to me, I'm falling, she wanted to scream, but had forgotten all of her English words,

198

s at all any more, and could only scream wordlessly.
d, a kind woman with plump arms who held her
sodden nightgown off over her shivering, shudder-
ing to let you go for just a moment, she said. No,
can't, I can't!

the nurse softly, you can do it, just hold on to the
took the hands of this pitiful young woman and
n either side. Don't let go! Marjorie screamed. You
eetly, you can do it. Now I'll go get a wash basin and
shened up. Don't leave me here by myself, Marjorie
m falling, I can't.

e nurse when she returned, see? you can do it. Then
el in warm water and rubbed it over the heaving
neck. So, that's better. You've had quite a fright. Do
er now? Marjorie could feel the flannel under her
ars. Felt a clean, dry nightgown slip over her head,
ght, now the other arm, good. See? It's better already.
it will help you fall asleep again. Have something to

oft noises, there, there, it's all right, and covered her
ng when she was alone again, and wished she could
the warmth of those anonymous arms, surrounded
athetic sweat.

*

ul. Under no circumstances did she want people to
be hateful. The hate, which had entered in a molten
and unyielding. Straight-backed and stiff, she left the
she and Hans sat across from each other in silence,
little as they could because there wasn't enough
he middle of the table was the letter home that would
saw her looking and put the sheets of stationery in

the drawer of the sideboard. His thoughtfulness only intensified her hate. No-one had to take any pains on her account.

She hated her failure of a body. Disgusted, she slid it between the sheets. He didn't dare touch her. Why would he want to touch me anyway. In the morning he hurried off to work. Then she'd lie down on the floor, her thoughts too heavy to remain upright. Lie on the dirty yellow carpet with the dark brown checks, breathing in the smell of mildew. For hours she followed a modest ray of sunlight – which had come in through the high window and landed halfway down the wall – until the light completed its trajectory and withdrew. It wasn't your fault, she said to the child, you were a good child, a good child in the wrong place. It was my fault. There's nothing you can do about it. She lay in the same position the whole time, and observed coolly that her neck had started to hurt and then her back and finally her legs and the rest of that dead body. Listened to the sounds of the city. To all of those fools riding their bicycles on the left-hand side and sometimes calling things out to one another, to trams that went past (with prams hanging from them), to the trolleybus. Everyone going about their stupid business. Sometimes she crawled over to the radiogram, a huge piece of furniture, in the same way that everything here was huge and unwieldy, and listened to Radio Netherlands. She had no idea why. She'd never be able to go back home. Couldn't face them any more. There was no way back.

Often she would think it hadn't really happened, that the child was still alive, that it was hidden away somewhere deep inside her body and would emerge before long. In the bathroom she stared at the raw scar on her belly – a rush job that had left a jagged trail from pubic hair to navel – and didn't really believe it was in there. Or that it was her. But if she looked in the mirror long enough, she had to acknowledge that she corresponded with the creature who was standing there. For the first time she could see how ugly she was, from head to toe, she'd never realized, almost repellent. This discovery kept her glued to the mirror. If one of the other tenants knocked impatiently on the door because they wanted to take a

l motionless and wouldn't reply. If the person per-
ıt wildly, not recognizing herself. You just have to
you? Even her voice was ugly. At the end of every
get dressed and do the shopping, a huge effort with
ody out of order like that. In the shops she kept as
e hope that no-one would touch her. By the time it
dn't remember why she'd come. Couldn't think of a
r to make. My name is don't-know-don't-care and
standstill right here in front of this counter. There
ound me. That's all right, we're not bothering each
isappear into thin air, either. I don't need anything.
uld I also have that pumpkin, which we feed to the
pite of all of this, she somehow always managed to
teps to the earth's surface, and in the evening would
st before Hans. No-one would be able to say she'd
r as well.

vas saying that. Their Kiwi friends, the ones they'd
th so often, the ones they'd had such laughs with,
She wouldn't open the door. Esther stayed away.
would once again refuse to go to church. The curate
re she'd been was given tea and afterwards politely
me back. The God who did this to her could count
ind she was a fierce opponent. The following Sunday
rch either out of solidarity, which made her furious,
oking for solidarity. Just go. But he'd never been such
ıyway.

*

ound had healed sufficiently, Hans drove with her
motorcycle to the place outside town where their
umped him on his back a little too hard: 'Why are
?' She wasn't made of glass. He gunned the engine –

if that's what she wanted, then that's what she'd get – she grabbed on to his jacket in the nick of time, and the dust from the gravel road flew up into her face. He'll start to hate me but he's stuck with me. She slid up next to him, laid her cheek on his back, and stayed that way the whole time they were on the road. 'It seems there are other Dutch people living in the park,' he shouted after ten minutes. The motorcycle bumped along into vast and desolate hills. A rectangular wooden caravan stood near a river, amidst the high pines. He stopped there and turned off the engine. They disturbed a crow that had been picking at something dead under a bush, a partially decomposed cat or a hare, and it flew up cawing. Then silence.

'This is it.'

From the tail you could tell it had been a cat. She knew she should sit up and say something about their caravan, that she should get off and walk over to it. Neither of them moved and they sat there, her cheek against his back. After a few minutes, Hans put his hand on her knee.

A soft, autumn drizzle, the harbinger of winter.

*

It was just before they moved, their few possessions in suitcases in a corner of the flat, their clothes tied inside a sheet and placed on top of her crate with the household goods. 'Dear Pa and Ma' is how she'd started the letter home, informing them of the situation. She'd written this three hours ago, slowly, uncertain as to what should come next. That was as far as she'd got. The whole time she just sat there staring at the letters, her elbows on the table and her head in her hands, thinking about the quarrel they'd had that morning, about scrubbing the bathroom. Hans had barely finished washing and shaving when she came in with a bucket that was far too heavy and sloshed the soapy water over the tiles on the bathroom floor, forcing him into the corner, where he watched helplessly as the distance between them became unbridgeable. He had to go to work, was still putting up fencing for a prosperous sheep farmer. It was a good job, it paid well, and afterwards a beer with the blokes. He was happy as long as he

if she wasn't wise to that. They didn't talk about it.
anything any more. She made the preparations for
gence bordering on fanaticism. 'What are you doing,
tanding on tiptoe to keep his socks from getting any
surgery.' She didn't know why she was doing it, why
every inch of the rooms they were going to leave
right. 'I don't want them to say I left it dirty.' 'Why
He watched as his wife got down on her hands and
ush to scrub her rage into the tiles. How she scraped
st go to work then, she thought, and pretended she
of his presence. Not that he'd been unkind. But she
completely ruin everything at a dizzying pace. She
the soapy water and picked up the bucket, which
ood at all. 'Let me do it,' he said. As if he'd been able
ce. 'Why? Nothing can go wrong now.' She hated
things like that. Hurled the bucket onto the floor
of soapy water splashed back up and drenched
still go wrong, then. She gave a shrill laugh. 'When
wiped the soapsuds from her face. Maybe he mis-
re, maybe he thought she was crying, because he
her and tried to take her in his arms, and said in a
passion that it didn't matter, it didn't matter at all.
hed him away. 'I'm not crippled! I'm not an invalid!'
nd fell back onto the wet floor in his clean trousers.
up quickly.
othes in the sheet; she'd washed, ironed, and folded
uch force that their things would think twice before
want to… I have to…' She squeezed past him, and
attempt to hold her. Standing at the front door a
ooked so miserable it almost made her laugh. 'What
ou're going to be late.' 'Marjorie…' She could see he
to sound cheerful. 'You don't have to stay on my

account, you know.' Although it didn't sound entirely convincing, he gladly accepted the opening and slipped out into the world.

'Dear Pa and Ma...' There was no way she could write about what had happened. Putting it down on paper would make it real. She would never be able to write to her parents again. Well, maybe postcards with Hello from Canterbury.

'Dear Pa and Ma, I've lost my child and am now well on my way to losing my husband as well. Every night I set before him a steaming plate of scar tissue; he doesn't like it, but he eats it anyway. The day will come when he'll refuse. How are you? Thanks, Ma, for writing about how our Greet is expecting her third and that Rietje's twins are so mischievous. I think you already have plenty of grandchildren, don't you? Pa must be pleased. The proud grandad? Does he still know I exist? No? So much the better, because I don't exist any more.'

She breathed heavily as she scrawled and scribbled, covering the paper with clumps of lines and squiggles, hooks and curves, scarred, illegible language. It was unacceptable. The decision had been taken for her in some sinister headquarters. A faceless force that was impossible to fight and so could not be defeated. There were shackles on her neck and feet and she pulled a ball and chain, condemned to a barren existence. But deep in her heart, she – always the first to stand up against injustice – could not imagine there was no way to escape from this sentence, which was undoubtedly the height of injustice.

She was still scribbling when someone knocked on the door. Because she wasn't planning to open it, she stopped moving her pen, sat motionless, inhaled, waited for the second knock and then the third, after which the intruder would realize no-one was home and go away. Then came a woman's voice, deep and husky.

'Marjorie?'

For a moment she was glad in spite of it all and wanted to call out 'come in' because of the carefree time they'd once shared in a room with tea roses and open windows. But her jaws were clamped shut and so she

door. Just like Esther to then open the door un-
head round the corner. She looked strange and
diately know why, until she realized it was because
ry, almost plain, in a wide jacket and wearing flat
red lipstick. 'Hi,' said the pale lips.
the hospital, knew all about it. They didn't have to
hank God for that. Even though she hadn't spoken,
down across from her at the table with her coat on.
t.

the letter with the scrawls. 'Fine.'
t glint in her eyes, so that you could never be com-

e tea?' I'm a good hostess.
the suitcases and the crate. 'Do you still have any?'
she'd even baked biscuits, a recipe from her domes-
tebook. There are other ways for a woman to find
stiffly to the tiny kitchen, where she went through
ns, aware she was being watched the entire time.
e until the tea and biscuits were in between them on
going to take off your coat?' 'In a bit.' The biscuits
t was hard to botch up sand biscuits. 'They're good.'

ch other as they chewed. Esther burst out laughing.
she really wanted to know. 'Look at us sitting here,'
ple of old biddies taking tea.'
. She laughed along dutifully and accepted the cig-
her. They smoked.
usiness,' Esther said as she tried to blow smoke rings.
goes here?' Then she told at length about Rose, the
shel Street from whom Esther had learned little more
' at the drop of a hat. Although Rose might once

have been the very best here in Christchurch, according to Esther she was twenty-five years behind as far as techniques and styles went. Rose realized this as well, so she called her clients to tell them the shop now had a 'continental dressmaker' and that instead of having to wait three months, their orders would now be ready in two weeks. Esther stepped up her already gruelling pace and worked like a madwoman, earning enough to be able to quit her job at the clothing factory. Her creations had gone down very well. By this time Rose herself was doing very little. She kept nodding off as she worked, and would burst into a kind of rapturous alto humming at the oddest moments. She'd probably been alone too long. Anyway, one day Rose told Esther she should just take over the shop.

'Did you have the money for that?' Marjorie asked. Not that it mattered to her. The story didn't interest her in the slightest. She put out her cigarette. The ashtray slid over the table.

'The rent for the building is next to nothing, and she let me pay for the business itself in instalments. Of course, she asked far too much, the business was on its last legs and her machines, too, just like she was. So I got her to come down by half.' So Jewish, thought Marjorie, always bargaining. 'So I went down to the Labour Department to find out just what kind of qualifications and diplomas I needed to start my own business here. Nice man, cigar smoker, sweat-stained shirt, asked if I had a name already. I'd actually wanted to name it Pacific Lady, but Peggy advised me against it. That Kiwis would get the idea it was for Polynesian women and they're very large, so it would put people off.'

'How is Peggy?' Marjorie asked.

'I don't know. So I came up with another name. Lady Esther. Nice, huh?'

'What do you mean you don't know?'

'So I said to the man, Lady Esther, and braced myself for the mountain of paperwork I'd have to deal with, you know the kind of thing, diplomas that of course aren't recognized here, or documents that have to be sent from Holland, or forms you have to wait months for, permits that don't

…nan says, Lady Esther, good name, that will be ten
… shakes my hand and wishes me "the very best and
…s". I just keep staring at him. He says, is there a
…about the permits? He looks at me and I say, the
…keeps looking at me, and I say, the business plan in
…ment certificates I don't have, the exams I still have
…his cigar, now I'm almost shouting: and the starting
…starting capital I'll never be able to raise? He says,
…n business. That was it! Ten pounds! He didn't even
…a from the fashion academy or a reference or any-
…untry!' The familiar, throaty laugh. 'So I say, then at
…our office!'

…ugh and heard how that sounded. If only they could
…ree months and were smoking their cigarettes with
…om the windowsill. They both took another biscuit.
…r own shop,' she said to have something to say, and
…uld ever get married. Esther focused all of her pow-
…n dunking her biscuit into the tea. You shouldn't do
…e, sand biscuits are too crumbly, and sure enough,
…to the cup edged in blue. The misery crept back in.
…aid, 'nice.'
…nush out of her cup with a teaspoon.
…eggy any more.'

…a in the office behind the atelier. That's where I sleep

…es were raised, followed by a long, probing look, an
…le asked Esther what colour her eyes were she always
…Marjorie found pretentious. Now she wondered what
…was something very complicated taking place on the
…le. Suspicious and wary, she waited. Watched how

Esther got up and slowly, almost hesitantly, unbuttoned her coat. What an odd way to go about it, she thought, she always has to make such a show of everything, and watched the movements of the long, slender fingers in fascination, one button after the other, and then the opening of the coat, and how Esther let it slide down, draped it over her arm, and put it on the chair. She could see the belly, but the image didn't reach her brain.

'Don't be shocked,' Esther said.

The shock exploded inside of her. Somewhere far away, Esther turned to one side so her profile was clearly visible. Light years away from each other. Sickened by the girl across from her, she tried to concentrate on what the husky voice was saying. She hated her. Truly, deeply hated her. She tried to listen nonetheless and not to scream.

'I'm twenty-five or twenty-six weeks along.'

It was impossible to do any quick mental arithmetic with so much hate inside your head. But she *was* able to figure out it had happened not long after their arrival in New Zealand. Now Leon would have to marry someone who'd pushed him into the river after all.

'It will be born sometime in the middle of July.'

In her mind, a fury leapt to the other side of the table, sharp claws ripped at the curly hair, slammed that head so hard against the tabletop that shards of skull fused with the wood. In July a child would be born over there. 'Gosh,' she said feebly. 'How long have you known?' Esther had been pregnant the whole time, in the room she'd shared with her so generously, *her* room. Mortified, she thought back to the talks they'd had right before her wedding, the references she'd made to the coming wedding night, about her status as an adult woman when she thought she was ahead of Esther on that front. The whole time, her so-called girlfriend hadn't breathed a word. She'd told her everything, the nuns, the stolen bread, everything, hadn't kept anything back. But nothing had ever been offered in return.

'Right after your wedding, I started to suspect something. Everything smelled so different. In January I knew for sure.'

een months since you'd had your last period.'
en erratic. I thought it came from all that flying. To
'I didn't think about it at all.'
d around the room full of glass so thin it could be
en noise and might cause them to hurt themselves
. 'Gosh.' She stared at those long hands that uncon-
elly and tried to feel nothing at seeing this. 'And

n't you dare ask, said the amber. Her heart pounded
aced down the list of potential candidates, from Ray
of Hans's *mates* and their friends from the beach to
don – anything was possible with that incessant
ose open blouses. Disgusting.

s if it were irrelevant. 'Oh, it's hard to say.' Of course,
ed, an evening here, an evening there, and all that
ich. Father unknown. Esther shrugged her shoulders
t matter to her. Still, she suddenly seemed terribly
truck by the full impact of this. An unwed mother.
front of her mouth. 'How are you going to manage?

silence. Esther crossed her arms above her belly and
ight. Marjorie saw her wandering the streets, jeered
ast.

hought of that before. If you want to be so careless
ght ahead. But don't come crying to me later. The
drummed her fingers on the table furiously, knocked
oblivion. 'Why didn't you get rid of it, then, while
ure you know where to go for things like that.' The
cheeks, she could feel she'd gone too far. But she
and endured the look.

'No-one's going to be got rid of here,' said Esther at last in a calm voice.

Marjorie thought of the family portrait, the father, the mother, and the little brother. She'd had her suspicions, but you don't ask a question like that, and Esther never shared anything. 'Sorry,' she said, to be on the safe side. Now here she was apologizing. All the same, she said it again: 'Sorry.' Esther nodded.

'I was able to hide it for three months, then Peggy figured it out and I was kindly requested to leave... she hated to do it, she hoped I'd understand... an unwed mother would damage her reputation.' A throaty, cynical laugh. Yes, go ahead and laugh, Marjorie thought, that's what you've got to look forward to, pointing fingers wherever you go, welcome nowhere.

But she *would* have a child.

She planted her elbows on the table abruptly and put her head in her hands. Stared at the biscuit crumbs on the table and tried not to scream. Far away, Esther went on. As soon as the old dressmaker Rose (who hadn't noticed a thing) had gone to live in the home for the elderly, she'd moved into the shop and put up a sign: 'Closed Temporarily'. It would be better if her clientele didn't find out about her current condition. She was living off her savings, spending as little money as possible, you could call it poverty. 'But,' she said, 'that's not the point. I can handle that.' No idea what the point actually was, then. Leave me out of this, why don't you. They didn't speak. Then came a voice so hoarse it was nearly inaudible.

'I don't want to bring a Jewish child into the world.'

In the silence that followed, Marjorie raised her head and thought: she really doesn't want the child. An outrageous possibility occurred to her, so outrageous that the thought wouldn't allow itself to be thought through to the end.

'Why not?'

Esther dismissed the question with a wave of her hand, a hard, conclusive gesture, a decision against which no appeal was possible. She had never confided in her. So be it. In the midst of this, the growing realiza-

210

that Esther didn't want the child. And that it was
 ay. And that it would have to stay somewhere.
 t it up for adoption?'
 sther spoke. 'With adoption, it would be possible to
 mother.'
 olution. 'What do you want to do, then?' she whis-
 ne, she gingerly inserted the secret key into the lock
 y tiny bit, and turned it with excruciating slowness
 ound. She'd made a spectacular escape once before.

*

 rned home she had the whole plan worked out, and
 a sparkle in her eyes he hadn't seen for a long time,
 with a surprise, a special Dutch meal of steaming
 s he was having his second beer, she told him about
 dy hell,' he said. How did she plan to carry that off?
 nim step by step. 'Bloody hell,' he said again, and this
 just like hers. She didn't like that. She'd anticipated
 uments and objections, but not the eagerness with
 oraced her plan. As if he'd given up on the possibil-
 lim – of having their own child. As if he'd accepted
 ourse was *her* failure, not his. This was going too fast
 ance isn't the same as no chance at all,' she stressed.
 mouth full, 'but there is almost no chance just the
 ner knife and fork down onto her plate. 'Shall I just
 then?' He flinched and started to stammer, that's not
 This could be their eldest child, and then it would
 had more, wouldn't it?
 what if we don't have any more?'
 ll have *one* child.' It was exactly the same train of
 rself all afternoon. But now, hearing him say it out
 ; her own failure thrown into her face like a wet

211

rag. 'Sure, because otherwise you're married to a barren woman. Then you won't have *any* children! Then you'll be sorry! Then you'll start to hate me!'

He pushed back his chair, threw his napkin down on the table.

'All right,' he said. 'We won't do it.'

*

They glowered as they folded out the bed, a routine procedure that no longer held any promise. Then she took off her clothes while he turned his back to her, and there amidst the heavy furniture he packed the last of his things for their move. Why should he still have any interest in her body? She crawled under the blankets with indifference and inched over to the wall; she lay there stiffly and listened to him shuffling about and to the rustling of large sheets of paper in the hope she would be suddenly, mercifully overcome by a long, long sleep.

But after a time the room was silent, and the silence lasted too long. Her entire nervous system went on alert. She turned over abruptly. He sat bent over the drawings of their dream house, crying soundlessly in such a restrained way it frightened her. Private crying in the night, nearly noiseless, only peristalsis.

His sorrow. She'd never thought about that.

She shot out of bed, rushed over to him, slipped onto his lap, and put her arms around him. 'Don't cry,' she pleaded, and she kept repeating it, more and more softly, 'don't cry, don't cry', even though she was crying just as hard herself and before long you couldn't tell who was comforting whom. Maybe they were comforting each other. They rubbed their wet cheeks together and sobbed, and licked at the salt that just kept coming, new tears mingling with the old, and they licked and they rubbed and they sobbed. By the time the flow of tears gradually abated, they were stuck together by a good deal of dampness and neither one of them was capable of disengaging from the other. There on that unwieldy dining room chair with hard plush upholstery that chafed her skin raw and red, Marjorie

his trousers and wriggled on top of her husband,
evening they were husband and wife in a superior
me in four months, in a variety of ways that were
nature, and they both knew, without saying it aloud,
n conceived that night. Whether it was their own
en conceived that night.

14

FIRST CAME ESTHER'S HAND, WITH fingers so flexible she could bend back her thumb and touch the fingernail to her lower arm. The palm of the hand faced upwards as it slid over the table in a slow and meaningful gesture. In the middle of the table, the fingers opened out further and stretched. The nails drummed softly as they made contact with the oak. The hand, a cool, sad hand, lay waiting quietly, unadorned by rings or bracelets. The room was hushed. Someone's fate was being decided. The walls of the flat looked on and were their witnesses.

Marjorie's hand was shorter and not as supple. A strong, athletic hand with short fingernails and a smooth wedding band. A hand for deeds, not dreams, and which now landed resolutely across Esther's open hand with an abrupt little plop and without the slightest show of hesitation (although she did feel this). The hands exchanged warmth, and waited. Then came Hans's hand, covering them almost protectively. His hand, a large male hand calloused from two years of working with hammers and planes, fit Marjorie's like a glove. Their wedding rings collided briefly, but this was accidental and had no significance. Now the hand on the bottom carried the other two, a solemn reception in a sad room. Three hands. All things considered, they were more than anything very young hands.

Marjorie couldn't help herself, she *had* to say something, as if she were

one,' she said, and cleared her throat because the
ink in them, 'no-one will ever find out.'
laughable. At another time.
Esther.
d?' Hans asked. He had his doubts on this point.
for hours. But Esther wouldn't budge, and Marjorie
r.
tion,' said Esther, 'the one essential condition.

asped each other more firmly, and it was no longer
the warmth was coming from. One ball of deter-

ns.
ther.
arjorie, and right away she wanted to add, 'It's *our*
nild,' because that was also part of their agreement
ed that more than anything in the whole world, but
The child would be inside Esther for almost three

w been said. Even so, none of the hands made any
. 'You have to understand...' Esther said after a
arjorie kept giving the bottom hand little squeezes,
re of the trust Esther had placed in them. They
came.
nclusion, to show it was all right. The hands let go
hdrew. At the same time they would remain there,
he centre of the table.

*

on an autumn day that had started with thin, cold
tation wagon drove into the park where the caravan
r, which was packed with possessions and pressure,

bumped carefully over the unpaved lane – lined on both sides with high plumes of grass that had already turned yellow – and drove onto the river's edge. At a remote spot in the middle of the park beneath a stand of pines stood the wooden mobile home. The desolation fit in with their plan. The caravan was set onto a concrete base and had an asbestos roof; Hans had done the cleaning and made the other preparations for their stay. A generator would provide them with electricity. He'd sold his motorcycle with a heavy heart, but hadn't complained. He used the money to buy the Vauxhall. Although it was a good car and very roomy, it was also very battered, so he'd been able to get it cheaply. This was also part of the plan. Now he turned off the ignition and got out, had a look around. Was glad to get off on his own for a bit.

Marjorie saw that there wasn't much left of the dead thing under the wet bushes.

'Are you coming?' asked Esther. She was watching Hans. 'The coast is clear.'

*

They unloaded the car as quickly as they could and got their belongings into the caravan. In spite of Hans's efforts, there was a pervasive smell of damp. A cast-iron stove stood in the middle up against the back wall. Hans said it would get the place warm and dry. Other than that, they only spoke when absolutely necessary, their ears pricked for any sounds that would announce the arrival of unwanted visitors. They knew there were other caravans scattered throughout the park, even that there were other Dutch people living there, but hoped that the vast size and ruggedness of the place would prevent any contact. Nonetheless, they didn't rest until everything was inside and Esther could retreat into her little room at the back of the caravan, invisible to the outside world. It was the smallest bedroom imaginable, partitioned off with a thin wall Hans had built to provide some privacy. 'Here I go again,' she said airily, plopping down onto the squeaky bed. Marjorie knew what she meant. 'It's only for three

...eer her up, and closed the curtain, which made the
... not costing you a cent.'

*

...ld plan, and they couldn't allow it to fail. All three
...d of this. So they'd prepared themselves for a three-
...n they would have to somehow stick it out with each
...ditions. Hans was lucky in that he could drive away
...eturn only at night. Marjorie tried not think about
...rated on Esther, a friend in need whose appeal for
...answered.

*

...ravan seemed endless. Especially during the day,
...wo of them. They drank tea and smoked cigarettes.
...y loved being able to speak Dutch to her heart's
...gth about her knowledge of pregnancy both to re-
...prepare her for what was to come. It was mainly
...sured. She showed Esther how to do exercises (which
...g with her), took Esther's blood pressure with the
...from the pharmacy, listened to the baby's heart with
...nd told one anecdote after another about the time
...bstetrics department in Our Lady Hospital. Almost
...etell the story of the heavyset young farmwife who'd
...because she had such excruciating pain in her lower
...hours later lay staring in shock at the baby in her
...thing for nine months,' she would say in conclusion.
...thing she'd eaten.' She wisely refrained from telling
...very had gone on for ever, when it had been difficult
...it had all gone wrong right before her eyes. It had
...ered how much pain Esther would be able to bear.
...uch, nor did she seem all that interested in her preg-

nancy. But her hands were always busy. She placed her sewing machine on the wobbly camping table and sewed baby sheets, embroidered pillowcases, and threaded elastic through the openings of nappy pants. She suggested that Marjorie donate her wedding dress so she could make sleepsuits. Marjorie asked if she'd lost her mind. It's for the little one, Esther said (they never spoke of your child or my child but always of 'the little one'). This argument carried a lot of weight, and a short time later, Marjorie grumbled as she took the crumpled white piqué from the suitcase. 'Then at least make a christening gown from it,' she fussed. Esther refused. She would hear nothing of baptism. Nonetheless, before long she was sitting there sketching intently – biting her lip, humming softly – because she'd had a vision of the most beautiful christening gown ever, she just couldn't resist, and this is how in the weeks that followed an exquisite little gown came into being, with frills and tiny covered buttons and endless layers of gathered lace (which she'd cut from the veil) and a bodice covered with delicate smocking. 'Oh dear, oh dear,' she would say, sighing in satisfaction, and when she was finished she handed her creation to Marjorie with a disdainful little nod and the words, 'But don't you dare have the little one baptized.' She knitted small sweaters in fantastic patterns that she would pull out of her head as she went along, almost in a trance. She was less inspired when it came to herself. Marjorie's offer to buy her a maternity smock in town was turned down in disgust. I was just trying to help, you know, said Marjorie, insulted. Esther shrugged, and sewed inserts into the side seams of a purple bouclé dress she referred to as a failed experiment (something Marjorie could only agree with). Over the dress she wore a red cardigan that could expand along with her belly until the end. She put on lipstick and looked striking. But she made it perfectly clear that these clothes would disappear into the fire after, after. That this entire episode would go up in smoke. To Marjorie's annoyance she continued to wear high heels, which clacked noisily over the hard floor. She'd topple over if she wore flat shoes, she explained. Which was nonsense. There was no reason she couldn't wear slippers, just like she did.

ays when Esther would lapse into silent brooding.
cross from her would get under Marjorie's skin. So
down in endless bickering, she threw herself into
and although she didn't quite lie, there were many

*

d Ma, *Everything is fine here. Hans and I now have
ust the way we like it. Outside winter has set in, but
ng cheerfully and keeps us nice and warm. It's so beau-
us live like free spirits, out in nature. Of course, a
emporary and we're probably going to be moving
applied for a job up in the north. We still want to
ed country, and the climate there seems to be very*

*

well. The wood was wet. If they wanted to be warm,
with smoke, making their eyes and throats burn.
n the door and windows a crack and before long
They put on as many sweaters as they could. If they
m the stove their breath would come out in little
fingers from her gloves and went on embroidering.
tears and studied her closely. She became curious
, because of the child, but Esther didn't want to talk
ing special,' was the only thing she said. 'Tailors and
m. Hard taskmasters – I was taught how to stitch by
If it tore, I had to do it over again, *hopla*.'
rie didn't want to appear too eager. As long as the
Esther, nothing was certain nor could she lay claim
ing the baby's heart didn't bring it any closer. So she
about irritably as she made yet another pot of tea.

219

Felt rejected. And to think that she'd had Hans drive her to town on two separate occasions to buy her a larger brassiere. For my friend, she told the saleswoman, she's having a difficult pregnancy and isn't allowed out of bed. I do everything for her, that's what friends are for. The saleswoman showered her with praise.

*

Things were easier with Hans there in the evenings. He brought fresh air and optimism along with him, and the groceries she'd ordered. She and Esther took turns making the meals on the paraffin stove as they listened to his stories from the outside world. Laughed at his jokes. Marjorie continued to feel slighted; Esther bent over backwards for Hans, her laughter loud and throaty, her gestures exaggerated. And she didn't like anything Marjorie cooked: she would put down her fork after only three bites with one of those looks on her face and never a word of appreciation. Matters didn't improve any when it turned out her blood pressure was too high and her food had to be cooked without any salt. A little gratitude wouldn't have gone amiss, thought Marjorie, after all, they were paying the bills. But she did her best to control her irritation, and time and again she managed to see Esther in a softer light. What helped was the awareness that she'd put so much trust in them. The child would have a good life with them, which was no small thing, and the thought of this could make her feel completely warm inside. And actually the three of them usually had a lot of fun together, as if time had stood still and they were still living in the room with the tea roses, but then without Leon.

They wondered how he was doing.

Esther told how she'd felt guilty later on. She'd had absolutely no right to push him into the river: he'd done nothing to deserve such treatment. She'd written him a long letter of apology, but he never wrote back. 'That doesn't surprise me one bit,' said Marjorie, 'after being jilted like that.' 'You're lucky he was such a good fellow,' said Hans. 'Who knows what someone else might have done.' Then they all fell silent, and the three of

ympathy for that poor Leon. Looked at each other.
ed.

*

he caravan, as far as possible from Esther's little
room, not much bigger and just as musty. In the
at was too small and sagged dangerously down the
egularly celebrate the marriage they'd won back.
eaking of the springs and their own moans to a
badly, because of the tension and the cold. They
over the plan one more time. Sometimes Hans had
ve doing, for God's sake? Then she would talk him
she would find it hard to fall asleep. Elsewhere in
lse was finding it even harder to sleep. At least once
d wake up because she heard movement, and sighs.
. Then she would lie there and listen until the front
d. She was usually asleep by the time the front door
must have spent many hours outside in the cold
poke of it.

*

mething goes wrong during the delivery?' Esther
g their evening meal. The baby was moving around
, and she'd placed their hands on her belly so they
thing's going to go wrong,' said Marjorie, recalling
Hospital when the head nurse, a woman they called
herself down in between the unfortunate woman's
d her entire weight to push the baby out while the
ortured for two days and nights already – screamed.
ong,' said Hans, 'we'll drive full speed to the hos-
he end of our plan.' 'Nothing's going to go wrong,'

221

Hans spent every free minute working on the Vauxhall out in front of the caravan. He cleaned, sanded and soldered, and every individual part passed through his hands.

On the last Saturday in June he went to town with Marjorie and drove up close to the door of the large hospital where at one time – hard to believe it was only nine months ago – she'd been assigned to work in the laundry room, to her great indignation. Right at the start of visiting hours. With her head held high and her husband on her arm, she walked straight to the obstetrics ward, strolled up and down the hall three times until she saw that the nurses had left the new mothers to their visitors and had gone to have their own afternoon tea, dashed into the storeroom and, made lucid by the tension, quickly stuffed everything she might need into her generous shopping bag and the pockets of her coat. Navel bandages, infant nappies, she didn't miss a thing. In the meantime, Hans kept watch in the hallway. 'I've aged ten years,' he sighed when they drove away from the car park a short time later. 'The sweat is pouring off me.' But she thumped the dashboard with delight, and was filled with an old, familiar pleasure.

In July, winter grew colder, and all three of them grew weary. Were fed up with walking on eggshells and drinking cups of tea. Found it hard to put up with each other. Esther sank into an odd indifference. Her face looked puffy. She sat sprawled in the chair and seemed incapable of remembering anything. Hans would sit bolt upright at the slightest sigh. He'd been offered an office job in Wellington, with Woolworths, and had to start in three weeks' time. He'd quit his carpentry job in Christchurch and was around all day now, he didn't really know what to do with himself. He chopped a huge supply of wood for the stove. Touched up the last of the scratches on the car. From nerves alone, no-one had an appetite. Marjorie complained of stomach pain. It shouldn't go on much longer. Everything was ready, the suitcases were packed. They'd gone over the plan and refined it again and again. They'd given notice for the caravan. It couldn't go on much longer. Esther constantly had cramps in her legs, pain in her lower back, and her stomach would get hard. When she lay

comfortable. The baby had dropped and weighed

*

bid any contact with the other residents in the park.
ig that this hadn't been difficult. They remained on
nally they would hear a car in the distance. Then
they were doing (Esther would go to her room to
nd listened until the only sounds they could hear
rds, wind, trees, and water.
led the sounds. And the snow made them think of
The first flakes had fallen during the night. That
Marjorie pelted each other with snowballs. Esther
, her wide cardigan over her bulging dress, and
musement. The sky was leaden; there was bound
pping and sliding, Hans got hold of Marjorie and
to her neck while she shrieked with laughter and
r!' while in the meantime trying to trip him up. In
both feel that their gaiety wasn't genuine, as if they
thing remembered from the past. Afterwards, they
f their clothes. Together they cleaned the snow off
rate – which contained as many of their possessions
back. Today Hans was going to bring it to the boat
o town to do the shopping. They kissed each other
iff lips, and she stood waving as the car drove off.
hands tucked into her armpits to warm them up, she
and closed the door behind her, locking it, as she
know. Esther was making coffee. Lately she felt like
every so often. Marjorie took a wet towel from the
the stove and dried her hair and neck. She yawned;
the night before. 'I think I'll go back to bed again
sat down at the table, where the remains of their

223

breakfast had not yet been cleared away. Waited for the coffee. Yawned again, which made her eyes fill with tears. 'I don't like the smell of the coffee,' Esther said. 'I won't drink it.' Marjorie looked out the window and grew sombre; she thought about last night, when she lay brooding in the dark and knew for certain she could never have a baby and that once her own baby was born Esther wouldn't want to give it up, so that she, that she... Traces of this still clung to her, the threat of having a failed life. That's when she saw the man and woman. They were warmly dressed and walking through the snow straight towards their caravan. They were close enough to see her sitting there. They'd probably left their car a bit further down the lane.

'Esther,' she said flatly.

Esther turned around. Marjorie stood part-way up and leaned towards the window, taking up as much space as she could, and returned their greeting. '*Quick,*' she said, but Esther had understood. She got down on her hands and knees, groaning softly because it was hard for her to make those kinds of movements, and crawled as close to the wall as she could get, under the window and on to her room, the skirt of her dress dragging along and getting in the way and sometimes pulling her down. 'The plates – the plates,' she hissed. Marjorie didn't know what she meant. She waited uncertainly until the man and woman had reached the window. Good morning! They smiled at each other at length. The man's protruding ears stuck out at an angle from beneath his woolly hat, and their outside edges were red from the cold. He had a large, astonished head. The woman had beady brown eyes. You could see a lot of gums when she smiled. The man and woman weren't much older than she was. They went back and forth for a while, grimacing enthusiastically at each other; it started to get a little strange, and she realized they weren't going to leave. Behind her she heard the door to Esther's room open and close softly. The woman gestured, coffee, do you have coffee? Marjorie laughed and shook her head no. 'Sorry, no time!' she called out through the window, and pointed to the suitcases that stood waiting in the caravan. The beady eyes

their sockets in surprise. The man pointed to the

r her breath, but had no choice but to go and open

hey introduced themselves at length, but the names

nto her head. The whole time she was thinking of

had left behind as she crawled across the floor, and

sh odour. 'Are you leaving already?' the man said.

le had a Frisian accent, from the north of Holland.

collect her thoughts. 'Yes,' she said, 'but my husband

job.' In Wellington, she'd wanted to add, but caught

h,' the man said with interest, 'a new job, that's nice.

be?'

owed never to know anything about each other.

Esther would never know where they'd gone. Now

a thin partition, listening in. Marjorie stared over

e to the pine trees, where snow was sliding off the

he ground with dull plops.

said.

. And when are you leaving?'

making an odd impression.

an seemed deeply disappointed, as if her departure

le world to collapse.

yes looked for the place where the bones and skull

covered everything.

id moronically.

s that we really wanted to invite you over,' said the

ed. We're from Reitsum, near Dokkum.' She recog-

ody of homesickness.

id, and pushed the door almost closed because

ning from Esther's room, 'but not now.'

'Dokkum's not far by bicycle if you have the wind at your back. Where are you from?'

'I smell coffee,' said the woman.

'Saint Boniface was murdered by the Frisians in Dokkum,' said Marjorie, repeating a phrase every Dutch child learns at school, her twisted face a reflection of the despair she felt inside. The woman nodded happily.

'Keep us posted, won't you?' said the man. 'Then the four of us can still drink a toast to the future with a flagon. Our boy is called Lewis.'

She nodded.

'His name is actually Lieuwe,' said the woman.

'Make sure you do come over, all right?' the man urged. '*Before* you leave.'

She laughed politely at his joke.

He made an attempt to explain where they lived but she shut the door, smiling and nodding the whole while. Then realized that perhaps it hadn't been a joke. Soft moaning came from the little room. She looked at the wet trail on the floor, which went all the way to the door of the room. The couple crunched through the snow. She went to the window, waved again, watched them closely until they were completely out of sight. Only when she heard a car drive off in the distance did she emerge from her stupor. 'Gone,' she said, and saw the three breakfast plates on the table.

'Marjorie... can you come.'

Esther was standing in her high heels in a pool of amniotic fluid, holding up her skirt.

*

'You're not groggy enough yet,' said Marjorie six hours later as she pushed a new supply of wood into the stove, because she remembered the dazed condition of the women in the obstetrics ward, the inward-looking expressions, as if they were on another planet and were no longer aware of how they appeared to others, legs open wide, the crotch in full view, the

oss of decorum. Esther, however, stubbornly refused
d high heels, shuffled through the caravan between
, and wanted no part of the internal examination
g upon. 'What a predicament,' she kept repeating.
uch slower,' said Marjorie. 'You have to save your
on she'd tried to quietly make herself a sandwich,
having a contraction at that moment, crawling
n her hands and knees roaring like a lion, snapped
e should get that sandwich the hell out of here. Get
y from her. She quickly put the bread back into the
gh her stomach burned, she wasn't hungry. She
after every contraction. Sometimes Esther wanted
inst her lower back so she didn't feel the pain as
t they hardly spoke, and allowed the time to pass.
see your hand in front of your face, it just kept
asn't back. They hadn't included that in their plan.
been back to church since her operation, sent up a
ayers.

*

g to last?' Esther moaned hours later. She leaned on
ith both hands while Marjorie stood behind her and
y had their coats on, and could see their breath. I
ie stove going in a bit, thought Marjorie, the baby
et me examine you,' she said, 'I'll know how much
ext contraction announced itself.

*

top of the mattress on the big bed. On top of this
s late at night. Esther moaned as she lay on her side,
f how much time had elapsed between contractions,
trol. She howled, deeply affronted she was no longer

227

in charge of her own body and astonished by so much pain; she breathed high and fast, gasped for air. Marjorie, inwardly frozen with fear, sat on the edge of the bed giving short instructions in a calm, authoritative voice like she'd seen the gynaecologists do. 'Breathe… breathe…' Hans had not come home. No car, no help. Snow. Nothing was allowed to go wrong. Don't let anything go wrong.

'Breathe… breathe…'

She rubbed Esther's back non-stop and spoke to her with words that were gentle and encouraging. 'Just let it come,' she said. 'Surrender to the pain, go with it.' She used a wet flannel to wipe off the sweaty, tortured face. Esther gradually slipped deep down inside herself. Trapped within a raging body, dazed by the pain, she slipped into another world. She whimpered the whole time, soft and plaintive, it almost became singing, a delirious song. Marjorie kept encouraging her in a calm voice. 'You're doing fine. It's going just fine.' She hardly dared take her eyes off her body, afraid it would get away from her. But still she somehow managed to get the stove going again for the fourth time. To fill the oil lamp, put fresh candles in the candleholders. To put her head out the door for a moment to get some air, in the hope she'd see headlights appear.

Near dawn a transition, as if Esther had woken up. A very worried look. 'Where's Hans?' The nest had to be safe, and it wasn't. She sat up. 'So. I quit. I'm leaving.' Marjorie knew this heralded the final stage of labour, and now Esther could push. 'That's fine,' she said, 'just go ahead and do whatever you feel you need to do right now.'

*

These contractions went on for a long time, and she wondered how long they should be allowed to last. Esther lay propped up against the pillows with her legs wide apart, and she kneeled in front of her on the bed, using force to push back her lower legs during every contraction. The blood, the humiliation, the smell, the physical contact, all of this intimacy, it no longer mattered. Even so, Esther was still wearing her high heels and

ssiere to come off, nor her dress, which had been
under her armpits.

was going on too long. Marjorie tried her best to
ouldn't remember, couldn't remember exactly how
what she was supposed to do then. She saw herself
snow in the dark across the immense unlit park,
e place where the man and woman lived. Cursed
attention to their directions. And then what? What
There was no way she could leave. Esther would be
clear instructions.

. keep going… not too hard… good… and now

go wrong, please don't let anything go wrong. A
age. She saw one dead body, then she saw two. We
e out of our minds. In between the contractions
e couldn't do it, that she was going to burst open
with that odd, unruffled gynaecologist voice: 'Don't
ocused, concentrate, it's going fine…' and thought:

ged contraction. In a sudden burst of clarity, she
any longer. I have to do something. When the con-
er, Esther collapsed terrified into the pillows and
while, to take a break, to not be tortured like that
uld see the black hair on the baby's head.
it,' she said. 'It won't be long now,' she said, 'the next
at. And now push as hard as you can.'
s a Herculean task. Esther pushed for dear life. This
orst one yet, but by the time it ended the head had
difficult work had been done. The room was filled
n. Marjorie slid her finger along the neck, checking
ical cord was not wrapped around it, and hooked her
der. During the next contraction the child slipped

out with a twist into her open hands. She felt the small body, warm and alive. She looked at the alarm clock – it was twenty-two minutes to five. 'It's a boy,' she said. His feet were blue. He opened his eyes immediately. Then he drew a breath and made a sound that seemed remotely like crying but remained indescribable. She couldn't imagine him ever not being there. Hello, sweetheart, she said wordlessly. But he wasn't hers. She wrapped him in the clean towels she'd warmed for him with the hot water bottles. She didn't dare think about anything and, as if she were in a film, performed all of the procedures she could remember. Used a thin rubber tube to suction out his nose and mouth. Tied off the greyish umbilical cord. Cut through it with a couple of snips and a ringing silence inside her head. She wiped the baby clean, checked his reflexes, counted his fingers and toes. Her hands were enormous next to his own. She wrapped him in the warm blankets. Every image etched itself into her mind. Then she put the baby into Esther's arms without speaking. There was no other way.

Next she turned her attention to the lower part of the mother's body. Removed the high heels from the icy feet. Waited for the contraction that would push out the placenta. It took about ten minutes. The contraction caught Esther off guard and she protested, she'd had enough. Marjorie removed the blood-soaked towel. She washed her hands with disinfectant soap for the umpteenth time. Turned her attention to the mother, washed her, and saw she needed stitches. She'd seen it done often enough. She calmly unwrapped the curved suture needle and threaded it. A steely inner voice commanded her hands not to shake. She put in three small stitches as if she did this every day, it wasn't so bad, nothing unusual, she'd seen worse. Esther didn't feel a thing and looked at the child. They were silent the whole time. Marjorie went about her work and knew that Esther wouldn't give up the child.

*

It had all ended well, that was the only thing that registered with her. From time to time she sent up tattered thankful thoughts in repayment. Outside

g. Morning came. She felt nothing now except
erself. Mechanically, she got the stove going again,
sther tea and a cracker. She wasn't able to eat any-
ck at her from the mirror was the haggard face of
cognize. She refilled the hot water bottles and
blankets next to Esther. Esther's teeth chattered as
es closed and the child wrapped up warmly in her
old.' She didn't open her eyes. Marjorie covered
et. 'That's because you worked so hard,' she said.
atterhorn, that's how you have to look at it.' The
She sat down at the foot of the bed and looked at
dea what she could possibly say. The floor came
again. Occasionally she changed position. It went

*

g outside by the time Hans came in. She gave him
just as haggard and pale as she did, as if during
rough exactly the same thing. 'Bloody hell,' he said
unt. 'I knew it, I was afraid that might have hap-
been impassable and the car had broken down,
he coolant. 'You couldn't have made it up,' he said.
w with an overheating engine.' He'd spent the night
olleague and his wife, and had been so worried he
rly this morning he'd picked up the car from the

reassure him. It had all gone well. The baby had
tay with Esther. It had all gone well and they should
What was wrong with us, she wanted to ask him,
? Why didn't we see it was insane? But she saved all
because she was incapable of speech.

Something had happened to all three of their faces. They could see it when they looked at each other. They stood next to the bed in the small room, their shins pressed up against the metal edge, in the concentrated atmosphere in which you could smell every hour of the previous night. From the bundle in Esther's arms came barely audible noises. 'Hi,' said Hans softly. 'Hi,' said Esther. Her voice was weak and a little offended. She'd had to endure too much pain.

All three of them bent over the child. Calm, alert eyes.

'It was quite a predicament,' Esther said after a time. Then she looked at Marjorie and smiled, said quietly, 'Well done.' Something inside that had been completely shrivelled began to swell just the tiniest bit. 'You, too,' she said.

Esther took the bundle in both hands and gave it to Hans.

'Here's your son.'

He took the baby from her, stunned. Marjorie, who'd had nothing to eat for twenty-four hours and hadn't slept for thirty-two, couldn't get the picture to focus, but suddenly understood it all. You can't give your child to another mother.

Esther pulled herself up with difficulty; she tried to stand, but dizziness forced her back down. 'What would you like to do?' She wanted to go to her own room. Marjorie wrapped her in the blanket and helped her along. 'Hold on to your belly,' she said. They inched forward through the caravan. Behind them stood Hans with his son in his arms. She got Esther – who didn't want to take off her dress – into the cold bed and tucked her in as best she could. She looked with new eyes at the family portrait that stood on the nightstand together with the menorah, closed the door behind her, and walked back to get hot water bottles out of the other bed. Hans was sitting on the bed with his knees pulled up, with the bundle in front of him on his thighs. 'Look,' he said. Both of his enormous fingers were extended outward, and the tiny hands were clasped around them.

ɔked at his son. The baby lay with his eyes closed,
mes a dainty little tongue would slip out. She went
, filled the hot water bottles from the kettle, closed
d them in between the blankets next to Esther, who
to the wall, her teeth still chattering. She pulled the
vering body as far as she could, tucked it in firmly
checked to see if the hot water bottle was right up
er feet. Stroked the defeated curls. There was no
hivering. A strangled voice from beneath the blan-
l over to hear. 'What did you say?' she whispered.
ɔ do with 'a safe life', the words muffled by a snowy

l, and knew she was being watched by the solemn
mother, and the little brother in the picture frame.
ne door behind her and started cleaning up the
nuch time. Her son was going to be born this after-
inutes to five.

15

JUST OUTSIDE CHRISTCHURCH THE BUILDINGS gave way to an indefinable landscape, large areas of which were covered with steadily melting snow. 'I consider this to be a no-man's-land,' she said, and she could hear she was speaking with the thick tongue of a drunk. 'That's fine, love,' said Hans, who wasn't listening because he was too nervous and too moved and was trying to pay attention to the slippery road. He didn't dare drive very fast, because wedged on the floor between the front and back seats was a cardboard box, and there, inside thick blankets bolstered by hot water bottles, was the baby. Invisible to the outside world because he did not yet officially exist. The few times another car overtook them, Marjorie made sure she was clearly visible, sprawled in the passenger seat with a pained expression on her face. Hans's face was already wearing the corresponding worried look. Not that anyone noticed them, but they weren't taking any chances. After some time she spoke again. 'I consider this to be a non-existent point in time in which the cards are reshuffled.' The words came out slurred, but in a strange, hallucinatory way she was wide awake. 'You vanish into a green expanse,' she went on, 'all right then, green and white, and when you come out you have a baby.' She looked between the seats. The baby was asleep. She'd fed him his first bottle while they were still in the caravan, just before they'd driven to Christchurch to take Esther home.

red, and the railway line next to the road. 'I was
here,' she said. She'd worked out their drive north
ap opened up on the table. Now she was putting
h grim determination, the dress rehearsal. Hans

f this?'
about pain in my lower back.'

ng about it for weeks.'
caused it?'
food here. I'd had an upset stomach for months.'

s you, because you've been here much longer than

*

eriod for months.'
spect anything?'
unts of blood. That made me think I had my period.'

very long.'
nt for that?'
rom all that flying.'

*

elly was getting bigger.'

nstipation, from the food.'
st from constipation?'
at big, you know.'

235

'How could that be, anyway?'

'What?'

'That your belly stayed so small. If you were pregnant. Which we didn't realize. But you were. Even though you weren't really pregnant, of course.'

'I was really pregnant, you know.'

'Yes, but… Now it's getting too complicated.'

✶

'Back to my belly, why my belly didn't get big.'

'Well?'

'Because I have strong muscles, played a lot of sports, strong abdominal muscles. They held my belly in. That's possible. That's why I didn't know.'

'But if you'd been complaining of pain for weeks…'

'Yes?'

'Why didn't you go see a doctor, then?'

'Because I'm a headstrong nurse who thinks she knows it all.'

'Yes, that's true.'

'No, that's our *story*.'

In between they were silent. They listened intently to the sounds the baby made. And had anxious thoughts.

✶

The road wound high into the hills. Below lay a rolling valley. Beautiful, watery afternoon light. At the bottom, a ribbon of river. Pine trees with dripping branches. Marjorie watched the road keep getting smaller and then wider again, funny what lack of sleep can do to you. 'This is where I gradually started to panic. I didn't know what was happening to me. The shooting pains were coming faster and faster. I couldn't stand it any more.'

on driving as fast as you could. There's nothing

*

ie road there was the South Pacific, the water wild
on the rocks. She got excited in spite of the tension.
!' The road became winding, with the railway line
on the right. They drove through narrow tunnels
s in the sea, with seagulls around them in the air.
ind turned to such an extent that it made her nau-
regnant woman. In Kaikoura they stopped near a
one would see them. They stood next to the car for
arched her back and went through the motions of
er back pain and nausea. She still hadn't been able
r stomach was so empty it actually *had* started to
e sheet metal from the strain. She leaned her fore-
f the car, stomped her feet like she'd seen Esther
lf into her role. I could be an actress, she thought,
iding more than one life. Hans stood there looking
mp and cold. Because they couldn't tell whether
house, they continued on their way after a short
the hot water bottles, which were still giving off
iby was sleeping. The tiny hands were sticking out,
s at the wrist. She tucked them carefully beneath
pt crossing. She liked the blurriness this produced,
e convincing.
after your father first and then after mine, or the
is asked.
v we're going to have a child,' she replied.

*

237

The road was empty between Kaikoura and Blenheim. They hadn't met any other cars for a very long time now. A vast landscape of dunes. The road went up and down. She became nauseous again.

'Why were we driving here?' Hans asked.

She laughed weakly. 'It's like catechism. Why are we here on this earth?'

'Well?'

'We were moving from the South Island to the North Island because you'd got a new job in Wellington, and we wanted to see the sights along the way.'

'See something of the country.'

'Exactly.' It came out 'eshackly' because her tongue wouldn't cooperate. She giggled.

'Why didn't we take the boat to Wellington along with our things?'

'Then we wouldn't be able to see anything. The boat goes at night.'

'Hmm.'

'We also wanted to fly over the Marlborough Sounds.'

'I thought you never wanted to fly again after the air race?'

'You talked me into it.'

'*I* talked *you* into it?'

'That's right.'

'How did I manage that?'

She laughed and tickled the back of his neck. There were tears in her eyes. I'm emotionally just as up and down as an expectant mother, she thought. And I look just as puffy. This is going to work.

*

'Why did we have so many blankets with us? And hot water bottles?'

'Because it was cold in the car. You shouldn't ask unnecessary questions.'

She would occasionally slip off into a dreamlike state and was at the same time more wide awake than ever before. But he couldn't stop, because the closer they got to Blenheim the more nervous he got.

d the milk powder, and the clothes?'
ind out about that, silly.'

*

tartled, he slammed on the brakes. The car stopped
es. As if prearranged, they both turned round and
ts, but the baby hadn't noticed and was still asleep.
'It's four o'clock – this is the place, here's where it's

?'
ne out of a daze,' she said, 'and suddenly had an
n.'
say to me?'
the car, somewhere at the side of the road. I said I

knew that now?'
enly understood what was happening to me.'
our waters broke?'
ourse.'
y toes, I can't slack off. She sprinkled water from the
. Onto the floor.
?'
nstructions. I'm a nurse. There was no other way.'
driven on quickly to Blenheim, to a hospital?'
that. The baby was on the way and wouldn't wait. I

*

him in detail, sprawled over the front seat. Showed
cribed the process. What he'd done. How he'd tied
with the gauze from the first aid kit they always had

239

in the car, and how he'd cut the thick cord with the bandage scissors. She took the bloody towel out of her bag and opened it up, showed Hans the placenta. He didn't want to look at it too long. 'Bloody hell,' he sighed. At twenty-two minutes to five, he lifted their baby out of the box, blanket and all, and handed him to her.

Outside Hans dug a hole in the cold sandy soil of the dunes and buried the bloody towels and the placenta. Marked the spot with a stick so they could find it again if they had to. In the quiet of the car she got acquainted with her child. 'Hello, sweetheart,' she said, 'I'm so glad you're here,' and suddenly she was able to focus her eyes on every square inch, and made her way over the little face, the delicate eyebrows, the turned-up nose, and then down to his hands, which lay beneath his chin, completely relaxed, without the slightest bit of resistance, why do we resist things so much, and her eyes zoomed in on the long fingers with nails like the gothic windows of a tiny cathedral. A snip out of time. She jerked back her head, pulled herself together, sighed deeply, flexed her muscles and made strange sounds to wake herself up. The baby yawned. It was un-believable he was able to make a human gesture like that, unbelievable. Everyone should see it. She stroked his cheek with her index finger and felt its sublime perfection. In a reflex he opened his mouth wide and turned it towards her hand, looked furiously and full of life for a nipple, without ever waking up. Love like liquid concrete trickled in. But it wasn't the time to rest assured, it wasn't over yet, and they still had a major hurdle to take.

*

Just before closing time, they staggered into the small town hall in Blenheim. Hans held the bundle with the infant in his left arm, and with his right he supported his shivering wife, who had just given birth. The shivering was genuine, hunger and lack of sleep having robbed her of all her body heat. Strange things were happening to her and she just let them happen, like when she stepped out of her body sideways and walked on in

ulating carpet. They walked gingerly towards the

aired woman was getting ready to close for the day.

ee got a chair for the young woman. There was no

story. You only had to look at their ashen faces to

people were in a state of shock. *Baby present*, she

gistered under the name of Robertus Johannes

obby. You should go to the doctor now, she urged,

t needed to rest, so she helpfully explained where

tel.

*

was a demand for cars that were in reasonable

erested in the station wagon at the garage in

t the plane tickets from the money they got for it.

hotel lobby, as an official mother with her baby in

shed. All three of them had slept soundly, although

d still been tense. The tiny boy lay between them.

s and let out burps. The contents of his nappies

delighted by everything he did.

ce they'd taken off from the South Island in the

hat she allowed herself to feel euphoric. The baby

ected. Fussing with a crying baby felt wonderfully

e most beautiful landscape she'd ever seen, snow-

ds that seemed to rise straight up out of the sea.

d had changed. The sun was shining differently. She

usband's shoulder. He was still somewhat uneasy.

and see a doctor the next day, why did we fly out

ught for a moment. 'You know what,' she said, 'if

question, we'll say: where we come from, women

me. There's no doctor involved.'

erly at their child, who was already falling asleep

again with a worried little wrinkle on his forehead, and it made both of them laugh. You're going to have a good and a safe life, she said inside her head, I'll see to that, and her eyes filled with tears because it occurred to her just how she'd saved this child. She smiled as she wiped away the tears. Hans saw this, and pulled her close to him. Sweetheart, he said.

They didn't talk much, though.

Something kept bothering her.

The sign 'Closed Temporarily'. Esther, who had stumbled through the airless atelier to the sofa in the back and lay down with her coat on. The silence. The bound breasts that would start to hurt. The silence. The smell of yellowed pattern pieces. They hadn't left her unprovided for by any means, come now, there were bags full of food for the coming days in the small kitchen, and half of Hans's monthly salary lay on the cutting table, because of course she hadn't earned any money over the past few months. You couldn't say they hadn't done anything for her. But she was lying so quietly on the sofa. When we left.

She shook her head and gazed out the window at the Marlborough Sounds below, at the sun glittering on the azure blue and on the snow-caps. It was magnificent, it was a reward. Everything had gone well. She'd got the better of fate once more. Now she had to rid herself of the ridiculous notion that not only had she saved a child, she'd also abandoned one.

16

HAT MIGHT have been Frank's living room is
folding chairs have been set up everywhere, many
nd. Because of their age, Kris has seated the three
ble sofa. Even though her arm is in a cast, Marjorie
euvre Ada in between Esther and herself. At the
nst the backdrop of the display cases with the guns,
h is now closed. On top of it are large floral arrange-
ribbons that urge him to rest in peace, that say
in is a lectern on a raised platform. Quite a number
er friends from the area who have to take sips of
ntinue, a winemaker who says he never had a better
er who recalls his sense of humour, an Asian cellar
ligible accent, and a blonde-haired student work-
chool who sings the college's praises in such a way
r if she'd actually wanted to say something else.
g too low to be able to really see the speakers in the
ffort to follow their words as best she can, because
o he had been. Amidst the flattering words of praise
he searches for what is really being said about him.
hears: 'inspiring man... dedicated winegrower...
uthority... tireless... a loss for the region...' and her

heart breaks along the old lines, because with every tribute she sees him sink further into loneliness. No child to stand at the lectern and say 'Papa', no matter how grown-up, no wife to say 'my darling', no brother or sister to talk about 'our Frank'. She gratefully accepts the tissue Esther offers her and wipes away her tears. Nonetheless, funny remarks keep cropping up in the speeches from which you can conclude that he'd had a great many girlfriends. And indeed, when she looks around she sees quite a few women with faces just as tear-stained as her own. Some of them are her own age. Most of them are quite a bit younger, which stings a bit. But if her observations are accurate, there's no-one special, no-one who took away his loneliness. She blows her nose and tries to calm her breathing.

Marjorie is uncomfortable. I shouldn't have come, throbs in her head. Now everything has become inevitable. Any minute now, Bob will come back with Hannah. She's dreadfully hot. Moreover, the sofa's too low and she can't see a thing and her skirt is too tight and her cast makes her itch, and it irritates her that Ada's so sad and also that she's managed to keep her figure, and she could do with a glass of sherry and something to nibble on, and that confident look on Esther's face is making her extremely nervous. The speakers go on and on, there's no end to it. '... They're such hard workers, the bloody Dutchies...' Around her the Kiwis laugh, ha ha ha, those darn Dutchies. You see? she thinks, in the end you're still an outsider. She can't stand it in a way that there are so many more people here than at Hans's cremation and that they're all acting as if the great Frank de Rooy was so terribly important.

Esther is only half listening to the eulogies. She's studying the young people gathered together next to the wall. They might be students from elsewhere who've come to help with the harvest, or those attending the Druivebloed Viticulture College. Some of the faces are Asian, along with white and Polynesian ones, and she sees Kris standing between two girls who appear to be English, who have on cowboy boots and carry their bags angled over their bellies. The boys wear their trousers low. A couple of them have goatees, which to her seems old-fashioned but is apparently all

bellies peek out between T-shirts and skirts. Esther
sloppy and unbecoming, but the children them-
not that they're all nice-looking, far from it, but
nder of youth. They stand apart from the adults
d every gesture, every look, every whispered word
e only they can understand. They know they are
n full of older people. Their mistake is to believe
s, and to assume it will always be this way. Esther
race. She wonders if their group made the same
er people in the crowd when they arrived at the
ossible to imagine.

rs are slowly pushed open from the middle, and a
e step to one side to allow one of their contempor-
tty girl with an energetic air about her, dark curly
look in her eyes. The girl stays close to the door.
ddle-aged man with a contented face and a casual
-grey jacket that doesn't look to Esther as if it was
She's quite sure she saw the man reading a news-
morning, because she'd noticed the jacket then as
ve similar features; he must be her father. It's clear
now the other young people – curious looks are
ys are interested. The girl is aware of this, because
s comes into her eyes as she scans the room as if
Kris manoeuvres himself into a position near the
, thinks Esther, this glorious game. She can't take
's like seeing her long-ago self standing there. And
ve the child she'd been, she closes her eyes and
or these youngsters, right from the bottom of her
t the other end of the sofa, Marjorie moves rest-
oan beneath the weight. When she opens her eyes,
r direction, discreetly but unmistakably, her face lit
ed delight, as if she was seeing her again after a long

absence. The man is also looking towards her, smiling broadly. But she doesn't know these people. She turns around to find out who this might be meant for. Marjorie is also waving.

They're with Marjorie.

The room drops away, the voices of the speakers fade into the distance, her head slumps forward and her eyes look for support from the toes of her shoes, which are stationed somewhere miles away on the ground. 'Who's that?' she hears Ada whisper. 'That's my son,' Marjorie whispers back, 'and my youngest granddaughter.' Ada makes a squeaking sound, something Esther remembers from the past. 'Oh, how nice!' They're shushed by those around them.

*

Once they've made their way outside, after shuffling out of the steamy hall with the stream of mourners, Hannah throws her arms around her grandmother's neck. Marjorie holds her cast off to one side as best she can to keep it out of harm's way, and clasps her left arm around the slender body. 'My dear girl,' she says, her throat squeezed shut, 'you've got so thin. And you smell like horses.' Over the shoulders of her favourite grandchild she keeps an eye on Esther, who is digging a pack of cigarettes out of her bag a short distance away. Hannah steps back and holds out her hands with the long, tapered fingers. The palms have taken on an orangey hue. 'Look,' she says triumphantly, 'from the reins.'

Ada has stayed close to them. She doesn't know anyone else here and is dreading what comes next, the burial. Marjorie introduces her to Hannah. 'She was going to travel through Australia for a year,' she says, 'working here and there, but she's been on a horse farm somewhere in the bush for months now. And if you ask me, it's not just because of the horses.' Hannah laughs, a deep, throaty laugh, and tells Ada how she waded barefoot through the river in the morning to get the horses, how she rode through the bush with groups of Japanese tourists, some of whom had never been on a horse before. She says she also really wants to

246

till got four months.' Her eyes wander over to Kris,

s friends further along.

ed and independent, thinks Ada.

lighter. It's as if her eyes aren't relaying any infor-

are numb. Then a charcoal-grey sleeve moves into

olds up a light. Now she really has a problem. She's

afraid she won't be able to get the cigarette into

l fashion, let alone into the flame. She plants her

her side and holds her right wrist with her left

teeth on to the filter before the cigarette between

e to swerve too much to one side. This construct

ard towards the lighter. She takes hold of his wrist

grasps it tightly. A broad masculine wrist, warm

of her son. She draws the fire through her cigarette

he straightens up, she finds herself looking into

eyes. After two or three puffs she calms down

n if he'd like one, too. He accepts, and introduces

lish: 'I'm Robert.' Nearby, Ada and Marjorie are

How many children do you have?' Esther asks once

king. Her hands are still shaking, and she keeps

against her body. Her muscles feel like steel cables

nsioned, and she knows that tonight in the hotel

k in the bath to settle down. 'Three,' he answers.

a wife. I'm lucky.' His voice has a pleasant, deep

e her head, three, three daughters, three children,

have three grandchildren. She knows Marjorie is

people everywhere, the hum of voices is subdued

. The mourners part respectfully as the coffin is

to walk behind the coffin in a long line through

tery. Marjorie takes her son's arm. 'Did I see you

r hand reassuringly. 'No, you must be mistaken.'

Then Marjorie puts her good arm through his and leads him away from Esther.

Robert, thinks Esther, Robert. And then: Bobby darling.

*

Death makes everything final. The procession moves slowly through the fields and Ada has plenty of time to take in the countryside, to see the white nets draped over the vines. She'd always imagined she would come back sooner. She'd been held back by fear and look what happened, now it's been decided for her and she's walking next to Esther behind his coffin. Marjorie walks in front of them, flanked by her son and granddaughter. The sun is lower in the sky and in spite of everything, Ada enjoys the warmth, which is now soft as velvet. The coffin has been placed on a wheeled bier and is being rolled along slowly by six young men, three on either side, cellar hands from the winery. Directly behind the coffin walks the elderly Maori woman who kept a vigil next to Frank. Next to her a Maori man of the same age; he must be her husband. Ada is somewhere in the middle of the long line and can't see him very well, but deep in her heart she knows who he is. And also that she'll come face to face with him soon. Mozie.

But she doesn't know what she will say.

She directs her gaze at Marjorie's heels, at the swollen ankles that go straight down into the shoes. Marjorie's son became an architect. Her own children haven't gone quite as far. Julie, in Hokitika, works at the visitor information centre now that the children are grown. Son-in-law Gary drives a truck when he's not drinking. Julie is a sweet, considerate daughter but a little bossy, with a voice that gets louder when she's overwrought, something she almost always is. If Ada doesn't follow up on her good advice, she gets angry. She means well.

Pete, in Kerikeri, lives alone in a house that smells of scorched coffee. She worries most about him. He left his wife and children when he found out which way he was inclined. Since then Derk has refused to have any

ere once a year. More often isn't possible. It's quite
et is expensive. Even so, she's not sure that's why.
ce agent for a large company. In his free time he
hurch, just like his father has always done. At his
w why he lives by himself. Or they do know, but
s. Last year he went on holiday to Bali, by himself.
Ada a little sad. He's a gentle person, but gloomy
und a pile of photographs in his closet, of young
clothes. It's not easy. If she tries to talk about it, he
uch like Derk, the father who doesn't want to see

, is the child she's secretly most proud of, who has
eart. It's always been that way, although if someone
uld deny it completely. To everyone's surprise, he
ll, heavy, clumsy little boy into a gangly beanpole,
and then once he turned twenty he gradually sank
til he took on his true form and turned out to be
llow, the best-looking of the three. He became a
a gregarious, warm-hearted disposition. He and
ends, the children like to come home, and do so
noisy and cheerful, with dogs and music. Danny
ne one for years, a group of friends, nowadays they
r's parties, where their children laugh them down.
rch in years, and the children know nothing about
aughter plays the piano beautifully and went to the

o lives nearby – looks after her the most, it's Danny
ly is, and he always has. He sees how quiet her life
Mum, he says regularly, why don't you and Dad
land, in Ons Dorp with the other Dutch pension-
e and being together with all the others? I could
o time. Ada would love to, but Derk doesn't see why

they should. A move like that costs money, it's a lot of bother, and you never know what your new neighbours will be like.

Anyway, she'll go and see both of her sons after the funeral and tell them the whole story, just like she did with Julie the day before yesterday on the beach. She'll be honest, without going into too much detail. Although they might be adults, children don't want to know that a man who was not their father saw their mother without any underwear. That she draped white bird netting around her naked body like a bridal veil and that the man fell back onto the bed so he could watch her spin slowly out of the veils in a sultry dance.

But she *will* tell them the truth. They'll be shocked, just like Julie was, but she can't help but think it will also come as a relief to them, because they'll be better able to understand some of the things that happened, things that never became completely clear to them inside their heads. Things that took place after their mother came back to them following a mysterious trip. Such as the times they found her on the bed in the middle of the day, flat on her belly, moaning softly as if she were in pain, frantically rubbing her face into a summer dress with colourful stripes, one that was unfamiliar to them because their mother never, ever wore it.

17

DDRESSED TO her. Ada van Holland. Not as a
as Mrs Visser, or Mrs van Holland-Visser for that
essed to 'Ada van Holland'. It was a thick envelope,
rable sum in postage stamps. Because she delivered
as the first to get it. When she turned it over and
ender, she knew she wouldn't be putting this letter
She pedalled hard into the wind as she made her
wspapers, letters, cards and packages into the cor-
s, house after house. The entire time, the envelope
d pouch of the heavy postbag slung over her bike
ay for a couple of hours she reached the river, and
he rocks below. Only then did she dare open the
us eyes.

*

ril 1961

d, who sat next to me during the flight to New
've thought of so often since then.

iom am I writing these words? Back then, you and

I didn't have the chance to get to know each other very well. It's now eight years later and we're no longer who we were when we met. It's possible that the hands in which this letter finds itself are no longer the hands I held as we landed.

The last picture I have of you – you were sitting in the back of a pickup truck – has stayed with me. More pictures have stayed with me.

I got your address from Marjorie. (She thought you would still know who she was.) I ran into her on a rugby pitch in Wellington where her son was playing in a junior match. It turned out that for the past couple of years we've been living just an hour and a half from each other, she in Khandallah Village and me on my farm in Martinborough.

I think it's best if I tell you a little bit about my time here, in broad brushstrokes, starting from the moment we parted without being able to say goodbye.

I stayed the first night in Christchurch. Our meeting had touched me. That evening I went for a walk (together with Esther, I'm sure you remember her) along the Avon River, unhappy with myself because I shouldn't have let you go. This has been troubling me for a long time. The question is, can I tell you this now?

That night I didn't sleep. The next day I took the train to the harbour. Lyttelton reminded me of the East Indies, maybe because of how it smelled. I still remember thinking: the adventure has now begun, and I stepped onto the gangway of the Maori. Towards evening we cast off. I shared the small, cramped cabin with three men. I was so tired I fell into a dreamless sleep and only woke up as we were approaching Wellington harbour the next morning. I dressed quickly and went on deck, inwardly cursing myself that I'd missed seeing the sun come up as we passed through Cook Strait. There, where I was greeted by the most exquisite scenery and a glorious day, I was overcome for the first time by the emotion that comes with arriving in a new country, so different from our actual arrival, which had left me with the sad taste of goodbye.

afternoon I arrived by train in Masterton, where

der man, the boss, who said I should call him

rton we drove nearly seventeen miles over gravel

st, to his sheep station near Riversdale. I was dis-

abour Department had assigned me to a sheep

rs made me think of the smallholders in Drenthe,

overty. But when we got there I saw a huge prop-

f sheep, as far as the eye could see, and I decided

gement.

me at the start. The noise alone! There were

heep right around the farm. I was surrounded by

ht – there was a wall of bleating around every-

t you couldn't think straight. It was impossible to

en in the dark. I started having nightmares in

wailing as they awaited execution.

ew days there would be a magical moment when

happen to fall silent at the same time. Dogs,

uld stop what they were doing and look up. An

t would last for a few seconds. Then one sheep

other would join in, and five seconds later there

I couldn't understand why people would want to

nere was the smell, the greasy smell of sheep, which

res of your skin and into your clothes.

nost unpleasant surprise of all was the homesick-

had my share of homesickness for the East Indies,

l on being homesick for Holland – there's nothing

et that's what happened. There were old bicycle

's barn. When I heard another Dutchman was

down the road, I put together a makeshift bike

ut parts and rode twenty-five miles down the road

e I got there it turned out the man had been

else. I was heartbroken on the ride back, that's the

only way I can describe it, even though I didn't know him. Two months later, at Christmas, it really got to me. I travelled for hours by train to Wellington to go to midnight mass at Saint Mary's – me, who doesn't believe in anything – because someone had told me a lot of Dutch people would be there. That day, up in the north, a train had gone through a bridge, right into the wild currents of the Wangaehu River and there were many Dutch passengers on board, on their way to the same mass. Hundreds were said to have died, and the people in the church were desperate. In his sermon, the priest tried to be encouraging, such things always happened for a reason, God had his own plan, and it would purify us all. In spite of these edifying words, there was panic among the churchgoers about the fate of their relatives. Asking for attention felt inappropriate, so I let go of my hope of an invitation and trudged back to my hotel, where a couple of drunken, beer-drinking Kiwis were celebrating Christmas in a large, bleak hall. My hotel room smelled of the countless cigarettes that had been smoked there in solitude, and I did my bit as well. The next day I went back to the farm and found it deserted – everyone had gone to visit relatives for Boxing Day.

But I gradually began to appreciate life in the Wairarapa. Galloping on horseback over the open plains at sunrise mustering sheep. No obstacles before you except the hills in the distance, and you would soon pass through them with your flock, your dog, and your horse. It's a good country. Once you made it to the top of the hills, you could see the Pacific glistening in the distance. We moved over the plains the whole day. We told ourselves we were free, which is easy to do when you're out in the open. Once in a while a farm plane would drone overhead. The flock, the horses, the shepherds, the dog, we would all stop in our tracks and follow the plane with our eyes – it was the high point of our day. At sundown we would arrive back at the farm with four hundred sheep. And that was just the sheep from a single paddock.

254

ed on me that in this country, sheep farmers were
ler. All right then, I thought, I'll become a sheep

clean and sort wool and I took shearing lessons
dustrious, everyone thought I was a real Dutchie,
been before coming here). Shearing was left to
shearers, usually Maoris. For days on end, five
dy types, big strapping fellows, would set the tone
tarted at five in the morning. Then an hour for
on the occasional smoko. Shearing is gruelling
reason than the unrelenting racket produced by
kes it impossible to talk. And they didn't talk —
Eight hours at a stretch, and longer if need be.
sheep could even blink, they would turn it onto
nimal up into a half-standing position, and using
eavy, razor-sharp shears, cut the fleece from the
were rough with the sheep, I saw blood, the blades
didn't concern them. It's business. In this way they
a hundred sheep a day, bent over the whole time,
he women spread the wool out onto a curved table
hell, which could turn. They picked out any irreg-
s the shearers were able to remove the wool in a
it resembled a hide, and the women would then
a blanket. These blankets piled up, first in the
of the corners and finally the blankets crept closer

earing was over for the year.
admit I had no talent for this. I was too afraid of
. I had visions of the nipples I might nick with the
antically tried to shear around all of the bones. At
zor-sharp blades that would get out of control and
ked.

Not to worry; I would become a farmer, and hire shearers to do that work. I joined the Young Farmers Club, which met every month. The first few times I sat back the entire evening with an intelligent look on my face, acting like none of that jargon – pronounced in those strong accents – held any secrets for me. But on the night of the first social evening I was going to have to join in the discussion myself and suddenly dreaded it so much I stayed home. So I said to myself, if you don't seize upon opportunities like this, you'll never integrate. At the next meeting I was put on a team for a debating competition. Don't ask me how I pulled it off, but we won. I kept at it, and learned the basics of rugby and went to the Saturday night dances in the country hall. I was determined not to remain an outcast. But even so.

I couldn't settle in. There were three of us shepherds: William, another man, and me. William was a decent chap, but quite a bit older than I was. The other man didn't want anything to do with foreigners who came and snapped up all the jobs. The station hands were nice enough fellows, but my contact with them remained superficial as well.

I liked the Wairarapa, which is hot and dry. I could have got more experience, while saving up to buy my first sheep, then a second, then a flock, a piece of property, my own sheep station and the farmer's daughter. But I got restless and decided to try to get another job.

Farther north, in Whangarei, I was assigned to a farmer who'd fought against the Germans in Egypt and had returned home with a paralysed leg and a foul temper. He walked with crutches. As compensation, the government had given him some land, parts of which were still wooded. The work consisted of cutting down kauri trees – giants a thousand years old – to turn the land into pasture for livestock. They call this 'breaking in the land'. That's where I met Mozie. His real name is Wiremu Moses Mauriohooho and he's a full-blooded Maori. Mozie also fought in the war, in France. He started talking about wine. He missed the pinot noir. A Maori who learned to drink

ndy and still misses it, that's the kind of person

ds. On our days off he would teach me the finer
ort of rugby, which meant I regularly went to bed
g from muscle pain. On workdays we battled
ooded Wilderness. During that period I think I
tronger than I had been.

, I tried to ignore the crutch man as much as I
dn't pay well and was always carping about some-
e got into an argument. I had to spread manure
aining cats and dogs and blowing a gale, and after
en my soul was soaked through, and the tractor
the thick layers of mud, and I said: I can't work
o quit till it stops raining. He threatened that if I
uld fire me. Fine, I said. And I could pack my bags.
o his ankles in mud, shouting at me and waving
it had been our war, and it had ruined his life.
g doesn't agree with me.

y goodbye to Mozie. This time I was assigned to a
as manager of a dairy farm, in a village with
many Maori people lived. The only Pakehas were
family, and a neighbour who lived eighty kilo-
ly got used to life among the Maoris. They didn't
farm manager, where my job involved taking care
d. Too industrious, too efficient, too Dutch. Aside
ong well – I played sports with them, tried to learn
l with the girls in the country hall and during the
o drink beer with their brothers behind the fogged-
ebody's car.

n longer I would undoubtedly have been afflicted
ease: 'Nice day for work… yeah… let's go fishing.'
there on the edge of the ocean was a pleasant one.

But I gradually had to admit that working with livestock was not my cup of tea. Nor was working with cows. In the end, it becomes monotonous – you slap an animal on its flank, attach a suction cup to a teat, gallop three times around it on your horse, and that's about as varied as it gets. What's left is the drive to earn money: more land, more livestock, more business. That wasn't enough for me, but I no longer knew what I did want.

On one of my days off I went on my motorcycle to visit Mozie, who was still working for the crutch man. We talked about my restlessness and my doubts. Suddenly he said, 'Why don't you plant pinot noir?'

Nobody drinks wine in this country. Sherry they know, and plonk like Bakano red and Cresta Doré white. They're not allowed to serve wine in pubs. Even so, right away I knew this was it, that this was what I'd been looking for and that at an unconscious level I'd known it all along, like something waiting to be dug up. I'm not a stockman, I'm a planter. I want to grow crops. When I was a child on Java I would watch for hours as our gardener worked, taking cuttings and grafting. I helped him when he let me. It was an intense longing, and the reason why I studied tropical agriculture. Why couldn't I do something like that here? Looking back it seems strange I hadn't come up with the idea on my own.

I drew up a plan and asked Mozie if he wanted to help me. I also immediately knew where I wanted to implement my plan (that's how you can tell it's a good idea): in the Wairarapa, where I'd begun. It has a climate similar to Burgundy. That's where my vineyard would be. I wasn't that far yet, but my goal was clear. And then I realized how all along I'd seen my farm in my mind's eye, large and prosperous, with fertile land among the rolling hills, and that there wasn't a single living creature in that picture. Livestock had never grazed in the fields of my dreams.

And now, briefly. For three years we worked for an English winegrower in Marlborough and learned by experience. During this same

espondence course to become a viticulturist and
Roseworthy Agriculture College in Australia, and
n the evenings. In '58 I got a loan from the bank
es of land near Martinborough I now own, flat
l and backed by mountains. Ideal conditions for
, three years on, we've had our first harvest. I've
rt of this for myself so I can keep experimenting.
before the wine is good enough to bring out under
arn money, Mozie and I work for the farmers
apples. Tar sheds. Bring in hay. That's all right,
y we're doing it.

less where I am right now. I could be contented.
nto the picture again, or rather, this is where the
the back of the pickup comes in, the picture that
ecause I can't stop myself from conjuring up that
hat moment, over and over again, and every time
crucial moment, the moment when in fact I did
from behind a dirty bus window. This has been
for eight years now. Increasingly more so after
rie, until the moment I put pen to paper to share
erson who can ease my mind.

f could almost be called charming. There in the
a girl in the rain, jolting along, a striking contrast
d vulnerability on the one hand and the solid
h conditions on the other. Maybe I saw nothing
hat first instant, there behind the fogged-over bus
ving to justify my behaviour. I could have known
eant, I'd listened to your hesitations about your
n who was waiting for you. But it was only when
e truck behind and you'd disappeared from sight
ng of what I saw sank in.

moment countless times. From behind the window

I see you being jostled and jolted in the back of the truck; and rather than it happening much later, I explode instantly with a kind of primitive outrage, time and again; can a person who would do something like this make her happy? Thousands of times I've stopped the bus. Got the bus to stop in front of the truck. Jumped out in front of it. Walked around it. Reached out my hand to you, thousands of times. Taken your hand in mine, the hand I held while we were landing and that I still held as the aeroplane slowed down, the hand I should never have let go of.

Why didn't you jump out of the truck on your own? Why did you let him carry you off like that?

I can't change what happened. I can no longer stop the bus and jump out in front of the truck like a hero. I missed my chance, not knowing how it would affect my life. A short time later, the bus dropped me off on a silent Sunday morning at the square in Christchurch, and I started my life as an immigrant, just like I'd planned. The way I've described it to you here is the way lives can also be described: as a series of events whereby the things that really mattered to you remain unsaid.

So, girl in the back of the truck – won't you at least tell me everything turned out all right?

*

She remembered his prominent nose, the strong profile. She remembered that his voice was deep and pleasant. But what she remembered most of all were his eyes, and the way he had looked at her, and how she had taken shape beneath his gaze.

His words had the same effect. She hadn't given another thought to her ride in the back of the pickup. What remained was a vague memory of a miserable period filled with homesickness and disappointment and which she preferred not to think about, and now his words had conjured up a picture and it turned out she was the tragic heroine in a film.

cycled past she would say hello to the spot along
ead the first letter. She read his next letter at the
the letters that followed, which gradually became
ned words that would keep her awake at night. She
er head constantly, with an inner voice that was
. She used complete sentences to describe for him
d thought, continually correcting herself, looking
ost precision.

been much of a talker, and this hadn't improved
hen she arrived she didn't speak a word of English,
told her she shouldn't speak Dutch when Kiwis
they don't like that' – the first months she hardly
e. If she was forced to venture out, she didn't say a
Frisian woman from their church had taught her
nan had befriended her for a time, until they both
too busy to visit each other – to Ada's relief. But
ot much further. Although she occasionally learned
of times she found out later that she'd misunder-
he knew she spoke horribly broken English, with
ver of grammar, and she was ashamed of this. She
stand the Kiwi accent, which made her feel insecure
ldren's school. 'Seex acks, please,' she whispered to
counter, who first brought her ZigZag cigarette
thought she wanted six axes, until he understood
!', by which time she'd died a thousand deaths, and
he dreadful business of paying for her purchases
terly confused her, all those pennies and pounds.
s been shy, nowadays it seemed as though she'd
le. For a while she and Derk had spoken Dutch at
e children were getting bigger they did this less and

less. They had become native speakers – they thought Dutch was dumb and wanted nothing to do with it. Recently she'd noticed that she sometimes couldn't understand her own children.

But she talked plenty inside her head, non-stop, and since that first letter her thoughts had a purpose, a recipient. This went on all day long, and it changed how she saw her surroundings – as she talked she polished everything till it sparkled, and some of that sparkle rubbed off on reality.

She worked for quite a time on the letters she wrote to him. It wasn't easy to turn her thoughts into words on paper. She bought a notebook and carried it with her everywhere she went, making notes. What are you doing, anyway? Derk asked. Oh, nothing special, she said with a start.

*

She was secretly living on two different levels at once. As she cycled in all kinds of weather on her rounds to deliver the post, she would describe the river, the sea, the deep sound the steamships made and the splashing of the water and how she loved the silhouettes of the tall cranes in the harbour. It seems like they lead a life of their own, she wrote, high above our scratchings, a little lonely and detached, as if they've always been there and weren't made by human hands. She didn't write about the rain, or how tired she was. During the weekends she would drag her unwilling children along on windy walks in the mountains, something that had frightened her in the early years, but she'd grown to love it, the hiking and climbing, the expanse of the valleys and peaks, the cold wind on your cheeks, the commanding view of the ocean, being so close to birds of prey. Derk didn't see the point of walking without a destination, and would rather work on his trucks or do odd jobs for the church. She'd resigned herself to this years ago and now it worked to her advantage. This way, she didn't have to talk, and could describe for Frank every step she took during these mountain walks, without interruption. In her mind she crossed out sentences, erased them, and came up with other, better ones. When the children ran off ahead down a hill and she was sure no-one was

the little notebook out of her coat pocket and
w thoughts or nice sentences he was sure to enjoy,
im long for her even more.

*

wrote. And after a time, he did. She saw a man
a stack of crates, a cowboy hat on his head, with
he shadow under the brim of his hat. He'd filled
ular and had become even more handsome, and
s of love wash over her because after all, it was hap-
et, somewhere where it wouldn't hurt anyone. And
ote, where's your picture? She sent one that Derk
n the beach during which he'd complained non-
s. She was wearing a swimsuit she'd bought here,
her. The sun lit up her blonde hair. You could see
and shapely. A bit of a film-star snapshot. She also
of her with the three children.

*

rite about Derk – it felt like a betrayal to both of
he would end up tangled in deceitful descriptions
th what she wanted than with how she actually saw
id this as little as possible. Almost as if he didn't
ask.

*

her in her fantasies, and slowly started to stir. He
s desire, and she recalled how during the air race
he ease with which he touched her. Now his words
o the hayloft of long ago, which she'd lost touch

thing, and that made it even more exciting. If they

263

only knew what was going on right now, she thought, as she dutifully trudged through the mud with the shopping. Then for a moment her legs would freeze at the fear of being found out. Of course, her co-workers at the post office had noticed the steady flow of letters from Martinborough. Clive, who sorted the post and was always trying to tickle her, teased her about it: that person who was always writing to her, who was he, anyway, and did Derk know about this? Here – here's another one, grab it if you can. Then she would giggle and jump up in the direction of his outstretched arm, and tried to use the nearness of her body to divert his attention away from the letter. He's a distant relative of mine, she said, fiercely hoping he would never verify this with Derk, and counted herself lucky to have a husband who was so unapproachable. She would fret for days after such an incident. Although it would have been safest to burn Frank's letters, she couldn't bring herself to do it. As long as the words continued to reveal new meanings to her every time, it was as if they were alive. They would scream if thrown into the fire.

There was one place Derk would certainly never go. That was the drawer in which she kept the most intimate of her women's things, the sanitary napkins and her underwear. And that's where she hid the letters. This felt appropriate in a forbidden way. At night, the drawer glowed in the dark. Then she would communicate with it from her bed, while her husband slept beside her.

The only one who knew about it was God. He who could see through envelopes and behind words knew about her life below deck. He probably watched in sorrow as every day she fled from the life He had intended for her. She hardly dared think of it. Maybe it wasn't so very bad, she found herself hoping on a couple of occasions. After all, they're only fantasies. Sinful fantasies, but fantasies nonetheless. When she was feeling very optimistic, she hoped that if the two lines ever had to intersect, the matter would somehow take care of itself at that point and all would be well.

*

ters in secret, with no return address on the enve-
get suspicious when the post was being sorted.
he envelope into the slot she always made sure no-
nd, and afterwards she was always overcome by a
uilt and rationalization – although it was against
hurting anyone and it would never come to any-
e weeks that followed, she would keep imagining
when he read this particular sentence, or that par-
lay she would see another letter from him held in
and could afterwards slip into that other world
by the river. This would be followed by weeks of
d been in that last letter, and what a pity that the
and wasn't it a good thing we would never meet.
e longer and longer, and because by now both of
form out of making them as attractive as possible
nd attention) and because they were impatient,
ne took longer as well. They weren't exchanging
She told him about the village where she'd grown
ut the East Indies and returning to Holland with
she was startled by what she could read between

*

parents sitting side by side on wide chairs, the arms
h are decorated with woodcarvings. The picture was
rs stand beneath the foliage of a flamboyant tree; my
he shade, and the sun shines white on my mother's
n serious faces. My father's watch chain loops over his
olds a small bag in her right hand. Behind them you
ter on the wall around our garden. My parents are
ay from each other, my mother years after my father's
airs shipped over as soon as I settled here in

265

Martinborough, together with some other East Indian things from our house, including a mask with bulging eyes that wards off evil spirits for those who believe in them. My mother believed in them till her last lonely second. If you ask me, the mask didn't do its job. It wasn't able to ward off the evil spirits inside her head. Here it hangs on a nail and no-one believes in it, a decorative wooden object from a faraway place and a time long gone. To call this revenge would mean you believed in it.

*

She didn't dare come right out and ask him to explain, though she did start to love him even more. In this way she managed to make it through her days. By now, this had been going on for two years.

18

E rare and wonderful Saturdays. One of those days
irds singing in the garden, birds who came to sit
unlight filtered in through the spikes of wheat on
iffused the bedroom with a glow of golden fields
ful, and content. Downstairs Marjorie could hear
he juicer, Hans's deep voice, and Bobby's husky
hed and turned onto her side; the bed complied
using for a while. If he's chosen, I'll make choco-
ears welled up behind her eyelids at the thought.
ught. I can be contented, because I've earned it.
l. After breakfast the three of them drove to the
was to play in the junior tournament. In the
xchanged tender glances because the child on the
o bravely to hide his nervousness. A scout was
players for Wellington's junior team and he stood
selected. Because it was a special occasion, Frank
He joined them on the hard benches of the stand
iothing about rugby, and had no interest in all the
t during the entire match she enjoyed the sight of
vho was so keen and determined and distracted by
y his mother's high-pitched squeals and shouts of

encouragement. Her neck was splotchy from all the excitement. He gets his determination from me, she thought, it's in our blood. She'd become so accustomed to making these kinds of observations that she no longer thought about their impossibility. Afterwards, she laughed as she took him into her arms when he came out of the changing rooms and ran towards her with the good news: Mum, they picked me, they picked me! And afterwards she was proud as a peacock as she walked with her three men through the centre of Wellington to do a bit of shopping since they were here. She'd promised Bobby a comic book, the latest *Roy of the Rovers*. Enveloped by a cloud of contentment, she linked arms with Hans. She was entitled to that cloud.

Because she liked to think of herself as courageous, for a long time Marjorie was dismayed to find that fear was the downside of the love she felt for the child. For the first few years it had been sheer torture. If she were leaning over the changing table gazing adoringly at the baby's bottom, she couldn't help but imagine that his real mother was feeling something similar, even if it was at a distance. While breathing in the intoxicating scent of the baby's body she knew for certain it would make its way along the roads of the North Island to the South Island, where it would ultimately reach Esther's nostrils in Christchurch. Regret, regret, she heard her sob, give me back my child. When they refused, this regret would quickly turn to rage, and then would come the threats. It wouldn't take much for a desperate mother to bring the illegal nature of the birth registration to light. The only thing necessary would be the hospital files from Christchurch showing that shortly before her so-called son was born, a wandering fetus had been removed from Marjorie. Then she would have to put her head under the cold-water tap to rinse the heat from her cheeks. Her fear kept watch at the front door of their house like a warrior, and her love for the infant increased in direct proportion to this. You-are-mine, she blew onto the chubby little cheeks. She tirelessly sang Dutch songs in funny voices, which made him shriek with laughter. 'Clap your hands together, be glad, glad, glad.' She didn't dare to be glad herself.

sk someone would become suspicious. Her nerves
at with the baby on her lap in the warm waiting
ciety with the other young mothers, imitating the
ions that came naturally to them. She joined in
about engorged breasts. Oh yes, she agreed com-
witing any opposition, infant care is *much* better
he would come home completely exhausted.
stand this. It wasn't in his nature to get worked up
nay or may not happen. He enjoyed the little boy,
o the air – the child crowed with pleasure and
and caught him in his large hands. Every night in
her. They'd made a clear agreement with Esther,
th in this. Why would anyone be able to see she
He didn't know of a more genuine mother than
hing always seemed so simple when he was there,
e to fall asleep. But the next morning, as soon as
– who would be standing up in his bed, dancing
tiny flecks of amber in the grey-green of his eyes,
t once again.

⋆

le to turn off the fear. You know what, she would
sther, he's got chicken pox *now*, he's vomiting, he
v, and you're not here. There's so much happen-
. And you're not here.

⋆

n Wellington, in a rented furnished flat that was
ed as a bookkeeper in the purchasing department
enings he also took on as many carpentry jobs as
ful with their money, and saved until they had a
nds. Marjorie had found out they could use this

269

to get a loan from the government for a new house. The state didn't invest in second-hand houses. Well, that was a good thing, because she'd had her fill of boarding houses, caravans, and rental flats. The new houses were being built outside town. Because there was still a housing shortage, 'home viewing' was a popular leisure activity. On Sundays she would make sure her family was nicely dressed and they would go by public transport to join the lines of house hunters who were being shown around the model homes. In the presence of Hans she actually managed to enjoy the compliments they received for their lively child, 'but how could it be otherwise with parents like that!'

They decided on Khandallah Village because everything in the neighbourhood – which was attractively laid out with an abundance of space and set high in the wooded hills above the city – held the promise of prosperity. The house, a 'three-bedroom, spacious open-plan home' with a garage and a view out over the bay, was much too expensive for them and they were only able to buy it by taking out a large mortgage. Her father kicked up a fuss about this in his letters from Holland, but she didn't give up, because, she reasoned, in twenty-five years it will be ours and then we'll sell it at a large profit and buy an even bigger house. Hans took her advice. She was much shrewder and more thorough in this kind of thing than he was.

There was no sewer system. A small outbuilding served as the toilet. Every evening 'the nightman' – which is how she referred to him to Bobby – would come and hoist the barrel up onto his shoulder, and empty it into a cart. She sent a cheerful account of this back home, and even before receiving Pa's scornful reply, she knew she shouldn't have done so. He sarcastically praised their expensive investment in such a house. You know what he's like, said Hans in amazement when she would once again furiously stamp her feet. After three years, the district got a sewer system. They had to pay extra for this, but they were also allowed to buy the piece of land around their house. Their garden.

es of having their own child, her own pregnancy,
dfully for a long time. It didn't happen. Almost no
e no chance at all. Over time, the third bedroom
Hans's fishing rods, her canning jars, the ironing
d. She couldn't write home about it. That hurt, too,
ted. Her letters were filled with half-truths and
ade the distance unbridgeable. How can I ever face
nt, carrying so much deception. Then fear would
father's sermons about their child's birth date still
so careful not to let things get out of hand,' she
l only cuddled until the wedding, but now every-
get married and I can't say anything to change it.'
bout the necessity of the deceit. Because the clearer
be no second child, the more important Bobby

etely hers.
lf seemed to do everything he could to help her in
behind her lovingly – so much Mama, all to myself
e up in the air in the same way she did. The black
a fell out before long, and his new hair grew in
those few flecks of amber, his irises really were
t part, the kind that could pass for Dutch, and that
ould see in their own eyes. She knew it wasn't pos-
could see her own spirit in him. If he was told he
he would fling himself to the ground in such deep
rd not to laugh. In exactly the same way, he would
ticky toddler love out over them. As soon as he was
er the bars of his crib, he would crawl into bed with
nd wouldn't rest until he'd nestled down comfort-
his parents. What he liked most of all was to then

pull the other parent's arm around him. Hot childish breath in her ear, 'Mum, want to play a game?' 'It's half past five,' Hans groaned tenderly. 'Yes, but it's a veeery quiet game...' whispered the husky little voice. It became one of many rituals. Family life proved to be made up of rituals that affirmed your common bond and left the outside world behind. With time, you grew accustomed to this and ultimately it became a goal in itself.

*

In her contact with others – the neighbours, Hans's colleagues, the mothers at school – the fear of being discovered stood in her way for a long time. The New Zealanders' polite British aloofness worked to her advantage. She was so terrified that one day someone would question her motherhood that she wore a corset of perfection and was often only able to breathe once she was safely within the walls of her own home. Her heart ached when she thought back to all the light-hearted fun she'd had with her girlfriends in Holland, skating in chains over the ice, the intense whispered conversations at night in the nurses' residence. When no-one was looking, she wept from homesickness. In spite of this, she resolutely built up a social life for her family that was above reproach. That didn't arouse the slightest suspicion.

The way she kept house also had to be above reproach. This didn't happen of its own accord. During the early years, she could be overcome by a grim feeling of hopelessness as she folded the laundry or vacuumed the house for the umpteenth time, or wiped up the remains of the fruit the toddler had spat out around him on the kitchen floor. She found housework dull, and missed nursing. So is this it, then? she wondered as she sat on the edge of the sandbox watching the sand trickle through her fingers. She wrote to her mother about it, and this time her letter was honest and unhappy. Weeks later, a package arrived by surface mail. It contained a brightly coloured checked apron, with ruffles along the edges and two large patch pockets. 'Sweetheart,' her mother wrote, 'I'm sending you this apron because you're having a hard time. Go and quietly wash the

272

small, and stop wanting things. It will bring you
be of service. Washing the dishes, that's your job.
I'll find happiness again. No ambition, not even an
ches. You'll see.' The tender, loving tone made her
she put on the apron. She briefly considered a job
obby went to primary school. Working mothers
y, she read in the magazines her mother sent, over-
Domestic happiness could suffer as a result. This
arguments between the couple. This idea put her
her father's fits of rage, the fights he would start
ild will never have to lock himself in the toilet. I'll
start fights. With the women's magazines in hand,
er power to 'bring inspiration to the home and
ds of delight that break up the dull sameness,
garden and artistic endeavours of all kinds'.
s, she doggedly threw herself into preserving fruit
roses, into hobbies like flower arranging and col-
verything to bestow 'that special glow' upon her
nan's Weekly maintained that her family could not
she'd make sure they got vitamin B, and Bobby
s he liked, but he wouldn't be allowed to leave the
d his Vegemite sandwich. There was a reason that
ong and healthy. She worked at improving her
clenched and her old domestic science school
ase-stained pages opened out on the kitchen
tried a new recipe she'd make another mistake,
nfuriate her. She puffed and perspired as she
ough for currant loaf, and when it was finally
e turned around towards the counter in her over-
all the ingredients that should have gone into it
rrants, and the almonds. And then there was the
n simmering for hours on the heat diffuser that

she strained through a colander in the sink. But she never repeated her mistakes and never allowed herself to become discouraged, because she was convinced it was essential that her family be above reproach. The sparkle she bestowed upon this fortress would dazzle any adversaries.

⋆

Her efforts were rewarded. Khandallah Village grew into a leafy, thriving neighbourhood where the children rode their bicycles at full speed down the hilly streets to build dens in the woods behind the swimming pool. She watched Bobby from the garden and knew she was giving him a wonderful childhood. Her door was always open to his friends. She was good with children. He went to a private school, which was more expensive and thus better, something she liked to mention if it came up. In keeping with this, the school uniforms were also more expensive and he grew so fast he was always needing a new one. All of these things filled her with pride.

The adversaries never showed up. Esther's ghost faded away with the years and disappeared to the furthest reaches of Marjorie's consciousness. The idea that anyone – no matter who – could break the bond between the three of them gradually became ridiculous.

They were an ordinary family.

⋆

This is how she came to be walking through Wellington that Saturday, relaxed and content, in her young son's wake and on the arm of her man.

'Do you still love me?' she asked.

'Do I have a choice?'

She loved his jokes. Although he certainly wasn't the most exciting man on earth, they had a good life together and she couldn't imagine herself married to anyone else. That must be love. She loved his constant care and attention. He made things, planed and painted, designed a sunroom, built a pantry. In the meantime, he'd worked his way up to head of the purchasing department at Woolworths. He bought her all the modern

274

They were the first in their neighbourhood to own
wood cabinet model with jaunty angled legs. The
n came to watch television with Bobby. When they
et and she turned the big knob, she felt herself to
good fairy.

he took care of Hans. Her meals had lulled the TB
to an eternal sleep and tucked them in beneath a
starting to develop a paunch, and she saw this as
er death. It lent him an unwieldiness she wasn't
ut she preferred that to, to.

loved her. He still put his hands around her waist.
since the tips of his fingers had been able to touch.
d coquettishly. 'Excellent,' was his standard reply.
you.' When she looked into the mirror, she could
here stood a woman in the prime of her life. The
ed good on her. She loved dressing like an adult.
ially if you draped the cardigan over your shoul-
button fastened. Every week she would have her
ed. Luckily, it didn't rain very often here.

more than words could express, loved that bright
r on the pitch, her child, who thought she didn't
out of his bedroom window and over the garage
go to the swimming pool. She loved herself
his secret freedom. Then she would think of her
mb her nose at him, have a look at this, Pa, your
And afterwards she would sometimes burst into
o why.

loved the choices they'd made, the light Swedish
e shelves, and the white of the window frames.
with a white rain gutter. Just like the garage. On
d climb up the ladder with his paintbrush to add
en she'd bring him coffee (they'd never been able

275

to give up drinking coffee) with her home-made cake and they'd sit together on the porch enjoying the view over the city and the harbour and the bay. Wonderful, they'd nod with their mouths full of cake, listening to the dreamy sound of a neighbours' lawnmower further down. Her garden sloped upward, and in it grew palm trees, large ferns, and the roses she'd planted. The breeze brushed past them, carrying whiffs of perfume that mingled with the smell of coffee. Then she would squeeze her husband's knees with delight. The large mortgage was part of a sensible plan, a far-sighted vision. *Her* plan, *her* vision. Pa still disagreed. She had pushed ahead with it, if only because of the tone of his letters.

She loved their life. A telephone, a television. The Zephyr, and how she felt when she placed her arm casually in the open window and drove out of their very own garage. Their friends had names like Ian and Kathleen and Norman and Edna, and they would often all go out for a Sunday picnic, when the men would discuss the nuclear threat, the women would discuss the children, and the children would run and play. After a couple of beers, Hans would start telling jokes. Sometimes they sang Cliff Richard songs or the comic numbers by the Howard Morrison Quartet. '*My Old Man's an All Black!*' (That was usually the moment when the children would go and play somewhere else.) It always ended in merriment. During the winter she'd invite everyone over to their house and would make her Sunday roast, which was just as good as Kathleen's or Edna's. To be honest, and it wasn't boasting, hers was better. Seasoned with more determination. It was debatable whether as a foreigner you could ever become a real Kiwi – you could always feel a degree of reserve there – but everyone would have to admit they'd made great strides. Their application for naturalization was being processed.

*

Not that she was thinking about any of these things in particular as she walked through the streets of 'windy Wellington' that Saturday after the match. She was thinking about getting new plastic sandals for everyone,

she wanted to make for supper, but in fact she

hese kinds of things at all because they'd become

er reality. She poked her husband in the ribs with

attention to their child out in front of them, who

attempt to walk in a way that was just as self-

his big hero Frank. She thought about how fast

that it was quite possible he would end up taller

't even notice that such a thought no longer made

are in the world, she enjoyed the childish chatter

y he moved his hands, the small voice that rose in

seen that the back was a big boy, already in sec-

t he'd been able to get by him anyway? Luckily

s. And he'd seen much more, how Bobby had then

ored a try. The deep voice flattered. 'That would

ut if he hadn't picked you.' It galled her. 'Hey,' she

, he'll be too big for his boots before you know it.'

rds her with a wink, and continued his conversa-

me she'd been joking. The blood rushed to her

husband's arm, she stared at the lazy walk of the

heir friend but with whom she never felt entirely

had been her who'd recognized him on the field

called his name. Sometimes she wished she'd let

s didn't understand this, he saw only the good in

k could sit for hours bent over the drawings of

rd, mumbling mysterious man-talk. Actually, she

ther. Frank was pleasant and well-mannered. A

her heart, she couldn't bear it that he was better-

looked for flaws – he has strange, slanty eyebrows

is eyes. And he walks so sluggishly. It annoyed her

acted differently when he was around. She herself

h silliness. But it set her teeth on edge, the way he

he ran her household, as if he had his own private

thoughts on this matter. He doesn't have to look at me like that, she would often say to Hans. How does he look at you then? She wasn't able to explain it. Maybe he feels like he's better than we are. Nonsense, said Hans, I've never noticed anything of the kind, and then he would give her a cheerful slap on her backside. Nothing bothered him. Nor was he jealous, either, when Bobby came home full of stories after a day at the vineyard, that he'd practised rugby passes with Mozie and that Frank had let him go along in the jeep when he went bird shooting. Hans was able to stroll contentedly through Wellington with her on his arm, in no way begrudging his friend the admiration of his son. That's how he was and that's why she'd married him. She breathed deeply, conscious of her happiness that sunny Saturday. One of those extraordinary moments when you suddenly become aware of this. Yes, tonight there'll be chocolate pudding. She linked her arm more firmly through Hans's, and their bodies pressed briefly together in recognition. The night before she'd put on her pink nylon baby-doll, a signal he'd been quick to understand. A day edged in gold.

*

In Cuba Street, just before they had to cross over on their way to the bookshop, her attention was drawn to a group of people standing in front of a building further down the street. She saw a construction worker on a ladder painting large letters onto the facade. In front of the shop stood a moving van with the tailgate ramp lowered. Men in overalls were carrying things from the van into the shop. Garment racks, mannequins, mirrors, it looked to her like fixtures and furnishings for a new, modern sort of ladies' clothing shop. 'I just want to have a quick look at what's going on over there,' she said.

'Mum, come on.'

You go on ahead, she motioned, and walked on. Men aren't interested in these kinds of things.

It was a wide building, and the glass in the double doors was enclosed

ies. To either side of the doors were large display
brown paper. She directed her gaze upwards, to the
Through the windows you could see the movers
s and mirrors and rolled-up rugs there as well.
pening here. This was going to be a shop unlike
own. She made up her mind to be one of the first
new good skirt and blouse anyway, and she would
t to Edna and Kathleen, such a lovely little shop,
nporary, funny you haven't heard of it. Then the
m the ladder and she could see the lettering he'd
he slender black letters were modern, and curved
e top; if you narrowed your eyes they bore a slight
models.
e.
When she looked again the words were still there.
siren began to wail. Of its own accord, her gaze
hop through the open doors, like a scout on the
the back, where people moved back and forth
, patches of colour that flashed by like they did
a train. Someone put a hand on her back.
' said Hans. 'We're waiting.'
f colour she could now make out a woman in a
ou saw Jackie Kennedy wearing in photographs.
g with her back to them: she had dark curly hair
high heels. She stood like a beacon amidst the
ng a fan of colour samples in the direction of a
m that gesture alone she could tell it was Esther.
d to say to Hans, 'quick,' but no sound came out
o recognized Esther and stood there in surprise.
in the hot pink sleeve gestured dramatically
nd as she did so, Esther spun around and looked
re remained suspended in mid-air.

The child was there instantaneously.

Marjorie hoped, *prayed*, that Frank had walked on to the bookshop with him. 'Oh… oh,' she said, it was more like a moan being squeezed out of her windpipe, and once again, 'Oh… oh…'

There was no escape.

Esther was the first to regain her composure, you could see her pulling herself together and quickly slipping her old, bold image over the pieces. Could see her taking cover inside her suit. The large mouth with the painted lips opened wide to cry out gushing words of welcome while the teeth stood at attention. The arm shot up in greeting. Big bracelets clattered down to the middle of her forearm. Hello! The familiar throaty laugh. Oh, right, for this woman, affectation was the norm. In a matter of seconds she was sashaying her way to the door. But she could see from the way the slender ankles wobbled above the high heels that Esther was just as shocked as she was. The onlookers parted slightly, as if they could sense that this encounter was something special. Or because Esther cut an impressive figure, so that you had to move back a bit to take her in.

All three of them fumbled about awkwardly. This was never meant to happen and no-one knew how to act. So they sniffed at each other and ping-ponged greetings back and forth. Hello, hello, how are you, fine, gosh, well… oh dear.

'Esther,' said Hans, as if he couldn't believe it.

Long trembling fingers took a cigarette from a pack tucked brazenly into the waistband of the hot pink skirt. The things you can conceal under such a divine jacket. Hans took one, Marjorie declined silently. Watched how her husband hurried to offer her a light.

'What are you doing here?' The words were coughed out, smoke and all.

'We live here.'

'Oh… You do?'

'In Khandallah Village.'

She pointed back, to somewhere above and behind her. Esther looked at the sky in surprise.

in Auckland.'

that?'

ht.'

what I thought.'

that, while they tried to get their knocking knees

eantime, Marjorie studied the painted face oppo-

older than she remembered. Eyebrows pencilled

e amber in her eyes framed by dramatic false eye-

ression heavy and arrogant. A powdered face that

bold and striking, the mouth the same shade of

dislike was there immediately, because everything

her conscious of her own ordinary skirt and

ch she'd been strolling so contentedly just a short

ortable heels of her shoes. Her flat, comfortable

n with her name in huge letters on the front of a

s a wonderful area,' she said quickly. 'All of the

es. Not that many Indians live there. It's a good

use has three bedrooms and a big garden *and* a

ve their heads the entire time.

was busy. They were surrounded by curious

Esther the movers were squeezing through the

er. In the shop, the pale young man paced back

ing his neck towards his employer. A fabric sup-

on the brand-new counter and waited. Marjorie

same time, at the outermost corners of her eyes

he back of her head, she saw Bobby standing on

t with Frank. She only hoped she could manage

to a close before he came back to find out what

d. Her brain was going flat out. Across from her,

281

a huge question mark was suspended in the amber, the tension apparent in Esther's nervous puffing on her cigarette. She mustn't give her enough time to ask that question. It was none of that woman's business where the child was.

'Well,' she said, and put her hands together to announce their departure.

But once again, Hans was unaware of the dangers. At times, his faith in people was enough to drive her mad. As if it were a perfectly ordinary encounter, he wanted to know about Esther's business and got caught up in a conversation about how to keep demanding financiers happy and how to educate a conservative clientele, one of those conversations that's hard to cut short. Idiot, was all she could think, idiot, idiot, and in the meantime she could almost feel how on the other side of the street Bobby was looking to the right and then to the left, just like she'd taught him, and how he was waiting for the moment when the traffic would allow him to cross. She wanted to shout out to him: stay there! run for your life! and wave her arms wildly to make him realize that danger lurked here, but she didn't even dare look in his direction for fear that Esther would follow her gaze.

'This is my second shop now,' said Esther. 'Christchurch got too small for me,' and she fanned herself with the colour samples, as if what she'd really wanted to say was that things had got too hot for her there. Marjorie saw her fear become reality. Bobby and Frank crossed the street.

Esther started to stammer. She'd been in the middle of a sentence – explaining how her boutique was going to transform the entire shopping area – and the rest of it rolled feebly out of her mouth and smashed onto the pavement. She uttered a short, raspy cry. Then silence.

All three of them watched without speaking.

Frank draped his arm protectively over the child's shoulders and guided him safely to the other side. The boy had his hands in his pockets and was squinting his eyes against the sun. It seemed to Marjorie that he'd come into sharper focus, so that only now could you see just how perfect

282

boy imaginable, strong and sweet, with bright eyes
Over the past few years she'd convinced herself
n from her, but now the other shone through

weakly to Hans, and took him by the arm. Frank
re talking to when they were still several feet away.
he surge of pleasure at this unexpected encounter.
it stung with surprising sharpness to remember
ately recognized *her* two years ago when she'd
usiastically.
ashen beneath the powder, as if she were being
ns. Marjorie held her breath and squeezed Hans's
k at him. All of these people to be kept in the dark.
hers reassuringly, which made her livid, and she

ls Hans and Marjorie along invisible family lines.
wrapped the lines around them, ran her hand
He ducked away from her with a fluid movement,
e of the many. In the meantime, she closely fol-
to get over her shock and greet Frank like an
ugged each other, hello! hello! Then he took hold
arms in the air, and examined her from head to
ntimacy between them that Marjorie hadn't seen
en't changed a bit,' he said. Esther laughed her
e while her eyes kept straying over to the child,
parents, oblivious to it all and not terribly inter-
ght Marjorie, and it throbbed in her head, his
like an incantation, but the amber burned holes
ties. She grimly suppressed her desire to scream
wasn't going to give anything away. No removal
l notice anything strange about this scene, not
erved from the outside, this was just a chance

meeting between a group of immigrants who'd all arrived in this country together ten years earlier and whose mother tongue was now peppered with English.

It didn't escape her notice that Esther was hardly able to answer the questions Frank was asking her, that she took in great gulps of air and let out strange laughing noises. They were just ordinary expressions of interest, how was he to know, how are you, how nice to see you again, is all of this yours, my goodness, congratulations. She saw Esther's eyes dart nervously from the man to the boy, who was waiting behind her on the pavement until the adults were ready to join him. A cub who doesn't notice the hunter is stalking him.

'Bobby, darling...' she said loudly, and motioned to him. I'll show her. Esther's voice faltered in the middle of a sentence. Quickly now, take charge. She put her hands on the child's shoulders and pushed him forward. 'This is our son Bobby,' she said, and her words fell out of the sky like maternal swords and made Esther recoil.

Bobby didn't show much interest, but she'd brought him up well and he politely shook the extended hand. The bone bracelets clattered together.

'Hello, Bobby,' said the husky voice in Dutch. 'I'm Esther.'

'He only speaks English.'

She mercilessly observed the stilted conversation Esther was carrying on with the child. Oh dear, he liked rugby. Oh dear, the Wellington junior team. She doesn't know what to say, she thought, because she doesn't know him. She briefly wondered what was going through Esther's mind, whether it was hard for her, whether it hurt.

Inside the shop they were getting tired of waiting and the pale young man squeezed past the removal men, who were lugging a heavy glass display case, and stood there wringing his hands on the pavement behind Esther. He cleared his throat obsequiously to get her attention, his Adam's apple bobbing up and down. 'Esther, please...'

Esther ignored him.

ritical, he lisped, the supplier wanted to settle up
e where the storage cupboards should go without
s collarless jacket. 'You're busy,' she said in Dutch.
w.' She squeezed Hans's arm for the second time.
 on our way now.'
aid, 'the bloody Dutchies – we're not doing so

sther look from Frank to Bobby. 'See you, then,'
 nails deep into her husband's arm. 'Yes!' he
hook Esther's hand. 'Really nice… come and see
 phone book.' The urge to give him a hard smack
 Bobby close to her and he didn't protest, as if
s were being used as a lightning rod.
head in his hands. 'Look at us,' he said again
, as if he still wanted to say something but didn't
 spite of everything she became momentarily
er Ada? Ada van Holland?' His voice lower than
eaning.
?'
en writing letters… for some time now.'
rie this. Two years ago, shortly after they'd met
, he'd asked her for Ada's address. All those times
their home, all those times he'd joined them for
l that time he hadn't bothered to tell her this. He
'Bobby, darling, let's go,' she said pointedly, and
er, releasing a spray of deadly poison, dragging
ind her. Frank de Rooy could do as he pleased.
w on she was going to be indifferent. But on the
e didn't dare leave their sight, because they were
ering, and God only knew what Esther was
hings she *could* tell him, and she realized there
lged in gold. She cupped her hands around her

mouth and shouted across the road like a street vendor: 'Frank, are you coming?' When he rejoined them, she ignored him completely. She cut short every attempt he or Hans made to talk about running into Esther. I've got a headache, she snapped. A few streets on, the two men and the boy had miraculously managed to distance themselves from her and walked far out ahead, talking about sports as if nothing had happened. They hadn't noticed what was wrong with her. That she was choking on something caught in her throat, something painful and impossible to swallow. That her tongue was clinging fearfully to the roof of her mouth.

In the bookshop, she took Hans to one side. I want to go home, she said.

19

IED WHEN SHE pushed open the door that
barber' drifting down from the mountains in the
leaden clouds that were an accumulation of gales
ownpours. Clouds like these formed the backdrop
f they truly were harbingers of doom, so many
have happened over the past ten years that an ordi-
ave survived. It just rained a lot on the West Coast.
reatening clouds that made it seem like a very ordi-
of a day filled with routine, first bicycle to school
to the post office, fill the postbags, deliver post for
sure everything stays dry, then do the shopping,
se, open her drawer, revise and polish the letter she
n, or have yet another look at the photo with the
hat, or reread his letters, find new meanings in
various meanings, hide his letters away safely, close
bicycle, pick up the children from school, ride back,
ere home, think up things for them to do if the
always), prepare the evening meal, greet Derk and
mood he's in, pour him a beer, keep the children
ood mood (almost always), try to keep the evening
ear the table, wash the dishes, read to the children,

sing songs, put the children to bed, make tea for Derk, be nice to him. Describe everything to herself in glowing terms as if the life in question was an exceptional one. Once the children are asleep, read a library book, curled up in the brown chair by the fireplace. When the warmth brings on drowsiness remain in reading position, but escape again inside and fantasize about words in the letters. Chew gently on some of the words, taste them, or slide your tongue along them. Let words balance between your lips and then speak them soundlessly (dangerously near Derk, who has no idea and sits at the table writing to the local council that he's not stupid, who do they think they are?), special words that only Frank uses, like 'soft womanly breasts' and 'full shapely thighs'. Dream about what he describes in his letters as if it were reality and feel the effect such love can have on your body and soul. Go to bed dreaming, if possible much earlier than Derk, or otherwise later, you go on ahead, I'm not sleepy yet, so there doesn't have to be any of the touching that sets your nerves on edge, such as the meek way he pulls your hand down to his groin under the blanket as a sign that sexual intercourse is on the menu tonight after the meat and potatoes. A gesture that, precisely because of its meekness, won't take no for an answer. Better to avoid this. Push away the uncomfortable feeling that he's also entitled to something, he does his best for us, he loves me, his mood is my fault. Better to push away that feeling and go to bed before or after he does. Lay next to him with eyes closed and commit adultery. If that's adultery.

*

It seemed like it was going to be that kind of day, an ordinary day. The first gusts of wind and the cold raindrops did nothing to change this. She pushed her hair out of her eyes, tucked it behind her ears in a futile gesture, and quickly touched her coat pocket to see if the envelope containing her latest letter was there, something she was absolutely sure of but still wanted to check again and again, because just doing so gave her pleasure, offered an escape. Then three small bodies shot past her and out of

the hill, she saw her daughter's bare, thin calves
'Let's see who gets to the bottom first!' Little girls
clearly agreed to put a stop to the daily contest
of the hill because Danny, the littlest child, could
hat it wasn't fair. 'We weren't going to do that any
er and sister – so much more agile than he was –
ht, their cries sinking down deeper towards the
indignantly to his mother, also a daily ritual. She
ttle hand. She could hear the unshed tears in his
of pride, and just hoped that everything in life
y, this small, clumsy boy who always stumbled
ay as they went down the hill together and she
eight pull on her arm, the heavy clumsiness with
his feet from the wet sandy ground and bravely
mother. Lord, have mercy on this child.
iveway. On bad days, the hill was one big swampy
ays, there was sand everywhere, brought in on the
vn in by the wind. Although she'd abandoned her
d-free house, the driveway was a recurring subject
er and Derk. First there was no money. The wages
er for the railway were just enough to live on. When
school, Ada got a job as a postie. It was considered
woman to have a job, and sometimes this embar-
he earned they'd saved a sum of money that would
labour and materials. That was no longer the
was that the local council refused to sell the land,
to build a driveway for the local council. He was
battle over this, which didn't improve things at
e, she trudged up and down every day, with the
ing. He'd built a small shelter at the bottom of the
used to keep the pram when the children were
uldn't pull it up through the sand. Sometimes she

289

would think back to how she would inch her way up the hill when she was heavily pregnant – carrying bulky bags and a wobbly toddler, and holding the hand of a headstrong preschooler – afraid that this was her life and that it would never be any different. How she'd been unable to believe it back then.

Nowadays they kept the bicycles under the shelter. While she half listened to the chatter about who had won and that it hadn't been fair, Ada got her bicycle and lifted the small boy's astonishing weight onto the back. Not that Danny was fat. It was more as if everything about him reached out to the earth, or like gravity had more of a hold on him than on the other two, who moved like quicksilver and were almost always jumping. Oh, child, you *are* heavy, she said wordlessly, and with a sharp pang of tenderness in her heart. Peter nimbly took his place on the seat, while she balanced the bicycle by grabbing on to the handlebars and planting her feet firmly into the mud. Julie, who was already ten, had her own bike. They'd named her after the Dutch Queen Juliana. Every day when she saw her oldest child jumping around in good health, Ada would send up a grateful prayer. After Julie was born, Ada's panic only diminished once she'd seen for herself that the baby had ten fingers and ten toes, that she didn't have spina bifida, a cleft palate, a plague of locusts, hailstones big as boulders, or bubonic plague, all of which she could have expected considering the child was conceived in sin. A wonderful, healthy daughter, said the midwife, who was ignorant of the circumstances, but Ada was still convinced she could be punished through her children, and never dared to completely let her guard down. When Peter was born two years later, she was still apprehensive. But nothing happened, the children thrived, and when the third one arrived she thought, this one's mine. She leaned forward in the bed, scooped the small, sightless little creature from between her legs and slid him onto her belly, umbilical cord and all. He grunted softly, and she took him straight into the depths of her heart. Oh, was that you, she said, and licked the grease from his scalp until the midwife took him away. With this little boy she had the courage to simply

em like the Lord had forgiven her. The only thing
e the rest of her life without sinning. Anyone else

als as she cycled with the children to school, a dis-
school bus passed through their neighbourhood,
olics. Children from the reformed church weren't

*

n nervous, she'd got used to that, and even though
ond spontaneously, she enjoyed the looks of the
ped her children off at school and the clumsy jokes
at the post office, how they put themselves out for
h other to be allowed to carry the filled postbags
't understand it, though. Sometimes she could see
hunching her back as she bent into the wind, her
d her nose red from the cold, in her shapeless coat,
ng and slogging, bone-weary, and would wonder
at it could be. The Ada who emerged from Frank's
e barely recognized, someone with so much love
s reason alone she was entitled to a life that didn't
ghtest.

*

't see me, she thought as she cycled home with the
n after work in the driving rain and with a vicious
side, causing Julie to fall over, bicycle and all, such
o much wind, and her with the two boys. She'd also
k for quite a lot of the way, which meant the trip
r than usual. By the time they arrived at the bottom
n blown over inside and out. Good thing he can't
ot actually in so many words, but more as the only

blessing in a life in which the days were strung together into a waterwheel that circled slowly in squelching mud and would never actually arrive anywhere. Derk's truck was there already. 'Visser Transport', she'd done the lettering herself, six months ago now, when he lost his job at the railway because of his hard-headedness. She had supported him in his conflict with the union, of course, a wife should support her husband, he was absolutely right, a blinkered, obstinate kind of rightness that was completely fruitless and which caused him to suffer more and more each day, and after he was fired she'd agreed with him entirely when he wanted to buy a second-hand Bedford 5-ton truck and start his own transport company. Business still had to pick up. He was home, earlier than usual. With no other thoughts in her windswept mind, she started on her daily climb, while the two older children deftly skirted the pools of mud and Danny – strings of mucus blowing to either side of his chapped cheeks – held on to her coat and let himself be pulled up the hill. You can walk, love, she'd wanted to say, but the wind blew away her voice before she'd formed the words. For a moment, it was all too much. On the inside, a raging monster snapped the necks of little children into pieces. But by the time she arrived at the top of the hill with her little boy in tow and walked to the door of the bunker, she was breathless and chastened and the monsters had all shrivelled up.

*

The children were running around, as children do. Ada picked up a soggy jacket from the floor, as mothers do. She asked them to be a little quieter, because Dad was home – where was Dad, then? – and walked to the kitchen to make tea and saw the paint flaking on the concrete floor, just like yesterday and all the previous days – I really have to do something about that soon – dried her hair with a musty-smelling towel: it has to go in the wash; she blew her nose in it, too: it has to go in the wash anyway. Picked up the kettle, listened absently to the sound of the water from the tap, shivered with cold when her wet skirt touched her legs, glanced into

e sure all was well, and suddenly felt the goose-
ad swiftly over her entire body. The bedroom door
he, but hadn't come out nor made himself heard.

oice light, turn off tap, all the ordinary things, a
ake pancakes with them in a bit, it's been a while.
alled out, without looking up from his game and
ere his father was. Fathers and mothers are just

r. The door to the bedroom remained closed. She
ove, but didn't light the flame yet, it was a sense
r children were born, an instinct for the preserva-
n't put the kettle on and walk away when the

how long you'll be away.

*

r bedroom. He stood by the open drawer of her
There were more letters lying on the bed behind
ton bedspread was rumpled; he'd sat there, for who
ad read everything. She could also see the photo
cowboy hat. She slipped quickly into the bedroom
hind her by bumping it with her bottom, some-
a time when everything was ordinary – the door
use a little extra force, back then. He stared at her
e saw the woman she really was, a deceiver.
ooy?'
e groaning to a halt.
As if this could possibly turn out well. The blood
she stood there limply, exhausted, and a little blind
ut to happen was so inescapable that she fled with
ing room, behind the closed door, where she could

place every one of the sounds she heard, from start to finish. The youngest had been killed in a wild game of knights and dragons. Sacrificed, as always. And the dead knight or dragon, the gunned-down redskin, the executed spy, the Mussulman who'd been run through by the Crusaders, did not agree. He started to howl. I have to go to him.

'You're home early,' she said.

He was silent. He was trembling. The howls in the other room, the audible presence of their children, kept the outburst at bay. They stood staring at each other like this in the airless void before the storm, it gave her the giggles, which she was only able to check by clenching her teeth together, as if she was suppressing a yawn. A small squeak escaped.

Behind her, Julie the dragon-slayer pushed open the door.

'He fell,' she cried. 'I didn't push him!'

Neither she nor Derk was capable of responding. She stepped woodenly to one side and stood next to the door without speaking. Saw the child stiffen and thought, how are we ever going to find our way out of this, I disobeyed and look what's happening now, I went against what I was told and did as I pleased, like Lot's wife, and now I've turned into a pillar of salt. She had no idea where to go from here. She saw Julie hesitate, her antennae twitching skittishly as she felt her way through the fog, there was something going on between Mum and Dad.

I can't help you. I don't know how.

The fallen knight, wailing furiously because of the death blow he'd been dealt – once again, he was out of the game – pushed the door open in his own unwieldy way and rent the air. 'They're pushing me... They won't let me... They're cheating... It's mean!' I have to do something, she signalled wordlessly to Derk, and broke out of her salty crust, herded the children out in front of her back to the living room, all of her attention focused on ending their bloody battle. Make pancakes. All the wet clothes have to come off. Flour, eggs, and milk. A little beer to make it light. Fry them in butter. Get the fireplace going. Or vanilla nut pudding, they like that, too. It's cold and clammy in here. His nose is always running,

, the poor child, thick green strings perpetually
and an infected smell.

up when Derk came out of the bedroom and put
y, not when he pulled on his boots, not when he
oor. 'Explain it to the pastor tonight,' he called out
oke when they wanted to keep something from
then she didn't dare look up, not even when the
and she was left behind holding a canister of flour
ee children who, considering the pitched battle
t a short time earlier, seemed rather bewildered.
s with him, she knew this without looking. She felt
hrough the house and stared straight into that

*

when the children went to bed. Outside, the rain
st the windows. She wasn't able to keep the fire
everywhere was the smell of damp clothing. He'd
h him. Her hands were cold as she arranged her
neat pile and placed them into what once again
rdinary drawer. Someone had said something to
king, she saw an outstretched arm and knew who
to think about it, what difference did it make. She
out Frank, as if by losing the letters she'd also lost
ams.

*

wet, and stamping their feet, a bitter blast of wind
ne of the four dared to look straight at her or to
she was contaminated. She dashed into the kitchen
ed to them muttering gravely by the door. 'Visser,
vay?' The pastor was out of breath from the climb.

Four figures in black bent over to take off their shoes, which were covered in too much mud to leave them on. Yes, thought Ada, what about that driveway. She poured the boiling water into the teapot unsteadily, feeling only disgust. Why does he go to the pastor for everything?

In the living room, Derk placed four chairs in a row, and one chair facing the others. She didn't despise him.

The pastor cleaned his glasses and did the talking. He wanted to know how long they'd been writing to each other. She did despise the pastor, despised his receding chin, his receding form: a man who rubbed his hands self-deprecatingly but whose eyes were hard, and when he looked at her they always contained the sin with which she'd come to this country. On his left was the elder with the faulty stomach valve, a man who was beyond reproach if not beyond producing certain odours; and on the other side, the elder who was known as being jovial and who, during a home visitation, had once kept her pinned against the windowsill with his barrel belly as he leaned past her to enjoy the view, she hadn't dared move, hadn't even dared to think what she thought, but she had no faith he would judge her fairly today. The thought that these men had read the letters made her sick.

'How long has this been going on?'

'About two years.'

She stared at four pairs of dark socks and sensed that the tribunal wouldn't settle for this; she couldn't allow herself to give minimal answers. She couldn't allow herself anything. Her guilt was so obvious it made her laugh. Her shoulders shook. 'He was very friendly, back then, during the flight, he helped me. We don't mean anything by it.'

I'm not able to do this, she thought, this is going wrong, I don't feel any remorse and I can't pretend – what's happened to me? She was becoming more disgusted all the time, and had to keep an iron grip on herself so she wouldn't, wouldn't.

In the silence, Derk opened out one of the letters. Don't do it, she thought, but he did it anyway, started to read aloud from it at random.

ne, in the dark above Australia, I kneeled down next

two seats and you were awake. I could feel you were

hosen to keep your eyes closed so you could follow

ring to you and what my hand was doing as I spoke.

sed excitement travelled over your skin, an almost

the curtain you were hiding behind, a curious and

ed out the contours of your body with my hand like

staken. I couldn't have been mistaken. That hungry,

rtain was restless and ready.

y a long silence, filled with overt condemnation in

vdness in their haunches. She was stark naked. The

side the socks. But it hurt her to see the bewildered

is was about his wife. 'How can you say you didn't

he said bitterly.

e answer to this, either. This whole situation was

m do it?' He shouted this, and tore the letter into

n the door to the children's room and considered

etters were in Martinborough and couldn't be read.

penly about these kinds of things as Frank did, she

d to and as a married woman it wouldn't have been

adn't discouraged him, either, on the contrary.

ed to Derk that he should control himself. He made

off his glasses and paused. She braced herself. He

o be heard above the howling of the wind outside.

ay, daughter. You've forsaken your duty as a wife.

never covet another man or lead him into tempta-

forgiveness and mend your ways.' He waited. Now

t him and nod. But she wasn't able to lift her head

bornly on the socks. See who wins. This went on for

he could lose face he put on his glasses, folded his

mediately did the same – and closed his eyes. 'Lord,'

he prayed loudly, 'make this woman a better wife and make her see the error of her ways.'

The wind, which had strengthened to a gale, underscored the prayer that just kept going on and on. Corinthians, Romans, Galatians: it seemed as if the entire Bible was brought to bear.

'... And lest, when I come again, my God will humble me among you, and that I shall bewail many which have sinned already, and have not repented of the uncleanness and fornication and lasciviousness which they have committed...' The pastor's voice escalated to pulpit strength. '... Let us walk honestly, as in the day; not in rioting and drunkenness, not in chambering and wantonness, not in strife and envying...' She hated that chin, that sagging skin, all that rightness. '... Who can find a virtuous woman? For her price is far above rubies...' She looked at Derk, who was praying along fervently for a virtuous woman. I can see the error of my ways, she thought, but I've sunk so low I no longer feel any remorse. She turned to ice and didn't recognize herself. Something of the woman in Frank's letters had taken root, had changed her. Then that's just the way it was, she was too tired to fight it, I can't be saved, I've left the straight and narrow and lost my way. She closed her ears to the prayer and listened to the wind and the rain. Of course, this deluge was meant for her. If God wants to punish the sinners, He will send His seas wherever He likes. God will wash me off the hill. All right, then. I'm freezing and soaked and also incredibly angry. With complete and sudden clarity, she knew she wasn't prepared to give up her fantasies. Maybe not even the writing.

After the prayer, the eyeglasses turned towards her again. Something was expected of her. 'Do you have anything to say?'

They were still hopeful over there.

She slowly got up. Or it might have been someone else.

'The tea's getting cold,' she said, in a voice she'd borrowed from a woman she didn't know. Step by step she reached the kitchen, knowing she was being followed by four pairs of eyes.

She inclined her head politely over the teapot, good evening. In the

e hung like an icy cloud. Let it hang there. The
d.

be made an elder soon,' said the pastor, expertly
rds the back of her head. 'That is, if his home life
.'

*

each other in silence for a long time. Without the
Derk seemed to have shrunk. Ada noticed his inse-
o make the tiniest move in his direction. She stared
ht at the linen closet he'd built. He'd been so proud
er and she'd lavished him with praise, look at this,
helves here, and that rod there, only he'd never got
so the wood scratched at your skin and the damp
. They squeaked and groaned when you pushed
ng to us, too, we're all getting warped out of shape.
ards her, she smelled postage stamps. As she always
is place in the hollow of her arm, with his head
eathing anxious and high. He loves me, he's afraid.
in defence, and she hoped he wouldn't make any
vouldn't stand for it. That was nothing new. It was
was nothing new. For years now she'd avoided him,
ension at home, something she felt awful about it.
beyond this on occasion, letting him have his way
couldn't change it, nor could she tell him about it. It
, his skin that was always slightly clammy, but more
he way he approached her, fearfully, rapidly, frenet-
piece of flotsam he was clinging to as he floundered
pping off at any moment. She didn't know how it
actly, but she knew that it did have to be different.
her careful attempts in this direction ('If we were
ediately... we could also...'), and they'd come to

nothing. You have to keep these kinds of forces in check, he would say anxiously. Then she would nod dutifully and leave it at that. Love has to grow, her mother had said. In a certain way that had actually happened, she often felt sorry for him, his anger, his conflict, and she could suddenly find herself moved by him, when he showed a boyish pride in his bunker, his truck, his family, when she sat alongside him high up in the cab of the Bedford, his hands turning the large steering wheel with studied nonchalance, when they would joke with each other as they all walked home from church on a sunny day. The fact that they had children together gave a sense of connection that sometimes bordered on happiness. But in bed he repelled her.

'Ada,' he whispered.

She stroked his sandy hair to reassure him. To keep him quiet.

'I might not be the most...'

She interrupted him. 'I'm sorry,' she said, and meant it, she felt herself becoming nauseous with pity. He was also saddled with her.

'I'm doing my best,' he mumbled, and grabbed on to her breast, don't do it, don't do it. 'For you, for the children.' She nodded, I know, she wanted to say, but at that moment she felt his erection against her leg. Too late. For a moment she acted like she didn't feel it, prolonging the moment in which the erection as yet played no role. 'Let's go to sleep,' she said as sweetly as she could, gently leading his hand away from her breast, 'it was quite a...' But he wanted to kiss her and wriggled on top of her beneath the blankets. She jerked her head to one side, tried to soften the gesture, I can't refuse him now, not after tonight, but the resistance she'd felt all evening surged up, and she pushed him off.

'Not now,' she said shrilly, 'I'm menstruating.'

He sat up suddenly.

'Again?'

She saw him fighting the urge to hit her and waited for the blow. He had never hit her before. He was a God-fearing, righteous person, and he controlled himself now as well. The children were sleeping in the small room next door, separated from their bedroom by a thin wall.

He turned his back to her, moved to the other side
nced his stony silence.

rged with anger and unhappiness, the distance
their actual proximity to each other. Outside, the
bsided, though the rain continued to fall.

*

ht she awoke with a start, with a short scream and
. She wanted to sit up, but couldn't move. She was
nd someone was sitting on her back. All of the air
of her. Knees kept her arms pressed tightly against
hrough her. Before she realized what was happened back by the hair. Then she heard the sound of
snipping, two, maybe three times, and her head
illow. Once more a hand grabbed her hard by the
d was yanked up and back and she could barely
fled cries, the scissors ploughed through her hair,
he skin on her scalp to hurt dreadfully, two, three
ad shot free and fell forward onto the pillow. Then
back of her head, so that her cries were smothered.
uffled by the pillow next to her ear, she heard the
continue, roughly dragging clumps of hair along
ing. He could kill me, she knew instinctively, and
ep as quiet as possible, but it was hard to breathe
struggle for air; she pushed her head to one side
was able to free up her nose and mouth, gasping
he scissors flash by out of the corner of her eye,
t, heard the scissors fall to the ground. Then he
of the head, an impotent blow. She silently endured
me weaker and weaker, until he stood up sobbing
sed the door behind him.

The door didn't open again. She didn't know how long it had lasted, she'd lost all sense of time. Like an animal, she stared at the door in the dark, not daring to move, barely breathing. He stayed away; he must have been sitting in the living room, alone and terrified, just like she was. One on either side. After an hour, or longer, or shorter, when the worst of her fear had passed, she started to shake and her teeth began to chatter. It burned behind her eyes. She touched her head gingerly, the short tufts, the long strands that had been spared. Then came the tears. She was overcome by a crippling sadness about everything that had gone wrong. The better future should have begun long ago. She would never get used to it here. She would never feel at home in this country. Or in this house. Or in the church. She would never feel at home anywhere any more. Chilled to the bone, she pulled the blankets around her and stayed sitting like this, unable to stop crying for the rest of the night, a pain in her stomach because her sobs were becoming increasingly like vomiting, her mouth open wide, soundless, for the children and because of the silence in the living room.

*

'I got carried away,' he said when the daylight had banished the darkness and the shame had nowhere to hide. He put an ashen face in at the door, he hadn't slept, either. He had sat in the dark staring at their destruction, not knowing where to go from here, just as she had done. But it didn't help.

She stood before the mirror in her nightgown with a pounding headache, and he shuffled behind her into the room, got dressed, mumbled. 'It wasn't... I didn't want to... didn't mean to...'

In the other room, she heard the children laughing. She should do something, make breakfast, things from a faraway past, but she kept staring at the woman with the half-closed, swollen eyes in the blotchy face and a head full of haphazard tufts of hair and long straggling strands left behind at random, a ridiculous-looking woman, pitiful and frightening. It you look like this, who are you then? She belongs

The children shouldn't see her like this. 'We can't

id and was startled by her own voice, a raw voice.

alk again. 'No,' he said meekly. 'I'll…' Then a soft

or and she heard Julie's high-pitched voice, ques-

weren't there any plates on the table, why wasn't

quickly snatched a scarf from the chest and placed

ined standing like this in the hope that this would

invisible. Derk came to her aid. He was willing to

make it up to her and squeezed through a narrow

the children wouldn't be upset by the way she

ing so well,' he said. 'I'll take you to school today in

breathing beneath the scarf the whole time, in soft

bric moving gently in and out – a pretty pastel for

assistant had said. She heard the children cheering,

eard his childish panting near the door, she knew

ettle for this and would come looking for her. She

ok on the door. She saw the handle move down and

he might be clumsy, but he was persistent as a

d out, because he wanted to check to see how sick

was there to lure him away and she waited for him

to Mummy, and Derk's stern reprimand and the

She knew that the children would be swallowing

throats squeezed slightly shut, because everything

ain and so menacing, and she stood there listening

been put on, and to the search for Peter's school-

hat Julie didn't need a ribbon in her hair today,

now how to do that. Say goodbye to Mum. Bye,

back from under the scarf.

20

A MAN ON THE TRAIN offered her a cigarette. She leaned towards the pack and took one out. It was the first cigarette of her life. Everything was going to be different. She pushed the yellow scarf back slightly and held her cigarette into the flame of his lighter, inhaled the smoke, and nearly fainted. She smiled wanly at the man and turned her head towards the window to make clear to him their contact would go no further. She took an occasional puff on the cigarette, but made sure to keep the smoke in her mouth so she wouldn't get dizzy again. One, two, three, then out through pursed lips – people actually like how this tastes? Two voices in her head. One of them said: I'm a runaway wife, a mother who just goes off and leaves her children behind. The other voice thought this was an exaggeration, it was just that she had to get away after such an emotional episode, that's all. A couple of days at most, and I'll be back.

The train travelled slowly, climbed gradually. To get away from the fellow's stares she slid closer to the window and looked out at the mountains, which were rugged if not terribly high. Up above, a large grey raptor hovered in the air and a small creature down below was unaware of its fate.

The man pointed to the shrubs that covered the hills. Bloody weed, he said, English settlers had brought it along with them in the previous century. In the spring it had yellow blossoms but was otherwise a scourge.

If r ... ole country would be overgrown with it in
no ...

... strong accent. She couldn't understand him.
She ... yellow scarf under her chin and tied it in a
kn ... just like Audrey Hepburn. It felt slightly suf-
foc ... cigarette and tried to seem aloof, suppressed
a c ...

int ... ame higher and steeper the train disappeared
the ... here was no longer any point in looking out
dir ... s and thought about her journey in the other
pas ... ack of their old Ford pickup. But her fellow
wa ... alone. Did she know that Mount Alexander
... Everest?

aw ... gained ground. Of course she couldn't stay
ins ... be the peacekeeper in her home. This was
she ... igarette the man offered her. From a distance
... n.

her ... all station in the middle of Arthur's Pass. To
nant ... npartment. She saw him greet a heavily preg-
hill. ... er to a group of houses at the bottom of a
... ery soon.

A ... train passed a solitary house in the middle of a
field. A woman wearing an apron stood in front of the house and waved
at the train for a long time. Funny, Ada thought, someone in the train
knows that wave's meant for him. That must be a wonderful feeling to
have such a loving send-off. He might also be relieved.

Then the mountains became more bare, the landscape softened gradually into rolling hills, and the clouds broke up. She slowly realized she
was moving towards the sun and the warmth. Occasionally she would see
her reflection in the window, see the yellow of the scarf she'd used to cover
the hideous tufts of hair, and remember the events of last night. In her
purse was the driveway money.

I went to the hairdresser, said the hard scrawl on the note she'd left for Derk. Then, in parentheses, she'd added even more angrily: it might take a week.

From Springfield on, the countryside became increasingly gentle. She watched hedgerows and trees and groups of houses flash by. The closer the train got to Christchurch, the lovelier the light became. Broad shafts of sunshine streamed into the compartment and the temperature in the train rose. It was a while before she realized this. She took off her coat; she would have loved to take off the scarf as well, but that was impossible. She was seized by a light-hearted, worldly kind of excitement. The second voice got the upper hand. Calm down, everyone, of course I'll come back, I just have to get away for a while, I really need this.

In Christchurch she put on her sunglasses. She was a bit nervous as she walked through the busy streets of the city centre with her coat folded over her arm, and she tried to reassure herself: first she'd find a ladies' hairdresser and then a hotel, and she'd go back home tomorrow morning, so she could pick up the children from school herself. What nice shops they had here. Maybe they should come here as a family one day soon.

*

Everything at the hairdresser's was lavender. The smell matched the colour. And then came the awful moment when she had to take off the scarf. 'Well, madam,' said the hairdresser – who had introduced herself as Anne, 'just like our Princess Anne' (maybe *your* princess, Ada thought) – 'take your time, but we won't get very far like this.' When she finally removed the scarf, filled with shame, the scissors of the other hairdressers hung in mid-air as they stared in shock at the tufts. Flushed faces also turned towards her from beneath the hairdryers. The hairdresser backed away. Ada let out some laughing sounds, my daughter, she wants to become a hairdresser so badly.

Then Anne got down to work – this was what you called a challenge. And madam had such a lovely face. Truly lovely. And she was lucky that short hair was the latest thing, short hair was very fashionable, and with the tip of her comb she tapped the photo of a close-cropped, fair-haired film star that had been taped to the mirror at an angle.

An hour later, Ada stood regarding her new look in the window of a ladies' clothing store, unaccustomed to her reflection. Anne had outdone herself, everyone at the hairdresser's had agreed, the result was incredible if you considered how madam had come in. Anne had folded the yellow scarf into a narrow headband and tied this around madam's short hair, just like the film star in the photo except that hers was light blue, which would have been better for madam as well with her blue eyes, but you can't have everything. Ada touched her hair, which had been sprayed with a hard, sticky layer that smelled of salon. She was pleased by the face that looked back at her from the glass. A bold, modern young thing, if you didn't know better. Only, her old skirt and cardigan didn't go with it at all. I have to make a decision, she thought, I have to look for a hotel, not spend too much money, and go back early tomorrow. But she wasn't able to make her thoughts strong enough, as if their knees kept giving out.

*

The dress looked gorgeous on her. The colourful stripes accentuated her waist and swayed gently around her hips. The square bodice left her throat and arms bare, so she also bought a light blue mohair sweater with short sleeves. She just had to have the belt, and the white openwork shoes as well, and the soft undergarments, and those expensive stockings – could you give me three pairs, please, I'm always getting ladders in my stockings – suddenly, the sky was the limit. She bought lipstick for the first time in her life. She was doing so many things for the first time now – mascara, and powder in one of those fancy boxes, and then real perfume as well, she was in a shop filled with pastries and was gobbling them up one after the other.

Breathless from all her irresponsible spending and her metamorphosis, she went from street to street – swaying her hips slightly because the dress called for this – on the way to the hotel the saleslady had so helpfully recommended. And she would have certainly ended up there, if the river hadn't continually reappeared. But in Christchurch, the Avon winds its way right through the city and it was as if the river were looking for her and kept lying down at her feet, here I am, why don't you stop for a moment. And she did just that – oh, lovely – took off her new shoes and put her coat on the grass to keep her new dress clean, lay down in the late-afternoon sun, breathed in the smell of the grass, listened to the lapping of the water, and dozed off. And in this twilight state came thoughts of Frank. This is where he walked that first evening, unhappy with himself because he'd let her go (she knew it by heart). He'd walked here with Esther, who had bold red lips, but he'd paid no attention to this because he was thinking of the girl in the back of the pickup. And she was that girl. And now she was lying on the grass he'd walked on, listening to the sounds he'd listened to then. And it was as if this enabled her to touch him, and she could feel they had a great deal in common, that their bond was a deep one. And then she stopped fighting it, jumped up and hurried to the station, finally admitting she was on her way to Martinborough, that with a bit of luck she could catch the train to the night boat in Lyttelton: she'd worked all of this out some time ago, and had done so for a reason.

*

It was the *Maori*. She ran from the passenger terminal with the beautiful sandblasted window to Number 2 wharf, gasping for breath as she joined the queue of people waiting in front of the ferry's gangway. She was overcome with emotion. From this point on, every step she took was laden with meaning, because she was literally following in his footsteps of ten years ago. I'll make sure I'm up on time tomorrow morning, she resolved, so I can be on deck as we pass through Cook Strait, for you, I'll do it over, for you. It seemed only natural when she started talking to him inside her head again. The palms, she said, it was the palm trees that reminded you of the East Indies, back then. As she always did, she ignored the wink of the steward who tore her ticket, and while she walked up the gangway with her head held high – a new woman in a new dress – she described how the setting sun washed over the hills of Lyttelton. She realized too late that the new woman would have known how to respond to the wink.

She shared the small cabin with three older women with whom she exchanged only the bare minimum of conversation. The sea was calm and smooth, without the slightest breeze. She hung over the railing as long as she could and described with pleasure how insignificant the harbour seemed in the distance, and how endless the sea was, immense, dark, mysterious. When she got cold, she went to her cabin and stretched out beneath the sheet, in her new undergarments, feverish with excitement. Just like Frank back then, she'd barely slept a wink the night before. Everything corresponds, she thought contentedly, just before the swell rocked her to sleep. For hours now, she hadn't dared to think about home.

*

At five a.m., there was a sharp rap on the door of their cabin. The older women groaned and turned over. For a moment she thought she was lying in her own bed, but then the reality of her trip came back to her. She got dressed in the dark and stumbled outside, onto the deck. Yawning and shivering, she looked around. An icy deep blue sky still hung over the sea and between the dark hills that rose straight out of the water in the distance. Her teeth were chattering and she wondered what she was doing here, and whether Derk had tucked the children in before he went to bed. For a moment she was standing in the children's room. But before she'd bent down over Danny's bed, who just like always had somehow managed to get his forehead up against the wooden headboard, with his back arched, before she'd leaned over the sleeping child, taken hold of him with both hands and carefully pulled that heavy body down so that his head was on the pillow, before she'd covered him with his blanket again and touched her hand to his warm neck, stroked his broad little back, and thankfully also before the sharp pang of love could reach her heart and make her miserable, the first orange glow of the sun appeared behind the hills and coloured the water indigo blue. A short time later, gold satin slid down over the peaks and was reflected in the sea until the golds came together and touched on the surface of the water. And in the middle of the indigo was their ship, pulling a long shadow in its wake. She heard the sound of trumpets, there could be no doubt: forgiveness was possible. She had never seen anything so beautiful. The darkness of the children's room vanished, and she waxed lyrical as she described to Frank what he'd missed back then.

*

In Wellington there were gusts of wind at every street corner, and she had to hold tightly to the skirt of her striped dress. The buildings were higher and the streets busier than in Christchurch. So Marjorie lives here somewhere, she thought uneasily, and in his last letter he'd written about running into Esther, who'd recently opened up a shop here. She quickly asked how to get to the station.

The weather was so pleasant here on the North Island that the windows in the train were open wide, allowing a sultry wind to cool your neck. She hoped Derk hadn't forgotten to send Julie's sports gear along with her. She leaned back and put her hands on her thighs, ran them over the smooth fabric with the colourful stripes, and closed her eyes. She had the compartment all to herself. Actually, she was sure he'd forgotten. The face of a distressed little girl intruded upon her. She quickly opened her eyes.

During the final leg of the day's journey, on the bumpy bus ride to Martinborough, the entire undertaking started to develop an ugly character. What on earth was she doing? She didn't know Frank at all. Their lives had nothing in common. They would probably have nothing to say to each other. Writing letters was one thing, fantasizing was another, but carrying on conversations wasn't her strongest suit. She wanted to turn on her heels. While the bus sped on relentlessly, she prepared herself, inventing an excuse that would explain her visit. And after that visit she'd get a hotel room in Martinborough. It was important to maintain a sense of authority at all times.

The bus dropped her off some distance from the village, on a narrow gravel road near an extensive tract of land surrounded by mountains. She lingered at the bus stop, gathering her courage. Most of the land was still uncultivated, but a number of acres had been planted. Grapes hung from the vines in some of the fields, and others had been planted more recently. At some distance from the road, in the middle of the fields, she saw the yard, with a simple house that was still in the process of being built. A couple of trees, a shed. And far away in the fields, at the foot of the mountains, an old caravan. But no matter how hard she looked, she saw no signs of life.

It turned out to be quite a walk to the house. Although the sun was already lower in the sky, it was very warm. Her new shoes were ill-suited to such rough terrain. Teetering between the grapevines, she talked herself round. Listen, she said, I'm a married woman, the mother of three children, and he's a bachelor. I'm leading an adult life, he's not. As long as we keep these things in mind. Nevertheless, every nerve in her body twitched disagreeably, and she was now sorry for the intimacies they'd shared in their letters. She shouldn't have taken it so lightly. She might come to regret this deeply if she were to come face to face with him later. What was wrong with me anyway? In the distance she heard a dry crack. She stopped and listened, but it wasn't followed by a second. It might have been a gunshot. Shaken, she put her suitcase down on the dry earth, shaded her eyes with her hand, and looked out over the rows of vines, but she could see nothing.

The yard also seemed deserted. Boxes and crates. A mound of dirt, a cement mixer, large wooden casks, a jumbled pile of stakes. Further on a small tractor, with a plough behind it. An open jeep stood near the house. There's his jeep, she noted, and wished her heart wouldn't beat so furiously. The tension made her pull back deep inside her body. He was probably in the house. She covered the short distance to the porch in a curious kind of numbness, just let it happen, once the first moment has passed it will all be more normal. She saw her arm reach towards the dark green door and, somewhere far away, make the motions of a person who's come for a visit and knocks. There was no sound along with this. Then she turned aside and looked out over the fields, so that if you opened the door you might think that none of it mattered all that much to her.

But no-one answered the door, nor when she knocked again, and then again. He wasn't home. She walked hesitantly to the open shed and looked inside, although the silence there said enough. Stacks of wooden casks, which must be for the wine. Even more crates, and bottles. In the corner lay a mountain of white bird netting, like the stuff she'd seen draped over some of the grapevines. Wobbling on her high heels, she took a few uncertain steps back to the yard and stopped. Indecisiveness and the blazing sun were making her head spin. The bus wouldn't be back for quite some time. The hotel in Martinborough had to be more than an hour away on foot, not a pleasant prospect with the blisters on her heels from the tight leather straps. On the other hand, if she left immediately she could escape, and he would never have to know she'd been standing here. Maybe this was a sign. To Derk she would maintain she'd been in Christchurch for three days, he would forgive her such an outing: after all, he had something to make amends for. She wouldn't write any more, that was out of the question; she would devote herself to her family and find her happiness there, it couldn't be all that hard. Seen from here, their marriage didn't seem all that bad. She'd been gone two days already, she had to get back quickly. She hoped he wasn't upsetting the children. She hoped he wasn't coming after her. He doesn't know where I am, but he could work it out, the address was on the back of the envelopes. Fear pounded beneath her ribs. A thin stream of sweat trickled onto her throat from behind her ear, and she wiped it away. No, she thought, he can't do that, because there's no-one he could leave the children with. Just to be sure, she had to go back straight away. Well, then she'd walk, in these shoes. In this dress. If I stand here much longer I'll get sunstroke. The dress was made of a modern material that was rather warm. She kneeled down and opened her suitcase, rummaged and groped – her sunglasses were somewhere towards the bottom – stuffed her old jacket back in, shut the lid and stood up, feeling wretched. It was better this way. Then she saw him standing there.

He was leaning against a crooked old fruit tree that stood at the edge of the yard. He looked at her and smiled. He'd probably been watching her the whole time, watching her awkward fumbling. In the space of a single second her sense of authority deflated, like a balloon that flies spluttering from your fingers as you're trying to blow it up. A cowboy in shirtsleeves and work trousers, the hat low over his eyes, next to him a rifle leaning against the tree, and around his waist a belt hung with dead birds. He slowly separated himself from the tree and unbuckled the belt, laying the birds down next to the rifle. She looked at his heavy work shoes and stayed rooted to the spot until he was close to her, then she lifted her eyes, and recognized the smile.

'There you are.'

And the voice. She was unable to speak, had to clear her throat for sound. Then, before she could tumble down into the depths, she quickly grabbed hold of the railing.

'I was in the neighbourhood.'

It sounded artificially ladylike – as if she'd found herself acting in a play in which she had to sip a cup of tea with her pinkie extended – but she went on with her tale, had practised it, 'An aunt in Wellington...' – she saw his eyes start to twinkle – 'who asked...' and for a moment he laughed openly, soundlessly, his head tipped back slightly, 'of Derk's, an aunt of Derk's, who asked... she's sick, she asked...' he nodded in encouragement, go on, 'so I thought... it's not all that serious... but I'll have to be getting back soon, but I thought, I thought...'

Then she faltered, lost.

'You thought, you were in the neighbourhood anyway.'

'Yes!'

The smile deepened. He raised his arms and let them fall back to his sides.

'I can't stay long,' she said.

He nodded to show this was completely clear to him. They were silent, and looked at each other intently. The here and now took over, what was in the letters played no role, they had no past. She had to get away as soon as she could.

He motioned towards the house. 'Shall we have a cup of tea then?'

*

The windows were open, she heard birds, the rustling of leaves in the tree in the yard. Inside, the temperature was just right. She attempted to ignore the way he was looking at her from the kitchen, and tried to act relaxed as she wandered around the room. His house was nothing like what she'd imagined. Not the digs of a bachelor, messy, helpless, immature. Although it had been furnished simply and at no great expense, everything exuded culture and refinement. There was a large oil painting of a mysterious landscape in a heavy frame, there were wooden statues, she saw the mask he'd written about, the chairs with the woodcarvings, an old leather sofa, a writing desk – weathered pieces of furniture with stories attached to them.

These things are ridiculously out of place in my simple house. Everything is waiting for better times. My mother's writing desk has three drawers and a scuffed leather blotter. It's not a man's desk, to be honest, it's too dainty, and if I want to sit at it I have to hold my knees off to one side in an impossible fashion. The key below the desktop keeps falling out. Actually, I don't like old things at all! The fact that I sit at the desk anyway is because I hope it will provide me with the right words, with you in my memory just as lovely and lost as she was.

Scattered stacks of books. *The Cruel Sea, The Kon-Tiki Expedition.* A record player surrounded by rows of records. She saw the bunker in front of her, their nondescript, mismatched furnishings, none of which had any of the elegance she saw here. The birthday calendar her mother had sent from Holland, with pictures of the royal family. Their faded crocheted bedspread, the Formica table they had their meals at, which wobbled constantly on the rough floor and made an awful scraping sound when you moved it.

Her last letter lay on the leather blotter. And standing against the back of the desk was her photo with the swimsuit. He looks at me when he sits here. You have beautiful, full, shapely thighs, he'd written after she sent the photo. Beautiful, full, shapely thighs, those were some of the words he used. Now she saw him sitting there as he wrote.

'You haven't changed,' he said from the kitchen.

'Yes, I have.'

Above the desk hung a photo in a dark wooden frame. A man stood next to a palm in a copper pot, a serious man, with a blonde woman seated on a chair in front of him (beautiful and lost, Ada thought automatically), in a long, flowing dress like those that had been fashionable in the 1930s. The man had his hands on her shoulders. The woman had a baby on her lap. Next to her stood a boy who must have been around five years old. She recognized Frank from his eyes.

'How have you changed?'

'My hair!'

He came in with a tray. 'Oh, that,' he said, as he set the tray down on the table and walked over to her. 'It looks good on you.'

She ran her hands over her short hair, to give herself something to do and so she wouldn't have to feel how nervous she was becoming with every step he took in her direction. 'It's the latest thing,' she said as casually as she could, but then let out a startled squeak because he'd come over and stood very close to her indeed. He laughed, as if he suddenly recognized her. 'Ada van Holland,' he said. There it was again. Their eyes greeted each other joyfully, glad to see one another again, although their words were still skimming the surface.

From outside came the sound of a motorcycle approaching through the field. She turned towards the window, jumpy as a fugitive. 'Who's that?' The motorcycle stopped in front of the house and the engine was turned off. She walked to the window with her heart and conscience pounding. Frank came and stood next to her. She saw a dark young man with heart-throb good looks; he was wearing a checked shirt, and his shirtsleeves were also rolled up. Strong, muscular arms. 'A Maori,' she said in surprise.

*

And so it came to pass that a short time later she found herself wandering through the vineyard between two men, in the low evening sun, dizzy from the heat and the situation. We're going to give you a tour, they said, and Frank had taken her by the hips and sat her down on a chair and without so much as asking, had taken off her new shoes and slipped a pair of heavy work boots onto her feet, as he held her ankle firmly with his hand and then slid it up to encircle her calf. The boots were too big for her, of course, her feet slid forward, and occasionally she would step right out of them. Everything added to their enjoyment on this sultry late afternoon. She slowly gave in to it; she was twenty-eight, that wasn't so old, and right now she couldn't recall her weighty responsibilities, her head was too light for that. She was a little embarrassed by her English, though, but they had to speak English because of Mozie.

'This used to be an orchard,' Frank said, 'but when we came here it had been neglected for years, there was only a rusty old shed, over there, off to one side, so dilapidated it would collapse if you blew on it.'

'So we tried to look as if we weren't really interested,' said Mozie, and took hold of her arm so that she stopped and watched him give a demonstration of their indifference. He crossed his arms, arched an eyebrow, shifted his weight onto one leg, and gave an exaggerated yawn – 'and we said to the farmer: this soil is useless, it's full of pebbles, what would we do with it?' Frank put his arm around her waist and turned her away from

Mozie with a practised movement. 'But for all that,' he said, 'we really wanted the land. Because it's ideal, protected by the mountains and full of pebbles.'

'Full of pebbles?'

Mozie scooped a handful of pebbles from the soil and handed them to Ada, offering them to her as if they were wedding rings. She laughed. 'Take them,' Frank said gravely. 'We've got plenty.'

'Why is that important, these pebbles?'

Mozie gave her a penetrating look. 'It's no good without pebbles.'

'No pebbles, no pinot noir,' said Frank, and explained to her that the stones retain the warmth and release this to the grapevines at night.

She shuffled to the edge of the field in her seven-league boots and touched the plump bunches of grapes. 'Pinot noir,' she said, savouring the words. She could spend the rest of her life walking through this carefree afternoon, with her two gentlemen, her striped dress, and beneath her fingertips the velvety grapes containing all of the sun's warmth.

*

He's an owner. He was born to be an owner. Followed sharply by: I wasn't, and I never will be one. How he leaned against one of the oak casks, *his* oak casks, in which the previous year's vintage waited for his approval. 'This is the first vintage we've kept entirely for ourselves, the first in five years.'

'Why?' Suddenly, she wanted to know everything about wine, and would gladly stay with these men for ever, in the dusky shade of this shed. But at the back of her mind the bus schedule started to nag.

'The quality of the grapes is never good to start with, so you experiment with them.'

'It's ready now,' said Mozie, his eyes half shut as if he were having a vision.

'How do you know?'

Mozie looked at her intently. 'I sense things,' he said in a low voice. She

317

pushed him away playfully, glad of her own spontaneous reaction, I'm on to you, you don't fool me.

'We're going to taste it and see if it's good,' said Frank. 'And if it's good, we're finally going to make some money around here.' He kept an eye on the rival's ritual dance. 'So it'll be an exciting moment, when we taste it. For us. Very exciting, actually.'

She had a burning desire to be there when it happened. It was unbearable that there would be exciting moments here without her.

'But you won't be here when that happens. What a shame.'

'When is it?'

'Tomorrow.'

Mozie gave Frank a curious look, and Ada understood it was all one big game. 'Tomorrow?'

'Yes, tomorrow, but then you'll be at… what's the aunt's name?'

'Why not today, then? Why not now? What difference could one day make?'

But that was out of the question, all the wine would be ruined and so would their future, in one go. No, no, if she wanted to be there when it happened, she would just have to stay here tonight. 'How sick is that aunt? Do you think she'll make it through the night? What's wrong with her? Because I've got the same thing.'

She held her breath and considered all the possibilities. Suppose she didn't go to a hotel. She'd seen the large bed with the white sheets. Now the works of the flesh are manifest, which are these: adultery, fornication, uncleanness, lasciviousness.

'I have to go,' she said flatly, her eyes open wide.

*

Frank drove her to the bus stop in the jeep. They sat there side by side in the remaining sunlight, two respectable adults. In the distance, Mozie was riding his motorcycle to the old caravan. Rigid with righteousness, she stared out over the fields. 'We haven't said a word to each other yet,' said

Frank. He took her hand, and for a moment they were back on the plane. 'Why won't you stay?' With Mozie gone, his tone of voice had changed. 'I'll sleep on the sofa. You can have my bedroom.' She shook her head, it wasn't right. 'I'll change the sheets.' She gave a short laugh, with a sad ache in her belly for everything that couldn't be.

'It's not right,' she said, but this time out loud.

Because both of them were thinking about this in silence, they could clearly hear the bus approaching in the distance. They looked at their hands that fit together so naturally. Everything she'd wanted to ask him, everything she'd wanted to tell him. Everything that still had to happen, that still waited to be discovered. Everything they hadn't done.

'Are we going to keep writing?' He placed his other hand on hers, just as he had back then. She wanted to curl up and go to sleep in the palm of his hand. The bus driver had seen them and was slowing down. There was a huge cloud of dust in the bus's wake, and a shower of flying gravel. 'No,' she said quickly. 'It's not right. He was furious. No more letters.' The bus clamoured to a halt. The door sighed as it opened. She sighed as she took her hand from his. He gave her a searching look. 'But Ada,' he said. 'Did you come so you could say goodbye?'

21

SHE WAS WOUND UP LIKE a spring as she lay in the hot water and listened to the sounds of the house. He'd built himself a spacious bathroom and in this stood a bath. Every house in New Zealand had a bathroom with hot running water and a bath, something she'd been surprised to discover when she came to this country ten years earlier. In Holland such things were only for the wealthy. A washtub in the kitchen on Friday, a kettle on the stove, first Father, then Mother, then the children. Things should have improved for her here, but there was no hot running water in the bunker and no bath: she was the only person in New Zealand who had neither. And her mother had written from Holland to say that everyone there had bathrooms with hot running water 'now that things are picking up'. Even her parents did. Only in the bunker was there still no bathroom with hot running water and no bath, and things weren't picking up there either. She'd done something terribly wrong in the ten years that followed her emigration, but things were going to be different now. She slid down further into the water, lifted her feet, rested her heels on the edge of the bath, and closed her eyes, even though there was no lock on the bathroom door. Because she was going to become someone like Frank, who she could hear moving around in the living room, whistling along with the saxophone on the jazz record he'd put on as he went about making her a meal in a leisurely fashion (*he* was making a meal for *her*), the kind of

320

person who was at ease everywhere, even in this situation, in which a man and a woman were circling around each other although they both knew it would end in them taking off their clothes and getting very close to each other with their naked bodies although they didn't know each other all that well and without the sanction of any institution. Fornication, adultery, lasciviousness: it was about to take place and didn't seem to make him particularly nervous. And from now on, she wanted that as well. To be like that. This had to do with the spacious dimensions of his bathroom and the whole atmosphere in his house, which was exactly what she'd always wanted but had never come up with herself. That there was no lock on the door because you're too civilized to open a closed door without knocking. It had to do with the wide rectangular window in the metal frame, which had been opened out and provided a view of the stars from the bath. It had to do with the towel that lay waiting on a stool, a large linen towel with an embroidered monogram, threadbare and worn but which had once been expensive and used in a villa on Java by the beautiful, lost woman and the serious man who were his parents, people who were naturally well-mannered and thought elegant things, and who themselves came from impeccable backgrounds. You could be sure there had been a grand piano in the villa, which the mother had played for her two children. All kinds of classical concerts played by heart, imbued with her tragic story even then, so that the children's eyes would fill with tears as they listened without being able to understand what had brought them on. Children are shaped by such things. And if not a piano, a violin. You could see that from the threadbare towel. It had to do with the three candles he'd placed on the edge of the bath, with the music that rippled through the house, with the books that lay everywhere, with the table that stood behind the house, he was laying that table right now, because they were going to eat outside, *outside,* in the night air. It wasn't all Derk's fault, she realized big-heartedly, over the past years she'd been just as blind to the possibilities that life offered. Maybe it was because the weather was always bad, and because of the lack of light in the bunker. She hated the bunker. For the first time, she dared to come right out and think this. She hated the bunker with the cold, hard concrete beneath your feet, which wouldn't hold paint, and the walls that were so thick and strong it was impossible to hide the electrical wiring in them so that the wires lay out in the open throughout the house, and where at night it was so dark she would often wake up with a start, afraid. She hated it, and she'd hated it from the very first day, and lately she'd noticed that Derk couldn't take it any more either, but he was too proud and inflexible to admit it. It was bad for the children as well – they stayed up on the hill too much because Ada wasn't able to keep going down with them, and they weren't old enough to go off on their own. Life on the hill had isolated the children. She hated it, and hated Greymouth, a gloomy place where the coal mines made everything grimy and black, and which had the most dangerous harbour in New Zealand, where the ships that came to load coal for Auckland couldn't enter at low tide or during a storm, and had to wait out on the open sea. A filthy harbour town, busy and wet, where trains went in and out and the river regularly flooded its banks. They could have easily left when Derk finished his obligatory two years; there was no reason they had to stay. In the beginning she'd brought it up carefully, but Derk didn't understand what she was on about, it made him agitated – what did she want, anyway? – and silenced her with her own discontent. They stayed. It was called 'the wettest place on earth'. During the winter it could literally rain for months at a time. They must have been out of their minds.

That was all going to change, just you wait. They were going to move, leave the West Coast, maybe even leave the South Island, move here, for example, to the Wairarapa, and live in a normal, sunny house, maybe even in a bungalow, with big windows and rooms for all of the children, and of course a bathroom with a bath. They would get a record player, and jazz records, and then they would listen to more than just the short-wave broadcasts on Radio Netherlands from five to six. The names were all unfamiliar to them now, anyway. She knew for certain Frank didn't tune in. She would pile stacks of books everywhere. Derk would never have to know what she'd really done, he would see that she'd returned from Christchurch a changed person and would come to appreciate this, he would feel what happens when you throw open the windows and let in the warm breeze. It would do them all a world of good and the children would grow up to be people of the world. Everyone would benefit from what was going to happen tonight at this vineyard.

*

Circling around each other. Tell me about Marjorie, she said, lifting a bare leg so that her foot rested on the seat of her chair, covering it quickly with the smooth fabric of the striped dress. They talked and talked, during dinner and for a long time after, speaking softly so as not to disturb the night. The moon was nearly full and lit up the fields. He'd made a salad, and rice, and when she came outside after her bath, he'd just put skewers onto a grill above the fire, with pieces of lamb and tomato and bell pepper. Shish kebab, he said, and she repeated it under her breath so she wouldn't forget. Glasses of red wine stood next to their plates. Our own pinot noir, he said, from two years ago, not good enough to sell, but drinkable. It was the first time she'd ever tasted wine and she made a face, thought it tasted like medicine, then realized that such a reaction belonged to the woman she no longer wanted to be, so she emptied her glass without batting an eye. She could tell he was impressed. After dinner she felt better.

They talked and talked, searching diligently for the things they had in common. Tell me about Marjorie, she said, and he started to talk, as if they had the rest of their lives. We've become friends, he said. Had she heard of Khandallah Village? – no, of course she hadn't. Hans and Marjorie lived there, with their son Bobby. A good neighbourhood, Marjorie was always saying, a good neighbourhood is important for your child. Hans, who had wanted to become an architect, had done a lot of work on their house, all by himself, and he'd made it into a wonderful house, it really was, with a

323

letter box, a fence, and a beautiful gate, everything painted a cheerful blue, an optimistic house with large rooms and extra windows, a porch, a garden, and a garage for their Ford Zephyr. And the car had tick lights, so you didn't have to stick your arm out of the window when you took a corner.

Their house was almost finished. Marjorie was still moving the furniture around, but according to Hans, that would never change. A happy family. On summer evenings, Bobby made an art form of jumping out of his bedroom window onto the roof of the garage and then escaping unnoticed to the neighbourhood swimming pool, where he and his friends had made a secret opening in the fence so they could sneak off and go swimming while everyone else thought they were asleep. But she should never mention this to Marjorie, because Bobby had only told him in the strictest confidence. 'How old is he?' she asked, although she would have preferred not to talk about children.

'He's nine now,' said Frank, 'and mad about rugby, just like me. His father prefers trout fishing, but Bobby thinks that's boring. He wants to become an All Black.'

'That's what all the little boys here want.'

'But he's got talent, he was chosen for the Wellington junior team. Next weekend I'm taking him to Rotorua to celebrate. We're going to go camping and look at the geysers. Sometimes his mother drops him off here and when she's gone, we tear through the fields in the jeep – he loves that – and then I let him shoot at birds with my gun… by the way, don't mention that to his mother, either.' The fire had nearly gone out; he leapt up and poked at the fire with a stick, adding some large pieces of wood. Ada could see he was fond of the child, his eyes lit up when he talked about him, and she continued to look at him as she wondered yet again why there was no wife here, no sound of children's voices. He was already thirty-five. But it's not something you ask. All these years and he hadn't forgotten her. But she was a married woman, and he'd known that all along as well, surely he'd had no illusions about that, no matter how much she wanted to believe otherwise because of the wonderful warm feeling that came with it. Along with this same tender feeling came an image of her own Danny sitting next to him in the jeep, his little hands around the butt of a rifle that was far too large, bird shooting. Saw him with Peter, bending over a rugby ball. Saw slender girlish calves jumping excitedly around the fire.

'Has Marjorie changed?' she asked quickly. She couldn't remember much about her, well, that she was Catholic, with red cheeks and a funny little nose. No, said Frank, not really, just a little rounder. Even Hans was starting to develop a paunch. It seemed like Marjorie was fattening him up – he smiled at the thought as he walked slowly back to the other side of the table, sat down, and poured her some more wine – because she cooked enormous meals, and Hans enjoyed them. Roast dinners every Sunday, with sherry trifles for dessert, like they'd turned into real Kiwis. Successful immigrants who'd passed with flying colours. Hans had a good job at Woolworths, and Marjorie drove around in their car and bought the latest things. Like a television set. She's funny, he said, she tells you how much everything cost, and the more it cost, the more she glows.

A television set, thought Ada, impressed. He offered her a cigarette. She took it, it was her third, she would get used to it, because smoking was part of her life from now on. They looked at each other over the flame – what are we waiting for – she got a whiff of lighter fluid, he snapped the lighter shut, and leaned back. He savoured his cigarette, sure of how the evening would end. He ran a hand through his hair and let her look at him. She felt a jealous pang aimed at no-one in particular, something she didn't understand. *Now*, she thought, *now*, go and sit on his lap and start. Instead, a polite question came out of her mouth. 'Don't they want to go back to Holland?' Marjorie and Hans were finished with Holland. They'd never even gone there for a holiday. They used their money for the house and the garden and for taking trips here. 'They're thinking about becoming New Zealanders.'

'What about you?'

'I became a citizen years ago. I burned my bridges.' He sounded relieved, pleased even, as if his bridges had led back to a place it was better not to be. She herself had given up her Dutch passport with a heavy heart. Derk was set on their becoming citizens, but for years she would have liked nothing better than to go back to Holland for good. She had obeyed him, as befitted her as a wife. The homesickness didn't go away. But to be honest, now that she was sitting here, on this wonderful evening in Frank's garden, looking out over his fields, with behind her the open windows of the house reaching out to her like longing arms, she was starting to like it here in New Zealand. Do you feel like a New Zealander? she'd wanted to ask, but when she looked at him it seemed like a ridiculous question. He was too much himself to be something else as well. The way he slowly sat up, flicked his cigarette into the fire, and leaned back again. All of his movements filled her with desire, and sadness. Maybe it was time to go inside. Turn around, look at me, do something to stop me. As if he could read her mind, he turned around and looked at her.

'And Esther?' she asked. 'You wrote that you'd seen Esther.'

He smiled.

'Yes,' he said, 'about a month ago. She's very busy. It's already her second shop. Christchurch got too small for her. She hasn't changed a bit, the same wild curls, the same... vibrant clothing.'

So how well does he actually know her? She stubbed out her cigarette in the ashtray. 'Is she married?' she asked. 'Does she have children?' And she noticed she was hoping for a yes.

'No.'

He stretched, at ease and in good spirits. 'She has a shop,' was all he added. Ada put her foot back on the grass. They would remain on opposite sides of a table till daybreak. And then she would have to go home. 'And Hans?' she asked. 'What's he like?'

He put out his hand. Come with me.

*

326

Stand here. With her bare feet on the floorboards, the warm wood beneath the soles of her feet. Let the time pass, because this night will stretch along with us. The moon provides light so we can see what we're doing. Stand here, he said, and ran his hands down her bare arms and then left her to stand there, in the middle of the room, as he sank down onto the sofa, which creaked under his weight, old leather. Each second etched itself into her mind, it had to be old leather, it couldn't have been anything else. The windows had to be open. And exactly these sounds, the rustling, the way the sofa creaked when he changed position, his breathing, and somewhere out in the fields the yowling of a cat in heat. Her body weightless, almost numb with excitement. The game being played here was a serious one. He let her just stand there for a time, he did, and she just stood there, wasn't planning to go anywhere, let her arms vanish into the folds of her dress, and rubbed the ball of her foot over the smooth wood.

'Take off your clothes.' He spoke the words softly, but it wasn't a request.

The belt buckle, the buttons on the back of her dress, her right hand slipped the left side off her shoulder, her left hand did the same to the right, and the dress slipped down along her arms and over her breasts; with long, drawn-out movements she pulled two arms through the arm-holes, her two numb hands took hold of the fabric near her waist and helped the dress along, past hips and bottom, and the stripes swished further down into the depths on their own, goodbye, dear dress, go curl up down there, why don't you. The dress was an ally, an accomplice. Without the dress, she wouldn't be here. She stepped out of it.

'It's a lot warmer here than where we live,' she said.

She knew full well it wouldn't end here. She was wicked, standing here in her undergarments in front of a man, with her thoughts reduced to silence.

'Keep going,' he said.

'We don't get much sun,' she said, and pulled her panties down past her thighs and calves, lifted her feet out of the leg openings one at a time and slid them over towards the dress, keep each other company, wait for me, I'll be back sometime, though I can't say when.

Then she put her hands behind her back and unhooked the fasteners. A fetching C cup, madam, the saleslady had said. *I dreamed I was a social butterfly in my Maidenform bra.* Her breasts heaved a sigh of relief. But she was now very naked indeed. She looked past Frank at the moon, tried to cover up certain parts of her body by crossing her arms.

'Don't,' he said. 'I want to see you.'

'I've got three children.'

'Show me, then.' His voice gave her courage, she heard desire in it, and dark, hidden pain. Although she still didn't dare meet his gaze entirely, she dropped her arms. 'And yet,' she said, to reassure them both, 'and yet it's beautiful there, too. I love the ocean.' After she'd had the children, her body had become softer, rounder, more complete. She wasn't sure if it would hold up under scrutiny. 'Sometimes I walk all the way to Hokitika. At times like that... I *am* happy.'

She could tell what he thought of her from the way he was breathing. And at that moment her soul filled with happiness, so much happiness that for the rest of her life there would be more than enough for everyone, for Frank, for Derk, for the children, there was plenty for everyone, there was happiness in abundance. He moaned. She cradled her breasts in her hands. 'Beautiful woman,' he said with a voice full of pain.

She was certainly not his first woman. He must lead a sinful life, it was shocking just to think of it. There on the old sofa, in a variety of different positions, she, the married woman, did a number of things for the first time in her life. There were times when she became confused. Then she would look at him and see he was invulnerable to its filthiness. This set her mind at ease.

*

Hours later, they lay side by side on the rug in front of the fireplace. She was already finding it easier to drink the pinot noir. Do you have a photo album? she asked. I want to get to know you. The night was far from over, and she was determined to lay claim to all of it, down to the tiniest morsel. Which is why she lay with her legs spread apart as they went through the jumbled pile of photographs, so he would be able to reach everywhere. Mozie on a tractor, a girl behind him. Frank attacking a tree with a huge chainsaw. Frank shearing a sheep – 'Trying to shear a sheep,' he said.

'Yes,' she teased, 'shearing sheep is for real men.'

'Well, damn…' Before she knew what was happening, he jumped up and put her in a hold for a shearing demonstration. She yelped, thrashed about and fought back, didn't give up easily, but couldn't escape from his grip – he was strong as an ox – and his other hand moved rapidly over her body, that's how a real man does it, he growled, here, and here, in one skilled sweep of the shears, you can feel that, can't you, and then you go on, and you shear here, and then there, well, the sheep doesn't like that, what does a sheep know, but the sheep has nothing to say about it, you can feel that, can't you, and his hand moved over her entire body, also over places where you might wonder if sheep had any wool. And the sheep convulsed with laughter, squirmed and fought, fell in love with the shearer and after a time had to admit that here was a real man, say it again – no, really, a *real* man – I didn't hear you – a *real, real* man! – oh, that's what I thought, too.

When they settled down again, they assumed their original positions. Ada picked up another picture. Frank along with two other men, all of them on horseback, a paddock with sheep in the background. And a girl leaning against the fence and looking up at the men. 'That's me,' Frank indicated, 'that's the shepherd, and that's William.'

'And who's this?'

'That's his daughter.'

'William's daughter.'

'Yes.'

'Nice daughter?'

All of the photographs had been taken in New Zealand. Frank fishing on the ocean with Maori people. She saw a pioneer who enjoyed what he was doing. There were girls in almost all of the photos. Sitting on a log, leaning against a gate, one hip angled forward, one leg crossed over the other, sometimes dark-haired, sometimes fair, sometimes Maori, in the foreground, in the background, arm in arm with Frank, next to him on a bench, or wearing sunglasses, at a picnic.

He saw her looking. 'Sick aunts, all of them,' he said, and put his hand between her legs to distract her; she leaned her forehead against the photographs and slid back into the warm hay, and when desire became too strong she pushed her hips against his and their bodies came together of their own accord, surrendering completely, melting and dissolving, and when they finally returned to their solid shapes it was time to add more wood to the fire, and he put on another record.

They lay breathing with their noses pressed together.

'All those girls,' she said softly. He blew on her short hair.

'Yes… but… not the right one. Not yet.'

In the back of his eyes was a dark garden, a labyrinth, a place so secret she didn't dare tell him she would have liked to have seen his pictures from the past. She had something to do with that garden. The music had something to do with it as well. Trumpet and saxophone lifted their legs up high as they waded through a bog of bass, drums, and piano. '*Kind of Blue*,' said Frank in her ear. 'Miles Davis.' She wanted to repeat it to herself, so that when she went back to her own life in a little while she wouldn't forget it, but suddenly she could imagine no other life than this one.

*

He leaned on one elbow and studied her buttocks. It was quite well possible there were spots on them, or other blemishes, but she was feeling too relaxed to be concerned about this. There was a single mirror in the bunker, over the washbasin. She hadn't seen herself from the back for ten years. Her eyes turned inwards so that she was looking cross-eyed beneath her closed eyelids. He kneaded softly and caressed her, looked at her, while she dozed off in the warmth of the fireplace, intensely happy, in the delicious smell of fire and wine and sex and sweat. By now she had faith that he would greet every blemish that belonged to her with the same affectionate regard. You have the most beautiful bum, he said. Then he asked what those two spots were.

'What kind of spots?'

'On both of your cheeks there's a spot that's a little darker than the rest, and a little rougher,' he said.

'Why is that?'

'I have no idea. Are they ugly? Is it bad?' She pushed herself up and turned around, tried to look at her own backside.

'No,' he said, 'but I'm curious what they are.' She couldn't see a thing, her eyes so tired they wouldn't focus.

'I really have no idea,' she murmured and lay back down on the rug, put her heavy head onto her arms, and floated off in wanton contentment. He suddenly pressed his thumb and index finger firmly near the bottom of her buttocks. 'My bicycle seat!' she cried, and burst out laughing, peals of laughter that she recognized from long ago. He studied her laughter intently as well.

*

Dawn came in the end, of course, creeping up in stockinged feet, an uninvited guest who apologizes beforehand but enters all the same. They woke up shivering, the fire had gone out completely, and Frank fried bacon and eggs which they washed down with tea. They closed the curtains in the bedroom so it could be night for a little while longer, and rubbed each other warm under the blankets. Her bus would be leaving in an hour and a half.

22

IN THE EVENING, SHE WOULD make up her mind to leave the following day. She studied the bus schedule, learned the train times by heart, and knew when the ferry left. But every time she would stay. Both her legs and her willpower were paralysed by love.

*

She woke up late, she could sleep as long as she wanted, and would wake to find the spot next to hers empty. During the morning, he and Mozie worked for farmers around the area. In the emptiness of the bed she would be assailed by thoughts of home, her sad yearning for the children, the fear that Derk would come after her and by doing so, spoil everything. No, she thought, he won't do that, because then he would have to leave the children with someone, and he wouldn't be able to keep the scandal a secret. No, he certainly wouldn't do that. She would make feverish calculations inside her head, going back and forth until she was sure she could safely stay for one more day. Then she would jump out of bed and make tea, giving her inner head a good shake. In the hours that followed she would sit on the porch, reading a book and basking in the warmth. She read a few books one right after the other, in English, no longer willing to settle for her poor command of the language. Here's a dictionary, said Frank, if you see a word you don't know, look it up, at least that's what I always do. The books were too difficult for her even if she did look up words, but she continued to read hungrily. It was all going to be different.

When the men came back, they sat outside and ate the lunch she'd prepared. And as if they could sense that her hours spent alone had been filled with peril, they would try to outdo each other to make her laugh. They took her along with them into the fields and explained about growing grapes. Then they would work for a few hours on their own land. If she felt like it she would help, and the three of them would pull white bird netting over the vines, and Mozie would show her how to take care of the wound to the grapevine after grafting. Or she would go back to her reading. But she couldn't concentrate with Frank around, and her eyes would keep straying over to the fields if he was working there, or to the tractor if he was on it. He was without a doubt the most handsome man on earth. She couldn't imagine a more handsome man. A large, big-boned man with an ambling gait. His body firm and inviting. It seemed as if he'd grown; in her memory he'd appeared cold and thin. New Zealand had nourished him, and made him stronger. Every movement, every look, the way he stood, walked, sat, and lay, everything filled her with desire, a desire that made her sad because her longing was greater than what was actually possible, and went further than these few days. Every cell in her body pointed in his direction, like a compass, quivering and sighing. Please let this pass, because I'll be walking next to Derk before long and I'll stumble.

After he came back from the fields at the end of the afternoon they would first sleep and then make love under the open windows, wild with desire. Then, with the same care and attention with which he bent and trained the shoots on the grapevines in the fields during the day, he would spread her legs in bed and explore every inch of her body, touching her everywhere, and going on until she turned inside out and begged… He saw everything, described and praised it, used his earlier words along with many more, and all of these words licked and tickled her, he licked her body and her soul until they expanded from within and assumed their

333

true and finest form. So this is how love works, she thought, and she did the same to him. She delighted in looking for ways to excite him and followed her own old fantasies in this, eagerly making them come true. With her body draped in yards of white bird netting, she danced a veil dance for him. If she assumed certain positions as she moved slowly in front of the large mirror – he had to watch this from the bed and wasn't allowed to take any action – she could manipulate him like a marionette. 'Oh woman, don't do this to me,' he said hoarsely. Sometimes they dispensed with all of this and he would pull her to him straight away. There was an animal side to all this as well. She discovered things could get rough there in the hayloft, and that this was love too. When they reached the point that neither of them knew front from back, they would stumble to the bath like two exhausted marathon runners. They would stay there for a long time, looking at each other without speaking. She was sick with love. I want to have him. I want to be him.

I want to know who he is. In the intimacy of the warm steamy room, all of the layers peeled away, she plucked up her courage. What happened to your father, she asked, and to your sister, and to your mother? He immediately moved away from her, sat up. What's the point, he growled, it has nothing to do with anything. But she wouldn't be put off, and asked specific questions. What happened to you and your family?

'My father...' he said after a time. 'We had a camp guard, he was a sadist. He wasn't even Japanese – he was Korean. One day he closed the latrines. Everyone had dysentery. My father died in his own filth. Skin and bones. I didn't dare touch him for fear I'd get sick.'

Then he fell silent, as if the subject was now closed. His eyes were hard and forbidding. She went on. 'How old were you then?'

'Sixteen,' he said. 'And I got sick, too, so I escaped from being sent to work on the Burma Railway.' He splashed water onto his face.

'But you survived,' she said. 'And your sister and your mother, where were they?'

'In the women's camp,' he said reluctantly. 'But we didn't know that.

334

No-one knew where their families were, or who was still alive. My aunt told me the story later on. My mother never spoke to me about it. My sister was frail, a delicate little girl, and my mother managed to keep her alive by secretly trading some of her belongings for food, with villagers, through the fence. This was strictly forbidden. One day the guard caught her at it. She was flogged publicly and put into a bamboo cage she couldn't stand up in, and was put on display for seven days in the roll-call yard, wearing just her underwear. Under the burning sun, with a shaved head. In the meantime my sister died of meningitis.'

Ada trickled water over his knees and listened. With the help of the Allies, he and his mother were reunited in Singapore harbour after the war ended. They travelled back to Holland together on the big ship. But she had changed. His sweet, beautiful mother was gone.

'She had turned away from people,' he said flatly. In Holland they went to live with her parents, his grandparents. She passed her days in that big house sitting at the desk that now stood here. She was neatly dressed, but otherwise completely passive. 'Did she still play the piano?' Ada asked. 'My mother?' he asked in surprise. 'She never played the piano in her life. She rode her motorcycle, a lot of young women in the East Indies did. And once she'd been in Holland for a while, she picked it up again. She bought an old motorcycle that was far too heavy for her and would go off on long rides. But the Dutch winters are too cold. Sometimes when she came home she was nearly frozen. She would never say where she'd been. Then she would return to her sitting and staring again. Everyone tried to talk to her, tried to make her see that she should spend more time with her child, that after all he was still alive, and needed her, and she would smile sympathetically, but nothing would change.'

'And you?' asked Ada.

He made a half-hearted gesture. 'The usual, I finished secondary school and then went to the Colonial School of Agriculture in Deventer, with the intention of going back to the East Indies as soon as I could. Which was no longer the East Indies. And when that was no longer an option...'

'Yes, I know,' she interrupted. 'I meant something else.'

He was silent.

She could see his muscles tighten and turn stiff and cold, even though the water was warm.

'I wanted to make her happy,' he said. 'I really tried. I was the most attentive son there ever was. If she wouldn't eat, I'd stay at the table and joke with her until I managed to get her to take a couple of bites. We tiptoed through that house, my grandparents and I, we did everything we could. We brought her flowers. Even though I was seventeen, eighteen years old, every day I'd cycle home right after school so she wouldn't be sitting there on her own. And then I'd talk to her, and tell her funny stories I often made up on the spot, because not all that many nice things happened in my life. One day she didn't come down to breakfast. She would still get dressed, but she'd sit on the edge of her bed for the rest of the day, like a statue of a dreamy-eyed woman.'

He fell silent. She waited.

'And you?' she asked after a time.

'I got fed up with it,' he said angrily. 'She didn't even come to my graduation.'

He went to live with his aunt and uncle in Deventer, and he visited her less and less. And then came a bitterly cold winter. The temperatures dropped below freezing. Everyone told her she shouldn't go riding, but she did it anyway.

'I think riding her motorcycle made her feel better,' he said.

He rubbed his jaw, looked at the shaving things that stood on the washbasin.

'What happened?' asked Ada.

He sniffed, slid down into the water and leaned his head against the edge of the bath, looked out from half-closed eyes into another time. For the first time she saw how tired he was. She wondered if he always slept so little. She put her hands around his calves under the water, and gently stroked the hair on his legs.

'They found her in a lake, the Naardermeer. She'd driven onto the ice. A walker had seen it happen. Deliberately, he told the police, she'd deliberately driven onto the lake, at a terrifying speed. She slid for miles, then the man heard long cracks shoot through the ice and she sank into the depths, motorcycle and all.'

He slid down deeper into the water and blew cheerful bubbles with his mouth, plop, plop, plop. It surprised her. Then he slid back up slightly, his eyes squeezed shut because water had got into them. 'They dragged the lake for her body for a long time. I was called home from Deventer; I had to identify her. She was wearing one of my father's cardigans under her motorcycle suit, from before we went to the East Indies.' He pushed the wet hair out of his face. Lifted his eyes and looked right at her.

'Then I was free.'

We've all come here wounded. He splashed water at her. 'It was a long time ago, Ada,' he cautioned.

The water was getting cold. She leaned forward to pull the plug from the drain.

*

In the evening he would play records for her, telling her the names of musicians and why he was so fond of this book or that, and it was like she was electrified, she never got tired, and as he talked he would prepare dishes with herbs and spices she'd never heard of, and ask questions about her life, and listen closely to her answers. 'You're very rich,' he said. 'You're never bored, and you have a body that can make a man happy.' Feeling proud and strong, she walked over to the record player and picked out the next record, John Coltrane, *A Love Supreme*, she'd never heard of it, was curious, she was filled with boundless energy, ready to revitalize her own life, to inject it with currents of culture, a zest for life, happiness. What was happening to her here was wonderful and couldn't have anything to do with sin, on the contrary, it was a kind of energy that would work miracles, look at her, she was covering herself with new skin made from a modern and free kind of fabric.

She asked him why he was against religion. 'You're wrong,' he said. 'I have nothing against religion. It's wonderful if people find comfort in it, and that's something everyone has to decide for themselves. But what I don't understand is the claim to absolute truth. God created the earth in seven days. Mary had an immaculate conception and Jesus rose from the dead and if I don't believe this, all hell will break loose.'

She thought about this. All right then, you don't have to believe it. But it almost has to be true. Because otherwise how can you explain, how can you explain.

'What cannot be explained,' he said, 'is still unknown. It's something we don't understand yet. Maybe later. Nowadays we know more than we did a thousand years ago, and in a thousand years we'll know more than we do now. Knowledge is always expanding. I don't have a problem with not knowing something. I do have a problem with embracing an unprovable theory that was invented by humans and dictates to us how we have to live our lives. So that we're caught in an impossible bind if we fail.'

Then he took the steaming casserole dish from the oven and gave her a cheerful wink.

'Don't you believe in a soul, then?'

'Soul, spirit, consciousness, the thing that separates us from animals, yes I do.'

'But what do you think happens to this after we die?'

'I have no idea what happens after death,' he said. 'No-one does. I don't think anything happens, or we'd certainly have some kind of indication of it by now. Dead is dead. But... I like surprises.' She looked at the self-assured way he carried himself, the calm that emanated from everything he did, and saw that he didn't need anyone – she started, making a sudden movement because she was falling down into the depths, like just before dropping off to sleep. For a second she wondered if he would reach out his hands to her if she really did fall, and her heart leapt into

338

her mouth. He was carving the leg of lamb and didn't notice. Then it passed.

He arranged the meat on a serving dish. She was going to do that, too, once she was home. No more pans on the table. She said: 'But wouldn't life be meaningless if there is no hereafter, no heavenly kingdom, no reward?'

'On the contrary,' he said. 'That makes this life even more precious.'

She sat with her beautiful bum on the counter, dangling her legs, and told him about her fear of damnation, she with her tendency towards wickedness, and as she spoke and saw the reaction on his face, it also struck her as odd, because sitting there was so enjoyable and she felt like such a good and friendly person. Anyway, it was true. And she was at it again, she was an adulteress, and so she was caught in an impossible bind, and it was easy for him to talk because it wasn't his bind.

Later that evening, he said: 'Don't fall for it, Ada, deep down inside you know perfectly well what you want – it's important that you listen to this.'

She wondered if what he meant was that she would be better off staying with him. But he didn't say it.

He didn't beg her or cling to her in desperation. One time he came right out and said he would love it if she stayed, and for a moment her thoughts circled around this possibility, but right away pitch-black words came looming up: words like 'divorced woman' and 'mother who abandons her children'. It was completely out of the question.

*

Every night they would reverse the order, first make love, then sleep. He read pornographic poems to her in English, she couldn't believe she was actually listening to them, let alone that she was finding them so arousing, but a short time later they acted out the poem, holding their breath and looking at each other, it *was* possible, it *did* work, and she then had to admit she was also an eager audience for these kinds of bad books. He ran a long cord into the bedroom and put the record player next to the bed. As the music played, he whispered stories in her ear, about encounters between strangers in hot sand, stories that started off slowly and always ended the same way. Ada, the child who loved fairy tales, was finally where she belonged, in the arms of this mythical figure. Tomorrow, she murmured as she dropped off to sleep, her beautiful bum up against his hips, I'll leave tomorrow.

*

She would invariably wake up in the dead of night because Danny was crying for her. Mum! he would sob in high-pitched wails, nearly drowning in his own tears, his nose running furiously, because Derk wouldn't give him his raggie, you're too big for that now, and she wasn't there to secretly slip him the dirty piece of cloth, which contained all of the smells that calmed him down. Give him his raggie, she pleaded, please, please, and her tears fell quietly onto the pillow.

*

Every day it became more likely that Derk would show up. No, she told herself, he won't do it, he's too proud. And too afraid. But it was impossible to push away the pain she felt when she thought of the children. Her longing for them was accompanied by thoughts of the bunker and her marriage and her approaching departure, and then she would do her best to suppress them, because she didn't want to mix the one with the other, she wanted to squeeze all she could out of these days, to the very last drop, to the very last second. She had her story ready, she wanted to get it right, about the hotel in Christchurch, she'd made up the details of the interior – when you come in, the breakfast room for the guests is the first right after the door with the stained glass, you can smell the bacon and eggs from the hall, and on the left is the sitting area with the sagging old leather sofa, next to the telephone – anyway, we don't have a phone at home or I would have called, and later, if she were ever to find herself in Christchurch with Derk she would say she couldn't find the hotel any more, that she'd forgotten where it was. Coming up with a story for God would be trickier. But because He was all-seeing, He would also realize that this week was for everyone's good, that their lives would improve drastically after this. It almost made sense, except that it would have been better if this week had been a great personal sacrifice. She would just have to give it some more thought. Not now.

*

If she'd had enough of reading and Frank wasn't back yet, she would go skipping through the vineyard, not yet thirty years old, barefoot, wearing nothing under her dress because everything was in the wash. The sun shone through the colourful stripes on her dress and she remembered being under her mother's skirt as a toddler and how she'd seen a colourful circus tent, and the slap that followed, and felt herself to be a better mother, a better person even. But if Frank stayed away for a long time it became harder and harder to skip. Sometimes she would catch herself in the act and it would suddenly become ridiculous. I'm acting carefree, but I'm not. Then fear would steal up on her, the fear she wouldn't be able to take this week with her into the rest of her life, and that all the drudgery and all that grim cycling against the wind would get the better of her, and then her mother would descend upon her, silent, her thin lips pinched, fretting as she cooked and cleaned and scrubbed her way through life. Sighs and reproaches, a bitter, impoverished life, not just from lack of money but because your mind was too small; then fear would pounce onto her shoulders and weigh her down and put an end to her skipping, because, she thought with her head bowed, I'm like that, too. What I want to do, I'm not able to do. My arms are too short. It's wrong, it's not done, and I don't dare.

*

One night he borrowed Mozie's motorcycle and they rode through the mild evening towards a lake to go swimming. She put her arms around him and looked over his shoulder at his hand on the throttle, the broad

341

wrist, the veins meandering over the back of his hand, and wanted to die, really die, didn't want to keep on living after this.

*

And then the final evening arrived. The week had been stretched to the limit, and she couldn't justify staying away any longer. She'd told him early that morning. He said nothing and went on getting dressed, it was like he ignored it because he assumed it wasn't true. The rest of the day carried on in the same way. But now, here in the shed, tears burned at the back of her eyes. He removed the plug from the oak cask. Mozie handed him a long pipette. Concentrating intently, Frank plunged the pipette down into the cask, which had taken on the colour of the wine. The shed was filled with a sacred silence. Ada, who couldn't understand what they were doing here when every minute counted, tried to show interest and ignore the terrible sadness that was stealing over her. The pipette filled with clear red liquid. Frank lifted it high into the air, and an arc of droplets flew onto her striped dress. He apologized, but she shrugged it off. 'He washed his garments in wine,' she said, 'and his clothes in the blood of grapes.' And when she saw the surprised look on his face, she added casually: 'Genesis 49, verse 11,' but it broke her heart, because for a moment there they'd been strangers and she realized how everything could just disappear.

Mozie held up a glass, and Frank carefully allowed some of the wine to drain into it. Holding the glass by the bottom of the stem, Mozie lifted it towards the light, looked at the liquid, murmured approvingly, and swirled the wine gently to and fro. Then he put his nose over the glass and sniffed. Next, he took a small sip. She caught something of the excitement. Frank came and stood next to her and put his arm around her hips. Although Mozie was present, she pressed herself up against him. Mozie pursed his lips, sucked in a little air, moved the wine around in his mouth – he made chewing motions, as if you could chew on wine – then swallowed the wine and opened his mouth. Let the silence last, the tension mount. Next to her, for the first time – for the first time! – she felt Frank tense with inner impatience, and she realized she was witnessing an important moment in his life, and that this would form a bond between them that would last for ever.

Mozie said nothing. He wore a poker face as he put his own glass down on the table and picked up a second, clean one. Frank let go of her and allowed some of the wine from the pipette to drain into this glass. Why don't they say something? This one was for him, and the entire procedure repeated itself. She saw the concentration on his face, the rapt attention, his senses focused on the wine in the front of his mouth. I'm jealous of everything now. And then she knew. It was his attention. It was the way he looked at her, so that she felt seen, and loved. He sees who I really am, with my suitcase full of different roles. And all at once she was insanely jealous of everyone and everything in his life that would receive the same kind of attention from him. Yes, she sneered, if I was left to my own devices his attention would be mine and mine alone from now on. Maybe I need a lot of attention. Or I'm not used to getting much attention. Derk looked away in embarrassment if you looked straight at him. And the hard truth was, she had her own failings in this regard. It was nice to have fantasies, but you could safely say that wherever she was, she was only half there, and that her thoughts were only half (and often not even that) on the things she was doing or the people she was with. That had to change as well. She stood up straight and concentrated on the wine tasting, but something sad made her wilt again before too long.

He swallowed the wine. Opened his mouth, let in air. He leaned his head back as if trying to hear something in the distance. Then his eyes opened wide. Mozie started to laugh, yes, mate. The wine was good. We're in business, mate! But it was more than that, she saw their joy increase with every passing second, saw it sink in drop by drop, that their dream had seen the light of day. She saw them light up as well. Deep down inside she withdrew into the dark; that's how it goes, the light goes out here and somewhere else it goes on. The friends shook each other's hands. They took turns hugging and kissing her, and filled three glasses and then lifted

343

their glasses and made a toast to the wine. We don't have a name yet, Mozie cried. To the wine without a name. She took a sip, tasted the difference between this wine and the one they'd been drinking up till now, and shared in their joy. The wine was outstanding, the wine was ready to go out into the world, the winery was born. Without her. She smoothed the skirt of her dress defiantly, under no circumstances did she want to be sad now. The wine had left three purple stains on the stripes. These stains would travel with her and would soon be all she had left of him. She hoped they wouldn't wash out, and saw herself sitting across from Derk at the table, trying to find the stains with her fingers beneath the Formica so she could hold on to something that mustn't be lost. He washed his garments in wine, and his clothes in the blood of grapes. 'Druivebloed,' she said out loud, in Dutch. They looked at her in surprise. 'That's what you should call it,' she said. 'The wine.'

It was quiet for a time.

'What?' asked Mozie, mystified.

'Blood of grapes,' Frank translated. She was embarrassed already.

*

There was no way she could possibly get out of the festivities so she didn't even try. She drank and danced and sang along with them. While they were still bottling the wine and Frank was busily chalking the name onto all of the casks, Mozie dug a hole in the yard and prepared a *hangi* on hot stones. And when darkness fell and all three of them were tipsy from drinking as they bottled the wine, they lay next to the fire, eating the hangi, the vegetables, the sweet potatoes, the wonderful lamb wrapped in leaves. And everything was drenched in the wine, their wine, because they just couldn't get enough of it. 'Droo-vi-blued...?' Mozie kept shouting. At this moment, the fact that she was going home tomorrow could not be allowed to intrude. No-one mentioned it, so she didn't either, you don't want to spoil things on a night like this. She drank along with the men like a Templar from the Bible. Together with Frank she tried to teach Mozie a

Dutch children's song and she broke down into fits of laughter at the way he pronounced the words. She ran inside and cried her eyes out in the bathroom.

They became boys again there around the fire, a boyish circle she wasn't a part of, sharing memories of people she didn't know, and they didn't tire of their own stories, and she lay just outside the circle and waited. This was her last night.

*

Frank lugged his record player and a long cord outside to the yard, and the three of them danced the latest dance next to the fire, *come on let's twist again...* she threw caution to the wind and lost sight of everything she'd learned, and even though Mozie was there she dared to fall against Frank and lose herself in an embrace. She didn't give herself the time to be embarrassed when Mozie commented on this in a loud voice and played a funny musical accompaniment on his banjo as they kissed. The menacing cloud of imminent departure loomed, and to keep this at bay she became more and more reckless, laughing as she took another drink of the wine she'd named so Frank would always remember her. She licked her lips, stamped her bare feet on the ground next to the fire, lifted the skirt of her dress and danced, aware she was being watched by the two men circling around her. Out of the corner of her eye, she saw that Mozie was envious of Frank because of her, saw Frank looking at her like he owned her, whirled the skirt of her dress more wildly about her legs and thought: this will have to last me the rest of my life. She danced towards him provocatively, extending her arms to entice him, hips gyrating and breasts bouncing, shamelessly, come to me my love, come. Beads of sweat flew into her eyes. Everything changed shape. Their foreheads sprouted bumps. On cloven hooves, they danced with wild abandon beneath the full moon, their tails lifted, panting and laughing, the rumpled sheets still to come in their eyes, while Mozie stirred up the fire and the sparks flew up around their ears.

No-one heard the taxi drive up. It turned into the yard from out of the fields and threw its light out over them like a net. They stood there blinded, momentarily at a loss; Frank put his arm around her shoulders and they breathed heavily as they waited together for the person who was going to get out of the car. A trickle of sweat ran down between her breasts and she wiped it away with her finger. The dress clung to her legs. Mozie turned off the music, dragging the needle back over the record with an awful screech. Ada squinted. The music still throbbed inside her head. For a moment she hoped a stranger would emerge and then she knew she'd done something terribly wrong, in contrast to what she'd been telling herself all week. Frank started to move in the direction of the car. Just then the door on the passenger side opened and she recognized the angry shape. She reached out to Frank and pulled him back sharply.

*

Let us walk honestly, as in the day; not in rioting and drunkenness, not in chambering and wantonness, not in strife and envying.

*

'You'll have to answer to God for what you've done,' said Derk. 'I came to bring you back.'

He was surrounded by hosts of wrathful angels brandishing fiery swords. She was naked to the bone and forever unmasked. Still, alongside the disgust, she could also see loss in his eyes. He ignored Frank and Mozie, as if they weren't standing right next to her. Behind him, the taxi backed a short distance away, almost discreetly, sorry folks, this doesn't concern me, I'll just wait over here. It sat idling at the edge of the yard, the rumbling of the engine providing an ominous accompaniment to the scene.

She greeted her husband timidly and was overcome with pity for both of them. He had no idea how stupid it had been to come after her, how by doing so he'd ruined everything. He didn't return her greeting. The only thing open to her now was to repent her sins until the end of time with no hope of forgiveness. There would be no jazz, no veil dances. The windows would stay forever closed. 'Running away from your family is an act of the Devil,' he said.

Next to her, Frank crossed his arms in front of his chest and breathed deeply. 'I came to get you, for the children,' said Derk. 'There's no forgiveness for you. In the eyes of God, the sin remains. Don't you forget it.'

'That's criminal,' said Frank.

She saw the fury erupt inside Derk's slender body and slam into the walls on all sides. But he controlled himself and continued to ignore Frank. 'You should be thankful I'm willing to take you back,' he told her. It suddenly occurred to her he'd got this from the pastor, she should be thankful you're willing to take her back, maybe even practised saying it on the way here. But she knew he wouldn't make it without her, and that he knew it, too.

Frank swore under his breath and walked towards him. 'If God can't forgive her,' he said when he was close to Derk, 'then there's something wrong with that God of yours.' For the tiniest possible fraction of a second she found herself thinking the same thing, and realized that something had indeed changed this week, even though it was not yet clear what that was. Then it was gone, and her legs were trembling because she saw Derk's iron punch slice through the air between the two men. Frank staggered back.

'What the hell,' he said, dumbfounded, and touched his jaw.

Derk was smaller than Frank and not as strong, but he was at least as stubborn. Moreover, he had God on his side. They fought furiously, and their powerful blows hit home. Ada screamed and tried to run over to them, but Mozie pulled her back – leave them alone – she beat her fists against her thighs uselessly, over and over, stop! don't! In the meantime the cowardly taxi kept creeping back, away from the spectacle.

Frank kicked Derk so hard he wasn't able to get up immediately, and abruptly turned his back on him. She shouted his name, but he didn't look at her, wiped the blood from his face, or at least tried to. Then she fell silent, because she detected an icy rage in that movement. Behind him, Derk scrambled to his feet and limped off, towards the taxi. He kept looking back, stumbled, got up again, limped on. When he reached the taxi, he turned around. He coughed, and his chest heaved up and down. Out of breath, he made a few helpless gestures, sweeping his arm through the air, to make it clear to her she should come to him, now. Now. Now.

But she couldn't keep her eyes off Frank, who was still rubbing his forehead with the back of his hand, as if by doing so he could keep something awful from happening. In the yard around him, winter set in.

'Ada!'

She turned her eyes towards her husband, but couldn't make out a thing. He must have realized that his gestures were useless, that she hadn't moved, that she wasn't coming over to him, because he let his arm drop in confusion.

That was the deciding moment.

His arm shot up and he stabbed a finger into the air, pointed at her, his face twisted helplessly, and he shouted: 'If you don't come home…' He coughed, straining his thin voice. 'If you don't come home, you'll never see the children again!'

She sank down into the darkness, into a windowless cellar. In the distance, Frank turned sharply and ran to the tree he'd been leaning against when she'd arrived in this yard, in another life. He grabbed the gun. The ice cracked beneath his feet and long fissures spread rapidly to where she stood.

'Then it's my duty…' – Derk was still shouting, she was sorry she was making him shout, that he had to stand there looking like that, with his face all bloody – '… then it's my duty to God to keep you away from the children!'

348

Go to him, murmured someone in the cellar, go with him.

Mozie still had his arms firmly around her. But that wasn't it. Her brain wasn't transmitting any impulses, somewhere a barricade had gone up in the space between thinking and doing. She watched numbly how one man cocked his gun and the other dragged himself towards the reversing taxi as fast as he could, and nothing registered with her. This is how numb you can be as you witness one person trying to kill another.

It looked clumsy, almost childish. Derk, hobbling and hurrying, tugging at the car door. The taxi, which just kept backing up. Frank, who ran several feet in the direction of the taxi and then stopped in the middle of the yard and took aim. Even the shots sounded more like dull, dry pops than like the echoing gunfire of a hero in a film. Moreover, in the film you knew for certain that killing the villain was a good deed.

The car door swung open. Derk fell back and lost his balance, but he didn't let go and managed to drag himself around the door and worm his way into the car. A shoe slipped off his foot and rolled over the sandy ground, the left one of the pair they'd bought together at Hannahs, his brown Sunday shoes. He wore his good shoes to come and get me. A bullet ricocheted off the taxi, a dry, hard pop. Derk shut the door with all his might, his survival instinct focusing on keeping it shut, everything else having become unimportant, and she could imagine the strength in his fingers, and how his fingernails dug into his flesh, breaking the skin without him feeling it. Then the taxi stopped abruptly, the driver shifted gears, stepped on the accelerator, and the car squealed forward, right at Frank, who jumped back, then made a sharp U-turn in the yard, making sand and clumps of grass fly into the air. A stone or a bullet shattered the rear window, and the car sped off the premises. Ada saw the deep track in the ground and also how Frank jumped over this and ran after the taxi with his gun at the ready, how he finally stopped and emptied the entire magazine in the direction of the fading sound of the car that had already left them far behind. And when there were no more bullets left, he remained in the same position, frozen, and only after a long time had passed did he lower his gun. And Mozie lowered his arms, but not one of the three moved; they stood there like statues, caught off guard by the polar night, and sleet rained down upon the yard.

*

She leaned against the wall in the dark. Neither of them spoke. Frank sat frozen on the edge of the sofa and looked at something she couldn't see. Mozie had gone to his caravan. They'd spoken in whispers, crouched next to what remained of the smouldering fire: should they wait to see if the police would come, had Derk been hit, was he wounded, or had Frank missed? Do you think he was trying to kill him? she asked with a shudder. If he'd wanted to kill him, said Mozie, your husband would be dead. He shoots birds in flight out of the sky. It must have taken a lot of self-control for him to miss. What's wrong with him? she continued in a whisper. I don't know, said Mozie, and he shrugged his shoulders, I really don't know. We don't talk about things like that. When the last log collapsed into cold ash and the police hadn't shown up and Derk hadn't come back either, he left her with Frank. She used a wet tea towel to carefully dab at his battered face, saying nothing, because her words wouldn't reach him through that thick wall of ice. Then she leaned against the wall in the dark and was silent for a long time. When she got stiff she moved away from the wall and turned on the tap to fill the bath with hot water.

*

I can't bear it, he said, that man can't make you happy, he put you in the back of a pickup, for years that almost drove me insane. Why, she asked, why for years, what was so terrible, I was a healthy young woman, I'd survive a trip like that, I did survive. He hasn't made you happy, he said. No, she said, but I'm also to blame for that. Stop it! he roared, and shot up out of the bath and collapsed back into it just as forcefully, so that the water splashed into the farthest corners of the bathroom, stop talking about blame; she recoiled in fright with the sponge in her hands, her dress

350

soaked through; he roared like a madman, you're not to blame for any of it, don't fall for it, don't you bloody well fall for it, don't go back there, Ada, you'll be despised by the righteous and treated accordingly, there won't be any forgiveness waiting for you there, tied up with a bow as a homecoming surprise, no, far from it, you'll always be alone in that house, he'll put you in the back of a pickup for the rest of your life and loneliness will force you to live in your head and you'll start to believe him, him and all of those idiots, and you'll end up thinking you don't deserve to be alive.

'And that's what I can't bear,' he added, in a voice that frightened her even more. She went and sat on the edge of the bath and placed her hand on the back of his neck.

*

In bed, beneath the sheets, she guided him gently, carefully inside. Outside the blue hour had begun, that hour in which everything is uniformly lit by the same cold light. His jaw was swelling by the minute and turning purple. 'You look awful,' she said. He laughed painfully and his face went lopsided, which added to the crazy effect. 'Don't,' she said. 'Otherwise I'll have to laugh, too, and we won't be able to continue.' The laughter bubbled up at once. A little while later they tried again; she welcomed him from within, surrounded him, and there was nothing to keep them from coming together.

They were the last people on earth.

He started to move inside her. He got on top – ow – and thrust himself deep inside her with every sentence, in a way she would never forget.

'Who loves you?'

Leaning on his arms, trembling from exhaustion, he used his last bit of strength to push questions inside of her, used his words to push her body back, her head into the pillow. They were rhetorical questions, he was sure of himself. 'You…' she moaned, the only answer possible.

The sheets slid off the bed. She wrapped her legs around him. He pushed, all the while studying her face in a way that was almost clinical, arrogant.

'Who do you love?'

'You...'

'Do you feel me?'

'Yes...'

'Do you love me?'

'Yes...'

'Who loves you?'

'You...'

'Who do you love?'

'You...'

This was repeated, again and again, until they'd reached complete agreement. Afterwards, they lay with their eyes closed, but didn't sleep. Outside, the sun spread the first golden sheets out over the fields. Ada dozed off and thought about how happy he made her and how unhappy she would always be with Derk. As if he could read her thoughts, he said: 'I can't bear it, Ada, I can't bear it,' and she could hear the cracks shooting through the ice, as if he were running towards her and the ice was too thin. Shaken and wide awake, she looked up. He buried his face in his hands. I'll stay with you, she whispered to the raw knuckles.

23

ON SATURDAY MORNING, EXACTLY ONE month after running into
Esther in Wellington, Frank's jeep turned into their street at the appointed time, an ungodly early hour. At the same moment, the last breakfast
plate with the blue trim slipped out of Marjorie's hands. She put the tea
towel down on the counter and stared open-mouthed at the shards strewn
over the tile floor. Now the sugar and creamer set were the only things left
of her father's dishes. They'd lasted ten years; once in a while a tumbler
or bowl would break, but since that Saturday in Wellington she'd broken
something almost every day. The cups and saucers escaped from her
clenched hands. The plates wriggled out from between her clutching
fingers. The serving dishes leapt off the counter as soon as she came into
the kitchen. She straightened up and looked out through the kitchen
window at the garden. The jeep stopped in front of their house. 'Bobby,
darling,' she called out, but it hadn't been necessary, and she heard his
chair scrape back upstairs.

Of course, the dishes had broken in vain. Esther hadn't shown her face
after their meeting, nor would she. They'd made clear agreements back
then. But can you avoid each other in a city like Wellington? It was lucky
they didn't live in the centre and that you had to go quite a way up to get
to Khandallah Village. Marjorie had stayed up there the whole month.

Let her stay away from here, she implored, and bent over to get the

353

dustpan and brush out of the cabinet under the sink. Let her stay away from here. She had repeated this thought dozens of times a day ever since the encounter, and had said it out loud just as many times to Hans, who would then shrug his shoulders. Don't borrow trouble, he'd say, shaking his head, don't let it ruin your life, have a little faith. If you don't think about it, it will just disappear on its own. But she could think of nothing else.

The sound of childish footsteps pounded overhead. A horn honked outside. A door slammed and the pounding moved to the stairs. She'd put an overnight bag next to the front door, with food, his swimming trunks, pyjamas, plastic sandals, a sweater for cool evenings. Inside the sleeping bag was his polar bear Icy (now coal black and with hardly any stuffing), who had been pressed as flat as he could go. They'd had a serious talk last night on the edge of his bed, his worried face lifted towards hers. You know what we'll do, she said, we'll put him all the way at the bottom, and once you're in your sleeping bag and it's dark, you can reach down and get him. Frank won't notice. He gave a sigh of relief. It's not always easy being tough.

The horn honked again. She took off her apron and hurried through the hall to reach the front door at the same time as he did, because that suddenly seemed important. 'Darling,' she said, 'what about *The Lone Ranger*?' Every Saturday he watched his favourite television programme together with his friends. But he jerked open the door impatiently and ran over the porch and down the path. Nothing could compete with a trip to the geysers with Frank. She picked up his bag with an air of resignation and followed him out. The date for the trip had been her idea, because Hans was going trout fishing with Norman this weekend and she would 'finally have some time to herself' as she put it.

What she was planning to do with that time she prudently kept to herself.

For the entire month now, the city had been burning down below. Last night, they'd sat on their bench and looked out at the lights and at the bay, as they often did. Take care you don't let all kinds of vague fears spoil the view, he'd said. Yes, sir, she'd said, you've made that quite clear.

As she walked over the narrow path, held the bag up so it wouldn't catch on her roses, and bumped the white gate open from behind, she wondered yet again whether she would have the nerve to visit Esther. And what she would say if she did. We took an oath, she muttered angrily, as if Esther was right in front of her and challenging this.

Bobby was standing next to the jeep looking crestfallen. There was a woman sitting next to Frank, a blonde woman in a summer dress with colourful stripes. The fact that she didn't recognize her right away was because of the sunglasses and the short hairdo. She crossed the street to the jeep. It seemed as if by walking over she was embarrassing the woman, that she was trying to make herself invisible by nervously twisting a strand of short hair around her finger. Frank got out and walked towards her, good morning, his mouth lopsided and his jaw swollen and purple, and it occurred to her that he'd been in a fight. He took the bag from her and stowed it in the back along with the other things. Meanwhile, she walked over to the woman to introduce herself. She recognized her from the soft squeak. 'Ada…? Is that Ada?'

She was still shy. Her body deceptively voluptuous. The greeting almost a whisper, her eyes cast down behind the dark glasses.

'How are you?'

'Fine.' It was barely audible.

'And how is Derk?'

'He's fine, too.'

'Where is he?'

'At home, with the children.' She had to lean forward to hear the reply and looked from one to the other in search of an explanation.

'Ada was in the neighbourhood,' said Frank. 'Do you know Derk's aunt? She lives somewhere near here. She's sick.' He slid into the driver's seat and she could see that in spite of his cheerfulness he looked tired, with dark circles under his eyes. 'What's her name again, your aunt?' He waited

355

with interest for the answer, but it didn't come, and Ada rocked back and forth in her seat and laughed a soft, squeaky laugh. Marjorie didn't know what to make of it. There was something strange hanging in the air around those two. What an awkward business.

Bobby pointed awestruck at Frank's swollen jaw. 'What happened?' Ah, said Frank, well, he was horsing around a little with Mozie and he had the ball and was running away fast, and suddenly Mozie dove at his legs, but he managed to stay ahead of him and as he was running he looked back to keep an eye on Mozie and ran smack into a tree. 'You know the one,' he said, 'the crooked tree at the edge of the yard.' Bobby nodded, knew exactly which one he meant. Wide eyes. The injuries on his friend's face only added to his godlike status. But Marjorie started to feel uncomfortable. 'Are you going to take Ada to her aunt's?'

'No,' he said. 'Her aunt can do without her for a bit, she's going to keep us company.' Marjorie looked at her child and knew how deeply disappointed he must be. From behind the wheel, Frank leaned towards the boy. 'Don't worry, mate, if she causes any trouble, we'll throw her in a hot spring.' Bobby shrugged his shoulders in a magnanimous gesture and climbed onto the back seat. Frank said he could come and sit between them on the front seat. 'That's all right,' the child answered politely. She could see he was feeling bashful, because the woman was a stranger to him. 'We'll change in a little while,' Frank promised him. 'Then you can sit up front.'

Ada motioned towards the house. A profusion of pale pink roses hanging down over the white fence. 'What a nice neighbourhood,' she said softly, 'and what a beautiful house you have.' Again the insecure little laugh at the end of the sentence, like a puppy lying down on its back, don't hit me please, my belly is soft. Her accent is awful, thought Marjorie, but she's still a sweetheart. I just hope Frank leaves her alone. She walked around the jeep onto the pavement – wondering anxiously how many tents they had in the back – and leaned towards her son, who was sitting bolt upright on the back seat. 'Have a lovely time, darling,' she said. 'I'll miss you terribly.'

His hair was still wet from the shower and had been neatly combed and parted. She could smell the soap, the innocent sense of anticipation. Kissed him on his cheek and on his neck, kiss, kiss, one more kiss, finding it suddenly impossible to say goodbye. He pushed her away in embarrassment, *Mum*. She stepped back and waved. Frank saluted. She hated him. Said in a friendly tone of voice: 'Shall I tell you how to get to Highway 1 from here?' He started the engine and shook his head. 'That won't be necessary,' he said. 'We're going into town first to pick up Esther.'

Ada said a bashful goodbye. The jeep started to move. Bobby's arm in the air, bye Mum! She grabbed on to the door and ran alongside the jeep as it angled onto the street.

'What do you mean?!'

He stepped on the brakes. Three surprised faces in the jeep. She coughed from the sudden shouting. Shook her head furiously to get rid of the cough.

'Why?!'

The slanty eyebrows crept up slightly. 'She wanted to come along.' His expression cool, more than ever the aristocrat. He didn't like hysterical women. On the back seat, her child's bewildered face. I have to control myself. But she was in too much of a panic, and clutched the rim of the door with both hands.

'Why...? Why does she want to go along?'

Frank shrugged his shoulders in amazement.

'She's never been to Rotorua, either.'

She tried to catch her breath but nearly choked and couldn't say a thing. 'Mum...' said Bobby hesitantly. There was absolutely no way she could let him go. So she walked to the front of the jeep and spread out her arms, forming a steel fence a tank couldn't have got through.

*

Have a little faith. She put her arm firmly around Bobby and waited for the door of the shop to open. She ignored the irritating pounding of her heart. If Esther was at all surprised by her presence, she didn't let it show. She didn't bat an eyelid as she came out of the shop – long and leggy and swinging her hips – in an apple-green summer dress in the latest fashion, straight as an arrow, very simple, but with large showy bracelets on her bare arms and wearing shoes with pointed toes and a lowish narrow heel. Frank gave her a hug and greeted her warmly: 'Yes, that's an appropriate outfit for a hike in a volcanic area.' Whereupon Esther made a turn like a model on a catwalk and in the affected voice of a female presenter said, 'A slim shift dress, very easy, very *Vogue*,' and he burst out laughing, with that crooked jaw of his. Thought that nonsense was funny.

'It's madness to do this right before the show,' Esther went on in her normal voice, 'but I just had to get away for a while!' Nor did she seem to be surprised by Ada's presence. Marjorie looked her straight in the eye when she got in. For a moment she thought she saw a crack appear in the amber, but she might have imagined it. Then the long arms ran their hands through everyone's hair in greeting, causing the heavy ivory bracelets to make a clattering sound that might have embarrassed someone else or prompted them to be more restrained, but not Esther, who plopped down on the back seat, pulled a white raffia sun hat over her curls and started to smoke, with a face that revealed nothing more than that the make-up had been applied even more carefully than usual that morning.

*

Once they were on the highway, it didn't escape Marjorie's attention that from beneath the wide brim of her hat Esther's eyes were glued to the knees of the boy, who sat wedged in between them reading his comic book, leaning slightly away from the strange woman, up against his mother, her arm firmly around him. She held him as close to her as she possibly could, prepared to defend him against any and all dangers, but she could do nothing more than allow herself to be carried off with him in a speeding jeep. And while she racked her brain for new explanations and probabilities, she remained outwardly impassive, watching the countryside rush by, squinting her eyes against the wind and bright sunlight. She'd forgotten her sunglasses in her haste. She wished she could get her feet down onto the ground, that she could stop the wheels from constantly turning. No matter how hard she tried, she couldn't shake the feeling that this was a kidnapping and that she'd got mixed up in it by chance, much to the annoyance of the others. The child was supposed to have been alone. She pressed him even closer to her. 'Mum,' he said without looking up from his comic, squirming free somewhat.

No-one said much. The jeep jolted along State Highway 1 and the noise of the engine, the singing of the tyres on the road, the flapping of the canvas, and the whistling of the wind made conversation difficult. On both sides of the road the countryside was gently rolling and picturesque, with flocks of sheep under trees, wooden churches, and the British flag flying here and there. She had to suppress an urge to cry for help. On the other side of the seat, Esther leaned forward and she dug for a while in the bag at her feet before producing a Peanut Slab. 'Bobby,' she shouted above the wind, 'Do you like chocolate? Otherwise I also brought along a Buzz Bar for you, if you'd rather have that.' He picked the Peanut Slab.

*

Frank kept his word. They took a break, stretched their legs, ate a sandwich, and changed places. Bobby perked up. So, said Frank, we can finally talk man to man. In the back, they sat cramped together uncomfortably, six bare knees in a row, three skirts that had to be defended against the wind. Uneasy hips that couldn't keep their distance. Marjorie had manoeuvred Ada in between Esther and herself. In an attempt to make contact, looking for an ally, she asked about her children, forcing her voice to be heard above the noise, made large gestures. Do you have a picture? Ada took a wrinkled photograph from her bag, a blurry snapshot taken on the beach by an amateur photographer. She saw a girl and two boys (a brief twinge of old jealousy – why everyone else and not me?), they had Dutch faces framed in flaxen hair, and she showered her with compliments. Oh, what adorable little rascals, she cried, I'll bet they keep you busy. She asked about their personalities, their quirks, how they were doing at school, but Ada gave brief, unintelligible answers, and she couldn't keep the conversation going. She found this disquieting. Because she was sure Esther was listening, she threw in some of her own stories of motherhood. 'Well, you know,' she concluded breathlessly, leaning towards the two women and lowering her voice so that it would be drowned out by the sound of the engine and wouldn't reach the front seat, 'it's just as well I'm going along, because although he might act tough during the day, at night in bed he turns into a little boy again if his mum isn't around to tuck him in.' She waited for a response, but Ada leaned back and closed her eyes. Her hands were in her lap and she was squeezing the photo, which wasn't going to make it any less wrinkled. Marjorie had the impression she wasn't feeling well, maybe she was carsick, maybe that was it. Then she gave up. What Esther was thinking remained a mystery; she smoked cigarettes and divulged nothing, but beneath the hat her eyes were still fixed on the front seat and she followed each of the boy's movements intently, as if they might reveal something to her. Marjorie turned away abruptly and stared out at the countryside, which glared back at her. A river cascaded at the bottom of a gorge next to the road, right alongside a jagged ridge. 'Do you see that?' Frank called back. Of course she could see how spectacular it was. But she struggled with the notion that the silence in the back seat, the conversation that didn't go anywhere, was some kind of conspiracy.

*

The jeep drove on for hours through a vast, desert-like expanse with little variation. Mount Ruapehu loomed up in the distance, the only high mountain on the North Island. In the front seat, everything remotely rugby-related had been discussed at length. Bobby was starting to get bored, she recognized the signs. It's not easy to keep a child happy for six hours in a car. 'Darling,' she called out above the wind and the engine, and she was nearly screaming as she launched into a song by Harry Belafonte.

360

He turned towards her and sang along enthusiastically and out of tune. '*Oh, island in the sun...*' It was something they often did, singing together, and he was still enough of a child to enjoy it. They went through their entire repertoire. In the driver's seat, Frank hummed along, '... *mamma look a booboo, they shout, their mother tells them shut up your mouth, that is your daddy, o no, my daddy can't be ugly so...!*'

Everything felt like some kind of demonstration, as if she was looking for approval. But next to her, Ada was still leaning back with her eyes closed, her head vibrating against the hard edge of the seat back from the motion of the jeep, and it seemed to Marjorie she wanted nothing to do with their singing, which could mean she knew everything and utterly disapproved. '*But I'm sad to say I'm on my way, won't be back for many a day...*' Next to Ada, there was a constant twisting of bracelets. The clattering collided with the songs.

*

After the desert, the road wound its way though forested hills, with conifers and streams reminiscent of Switzerland. Then the landscape became more open again. The jolting and shaking of the jeep became almost unbearable. But suddenly an enormous lake appeared against a backdrop of volcanic mountains, Lake Taupo, and the sight affected them like the opening bars of a symphony. They sat up and looked at the water that glistened invitingly and at the white sails tacking in the distance. It was time for a picnic. They got out of the jeep stiffly, glad of the sudden silence and the physical space. Marjorie took off her shoes and felt the reassuring softness of the grass beneath her bare feet. She handed Bobby his swimming trunks. He and Frank changed behind the bushes and ran into the water. It took the women longer; they took turns holding up bath towels for each other while they changed, averting their eyes discreetly. You could get the wrong idea about the nature of their soft laughter and think they were relaxed. Marjorie kept noticing things. Esther had brought along an extra swimsuit for Ada, an old one from her time at the clothing

361

factory. That confirmed her suspicions. There had been phone calls, they'd been in touch. About God knows what. She watched closely how Esther sashayed down to the water in her sculpted swimsuit and waved at the man and the boy. She decided she wouldn't let her be alone with them and that she would stay close to her, even swimming after her to the other side of the lake if she had to, but to her relief, Esther only put one toe in the water, proclaimed it was far too wet, and then applied herself to setting out the picnic things.

Exhausted from wandering among her own suspicions, she went and sat down on the grass some distance away and looked out over the lake, so that you might think she was enjoying watching her child as he swam, without a care in the world. In fact, she was waiting for the moment when Ada would go into the water so she could be alone with Esther. If only her heart wouldn't beat so wildly. But Ada leaned absently against a wooden rowing boat that had been pulled up onto the shore, and moved her feet through the cool water. Esther's old swimsuit was too small for her and caused her breasts to bulge out; once again Marjorie noticed how volup-tuous she appeared, and what a contrast this was to her behaviour. Everything about her was shapely, she couldn't take her eyes off her, and she could see this was also true for the people sitting further along the lake; it was as if the entire lake was holding its breath and watching this woman move her feet back and forth in the water somewhat sadly. She stood there as if she herself was hidden somewhere inside that curvaceous body and was apologizing for it straight off. Forgive me, she seemed to be saying, but I can't help but move along with my breasts, my hips, my bottom. It was as if every move she made caused the air to quiver and as if this spread far and wide so that for miles around men were becoming agitated without knowing why.

Marjorie shaded her eyes with her hand. Frank emerged from the water and went over and stood next to Ada. Her lovely face lit up, and they talked and leaned towards each other and then he suddenly grabbed her and lifted her over his shoulder and walked back into the water. Bold as brass. She could see that Ada was protesting and struggling to get away. Nonetheless, she couldn't help but notice that they seemed to be surrounded by something fluid, something warm and sensual, that his hands were familiar with her hips.

Frank and Ada swam a long way out. She waited for her child with the towel. His skin was covered with goosebumps, his lips were blue, and his teeth were chattering. We went really far, he said proudly. She wrapped the bath towel around him and started to rub vigorously. He was straining at the leash to get back to his pal in the water, and she could feel his confusion about this day, which had gone so differently from how he'd imagined. He didn't want to take off his wet swimming trunks. He also rejected her suggestion to put on his sweater. 'But you're shivering,' she said. He flatly denied this. She planted a kiss on his wet hair. Why was it children never noticed they were cold? Mum, he said, look, over there, a climbing tree. She looked at where he was pointing. The tree seemed very high to her, and she wondered if she should allow it. Then down by the blanket she saw Esther watching them from beneath her sun hat.

*

'I suddenly remembered that time Peggy invited us to a picnic,' Esther said when she got closer. 'She said "bring a plate" and we turned up with two empty dinner plates, remember? How were we to know there was supposed to be food on them?' She sat with an open notebook, or sketch pad, in one hand, and with her other hand she sketched the contours of the landscape with a piece of charcoal.

Marjorie crossed her arms. 'What are you planning to do?' she said. 'What did you have in mind?' Esther was unfazed and continued to draw with long, artistic strokes.

'Nothing,' she replied. 'See Rotorua.'

'I'm not stupid.'

'Would you light a cigarette for me, please?' Hands smeared with charcoal were lifted gracefully into the air. Marjorie looked in the large bag.

Esther said she could have one, too, but she refused, said she no longer smoked, that it was bad for you and that she didn't miss it. She rummaged angrily in the bag. Some people. *She* had spent the whole of yesterday in the kitchen. She'd baked two cakes and a whole pile of scones, and two different kinds of pies, cold veal, and meat loaf they could cut into slices and eat cold, had made cranberry sauce to go with it and poured it into a jam jar, had boiled eggs, vegetables, and potatoes for the salads and had made her own mayonnaise, which had failed twice in a row because she'd been impatient and had added the oil too quickly. Worked herself to a frazzle, had stood on her feet too long. In Esther's bag there were only sweets, cigarettes, and a bottle of bourbon. Esther took the cigarette between her extended fingers, inhaled deeply, and slowly blew out the smoke. 'We accidentally happen to live in the same city,' she said. 'Am I not allowed to know who he's become?'

'Why? Why do you have to know?'

Esther slowly put down her notebook and stretched her long body out on the grass. She leaned on one elbow and looked out over the lake, where in the distance, two dark specks swam towards each other over the sparkling surface and formed a single speck. Then she asked, 'Have you ever wondered how it was for me?' Marjorie thought back to the motionless figure they'd left behind on the sofa in the atelier. 'Yes,' she answered truthfully.

'Mum, look!' They both turned round towards the tree. Bobby was almost completely out of sight amidst the dense foliage. She gave him a thumbs-up to let him know how terrific he was. 'Now it's time to come down,' she called. 'It's a little too high for me.' That was exactly what he'd wanted to achieve, that his mother would find it scary so he could climb a little higher. Long ago she'd learned to have confidence in his agility, in his strong muscles, but she played her role with gusto because she loved to let him have his fun. Now, though, it seemed as if something sinister was stalking him, hidden among the leaves, something that could impair his dexterity, and she called out again in a voice that was unexpectedly shrill that he had to come down. Esther flicked her cigarette butt into the water in an arc. 'You have nothing to worry about,' she said.

*

I have nothing to worry about. They lay stretched out on the grass, three young women and a young man, pleasantly lethargic after the picnic, in the drowsiness of a late-summer afternoon by the lake, just an ordinary carefree group, with the child playing with his ball on the grass behind them. She wanted nothing more than to believe what Esther had said. Frank had brought along a few bottles of red wine, his own wine, he'd offered it to them proudly and kept topping up their glasses. The wine warmed and relaxed her, and she gradually became reconciled to the situation, and it hadn't hurt that everyone had praised her food so profusely. Maybe there was nothing going on. Have a little faith. Who knows, maybe Hans was right and she'd got too many ideas into her head. She wanted nothing more than to let go of her cares. She lay on her belly with her head on her arms and let herself be lulled to sleep by the warmth of the sun. She listened dreamily to the soft lapping of the water and to Frank's steady voice talking about his wine. 'Druivebloed,' said Esther. 'Where did you get the name?' Esther was the only one who'd hardly eaten a thing, which reminded Marjorie of the time in the caravan, but she'd drunk quite a bit of wine and had continued to sketch without interruption, changing her position at intervals while keeping the sheets of paper under control with one hand and racing the charcoal over the paper with the other.

'From a Bible passage,' said Frank, and he tickled the bottom of Ada's foot with a blade of grass. Ada was sleeping, lying on her side with her light blue cardigan folded under her head. Or pretending to be, it was hard to say because of the sunglasses. The foot withdrew. The blade of grass was undeterred. Marjorie watched through her eyelashes and it made her think of the pencil Hans used to tease her with in the hospital, wagging it back and forth in front of her eyes. Then a realization that dispelled her drowsiness: he's trying to seduce her. She came up on her elbows to be

365

able to see him better, in the hope she could figure out what possessed him to do something so awful, wanting to seduce this devout, married woman, the mother of three children. He took no notice of her, and his entire being was focused on Ada; she saw a dark longing in his eyes and this confused her. This was not the look that made Edna and Kathleen nervous. And she'd certainly never seen him look at *her* like that. He turned towards her. She said the first thing that came to her, laughingly appealing to an intimacy that didn't exist between them. 'A Bible passage? Since when do you read the Bible?' He gave a mysterious smile. 'Someone suggested it. I liked the word.' Imprints of grass on his thighs near the edge of his shorts. 'That must have been one of your girlfriends,' she said bluntly, to warn Ada and also because of a vague feeling of regret, which she wanted to put behind her as quickly as she could. She came to her own rescue in just a couple of steps. In her life, love was sensible. In his, sensual. The words were so similar, yet there was a world of difference in terms of peace of mind. And then there was the moral side of the whole business.

'A girlfriend who's well versed in the Bible,' said Esther without looking up from her paper.

Frank decided to ignore their comments. The blade of grass continued to pursue the soles of Ada's feet. 'Don't you agree,' he said, 'from a completely objective, entirely scientific point of view, that Ada van Holland is the most beautiful woman on earth?'

'I was just wondering how I should draw her,' said Esther.

Ada yelped and sat up suddenly, and her sunglasses fell onto the blanket. Her dress was twisted around her hips; she tugged it back in place, covered her knees with the skirt and quickly put her sunglasses back on. But Marjorie could see it pleased her. 'Ada is as pretty as a picture,' she said, 'no-one could fail to notice that. I imagine her husband thinks so, too.'

All three of them looked at her.

Blood rushed to her cheeks. She couldn't stand having them stare at her and plucked at the grass, wishing she could disappear down into it. So at least you know what I think about it, Frank, she thought peevishly. Leave Ada alone. But a hostile silence hung over the blanket, as if she'd been put outside the city gate to live in exile from now on.

Frank stood up without a word and walked over to where Bobby was playing on the grass, and signalled that he should throw him the ball. Marjorie looked at his shorts and at the bruises on his body. Bobby let out an Indian war cry.

'Oh dear,' said Esther, and handed out cigarettes. Marjorie took one, too. They smoked in silence. Their bodies automatically turned towards the man and the boy on the grass, who grabbed on to each other and tugged at each other and dived on top of the ball, as they laughed and puffed and panted. You could see from the way she smoked that Ada hadn't done it very often and that she didn't have much of an aptitude for it. Marjorie saw there were purplish stains on the skirt of the striped dress and felt sorry for her. 'How long have you been taking care of your aunt?' Ada cleared her throat, mumbled: 'A week.' It seemed like everything startled her.

'Gosh, you must really miss your little ones. I wouldn't be able to do it. When are you going home?' She gave an ambiguous shrug, and looked rather pale. Nothing more. Esther hummed and sketched. This exchange wasn't going anywhere, either. Marjorie carefully assumed a relaxed pose and focused on the game. Bobby ran over the grass. Frank tossed the ball in his direction but the boy missed, and Frank waited for him, standing with his legs wide apart like a boy. He ran a hand through his hair and glanced in the direction of the women on the blanket. Ada sat up. Marjorie had clearly seen the confusion behind the dark glasses and kept issuing warnings. 'Such a nice man should get married and have children, don't you think?' she said casually. 'He's a heartbreaker. We've seen quite a procession of women over the years.'

'He's a loner,' said Esther without looking up.

It sounded ridiculous, just like Esther to say something like that, and to be honest she'd never noticed any signs of this in Frank. She didn't really believe in loners. Still, the remark alarmed her, and once again she wondered how well Esther actually knew Frank. Whether she'd been at his vineyard after they bumped into each other a month back. What they'd talked about.

You have nothing to worry about. If only she could believe that.

Ada tucked up her legs and wrapped her arms around them, put her chin on her knees and sighed. They didn't talk any more after that. All you could hear was the wind and the water and Esther's bracelets, which moved as she sketched. On top of these sounds came the war cries of the man and the boy.

*

Frank played like a dog trying to shake off his fleas and got Bobby all riled up. It turned into a show, a game that for lack of a team bore only a slight resemblance to rugby or football, and that was being played primarily according to the rules of a different, age-old ritual – impressing the girls. Balls were thrown hard from unexpected angles and the one on the receiving end would dive sharply and land on the grass in the most spectacular way possible. And of course wouldn't turn around if there were screams from the blanket.

As always, she became fascinated, couldn't help it; she was enjoying seeing her child so absorbed in the game. Enjoyed the peals of childish laughter – no-one could laugh like he did – and the stunts he executed to outdo the man. Inwardly she encouraged him, go on, go on. A boy honing his strength on an adult man and growing all the while without realizing it. She saw Frank regularly hold back and give the child a break without him noticing it, and liked him for that. Heard the dull thuds their bodies made as they fell, and the panting and snorts of laughter as they struggled to get up, each held back by the other. She knew she was watching a performance, the breathtaking ballet of a large and a small man in shorts, who butted each other fiercely, like stags in rutting season, and tried to tackle one other, until one of them captured the ball and carried it off with a crazy cry of triumph. Then they would chase each other, and turn and abruptly face each other in a surprise attack, would circle each other at a distance in challenge and then outfox the other with rapid feints, all of it purely from the joy of being in motion.

And she knew Bobby would show off his scrapes to Hans, secretly proud, and tell him in an indifferent tone of voice that they'd been horsing around a little, and she realized that in her whole life she would never love anyone as much as she loved this little boy, her child, and pain spread through her body, as if a thick, syrupy liquid were being injected into her veins. Her love would not stop the course of things, the child would grow up and go his own way, but she would, well, that's the way it goes. The only question was whether she would still be entitled to this feeling. Because on the other side of the blanket someone else was also obsessively watching the performance, someone with perhaps more of a right to this feeling than she had.

I have nothing to worry about. But then why is she looking at him like that?

She breathed deeply in and out, her mouth open to keep the tears at bay, and laughed and clapped her hands when Bobby got the ball away from Frank with a clownish dive. 'You win,' cried Frank, raising his arms to signal a break, and they stood next to each other huffing and puffing, their faces happy and hot and their eyes squinting against the light. The child danced the ball triumphantly on his hands.

'They kind of look like each other,' said Ada.

It was just a simple observation. No-one even looked up. Esther bent over her sketchbook, and the charcoal ate into the paper. Marjorie clapped twice more, planted her hands behind her on the grass as a support, and started to do the sums.

*

All at once, it was unbelievable she'd never noticed it before. How long had he been coming to their house? But she hadn't been looking for it.

369

The strong, solid build. The thick brown hair that had the tendency to fall over his forehead if it got too long. Bobby's knees, which were wide in relation to his legs, so that you knew he still had a lot of growing to do. The power of his boyish voice, in which you could hear how deep it would become later on.

'He doesn't seem to need anyone, and that's why the other children find him so appealing,' the teacher had said to her at the parents' evening. 'They look up to him and ask: Bobby, what shall we do? And he doesn't seem to be aware of his role.'

She nodded proudly, recognized this, when he was a toddler she would often find him sitting up in his bed jabbering away quietly, very pleased with himself. 'He seems to be above taking sides,' the teacher went on. 'That's why they all want to be his friend.'

24

IT WAS NEARLY EVENING WHEN they drove into the wide streets of Rotorua. Steam curled up from holes in the asphalt; there must be powerful forces at work down below the surface. 'It stinks here,' cried Bobby, and plugged his nose. There was the faint smell of rotten eggs in the streets of the town. 'Sulphur,' said Frank, 'you smell sulphur.' For the last leg of the journey he had Ada sit up in front again. This time Bobby had climbed in between them without the slightest hesitation. Marjorie no longer cared if Frank wanted to seduce Ada, they could do as they pleased.

Esther plugged her nose, too. 'Imagine having to live here, so close to Hell,' she exclaimed. Her pinched, nasal voice made Bobby laugh. She's being funny, thought Marjorie, the offensive has begun. Around her, everyone was getting excited. In spite of the late hour, they gave in to Bobby's pleas and decided to start their walk through Wai-O-Tapu Thermal Wonderland now instead of tomorrow. Marjorie stayed out of it. The main thing was to get through this weekend without something terrible happening, and where they were wasn't important. The child was wound up like a top and cheered as he squeezed out of the jeep and ran in circles around the empty car park with his arms outstretched. She was curious when the first irritated looks, the first careful remarks would present themselves. You can only be truly patient with your own child. 'Darling,' she cried, but he ran after Frank to a path that disappeared steeply up into the hills.

Most of the visitors had gone home. The few people who were still there were on their way to the car park. They were as good as alone. We're insane, it will be dark soon. But she had no choice but to trudge after the others, deeper and deeper into enemy territory. In the middle of a group of tall, dark bushes, a white cloud of steam hung motionless in the air like an enormous, indecisive ghost. The wind carefully unravelled the edges. They had to climb a long way and Marjorie fell behind because her thoughts were weighing down her legs. Here, too, the same sickening odour of decay. On both sides of the path the earth bubbled and plopped, and steam escaped from holes and crevices. Mist wandered over the paths and she lost sight of the others occasionally. Frank and Ada were far out ahead. Somewhere she could hear her little boy's voice, that you should never pass the ball out in front of you, always backwards, and she heard Esther's throaty laugh, and when the mist disintegrated into wisps she could see Esther off in the distance, running after the child on her narrow heels.

The trail led to a huge hot pool bordered by high trees, where thick clouds of steam rose from the shallow fluorescent green water. The white crust at the edge of the pool was eroded. The others were waiting for her there, with hair sticking to their sweaty faces from the climb. Dark patches on their clothes. Frank and Ada stood talking off to one side; they spoke softly and seriously, and she could see that Ada was drinking in every word he said as if it were his last.

There was no holding Bobby, and he jumped around Esther and challenged her and ran away with the ball under his arm over the narrow wooden walkway that ran the entire length of the lake. The heels followed him, click-clacking over the wood, disappearing into the mist. She had no faith in anything any more and went after them as fast as she could. 'Bobby, darling,' she cried, 'not so fast, that water is hot!' But halfway across she couldn't see a thing and had to slow down. Far behind her she heard the muffled voices of Frank and Ada. So it actually *was* possible to have a conversation with Ada.

At the largest geyser, which she was relieved to find had a fence around it, the boy ran boisterously up and down the empty wooden stands. Steam shot high into the air with a deafening roar. 'Mum, look!… A rainbow!' The light from the last rays of sun was refracted in the spray. She took his hand and climbed along with him up to the top of the stand to have the best possible view of the beautiful spectacle, because she didn't want to spoil it for him.

*

The craters had names like Devil's Home and Devil's Bath and the sulphur crystals on their walls made them shimmer with venomous yellows and greens. Slow clouds floated up from the depths. Thermal gas consisted of steam, carbon monoxide, and sulphur, she read in the brochure. Sulphur in particular could be lethal in high concentrations. A creeping gas that lies in wait for its victims in crevices and caves. Deep down in the craters you could be dead in three minutes. It was considered safe above ground. The area was fenced off and everywhere were warning signs with the skull and crossbones. She leaned over the wooden railing and in the gaps between the clouds of mist she peered at the cracks and crevices in the crusty white ground. Bobby climbed onto the bottom rung; she yanked him down with a sharp rebuke. This took him by surprise and he moved a short distance away.

After a time, Esther leaned over him and with her long arm pointed to the crystals far below. 'Do you know what they are?' The husky voice low and mysterious. There slithers the snake, thought Marjorie, and saw glints of yellow appear in the amber of her eyes. The child laughed and shook his head no.

'Those are diamonds. One hundred per cent pure diamond…' – the voice dropped even lower and told of the magical powers attributed to these diamonds, about the rumour that they would grant eternal life, of kings and sheiks who coveted this treasure and were willing to give up their kingdoms for it, and although Marjorie was sure that Bobby didn't believe it, that he was too old for such a story, she could see he was captivated. 'Whoever manages to lay their hands on these diamonds will be all-powerful. But… it's terribly dangerous' – the voice descended into even more mysterious regions – 'because it seems that the Devil himself lives in the caves to guard the diamonds, which is why no mortal has ever dared to attempt it.'

'Rubbish,' she said in a loud voice to break the spell. Frank grinned.

Still they stood there looking out, all of them impressed by this magical landscape, this rugged, crusty place with its black thickets and deep diabolical crevices, where dignified clouds of mist wandered about sedately like proud ghosts in a dark forest. As if wanting to take them aside for a moment, a cloud descended upon them and took away their vision. Although Marjorie opened her eyes wide, she stared into nothingness. A cold, damp veil slid over her face. Somewhere someone had deliberately turned off the sun. It gave her goosebumps and she shivered. Later she would return to this point in time, because she was certain it coincided with the moment the excited child decided to crawl under the railing and dare to do something no-one else had ever dared to do before.

The cloud of mist gradually dispersed into wispy ribbons and they could make each other out again, but the sun didn't return and dusk descended. Behind the railing, the next cloud came gliding in. 'Where's Bobby?' she said, trying to keep her voice as calm as she could. As long as you stay calm, everything's fine. They looked around, wearing their ordinary masks, walking back and forth along the path as if they were searching for a lost umbrella, or a trail map. Then she cupped her hands around her mouth.

'Bobby!'

'Don't panic,' said Frank softly.

They lifted their heads and listened. Marjorie stopped breathing, stopped time. Life could not be allowed to move on, not even by an inch.

For a moment there was only the rustling of the trees, and then from somewhere beyond the barrier came his cheerful voice: 'Mum, do you see me? Can you see me?' Her heart a bird flapping its wings to extricate itself from a bush. She seized hold of the railing.

'Keep your voice calm when you answer,' said Frank, but she knew this herself. 'No, darling,' she called out, casting her words into the mist like a fishing line in the hope the child would bite. 'I can't see you. Where are you then?'

'Here!'

They looked at each other. It provided nothing beyond a vague indication of an approximate direction in thick fog. Frank told her to keep the boy talking, and climbed over the railing. 'Darling,' she called. 'Come on back now, I can't see you, it frightens me.' Too late she realized that words like these usually spurred him on to be even more of a daredevil. 'I mean it, Bobby, come back!' she added sharply. But Frank shook his head. 'Don't,' he said. 'Don't try to get him to come back, it's too dangerous, he should stay put. Keep talking to him, then I can get my bearings.' He turned towards the direction the boy's voice had come from. 'Bobby,' he called. 'Can you hear me? Can you hear what I'm saying?'

From somewhere came a sound, it was hard to place, it could have been a branch falling from a tree, or a stone breaking loose from the wall of a crater.

'Bobby darling,' she cried, 'what are you doing?' She tried to penetrate the mist with her voice, with her eyes, and repeated her question.

There was only silence.

'Bobby, say something!'

Suddenly they were all calling his name at the same time. And listening. She tried to imagine him revelling in the fact that he was keeping all the adults in suspense. She didn't manage to.

She shouted: 'Bobby, answer me! This isn't funny!'

She shouted this again and got dizzy, had to grab on to the railing. 'Not so fast,' said Frank. 'The sulphur will make you faint.' They raised their heads and listened to the silence. None of them dared look at each other.

There was no sign of life from the boy.

'God damn it!' said Frank, and the sound of his voice dashed her hopes and pulled her into a different dimension. She climbed over the railing and stepped into the mist.

*

She inches forward through the mist, the ground beneath her feet a treacherous trapdoor that could open up at any moment. With her left hand she covers her mouth and nose, and with the right she feels for bushes and trees to hold on to. It's hard to breathe. When the dizziness allows, she uncovers her mouth and shouts his name two or three times, until the world starts to spin and she has to grab on to a bush, or stop and lean forward for a moment to look with unseeing eyes at her shoes, which are dirty and covered in white dust. The others also call out the child's name. The sound comes from everywhere. Frank's voice: 'You go that way, I'll go this way!' Although she has no idea which way to go, she knows exactly where she's headed. The whole story unfolds at the speed of light. They find him at the bottom of a crater, burned and lifeless, his skin peeled away by a caustic poison. A small, hopelessly mutilated body lying at an unnatural angle, the picture that will stay etched in her memory for ever and will pursue her into the farthest reaches of the night. She screams, or thinks she's screaming, or thinks she hears someone screaming, and lets herself sink down into the stench, down past the uneven edge that crumbles beneath her feet. Frank grabs hold of her arm, a vice-like grip, clutches at her clothes with his other hand and pulls her up and snaps something at her in a furious tone of voice, something that to her seems to be of no importance of all. He forces her to go back to Rotorua with him. Police, ambulance, rescue services. She keeps screaming, because what makes them so sure he's dead? They give her an injection. In the dark, men in special protective suits are lowered slowly into the depths, on their way to the little body that's been there all alone the whole time at the bottom of Hell, the noxious fumes eating away at it continually so that the only thing left is a charred, bloody stump. The coffin is closed immediately and won't be opened again. She keeps screaming, because what makes them so sure it's him? They give her an injection. At the funeral, Hans refuses to look at her. At home she rips the wallpaper into shreds with her fingernails. Before long she becomes impossible to live with. Then she sets off, because she still hasn't found the boy. Years later it turns out that all along he's been waiting underneath the metal bed in the mental institution. Peekaboo. They hide there together until the merciful day of her death. And that's where she's headed.

But at the same time she's here as well, and that here calls for her to pull herself together, requires an ice-cold head. She inches forward as fast as she can to the edge of the next crater and tries to see the bottom through the steam. She removes her hand and calls his name as long as she can still manage to stand up. Then she reaches back and feels for a tree or a bush. Several feet ahead, hidden from view by thick mist, she can hear Ada murmuring as she passes by.

*

It lasted about twenty minutes, the longest twenty minutes ever, spent in a hateful landscape that didn't take the slightest notice of her, that sneered at her through the skulls and crossbones on the signs. Then she heard Ada call out. 'I found him! Here!'

By the time she'd followed the trail of Ada's cries and arrived at the spot, Frank was already carrying the child in his arms. Ada stood facing him, with the child in between them. It seemed as if they were trying to convince each other of something, but they moved apart when they saw her coming and stopped talking. He's alive, he nodded. The child was unconscious and his face was bloody. His shirt clung to his body in an odd way. She ran her hands over his limbs ever so lightly, felt his ribs, his collarbone, his head. Come, said Frank. She took hold of the boy's sturdy ankle and didn't let go of him again because she could feel the warmth of the skin beneath her fingers, the life flowing through the cells, and wasn't sure this would continue if she let go. As fast as they could – but so terribly slowly – they made their way back through the mist. Esther had remained on the path and they proceeded in the direction of her shouts. Marjorie focused on what seemed to have remained unchanged: the saggy worn elastic at the top of his sock, washed one too many times, the dirty cotton shoelaces of his plimsoll, tied in a double bow like she'd taught him. In the middle of the path stood Esther, turned to stone, or bewitched. They immediately took the short route back down to the car park, their faces twisted into grimaces. Once in a while the child moaned, but he didn't open his eyes. She kept hold of his ankle, softly calling out non-existent words to lure him back. Around them it was quickly becoming dark. Ada and Esther ran on ahead, their shoes in their hands, and she could see the soles of their feet disappear into the mist. 'It could be we've been lucky,' Frank panted. He told her what happened in short, breathless sentences. The boy lay in the middle of a wide, fairly shallow crater. He'd probably fainted there somewhere and rolled down. A protruding ledge had broken his fall. They didn't talk about it further, because it was terrifying to put their hope into words. Except for the jeep, the car park was empty. Frank called out to the others that Marjorie should sit in front. She took the child from him in the jeep. Ada, whose swollen eyes were filled with tears, helped her cover him carefully with the blanket. Esther didn't exist. Then Frank started the engine and turned on the headlights. The jeep tore over the asphalt. She steadied herself by putting one hand against the windscreen, and leaned over the child. Darling, she whispered, darling, remember when the Lone Ranger climbed onto that roof and all the bandits down on the ground were looking for him? With her mouth just over his ear, she softly kept breathing in life.

*

The hospital in Rotorua was built on a hill and looked out over a large lake. Frank stopped the jeep right in front of the entrance, double glass doors beneath a canopy supported by posts. He ran around the jeep and lifted Bobby from her lap. During the ride, the child had suddenly corrected her – his speech slurred and his eyes still closed – when she mangled the name of a rugby player. But none of the crazy mispronunciations that followed brought forth any further responses. While Frank hurried towards the glass doors with the heavy body of the child in his arms, she tugged at the door of the jeep, couldn't figure out how it worked, couldn't figure out the simplest of things any more. Ada ran on ahead past Frank and held the door open for him. Then the door fell shut. Behind the glass, Bobby's shoes floated away into a dimly lit hall. Marjorie shouted and tugged, but couldn't get the door open. She cursed and swung her legs over the door, grazing the bottom of her thighs on the sharp edge. She stumbled and fell to her knees on the pavement, which was covered with small stones. Sharp pain shot up. Esther came round the back of the jeep to help her. She quickly got to her feet and ran to the hole of light beneath the canopy that had swallowed up the child. Her hand was already on the large, square handle when in the glass of the door she saw the reflection of a sneering skull with empty sockets for eyes. She knew it was Esther's pale face lit from above by the lights in the canopy. But she saw the face of death. In a split second she spun around screaming, prepared to saw into the scrawny stomach with a serrated bread knife. Esther jumped back and raised her arms in a defensive gesture. They stood facing each other, both of them shaken. Esther didn't look like herself any more, as if the structure beneath her skin had shifted.

'Marjorie, I...'

'Was he supposed to have died?! Was that it?!'

She turned around, pushed open the heavy door, and let it slam shut behind her.

*

The doctors used tweezers to remove the shirt from Bobby's skin. He screamed, and although this was unbearable, it was also a powerful, living sound. She stroked his hot forehead and distracted him with jokes. A nurse washed the blood from his face. It turned out that all of that blood came from a good-sized scrape on his cheek, that was all. The doctors asked the child questions and examined him. They placed salve-soaked gauze on his burns and bandaged them up. The child cried and his teeth chattered. It took forever for them to bring the morphine. Only when he was fast asleep on the ward, his cheeks flushed an unnatural red, a frame over his body so nothing would press against the burns, did she ask where the others were. The nurse told her how to get to the waiting room.

The first thing she noticed when she opened the door was that Frank was rubbing Esther's back with his hand. They were sitting close together on a bench at the back of the waiting room. It was a cheerless place illuminated with dim yellowish light, so that it seemed as if the sulphur had done its job here as well. Esther puffed on a cigarette – she saw the end glow brighter – and was saying something to Frank that she couldn't make out, but it sounded weepy and distressed. Then the door slammed shut behind her and they jumped up. Caught in the act, she thought. She became vaguely aware that someone was missing. A short way from the door she stopped. Frank came towards her, his heavy shoes squeaking as they moved over the polished floor, his face ashen in the dim light, and she could sense a shift in him as well. But she didn't want to be touched, not under any circumstances, and stood stock-still, enclosed in a protective suit. In the background, she saw Esther floating through the room. She addressed herself only to Frank, in sterile nursing terms. 'Three bruised ribs, and some second-degree burns on the upper part of his body. There's even a third-degree burn in one spot, there'll be a scar there, but luckily it's near his armpit. They've given him morphine; he's sleeping.'

'Does he have to stay?'

'A couple of days – they want to keep him under observation, to be able to rule out internal injuries. And it could get infected.' Who are we talking about here – she heard herself, heard the nurse, the doctor, was revolted by all of those yapping mouths. It was about her child. 'He's feverish,' she said furiously, 'and he's in pain…' She repeated the word, pain, pain, pain. Her mouth opening and closing like a fish. Frank took hold of her. 'There's morphine for that,' he said. 'What are you going to do?' Kind hands around her bare arms. 'How are you doing?' A sharp longing to let herself fall into his arms and have him stroke her back. To let herself go over the edge and slide down into the crater. She pulled away and sealed up the holes in her protective suit. Wiped the tears from her cheeks. 'They're letting me sleep here tonight.'

He hesitated as he gave her a handkerchief with an apologetic look: there were bloodstains on it. 'Can we do something for you?' She shook her head no as she blew her nose. 'In that case,' he said, 'I propose we set up our tent somewhere nearby and come back early tomorrow morning.'

She raised her head. 'Where's Ada?' Not that it made any difference to her, but it gave her some time. Ada had gone outside, said Frank, to get some air, it had really shaken her up, but she'd be back before long. Then they were going to Lake Rotorua to camp. He stroked her cheek reassuringly. Again the dangerous longing. 'We'll be nearby,' he said. 'And tomorrow morning we'll be back.' Creeping gas that waits patiently for its victim. She gave him back his handkerchief. 'No,' she said, 'that won't be necessary. Go on home…' (the lie presented itself effortlessly and felt familiar) '… Hans is coming, I just talked to him on the phone, he was leaving right away.'

He gave her a searching look. 'Was he already back from his fishing trip then?'

'Yes. They didn't have any luck… They couldn't see a thing, just wandered around in the mist.'

She couldn't care less that he didn't believe her. He slowly folded the handkerchief and put it in his pocket, as if needing time to think. 'Marjorie,' he said then, 'wouldn't it be nice for you if we came back tomorrow morning?'

381

'No,' she said, 'I'd rather you didn't.'

He gave her that penetrating gaze of his. She quickly zipped the protective suit all the way shut. Esther came and stood next to him. Even though Marjorie managed to keep from looking in her direction even once, the grimy apple green slipped into the corners of her eyes all the same.

'But don't you think…' He wavered and stroked the stubble on his swollen jaw. 'We're all very upset… wouldn't you feel better if you knew we were nearby?'

Creeping gas that lies in wait in crevices and caves.

'No.'

He raised his arms to the side and let them fall back against his body with a plop, a gesture of his she was familiar with. His eyes darkened. But always the gentleman, he bowed to her request.

'All right, we'll go then.'

He put on his jacket, gave Esther her handbag. His movements were blurred around the edges. Poisonous gas has eaten away at all of us, she thought. We've been hollowed out, and soon we'll drift away from each other like wisps of mist. Wherever the wind blows. Ada is floating around somewhere outside, there's a good chance she's dissolved into the haze.

He leaned towards her and gave her a kiss, but his lips barely brushed her cheek. You can't kiss a protective suit.

'Can we see Bobby before we leave?'

She shook her head. 'No-one outside the family.'

His eyes opened wide. He was visibly shaken and couldn't hide the fact that he was hurt. 'I'm not an outsider, am I?' For a moment she felt sorry for him. He'd always taken such pleasure in playing rugby with the child. The affectionate look in his eyes when the little boy came in.

Creeping gas.

'No visits from outsiders,' she repeated, 'only his father and mother.'

Oh, yes, she'd hurt him, the great Frank de Rooy. But Esther put her hand on his arm, to show him it was all right. Good girl, she thought. Still, she felt sorry for him. 'Just his father and mother,' she repeated, more softly this time, as if she were patting him on the head.

*

Still she didn't trust it, so she pressed her forehead against the window in the hall of the hospital, because she wanted to see them drive away. The empty jeep stood below next to the kerb, underneath the street lamp. Her eyes gradually became accustomed to the darkness beyond the window and she saw Esther standing in the middle of the street, an indecisive silhouette. What is she looking at? Frank came walking up from the left, agitated, taking large strides, stopped; they called out something to one another, those two, he shook his head and ran back in the direction he'd come from. Disappeared from sight because of the canopy. It was clear who he was looking for; the wind had caught hold of the striped dress and Ada had floated off. A couple of minutes passed in which nothing much happened. Esther walked around helplessly and called out something, probably a name, that of Ada. Of course, they can't leave without Ada. But the wind was coming from the wrong direction, and Ada wouldn't be blowing back that way. Esther walked to the jeep. She didn't get in, sort of leaned up against it, well, what else could you do. It went on for a long time, nothing happened, but she couldn't take her eyes off it, as if she were witnessing something important, even though she couldn't imagine what that might be. Ah, there's Frank again, running, taking giant steps to the left and to the right in the middle of the street, he ran past Esther, who was standing by the jeep, called out something to her as he passed, but didn't stop and ran on until he disappeared from sight on the other side. For goodness' sake, this could go on for hours. All the same, her forehead remained pressed up against the window. Esther lingered near the jeep, in the light of the street lamp. Look, Mummy, heaven is shining down, Bobby had said when he was small. Suddenly the long body leaned forward, that apple green, *very easy*, **very Vogue**, over the driver's seat, and picked something up, a piece of paper, a note, the white bracelets slid down to her wrist

and by now Marjorie could imagine the sound they made. Esther straightened up, wavered as she looked in the direction Frank had gone, unfolded
the piece of paper, and read. Marjorie wanted to know what it said as well,
but there was no way to find out. Esther shouted something. Shortly afterwards, Frank appeared from the right. He was no longer running. Esther
raised her arm reluctantly, with the note in her hand. He just stood there
in the dark and didn't come any closer, as if he were afraid of the message
that awaited him. As long as you haven't read it, it could be something else.
Something like that.

*

She spent the entire night sitting in a chair next to the hospital bed,
holding the child's small, limp hand in hers, squeezing it softly to let him
know that even in his sleep he wasn't alone. The child slept fitfully, with
Icy alongside him on the pillow. Thanks be to God for Icy. The night nurse
brought her a blanket, which she wrapped herself in. Her back hurt. Near
morning she slumped over the bed half asleep, her head nodding heavily,
the sounds of the hospital in the background. She wondered why Ada had
left without saying goodbye. Whether that meant something.

'Excuse me...'

Someone placed a hand on her shoulder; she opened her eyes with
difficulty and sat up, it was the night nurse. 'I'm going off duty now. I
wanted to say goodbye, and wish you all the best for your little boy.' She
stood up groggily and nodded, yes, yes, of course, is it that time already?
A foul taste in her mouth. It was still dark, and the ward was dimly lit by
the lights in the hall. Together they looked at the child. Marjorie smoothed
the blanket, too tired to speak. When the nurse was gone she started
walking around, yawning and stretching. She didn't want to fall asleep,
because she was familiar with hospital routines and knew that before long
the silence would be broken by thermometers and flannels. To stay awake,
she picked up Esther's sketchbook, which had been left behind, forgotten,
in the waiting room. She'd done so countless times that night.

The people in the front seat of the jeep, throats vulnerable and exposed. Profiles inclined towards one another, Frank's prominent nose, Ada's soft line, the fullness of her lips when she smiled at him. The two black specks in the middle of the lake. But the rest of the pages were filled with the child, she'd mainly drawn the child, one after the other, page after page, again and again, the child on the front seat of the jeep, the child high in the tree, playing on the grass, eating, laughing, a close-up of his face, full-figure drawings in different positions and with different expressions, the whole sketchbook was filled with Bobby, Bobby, Bobby, on both sides of the paper. As if she'd wanted to use this trip to capture the child and understand him, to recognize him, from the structure of the bones in his body and in the areas of shadow and light that he consisted of on paper; she drew him with obsessive lines, as if she were looking for something, she's looking for someone, someone hidden inside him who seems to be signalling to her through the flecks in his eyes and the glow of his skin, through the pores that soak up life, let me live, says the child on the paper, please, let me live.

It both was and wasn't him. Although the child in the sketchbook decidedly resembled Bobby, she didn't recognize his clothes – they were unfamiliar, and his hair was different, too, curly, as if Esther remembered the child differently when she took her eyes off him and looked down at the paper.

25

SALLIE DIDN'T REALLY CARE FOR *all those giggly women. He was too small to appreciate the uniqueness of the fashion house where their father worked as a tailor. Esther was four years older than he was, and she would spend the whole year before each visit looking forward to the day that they were allowed to go along. She would take hold of his impatient hand and try to get him to walk along quietly behind their father over the antique carpets on the ground floor. The only thing Sal was interested in was the twinkling of the enormous chandeliers above their heads, but she gazed in admiration at the accessories displayed in the glass cases, the gloves of leather and silk, the umbrellas, the delicate stockings, the hats and the evening bags. Satin lingerie and lace in dreamy hues. She studied the movements of the saleswomen as they leaned over the counter towards an elegant customer, letting cashmere scarves glide through their hands. She breathed in perfumes and the soft scents of powders and made solemn vows to herself in her intoxicated state. But a little hand would always tug insistently at her sleeve. Because Sal wanted to get to the basement as fast as he could.*

*

She drove them up the wall at the atelier. It was right before the show, and every day she'd come storming in with more additions and drastic changes. No-one had been able to understand why she'd found it necessary to take a trip to Rotorua precisely now, during this busy time, and afterwards it seemed like they were paying for that one lousy Saturday off by having to work even harder. For example, all of a sudden she wanted to have embroidered flowers on the wedding gown because she'd woken up with an image of white silk frost flowers being blown onto the gown by a polar wind. Objections all round when she showed them the design – sorry, but there's not enough time, it's impossible. Esther, please, said Rits. She went off on a rant about dedication and enthusiasm that ended with all of them, herself included, embroidering late into the evening as their eyes burned. We're a creative team, she said, we don't allow ourselves to be confined by the edges of the day. This wasn't her first collection, but it *was* her first show, the official opening of Lady Esther Boutique, well, then you want to present your best ideas, wouldn't you agree? No-one could argue with that. But in the eyes of the pattern cutters she could see that her behaviour was starting to take on unhealthy forms. And they didn't even know what she was getting up to in her kitchen at night.

Rits, with his flaccid hips, who was becoming paler and more British by the day, had been banned from her bed without an explanation. He seemed relieved rather than insulted. She knew it irritated him no end that she called him Rits, which she pronounced like a Dutch word, rolling the R and exaggerating the other consonants – he wanted to be called by his own name just like everyone else. But he never dared stand up to her.

*

Wealthy families came to the fashion house to order their wardrobes, or an expensive set of linen with embroidered monograms. The staff had to have some knowledge of French, because the ladies enjoyed being addressed as 'Madame'. Above the ground floor were two floors of ateliers, around eight altogether. That's where their father worked, in the fur department, where the ladies would be shown large pelts – would you like a three-quarter-length coat with an ermine collar, or were you thinking of something floor-length in astrakhan? Before they got married, her mother had also worked in the fashion house, in blouses and skirts and dresses. Coats and suits, that was men's work. Their parents had met in the staff canteen. The director, who had a French beard and was worshipped by everyone, demanded total dedication to the firm and gave girls the choice: they could either get married and leave, or not get married and continue to work there. There were those who broke off their engagements. But Mother chose Father. In the evening, though, when Esther and Salomon were in bed, she worked at home embroidering monograms of intertwined initials, that's how much a part of the fashion house she'd become.

*

Following the episode in the caravan with Marjorie and Hans Doorman, having reached the point of wanting to die, she dragged herself off the sofa in the back of the atelier and stood trembling as she once again took up her trusty tamer's whip. She had added every thought of that little bundle of gurgles to her collection of repressed memories and unwelcome emotions, the wild beasts she had to keep under control. During the years that followed she was once again the ringmaster in her own circus, and Lady Esther became an institution in Christchurch. She had to expand, the orders became larger, and clients came from outside the city as well. One day a pale, sharp-featured young man from London came in, introduced himself as Richard, and said he wanted to work for her as a designer and cutter. But the next day, as he watched her draping fabric on a model, he became even more pale and announced he could never work for her because he would never be able to do what she could. What a bootlicker, she thought, and said: so make simple, basic things. Oh no, he said mournfully, I could never compete with you, I can't work for you. She let him bow and scrape a bit longer, then said: be my personal assistant. He had a depraved look in his eyes she found attractive. He performed his duties with the utmost diligence.

After nearly ten years of Lady Esther, with the tiresome prospect of that anniversary on the horizon, she decided it was time to turn things on their heads. Her salon in Cashel Street – where the smell of the ancient Rose would come wafting up in unexpected places – was bursting at the seams, and the ateliers were spread out all over town for lack of space. Moreover, she was starting to tire of the repetition and routine. A collection twice a year: she could go on like that for ever. What her clients wanted from her had become predictable. Esther didn't want to be predictable. The fashions that found favour among the ladies of Christchurch were those dictated by conservative England. But she kept up with the European fashion magazines and knew that a fresh new wind was blowing through London, with exciting designers like Mary Quant, who made clothing with deceptively simple lines and unprecedented freedom of movement. This was the kind of freedom she was looking for, the kind of freedom she also got from the Pill. Her clients would keel over if they ever found out that unmarried Esther took the Pill and that Rits wasn't spending his nights in his rented room, and as long as this was the case it would keep her from taking the plunge into new and interesting designs. I have to move to a larger city, get out of this sleepy place. It has to swing. Lady Esther Boutique. At the thought of this her blood started to flow in double time, like it used to.

The scandal hastened her decision. Late one evening, one of her cutters had unexpectedly come into the atelier at the same moment that Mr Corbett, the well-endowed husband of her most distinguished client, was sitting on the cutting table and Esther – wearing only her tape measure – was bending forward with his member in her mouth and her bottom towards the full-length mirror, which he was ogling through half-closed eyes. In no time, her clientele was reduced by half.

Christchurch quickly became too small.

She decided on Wellington because no-one she knew lived there. Together with Rits, she flew back and forth a few times and found a suitable building in the centre. Although the neighbourhood didn't exactly exude the radical fashion culture she'd hoped for, she would take care of that. They planned the move well in advance, because the salon in Christchurch had to fetch a good price. Rits devoted himself to this. She started designing. She decided to mark the opening of Lady Esther Boutique with a fashion show, which stepped up the pressure considerably. Feeling as insecure as if it were her first time, she took to the streets to look for silhouettes and forms that could serve as inspiration. She sent for her regular fabric manufacturers and put together a palette as though she was creating a painting.

When she had to start making the drawings, she could put it off no longer. Her pen hung suspended over empty sheets of paper. What appeals to me, what would I like to see? A Russian had been sent into space, you couldn't ignore that. Contemporary, clean lines, light material. Poise, presence. A more powerful kind of woman on the catwalk, young, funny, sexy. Polo-neck sweaters in Bohemian black. Maybe with the Beatles in the background. Low waistlines, halter lines, supple jerseys, easy to wear. The evening gowns can be dramatic, the cocktail dresses, too, the skirts will creep up to the middle of the knee, and we'll hear a jazzy bossa nova. And to finish, romance – we have to be practical, how much modernity can New Zealand take, otherwise I'll be stuck with the whole lot, so we'll end with a wedding gown that leaves everyone in tears.

Then she started to draw. She was familiar with the process: in the beginning you have to get started, draw what you drew last time, you get irritable, and you irritate everyone around you, what do they know, the fear that this time you won't succeed, you can't share that fear with anyone, because then they'll lose faith, they have to think you always have all the answers, so you grind up the fear into irritation and in the meantime you keep drawing, because you've discovered that that's the secret: that you have to keep going, that you shouldn't stop. And then suddenly – sometimes it takes days, sometimes it takes weeks – something happens on the paper and you get excited about certain lines and start to sweat, and at night when you stare wide-eyed into the darkness the designs appear one after the other as if they were waiting there for you and all you have to do is pass them on. Light on, pee, cigarette, draw. Rits pulls the blanket over his head demonstratively.

Draw. Experience happiness.

She went on like this for weeks, it had to be her best collection yet, in keeping with her big plans for Wellington. Although a fashion show lasts half an hour at most, it has to make an indelible impression. Which was why she turned the designs into patterns herself. This was unusual, you had pattern cutters for this, but she thought she could do a better job. Like a true artist, she left the logistics of the move to Rits. Real designers are incapable of running a business.

*

Both she and Sallie were fascinated by the stuffed horse with the side saddle. They were only allowed to visit the horse if the fitting rooms were empty, if no ladies were being fitted for a riding outfit. And if they promised to be quiet as mice. Don't forget, their father would say, otherwise you won't ever be allowed to come back. He would speak softly to the woman from the department for a moment and motion to them conspiratorially, and they would then tiptoe stiffly over the Persian carpet, and when she and Sal were in the fitting room – which was as big as their parlour – their father would close the heavy curtain so that they were alone with the horse and he could continue his whispered conversation with the woman. They would carefully run their hands over the horse's mane, touch the bit and the reins, stroke the strange, dead hide and pretend he was theirs and still alive. She would have preferred to have been there on her own, without her little brother. When the woman had to go back to work, their father would join them and lift them into the saddle in turns, that was best of all, because then you got to sit with two legs on one side, and you could pretend you were somebody. But Sallie would keep whining that he wanted to go to the basement.

*

The move to Wellington was a happening. Like a queen bee, she whirled among the movers, the painters, the suppliers, enjoying herself immensely. Outside, passers-by stood gaping at the spectacle, which was exactly what she wanted: buzz. I can do this, I made it, she thought, waving her colour samples in the air.

She turned around and looked straight into Marjorie's eyes.

The brief encounter knocked her off her sky-high heels. The presence of Frank de Rooy, who knew nothing, was confusing enough. But the sight of the boy had touched her very soul. Caused a lot of commotion among the ranks of the wild beasts. She took a deep breath and cracked the whip even faster.

As daunting as the designing stage can be, there's a certain degree of calm in developing a collection. The cutters make the toiles and you discuss them. Together you keep refining the designs, adding more detail, and all the garments are fitted on models and made once in the actual fabric. During this process the fit is closely scrutinized, because not every fabric does what you thought it would. Then you make the final pattern. The usual, nothing out of the ordinary. But her clattering bracelets unsettled the cutters in Wellington, there was a pervasive smell of paint in the atelier and everyone complained of headaches. Rits was beside himself when the invitations for the show turned out to contain misprints not once but twice, and she... she didn't recognize herself any more. She was anxious and insecure, she suddenly wanted batiste interlining for the cocktail dresses that were already finished, rejected the cord trim on an evening gown (days of intricate work), shouted furiously that no-one could make a decent Cardin sleeve any more, and an hour later wondered in desperation why she was acting like this. To keep the commotion in her head at bay, she goaded everyone, including herself, into accomplishing even more.

During the evenings, she arranged to meet with potential financial backers. Look, she would say over her fourth glass of bourbon, Wellington should have one big swinging centre, we'll approach artists, musicians,

actors and actresses, opera singers, architects, the avant-garde, the intel-
lectuals. I've got boundless talent and I deserve to be able to do my
designing in peace, without having to worry about money. My own
fashion magazine. My patterns by mail order. So many plans. You're all
dears. After the show we'll have a private party. She didn't understand
herself why she drank so much, particularly now that she had to be clear-
headed during the day, and she danced wildly, as if she was trying to
frighten off the enemy. She would be brought home near dawn. Rits pretended he was hurt. She pretended she was sorry. The next time it would
happen just the same.

All the while she tried to force herself not to think about the boy. She
didn't dare think of Frank de Rooy, either, and couldn't really understand
why she phoned him. Maybe she expected some help. 'You know...' she
said sadly. 'You know... I thought... when I saw you...' The secret burned
like bourbon in her throat.

'What?' he asked sleepily. It was the middle of the night.

She suddenly sobered up.

'Well,' she said, 'I thought... he would look great in Italian-style clothing. Short jackets, narrow trousers. I thought.' His deep laugh. 'But if I
hear you laugh like that,' she went on, 'I get the idea it's a lost cause.'

He told her that Ada van Holland, the most beautiful girl in the air
race, was staying with him, and explained the situation. We're going to
Rotorua tomorrow, he said, with Bobby, you know, Hans and Marjorie's
son. Suddenly she saw her chance to see the child from close up without
Marjorie breathing suspiciously down her neck. Oh, how nice, she cried,
I've wanted to go there for so long!

At the crack of dawn she put on her apple-green shift and placed her
sketchbook in her bag. Are you sure you want to wear that to go to see the
geysers? said Rits from under the blanket. Which geysers? she asked in
surprise.

*

On the top floor, if the heavy door happened to be open, they could catch a *glimpse of the boardroom, the high wainscoting* made of dark wood, the *gleaming expanse of desk, the painted portraits,* the antique kilims. Sallie *wasn't interested in this, and their father didn't want* them peering inside, so *it was never more than a glimpse. Stamping papers* in the office was fun, too. *Only they weren't allowed to talk while they worked.* She could manage this, *but it was too hard for little Sal, and he would play* a short distance away on *the rocking horse from the boys' department, which* was next to the office. In *the meantime, she would be seated at one of the* desks and given a stack of *old orders and three stamps. Received, Seen, Approved.* She stamped her way *enthusiastically through the stack, and as she did so* made believe she was in *the boardroom, feared and admired. Received. Seen.* Approved. And always, *every year it was the same, just when she was having* such a good time, she *would see Sallie coming towards her out of the corner* of her eye, because after *all, you can't get anywhere on a rocking horse and* he wanted to get to the *basement.*

*

She could barely remember how she and Frank got back from Rotorua that night. The fear for the child's life, the hospital, and then – even though the message contained in the note had been clear – they had searched for hours, looking for Ada, in bus stations, train stations, hotels, because he couldn't accept that Ada had made a choice, he was furious, just furious – 'A mistake, a bloody mistake!' – left the jeep in the middle of the road and ran into a field like a moonstruck wolf. Afterwards, he didn't want to drive any more, didn't want to talk, didn't want to do anything. Then she drove. She stared blindly into the night and struggled with the play in the steering wheel, the loose gearstick, the big pedals, and all that flapping, that sarcastic snapping. Her head full of sulphur fumes, her eyes full of hot mist. Towards the end, he took over from her. It was already getting light when he dropped her at Lady Esther Boutique. Would you like to sleep here? she asked, but he wanted to go home, in case Ada had changed her mind along the way and was waiting for him at the vineyard. She could tell he didn't believe it but that he still had to act as if he did, that he was imprisoned and wouldn't be released any time soon. A tight embrace, their teeth collided, consolation impossible and unwanted. She watched until he was out of sight, and the memory of that one night in Christchurch, their walk along the Avon, and the hotel bed afterwards flowed from her body. Then she felt a massive paw descend upon her neck. Cold morning light in the shop, the mannequins smirked at her, where is the boy? She knew she would no longer be able to control the beasts. In the bedroom, she yanked open the curtain. Rits moaned indignantly. I'm sleeping alone from now on, she said, and put the family portrait and the picture of Sal right in front of the menorah on the nightstand.

*

If it had been up to her, they would have stayed in the ladies' department the longest. She would have liked to have been able to make herself invisible so she could wander through the ateliers unseen, among the dress forms bearing the names of the regular clients and the high cutting tables with pattern pieces, shears, and chalk, and the dressmakers who, their mouths full of pins, would kneel next to the ladies when they came for fittings for the gowns they were having made. Everything appealed to her imagination: the intimate, almost whispered exchanges about darts and hip lines, the quick, cursory way in which bits of fabric would be plucked from the thick carpet, half of a red silk ball gown that was pinned to a lone dress form and which no-one was working on, so that she could surreptitiously run her fingers along the diagonal pleating, the wall cabinets with supplies, shimmering material for linings, thread in every possible colour, trimmings, buttons, feathers, pearls and sequins, infinite quantities of ribbon and lace wound around cardboard. She couldn't help but touch them, and if no-one was watching she would wrap wide satin ribbons around her wrist and the back of her hand and rub her nose over them softly as she dreamt up a dress fit for a princess. Once her dreaming was interrupted by the director with the French beard. She was startled, but he wasn't angry and enquired about her interest. Fashion, he explained, isn't something you can actually learn. You have to have a natural feel for it in your fingers, it's something you're born with. Esther looked at her own long, tapered fingers and made a silent, fervent wish. You have to have the ability to understand what women want, he went on, fashion sense, that's what you need. And product knowledge, he told her and Sal as he took them to see the fabrics (he called them yard goods), explaining that the silk came from Lyon and the wool from Paris. Sal wasn't the slightest bit interested, but deep inside her eleven-year-old self a great love began to burn, and her wish became a vow. Their father thanked the director profusely, which she found slightly embarrassing. And she was deeply embarrassed by Sal's childish whining and tugging.

*

Things had gone wrong since that ill-fated day in Rotorua. In panic, she did everything she could to get the people at the atelier to work as late as possible. Had them embroider white silk frost flowers. But every night there came a time when the last weary cutter would bid her a polite good-night and close the door of the salon behind her. Arranging to meet people was now out of the question; there was no way she could bring herself to be light and breezy. She would lock the heavy shop door and go up the stairs to her own rooms, and only halfway up, razor-sharp claws would slice furrows into the wounds of the previous nights. She couldn't sleep, flew around the cage at her wits' end. To keep from going under in the loneliness of the night, she had to do something.

She decided to make latkes for the child.

They had to be potato latkes, like the ones Grandma Berthi would make for Hanukkah. The problem was that she didn't have a recipe, no written record had survived. She had to make them from memory. Because she'd often helped with this, she could call to mind peeling the potatoes, grating and rinsing and especially pressing the pulp into the colander. Press hard, Bubeleh, otherwise there'll be too much starch left

396

behind and they'll be soggy, and your brother doesn't like them like that. Everything that followed was hazy, there were eggs involved, I think – I should have paid attention, they should have taught me how. I would go and sit at the festively laid table and wait along with Sal, next to the burning candles. Play with candle wax.

She didn't want to ask anyone for help. There was sure to be a Jewish community in Wellington as well, but she wouldn't be putting in an appearance. Every night she'd try again, she'd stand in her slip frying latkes, a cigarette in the corner of her mouth, a glass of bourbon within reach, with the window open wide and the door closed shut to keep the collection in the atelier from smelling like oil. But one time they'd be too bland, and another time too salty, then the oil would be too hot and they'd burn, then not hot enough and they wouldn't get brown, and they were always soggy, no matter what she did.

During the day, she fell into the habit of sending someone out to the grocery at the strangest moments (for example, halfway through a chaotic rehearsal with the models, or in the middle of a meeting with the people who would be building the catwalk) to buy pounds and pounds of potatoes and cartons of eggs and more bottles of oil. Esther is losing her mind, she could read in everyone's eyes, now of all times. She wanted to apologize and explain, but instead would fly into uncontrollable fits of rage. One day, during one of her outbursts she fired her best seamstress. That night, she saw a complete stranger in the mirror. Why did I do it? What have I done? Something's wrong with me. She quickly heated some oil in the pan.

As she experimented in the dead of night, she discovered she had to add eggs to the grated potatoes after squeezing them out. First she used too many eggs, then not enough, and in the end she arrived at one egg for every pound of potatoes, and by that time, quite a few nights had passed. Press hard, Bubeleh, get it as dry as you can, your brother likes them crispy. She feverishly peeled and grated more potatoes and pressed the grated pulp into the colander with all her might, while scenes from the past played endlessly inside her head, but without ever changing form. Sometimes old European words would slip out of her mouth. 'Measures', she would say, or 'mass grave'. Tears streamed down over her cheeks, hung from her nose, and dripped into the colander. Keep going, Bubeleh, it has to be drier. When the potato pulp couldn't get any drier, she put clean plasters on her knuckles and poured a fresh layer of oil into the frying pan.

✶

The basement of the fashion house ran the whole length of the building and was made up of various departments. It was hot and steamy and terribly noisy because of the boilers for the central steam heating. They were great brutes of boilers connected by high walkways where the stoker would cross with his wheelbarrows full of coal, which he would then dump into the machines. Sal couldn't get enough of it, and actually neither could their father. Then they went to see a man with white fluffy hair, he was the head stoker, which meant he could leave all the dirty work to his junior, and he had his own room filled with tools for carrying out repairs on the machines. He was a garrulous man, who enjoyed Sallie and gave him pieces of wood and a hammer and nails so he could make things. Let him be, Bubeleh, their father would say to her, you don't come here that often. No, she thought, that's exactly the point. But she didn't dare say so because she knew it was childish, she was so much older and Sallie was just a little boy. And so every time she had to put up with the fact that they spent much more time down in the basement than up in the ateliers. We had a leak a while back, the head stoker told their father the time that in retrospect turned out to be the last, we had a leak in the main pipe, scalding hot steam came pouring out, someone could have been killed. Esther lowered her head and had horrible thoughts.

✶

During the day, the tension mounted. Nearly all the invitations had been filled in and returned. Rits, who took care of the post, showed her. There

398

would be a huge crowd, they would have to rent more chairs. Here they come, she thought, the important types, Wellington's self-appointed elite, most of them won't understand it in the slightest but will want to have been there, sitting up at the front. Live music, she snapped at Rits, make sure you find a jazz band somewhere. When he started on about the budget she slapped him, something that shocked her more than it did him. I'm doing things that don't make any sense, what is going on? She walked around with dark circles under her eyes and interfered with every-thing, hardly dared leave anything to others. Layer by layer, she assembled the wedding gown along with the cutters, and every layer was full of intri-cate details. Now! she cried, and the four of them cut the yards and yards of organza. Her hands smelled of oil and afterwards so did the dress.

The models, who were also just the girlfriends and cousins of the cutters, had to be taught everything about make-up and hairstyles, and especially about how to swing your hips and place your feet at exagger-ated angles to each other when you're walking on the catwalk. Most of them were afraid of her, didn't know how to wear her creations, and couldn't walk. But she didn't give up. Lift up your chin, she shouted with a voice that seemed to be made up entirely of smoke, and slide those feet forward, you're not walking in a paddock, and she thought, maybe it needs some garlic... why am I thinking about garlic...? I don't want to think about garlic right now. She was tired of herself.

Late in the evening, when her fabulous creations were hanging beneath their coverings, protected against all possible disasters, she would close the door behind the cutters, shut the curtains, and resolve to go to sleep like a normal person this time. But before long she would be laid low and would crawl howling to the kitchen on her hands and knees, where she would pull the sack of potatoes towards her and start to peel. She was getting better at it all the time. First turn the flame up high, a spoonful of grated potato mixture in the hot oil, flatten it down a bit, lower the flame slightly so that they brown evenly, turn them over, repeat on the other side. From the tornado of whirling memories this useful one had appeared: that Grandma Berthi had chopped onion on a cutting board and snipped parsley in a cup and ground black peppercorns in a mortar and had mixed all of this into the egg mixture. And one night she made perfect latkes.

*

The director with the French beard was Jewish. So were most of the employees. If they were observant Jews, they didn't have to work on Jewish holidays or on Saturday. Although this cost them money, it was an advantage compared with other firms. Her family wasn't observant. Once in a while, if it worked out that way.

When the war broke out, Esther was in her first year of grammar school. She gradually became aware she was different, that her presence would never again be a given. Over time, gaps began to appear in the class. One day their father came home pale as death. The Germans had assigned an administrator to the fashion house with the task of liquidating the business. The man had done this to the best of his abilities. All of the employees had been dismissed. The firm was closed, and the director had been banned from coming anywhere near it. The building had been expertly stripped. The entire inventory had been loaded onto a train bound for Germany, with a sign on the freight cars: Generous donations from the people of the Netherlands.

Esther often thought about the horse. She would see him toppling over in the freight car and how his dead hide would tear and was afraid that this would hurt him all the same. At home she made funny hats for Grandma Berthi from remnants of fabric and felt, and sewed the mandatory stars onto everyone's coats. She was angry and unhappy. At Sallie's primary school, the Jewish children had a separate classroom. Sal kicked his football against their fence for hours at a time. She often took her discontentment out on him, she couldn't help it. Sissy, she would hiss when he walked by, sissy. When he was lying in bed she would tell him blood-curdling horror stories. And then he would usually wet his bed during the night. At the table she couldn't bear the sound of her parents chewing, and no matter how sweet Grandma Berthi was, she also had long black hairs on her chin. She shuddered and resolved *to leave everyone in this* house far behind. Then she thought of the director *with the French beard.* During the winter that Sal would have turned ten, *their father said they* should maybe go into hiding. But they were too late.

*

'Wait here,' she said to Rits at the corner of the street. 'I'll be right back.' In fact she couldn't go on; she wanted to go and lie in a basket underneath a table and stay there. He turned off the Morris's engine and let out a deep sigh, because he had no idea what she was doing here in Khandallah Village when they were in the final stages of putting on an important show down in the city, but she ignored his sighs, got out of the car unsteadily with her steaming bag and started walking. What kind of shoes do I have on, anyway, you don't wear red high heels to pay a visit to a sick person. It was frightening that something like this had escaped her attention. The street sloped upward at an angle, and on both sides were large wooden houses set in lush gardens, and for a moment the comforting charm of the neighbourhood touched her, and she felt a vague sense of regret without knowing why. A profusion of roses hanging down over the white fence of the house she was headed for. She braced herself and pushed open the gate, prepared for hostility and even to be turned away. It went better than she'd expected. Hans was standing on a ladder painting a window and seemed genuinely pleased to see her. 'Esther!' He climbed down and wiped his hands off on a cloth. Marjorie was at her flower-arranging class. Bobby was upstairs in bed. 'How is he doing?' she asked. 'Good... better... you know, children heal so quickly. He's already getting restless. Another week, I think, and he'll be up and around again. He can't lift his arm all the way yet, the skin is tight because of the burns, it needs time, the doctor says. We do exercises with him. But things will be fine eventually, just fine. And how are you?'

She complimented him on the house. His kindly face began to glow, and he patted the blue boards like you'd stroke the flank of a favourite horse. 'We're not done yet,' he said. 'I want to build an addition to the sunroom in the back.' She complimented him once again. Only then did she dare ask. 'Could I see Bobby for a moment?'

She noticed his hesitation and thought: Marjorie's forbidden it. I don't want Esther here, she'd said. She held up her bag. 'I just want to bring him a gift, I'm very busy, I'll be gone before you know it.' He kept wiping his hands on the paint-stained cloth. It wasn't going to make them any cleaner.

*

A boy's room, with rugby heroes on the wall. Bobby was sitting up in bed in his pyjamas, his arm and upper body bandaged. Surrounded by comic books. Unfortunately the latkes had cooled off, but he liked them anyway, asked if he could have another one. 'Help yourself,' she said. 'They're for you. Just right.' In the meantime, she took the menorah out of her bag. Outside she could hear Hans moving the ladder. She pushed a glass of lemonade and some comics to one side and placed the menorah on the nightstand.

'What's that?'

'It's for you,' she said. 'Keep it always. It's a menorah.' She sat down on the edge of his bed and took the candles out of her bag. 'Eight candles for eight days,' she said. 'The ninth is for lighting the other eight, it goes in the middle.' He nodded as he ate his second latke with relish, crumbs in the corners of his mouth, crumbs on the bed. 'I'm going to have a scar,' he said proudly. She wondered if he'd heard what she said. Her hands trembled as she put the candles in the menorah one by one.

'At Hanukkah you light another candle every day for eight days until all the candles are lit. Hanukkah is the festival of light. That's when you make latkes fried in oil.'

'Why?'

'Well, why do Dutch people make those special doughnuts on New Year's Eve?' The truth was that it had never interested her. It had something to do with the desecration of the Temple, and jugs of consecrated oil that had been defiled, all except one, but that one contained barely enough oil to keep the lamps burning for a single day, and then, *hopla*, what do you know, a miracle happened and the lamps just kept on burning for eight days and they were able to clean the Temple and get a new supply of consecrated oil. 'They' were The Jews, and she wasn't interested in them either.

'May I have another one?' They've really raised him well, she thought.

'Good, aren't they? My grandma always made them at Hanukkah. Always at Hanukkah.'

'Is it Hanukkah now?' Funny, he couldn't pronounce the hard, guttural sound at the start of the word. He's a Kiwi, he's one hundred per cent Kiwi.

For a moment she was overcome with happiness. 'If we want it to be, sure it is.'

He gave a short laugh. That laugh. Everything else fell away in a flash.

She blindly twisted the eighth candle into the menorah and leaned over to get the matches out of her bag. 'You remind me so much of Sallie, did you know that?' she said. 'You're the absolute picture of our Sal.'

'Who's that?'

'My little brother. Same eyes, same voice. How you move. How you laugh.'

She struck the match and picked up the ninth candle.

'Is he good at rugby, too?'

'He's dead. They gassed him. The only difference is that your hair is lighter.'

She heard the words coming out of her mouth. Couldn't believe she'd said them. Stop. When the ninth candle was burning at last, she held it to the first of the other eight candles. She noticed that Bobby was looking at her wide-eyed, that he'd stopped chewing, that his hand with the latke lay motionless on top of the blanket, and she wanted to reassure him. 'They were always looking for people like us,' she said, 'and one day it was just our turn.'

Wax dripped from the ninth candle because she was holding it at too much of an angle. She concentrated desperately on getting the candles lit without making a mess. She watched how the flame of the candle in her hand lit the other candles, how the two flames became one for a moment, until her hand pulled the candle back.

*

They had to be fast, and were allowed to take very little with them. It was raining. First everyone had to get into the truck with their suitcase and then they had to wait in a building packed with people; the place smelled like wet coats. It took a long time. Esther went to the toilet and she had to wait a long time there as well, and the toilets stank and were dirty. Afterwards she couldn't find Sal and the others, that's how crowded it was. When she was standing on the stairway she could see them a little way off, in a corner. Grandma Berthi had been given a chair. Her father wasn't with them. Suddenly she felt his hand around her wrist, squeezing hard, he was hurting her, he pulled her down the stairs right through the crowd, she nearly fell, and at the bottom his arm shook as he pointed to a tall man with a cap who was standing near the door with a couple of little children, and he said she had to get over there and go with that man on the double. She was terrified, her father's face was strangely twisted and he pushed her away from him, and when she got to the door, the cap yelled: where have you been, the children have to get home. She had no idea what was going on but went along with the cap, and he walked straight out the door with her and the other children, into the rain. But it was only when they arrived at that house that she saw Sal wasn't with them.

*

Eight candles were now burning; she carefully placed the ninth candle in the middle, looked at the flames, and couldn't hold back the sorrow. She was beside herself as she sat on the edge of the boy's bed. It took a while before she found words again. The light from the candles shot out in every direction. 'I just couldn't understand,' she whispered huskily and turned towards the boy; he looked at her feverishly, his mouth slightly open. She looked for his hand, had to know. 'I still don't understand... Didn't he want to go? Did my mother keep him with her? But why not me, then?' Bobby's hand was warm and sticky with crumbs. She moved closer, pulled him towards her carefully, and hugged him. The room dissolved into nothingness. She put her wet cheek next to his ear, smelled the warm smell of pyjamas by his neck. Murdered, all of them. He changed position inside her arms, she could tell he wasn't sure what to do, maybe she was hurting him, no matter how careful she was trying to be, but she had to know, so she held him close and rocked him. Murdered, all of them. She felt his vertebrae and touched his shoulder blades and pushed her face into his short hair, because she was looking for something, a sign that would explain everything, a word, a key, a comforting smell, and all the while a thin, distant wailing was coming from her mouth, as if deep inside her someone was lying sick on a mattress. She felt the boy's muscles stiffen and heard his frightened breathing and thought, stop this, stop this, but she couldn't stop, in the warmth of his child's body she was searching for something that could deliver her from the question that had been destroying her for years.

Why without me.

Reality returned as soon as the door opened and she became aware of how things must look, her sitting there like that with the child, of the misunderstanding, of the explanation that wouldn't be understood, that was pointless.

'Mum,' said Bobby tentatively.

She let go of him, turned away. 'Oh, dear,' she murmured, wiping off her cheeks with sticky hands that smelled like the oil from the latkes, 'oh, dear.'

*

Strangely enough, Marjorie didn't ask for an explanation. She walked quietly to the menorah and blew out the candles one by one, not roughly, as you might expect her to do, splattering melted wax in all directions, but restrained, carefully.

'It's a gift,' said Bobby.

'How nice, darling.'

Esther stood up, wanting to say something, but didn't. She picked up her bag wordlessly, empty from exhaustion. Marjorie ignored her, cleared away the latkes from the bed, and plumped up the child's pillow. 'So, now you have to rest,' she said, and tucked him in. Out in the garden she repeated this to her in the same calm voice: so, now he has to rest, she didn't ask her to explain, she didn't lose her temper, none of that, just: so, now he has to rest, goodbye, and she pressed the lost sketchbook into her hands. Hans stood next to the ladder with the brush in one hand and scratched his head with the other. Yes, said Esther, goodbye.

They parted civilly, like well-mannered adults. She had nearly reached the Morris when she thought of something. She walked back quickly, to tell them it didn't matter that they hadn't returned their invitation because she would reserve a place for them in any case. But from behind the garden gate she saw a man and a woman facing each other in stony silence. Something in his wife's eyes made Hans put the brush back in the can of paint. She turned noiselessly on her heel and walked away.

26

TWO WEEKS LATER, THE SPECTACLE was set to begin. The buzz had done its job, and the guests excitedly squeezed in among the packed rows on the way to their seats. The curtains were closed to soften the daylight, and behind them the windows were steaming over. Esther greeted her guests wearing a seemingly simple but utterly refined tomato-red pinafore dress made from a thin wool fabric. She shook hands, accepted compliments and bouquets, and made bold statements to usher in the new era. 'Time for a breath of fresh air,' she cried, a remark that seemed rather misplaced considering the overheated stuffiness of the crowded salon, but it was eagerly received all the same. No-one wants to get left behind. In the meantime, she kept an eye on the entrance. The faces she was looking for didn't appear, which actually didn't surprise her.

In the corner, the musicians from the jazz combo were tuning their instruments one last time. ('You don't want to know me,' said the bass player darkly when they met, and his inebriated eyes had penetrated deeply into hers. They were in bed together that very same night. He called her Lady Potato because of the huge quantity of potatoes he'd come across in her kitchen. That's a Dutch thing, she said, we're potato eaters, they made Vincent Van Gogh famous.) The last few days before the show, she'd rehearsed rigorously with the musicians and models until they were charged with the right kind of fiery excitement that would make the show into something special.

'Esther!' Rits was making panicked gestures over everyone's heads and tapping wildly on his watch. There was no room for any more chairs on either side of the catwalk. Guests who hadn't been able to find seats were standing rows deep pressed up against the wall. It was hard to get the door closed. Necks were craned in anticipation. Ten minutes after the scheduled starting time, she could put it off no longer. 'Esther!' She kissed and greeted her way to the top of the catwalk, where the microphone stand had been placed. Behind this hung a large curtain she'd had students from the art academy paint with imaginative geometric designs. And behind the curtain she knew how nervous the models and modistes would be, whispering frantically about curlers snarled in strands of hair or a button that had suddenly popped off the waistband of a skirt. She held out her hand and allowed Rits to help her onto the catwalk. The din gradually subsided.

*

The night after her visit to Bobby had been a difficult one. She had finally fallen into an exhausted sleep near dawn. 'Don't ever forget, Bubeleh,' said her father in her dream, 'you only live ten times. I can see that you're often sad. So one way or the other, I'll make sure you get flowers.' As she was waking up she realized he hadn't told her which of her ten lives she was living right now. Then she woke up completely and had even felt relieved. The wild beasts retreated wearily and went into hibernation. Time to get back to work then, she thought somewhat tremulously, *hopla*. But she felt deeply ashamed towards the little boy, an uneasy feeling she didn't know what to do with. Hans and Marjorie didn't send in their invitation. She could imagine why they hadn't. I have to go and talk with them after the show, I have to reassure them. After the show.

She took up her position behind the microphone, knew that all eyes were upon her. Down below, next to the catwalk, the bass player used the flat of his hand to silence his string bass. He had forceful hands and a shifty nature – she'd manage to stick it out with him for a while. Too bad he was just as thin as she was, two thin people in bed was like throwing two ladders on top of each other, kaboom. She was poised as she took hold of the microphone stand and looked into the room, surveying the packed salon and passing her gaze over the upturned faces. Strings of pearls had been taken out of boxes, hairdos sprayed up high, lipstick applied. Everyone had done their best and come here full of expectation and it had all been her doing. She was standing on a podium she'd built herself. For one terrible moment she didn't know why she'd done it. In this room there was no-one she could truly relate to. None of these people who were regarding her with such curiosity loved her. And she didn't love any of them, either. For one terrible moment her life stretched out in front of her like a polar landscape in which one collection after another would hide the emptiness for a time. Then she saw the flowers.

On the counter at the back of the salon stood a colourful display of dozens of bouquets in buckets because there weren't enough vases. Extravagant, expensive bouquets – no-one had wanted to be outdone. An overwhelming quantity of flowers, too many for just one person, but even so, all for her. The flowers nodded to her.

She took a deep breath and tapped on the microphone. A hush fell over the room.

Go ahead, Bubeleh, we're listening.

'Every day,' she said huskily, 'and every day anew, we can choose to stop wearing yesterday's coat. We've wanted to get rid of it for so long now, but you know how it goes, it's become so familiar, we've grown so used to it, it's hanging right there, and we put it on without a second thought. The coat is dull and faded and withdrawn. On the street it's as though we're invisible, nothing happens in the eyes of those who cross our path. It's from another time and weighs heavily on our shoulders. If we happen to see our reflection in a shop window, we're startled by our shapeless silhouette. The coat is worn and tattered from years of wind and rain. It smells musty. We feel mild aversion as we hang it back up in the evening. We think to ourselves, as we've done countless times before, maybe I won't wear it tomorrow.

'I challenge you.

'Every day we can choose to put on a new coat. With elegant, sleek lines and strong, bright colours, like a flower. When we look in the mirror, we're pleasantly surprised. We walk out the door feeling invigorated. On the street, we see the eyes of passers-by light up as we walk past. A hemline with a mind of its own that might even creep up above the knee! Or on a playful note, a surprising sash that wraps around and forms a giant bow behind our backs, you didn't expect that, did you? People turn around – there's something about that coat. That girl. That woman. And we walk on with a spring in our step, because something has happened, a tiny earthquake has taken place, we are seen, we exist, we've been reborn.

'Every day. A dress that flutters cheerfully, a jacket with square shoulders, trousers that make our legs longer so we can take larger steps. Made from fabric we can move more freely in, fluid and light, with nothing to weigh us down. With a colour that attracts attention, and bees. Let's be poppies in the stubble field. Nothing less. Every day. All the days of our lives. How many days that will be, we don't know. Let's not waste any of them.

'My name is Esther. I want to add colour to life. There are all kinds of ways to do this, and this is mine. Today my dream has come true. New Zealand has given me the opportunity to make a fresh new start. I offer New Zealand my talent.'

She gave a short bow. Applause. Her words had sounded genuine in her own ears, and she didn't want to doubt them. Then she motioned to Rits that he could step up to the microphone and launch into his starring role as presenter. And while the jazz combo struck up a rousing number, she disappeared behind the painted curtain and held it to one side to let the first model pass.

*

'... in aquamarine jersey, finished with duchess pleats at the front, with lines that flow along the contours of the body and a V-neck that comes into its own with the addition of a chunky necklace...'

*

'... made from cherry-red Shetland wool, with raglan sleeves, and hand-finished with saddle stitching along the hem...'

*

When the show had been over for quite some time and the muscles in her face were starting to ache from her permanent smile of success, her arms bruised from the hands that had grabbed hold of her, her cheeks chapped from the congratulatory kisses, and her ears starting to ring with cries of superb, marvellous, daring, and so utterly talented, her throat raw from the half-shouted explanations above the music and the animated hum of the guests and the excited relief of the models who were discussing the show with their families, did you see this? did you notice that? what did you think of me? When she was finding it hard to breathe for lack of air in the overcrowded room, when her head was starting to spin from all of the unfamiliar faces, the introductions, the promises, the appointments, the praise, the jokes, the witty replies, that's when, through the display window where the curtain had been pushed to one side to let in some day-light, she saw Frank de Rooy approaching at a steady pace from the other side of the street. And her heart leapt, even though she knew better. Although she went on tirelessly toasting and clinking and clinching and promising, she kept an eye on him in the throng and saw how he recoiled from the airless salon full of excited female sweat and whiffs of perfume, and how he took off his cowboy hat and more or less pushed himself inside and how his presence set off a subdued shock wave in the group of models standing by the door. He apologized, gallant as always, but he

411

didn't flirt and his eyes were dark and scanned the room restlessly as if he were looking for someone he needed to speak to urgently. 'What a marvellous story about the brides in the great air race,' said the editor of *Woman's Weekly*. 'We'll have to do something with that. Were there really a hundred? And what a divine bridal gown, my compliments!' Rits, who'd remained glued to Esther's side to share in the glory, gave a self-deprecating laugh.

'Yes,' said Esther, 'that was quite something. The entire plane was just one big dreamy white cloud, from front to back.' She excused herself on a pretext and squeezed her way towards Frank, shaking hands and exchanging greetings.

Can I speak with you for a moment? he asked.

Outside she blinked against the unexpectedly bright sunlight, a misleading evening sensation of drink and smoke and jazz inside her body. What's wrong? He was agitated, paced back and forth over the pavement, raised his arms and let them fall back to his sides apologetically. She saw he was angry and was finding it hard to keep a grip on himself.

'I'm too late.'

'Not for the cocktails.'

'How did it go?'

'Standing ovation.'

'Hmm.'

'Whether they'll actually wear it is another thing. Let alone whether they're prepared to pay for it. We'll see.'

He hadn't been listening, because he turned towards her in the middle of her sentence.

'Have you talked with them recently?'

'With who?'

'Hans and Marjorie. And Bobby.'

'No... yes... two weeks ago. A short visit.'

'Notice anything odd?'

'Um... no.'

'And afterwards… have you spoken with them since then?'

'No, I haven't.'

'You didn't call them?'

'No.'

'Didn't see them either?'

'No.'

He ran his hand through his hair and cursed emphatically. A sobering feeling of dread crept up along her spine. This is not good.

'What about you?' she asked.

'A couple of phone calls about Bobby, how things were going. But I had to work non-stop, helping the farmers with the harvest, and then I had to pick my own grapes. So I thought, when I go to Esther's opening I'll go to Khandallah Village first, then I can visit Bobby.'

'Yes?'

'So I called yesterday afternoon to arrange it. But no-one answered the phone. I called last night again. And then again late in the evening. Early this morning. No answer. Then I got worried. I thought, something's wrong with Bobby.'

The success, the salon, everything fell away.

'And then?'

'This morning after work I called again. No answer. Then I drove over there.'

'And?'

'They're gone. The house is empty. They're gone.'

*

He told her the story. The first sentences didn't sink in, because she was sitting on the edge of the bed next to the boy.

'I parked my jeep in front of the house and noticed it was different, a strange atmosphere, eerie. I went through the gate and kept feeling like something was off. I called out hello like I usually did, a couple of times, but there was no response. And in the back garden as well, by the sunroom

413

and the patio, everything was so… neat, so… lifeless. All of the rattan furniture was gone, and the fishing things, and Bobby's bicycle, which always stood against the wall of the garage. The back door was locked. That door was always open, even when they weren't home. So I looked through the kitchen window. The kitchen table was gone, no chairs, no mixing bowls on the countertop, no frying pans on the stove, not like Marjorie at all. Spooky. And then something began to dawn on me. I walked to the sunroom and looked in through the glass, to the living room.' He gave a couple of sharp snorts, like a tormented bull with no way out. 'Everything's gone.'

*

'I thought I'd gone to the wrong house. So I walked to the front to see if it was the right house number. I hadn't been mistaken.

'I hung around the gate, didn't know what to think, didn't know what to do. Went to the back again to make sure I hadn't been seeing things. And then their next-door neighbour came walking up. I know her, she dropped in regularly when I was at Hans and Marjorie's. She said: you don't know what to make of all of this, do you? And she told me that yesterday a huge moving van had come driving into the street and that the movers had loaded up the entire contents of their house. It had come as a total surprise. Neither Hans nor Marjorie had said a thing about moving, even though they were on friendly terms with her. At least that's she'd always thought. So she went to find out what was going on and Marjorie mumbled something about a better job and told her they'd sold the house, cool as you please, said, sorry, we're very busy, and that was that. Shook her hand and said goodbye. The woman stood there looking at me with eyes big as saucers. They were all planning to go on a picnic next week.'

Too late. Too late. Too late.

'It just occurred to me that the phone had been disconnected, that's why there was no answer. Anyway, according to the neighbour, Bobby was fine and was up and about again. That was a relief, in any case. But honestly, I was completely bewildered as I stood there looking at that cheerful blue house and thought: how in God's name could they have left this all behind? It was almost like their second child!'

'Where did they go?'

'That's what I wanted to know, too. Their things are going to the harbour, the neighbour said, they're going by sea. I said: by sea? Yes, she said, and the family went by plane. Where to? Well, Esther, do you want to guess where they've gone?'

I should have talked with them right away.

'See if you can guess where my friends, the ones I spent so much time with, are headed without so much as a word?'

She made a helpless gesture, it could be anywhere, from Whangarei to Dunedin and back again.

'Let me tell you. My friends, along with their child who was over the moon because he'd just been selected for the Wellington junior team, my friends who recently applied for New Zealand citizenship, have gone back to Holland.

'You heard right. They flew from here to Auckland, and from there to Amsterdam.

'All of those proud stories, all of those plans for the future. What did it all mean? Were they maybe homesick and didn't have the courage to talk about it?'

'Are you sure?'

'Didn't mention it, didn't say goodbye, nothing. Gone.'

'Temporary. On holiday.'

'For good. Back to where we came from. Tell me why if you can, because I don't have the answer. It's totally beyond me.'

Marjorie, the coward.

'Do you know why?'

'No,' she said simply, and her hand flew up in front of her mouth and she watched as he wretchedly pulled a pack of cigarettes from his trouser pocket, his entire being a solid mass of icy incomprehension. But an oath is an oath, and she couldn't help him. She gratefully accepted the cigarette, and put up a protective smokescreen between them that would allow her to think in private for a moment. She wondered why this affected him so deeply.

He took a deep drag and blew out the smoke with a furious force. 'Why do people always abandon each other? I was going to do even more rugby practice with Bobby. I wasn't even able to tell him goodbye.'

She thought about Ada, beautiful, soft Ada, and suspected there was nothing left to help cushion the blow.

'Hans and I are right in the middle of working on my building plans. He's helping me design my house. Always pleasant, always joking. Such a good fellow. He didn't even give me a call.'

Marjorie, the tyrant.

'Esther,' he said, 'what do you think about all of this?'

She looked over her shoulder at Lady Esther Boutique. Her guests were wedged in together behind the fogged-over windows. A festive mood enclosed by glass, an aquarium dance of flushed faces. Rits threw his head back and roared with laughter at something the editor said. The models kept pushing up their hair and shifting their weight from one leg to the other. They'd only just risen from being ordinary girls to potential film stars. No-one showed any signs of leaving, the conversations too exhilarating, the music too sultry, the cocktails too sweet. The arrival of a new era had been heralded in their presence, and that had to be celebrated. Later on she would say goodbye to everyone individually and turn vague promises into something more concrete with a clever remark. Then things had to be cleaned up, the clothing put away, the catwalk dismantled, the salon swept. Life would have to go on.

'When it comes right down to it, we're a treacherous species,' said Frank. For the second time in ten years, she held out her hand to him.

27

SLOWLY, BIT BY BIT, THE coffin is lowered into the depths. The cemetery is an open grassy area fringed by trees and adjacent to the fields of
the vineyard. The graves are simple, with no displays of marble or showy
memorials, most of them covered by grass and marked with small head-
stones. The mourners shuffle in silence past the deep rectangular hole. If
you're somewhere halfway, like Marjorie, Bob, and Hannah, or all the way
at the back like Ada and Esther, you have to be very patient. Each pair of
feet comes to a halt in front of the hole. Next to the hole is a large pile of
sand mixed with soil and pebbles. Some people throw a handful onto the
coffin, others use the spade that stands ready in the pile. Every time the
earth hits the coffin you hear the same dull thud, and pebbles glancing off
of the wood. Roses are thrown onto the coffin and other flowers as well,
notes fall into the grave and even a key. Someone sprinkles red wine over
the coffin as if it were holy water. Many people close their eyes for a
moment. Others look intently at the coffin. Everyone says goodbye to
Frank in silence. Bye, mate.

*

*A bomb placed under their marriage. That's what their return to Holland
proved to be. Hans turned against her for the first time. He'd done what she
wanted like he always did, but he was furious and made no bones about it.*

He called her 'Marjorie' instead of 'sweetheart' and kept his hands off her waist. 'You're just like your father,' he said coldly. He couldn't have hurt her more. Because no matter how generous Pa had been in providing them with a place to stay in their home in Zaandam, he was still impossible to live with. They had to obey his rules like little children, and he took every opportunity to show he'd been right, made a great display of taking it out of the trophy case and polishing it up right in front of their noses. What did I tell you, back with your tails between your legs. What did I tell you, you had to sell that expensive house of yours at a loss. What did I tell you, you married a man with no standing in the world. It was an impossible situation. As soon as Hans found a job, they moved to a rented flat in a narrow street in Amsterdam. They lived three floors up, with small sliding windows and a tiny balcony covered in pigeon droppings. Once again she became terribly homesick, only this time for New Zealand. She stared out at the drab buildings across the street and could have wept when she thought of Khandallah Village, her beautiful blue house, the beautiful blue sky, their beautiful blue life. The spectacular view out over the ocean. Everything was a let-down in Holland. Everyone was busy with their own lives. The herring she'd craved for so long tasted like cod liver oil. And Bobby, her high-spirited little boy, found life in this country completely baffling: so where do they swim then? Where do they play rugby? Why don't they play rugby? Where do they play anyway? When are we going back? With his shoulders hunched forward he would trudge off to school, where he couldn't understand anyone and people gave him puzzled looks. He got out of sorts from being indoors so much and became unmanageable. For the very first time, she was finding him a handful. If she unburdened herself to Hans at night in bed, he would tell her frostily that she'd brought it on herself. In spite of it all, she continued to maintain that her decision had been the right one. Their life there wasn't safe with Esther around. Then Hans would shake his head. You're just like your father, he said, you want everything your own way. You want to have everything under control, just like your father.

The ultimate insult.

It was touch-and-go for a long time. Anger didn't come naturally to him. After just under a year they moved to the affluent Gooi region because he got a job there as supervisor for a construction company. Although they lived in a terraced house, it had a garden and was situated in a leafy neighbourhood, and marked the start of a return to normality. Bobby rode his bicycle over the heath and made friends. They got a dog, a cheeky little dachshund, which the child adored. Hans put his hands back around her waist. But the feeling they would never again belong anywhere didn't really diminish. The subject of their flight from New Zealand remained taboo. It also weighed heavily on Hans that they'd left without telling their friends, like thieves in the night. Norman and Edna, Ian and Kathleen, they hadn't said goodbye to anyone. Frank de Rooy, who'd been relying on him to help build his house. She kept her suspicions about Frank to herself. After quite some time, Hans wrote Frank a letter. He wasn't good at writing letters, and had worked hard on it. I'll drop it in the post tomorrow morning when I take the dog for a walk, she said.

*

Now she is looking right into the grave. She leans towards her son and whispers, asks if he would scoop some earth down onto the coffin for her. As she speaks, she taps on her cast. The earth slides off the spade and lands on the coffin with a heavy thud. She closes her eyes. Sorry about that, she says grudgingly to the dead man.

They don't remain at the grave for long.

Bob puts his arm around his daughter's shoulder. 'I didn't know the man at all,' Hannah whispers in his ear when they move on. He gives her a short squeeze, he's so glad to see her again.

*

Ada scoops up the earth with both hands. She allows it to trickle onto the coffin and as she does so, selects a pebble. Here you are. Thank you. She brushes the rest of the earth from the small, smooth stone as best she can,

419

the stone that still carries within it the warmth of the afternoon sun. She clasps the stone in the hollow of her hand and closes her eyes. The dirt is under her fingernails.

*

The beginning was dominated by despair, and loss. She was soaked to the skin when she came into the bunker; she hugged her children and felt grief take hold of her body. It was a physical pain, a phantom pain, an unrelenting agony she had to keep hidden from everyone. She could feel his hand in hers. She could see him sitting, standing, lying down, could almost touch him. She saw him everywhere. She couldn't believe he wouldn't be standing there in front of her later on, that he wouldn't be waiting for her there in bed. In the meantime she would get the children dressed and make Derk's lunch. She heard his voice constantly. His words. She felt his hand on her neck. If no-one was at home, she would take the striped dress out of the drawer, bury her face in it, and smell herself in his arms. The images this evoked would never change, and retained their intensity. She talked to him constantly, inside her head, like she was used to doing. And now he spoke back. His sentences never changed, either, nor did they lose their power. Don't fall for it, Ada, she would hear when she felt the pastor's cold eyes upon her during the sermon. He'll put you in the back of a pickup, she would hear when Derk assailed her with his bitter reproaches.

And one day – it had happened so gradually she'd barely been aware of it – she was standing up straight. We're moving, she said one day to Derk, it can't go on like this, we're going down, to the village, we're going to go and live in a normal house, with lots of light and central heating and a bath with hot water. I've already found it, it has a garden, all you have to do is sign. Something has to happen if you want me to stay.

His jaw dropped to his chest. Struck dumb, he signed the lease. So that's how that works, she thought, and made up her mind to be braver more often.

The pain turned into a permanent presence that guided her and made her stronger. Frank was always there. She moved together with him at her side.

He became her. He was inside her. Embodied in her. Or she became him. She wasn't exactly sure which.

Next door to their new house lived a lively, sociable family. Derk kept his distance – they weren't religious enough for him – but the children went back and forth freely between the two houses, and Ada asked the woman, Mona, if she would give her English lessons. They became friends. She went with Mona to the public library and asked about which books she should read. She read and read, because she wanted to get ahead, and she also checked out books for her children and read to them aloud. If Derk found fault with the worldly nature of a book, she would close the door to the children's room to silence him. She bought a record player with the money she earned as a postie. It's important that the children grow up with music, she told Derk. He complained, because he was always complaining, but his complaints touched her less and less and the record player provided so much enjoyment. The man at the record store always took time for her when she came in and made enthusiastic recommendations. She and the children danced through the room to Chopin's flower waltzes. They sang along with Rigoletto at the tops of their voices. When Derk wasn't home, they listened to the Beatles. No-one liked Coleman Hawkins or Dexter Gordon except for her.

She never became truly happy. To keep the peace she often lied to Derk. Although they were small, innocent lies, they left her feeling lonely. She also felt lonely in bed. She really did try to enjoy making love with Derk – after all, a woman was supposed to accommodate her husband – but the aversion remained. Every so often she would squeeze her eyes shut and imagine with all her might that she was in bed with Frank. Those were the times when for days afterwards Derk would be pleasant, almost cheerful, but it made her sad. During those rare moments when she was home alone, she would close the curtains and go up into the hayloft with Frank, filled with desire. The guilty conscience that followed diminished over the years.

The world around them was changing. The newspapers spoke of the sexual revolution. Ada quietly made sure Julie got the Pill. She also had the courage to confide in her friend about what had happened. She awaited

421

judgement anxiously. But Mona had tears in her eyes and hugged her. What a beautiful story, she said, it left me nearly speechless. Not one word about sin. A beautiful story.

Ada noticed that her thoughts were starting to wander when she was praying. She found it hard to talk to God. She was talking to someone else, maybe that was it. Even though they were always the same, she preferred Frank's answers to God's silence. She started to ask herself questions (or maybe Frank asked these questions inside her) about things she'd never doubted before. She was no longer willing to settle for a wrathful God, had no desire to crawl away in fear, and focused instead on Jesus, who was so much more human. She started to feel less guilty. This alarmed Derk. Also because she was giving the children more and more freedom. When Danny, the youngest, turned twelve she said: from now on you can decide for yourself whether or not you go to church. Derk flew into a rage but she stuck to her guns. Pete, an insecure adolescent who longed for his father's approval, continued to go, but Julie and Danny stopped going at once. At fourteen Danny started a rock band with his friends. When they practised in the shed she would bring them cola and cake and stay to listen for a bit. They're so much freer, she told Frank. Then her heart would swell up like a birthday balloon and float gaily up into the air. At times like this she was happy.

*

Now she stands before the coffin with her eyes closed and asks Frank for forgiveness. Not the Frank inside her head, who never changed, but the real Frank, who lived on without her and grew old without her and died without her. She feels the pebble's warmth in the hollow of her hand. Forgive me, she says, forgive me for my weakness. Then she opens her eyes and walks on.

Together with him, just like always.

Behind her, Esther takes hold of the spade. Shuffling along behind the others, she hasn't been able to take her eyes off Bob and Hannah. The coffin is almost completely covered with earth. She leans on the spade and bows her head. So long, pal. You should see them, our son and our granddaughter. They're fine people. And it seems we've got two more grandchildren. Please forgive me. I decided for you, without consulting you, guided only by my own panic. You know how that goes.

*

They went to bed with each other a few more times. But although they were very fond of each other and both of them longed to be comforted, it made them uneasy. While their bodies were busy, they avoided each other's eyes. She knew he yearned for Ada. She found his physical presence unsettling. They had a child together he knew nothing about. And she had decided for him. She kept her contact with him to a minimum as a result, which ran counter to what she really wanted. It was this, and also the fear that one day she would be tempted to tell him everything. A vineyard? That's not my cup of tea, she cried, and threw herself into Lady Esther Boutique. That salon? You'll never get me in there again, he joked, and devoted himself to his Druivebloed Estate. Busy, busy, busy, they would tell each other over the phone.

*

When all the feet have shuffled past the grave, the crowd fans out over the cemetery. Wine merchants and retailers. Owners of area restaurants where Druivebloed is served. The waiters from the hotel in Martinborough. Although not everyone knows each other, they're bound together for this one day by coming to say goodbye to Frank. The same soft breeze dries their tears. Then gradually the first jokes are told. Kris taps on shoulders and invites everyone for a glass of pinot noir in the estate's restaurant. As the setting sun turns everything a golden red, people walk back through the fields in changing configurations, towards the silver tanks that tower high above the rest.

*

'I still do everything myself,' says Esther, opening out the Cahn Couture brochure for Hannah. 'Consultations, drawings, styling, designing, just look at the circles under my eyes.' She'd had the brochure made at the height of her fame, somewhere in the mid-seventies, when sheiks from Saudi Arabia would fly their wives to New Zealand for an evening gown by Lady Esther and she was regularly invited to visit Beverly Hills. 'Look at that workmanship. All those layers, all of them cut on the bias, so intricate.' The glory years, long before the dispute with Rits, who'd been in charge of the day-to-day running of Lady Esther Boutique for decades and who over the years had gone his own sneaky little way with the bookkeeping that she'd been too artistic to concern herself with. Until well into the nineties, she'd been occupied with lawyers, paperwork, and an ulcer, but at a certain point she called it a day and bore the loss. It turned out Lady Esther Boutique was entirely in his name. So was the capital she'd built up. She moved to Auckland. The shop in Wellington is still there, although under a different name. Her triumph is that he couldn't steal her talent. Her defeat is that she never recovered financially and will have to keep working for the rest of her life.

But she'd been planning to do that in any case.

'Anyway,' she says, because she can see from the girl's eyes that the styles in the brochure are hopelessly outdated and of no interest to the young people of today, 'anyway, my business came mainly from theatre people and foreigners, because there was a huge gap between what I wanted and what New Zealand could handle. Now I'm old – oh, dear – now I just have Lady Esther Bridal.' Then she falls silent and sees herself pottering about among the lifeless bridal mannequins in the atelier. Most of the dresses are for girls from the Samoan Islands, where they like traditional weddings. I've remained a child of the dead, she thinks, I never came to life myself, only through my designs. It's a sad thought, but she's got used to it.

Hannah hands back the brochure. 'Cahn Couture,' she says. 'Are you Jewish?'

'Yes, dear,' Esther answers without the slightest hint of reserve. So much time has passed and the world is a different place.

'So am I,' says the girl who is her granddaughter.

Tok tok go the words in Esther's head, tok tok, like a squash ball in an empty court. She's probably gaping dumbly at the girl. 'My mother's Jewish,' says Hannah as she digs something out of her backpack. 'Not that we really do all that much with it in my family. Once in a while. She's always going on about Israel. But no-one else is supposed to! Look...' She pulls a crumpled colour photo out of her backpack and smoothes out the corners. 'I took this with me to Australia to show people. My family.'

Unable to speak, Esther holds out her hand and takes the photo. Her hands are shaking just as badly as they were a few hours earlier when Bob offered her a light. She can't hide it, and sees the girl looking at her. She slides her sunglasses back over her hair, which has been drawn back tightly, and raises the reading glasses that hang from a thin chain around her neck. She still can't see. Brings the photo up close to her face. Next to her Hannah waits patiently, and looks around to see where the Maori boy has got to. Kris. He's not far off.

A staggering silence descends in Esther's head as she's pulled into the photo, into the room where the family is gathered around a table laid for a festive occasion. Bob, the son, the husband, the father, leans back in his chair. His jacket hangs open, his hair is dishevelled. He glows with contentment. He has his arm around a pretty black-haired woman who's sitting next to him. The woman's face is small and round, with Slavic cheekbones and a sexy quality. Large, bold earrings. The woman is resting her chin on her hands, her elbows are on the table, and she looks impishly into the lens. The three daughters are draped over each other in a silly pose. Even though they're making funny faces for the camera, you can see they've inherited their mother's beauty. The meal is at an advanced stage, glasses empty and half full, bits of food on plates, napkins tossed carelessly to one side, there must be more people present, the person who's taking the picture and other guests who lean out of the way to allow the nuclear family to be in the photo, the photo that will be taken along on the trip. Everything in the scene sparkles and glows. Especially the menorah that stands in the centre of the table, with lighted candles.

Esther clears her throat, swallows and swallows, but her voice has disappeared, probably for ever. Her life tumbles down around her. Mocks her.

'Yes,' says Hannah, 'that was at Hanukkah.' And she takes back the photo. Then she notices the state Esther is in. 'Is something wrong?' she asks with concern. 'Do you feel all right?'

Esther is numb as she gathers up some broken fragments of herself. 'Oh, dear,' she murmurs, and the unbearable folly of life surges up within her. She hides her face in her hands. Her sunglasses fall to the ground, the reading glasses dangle helplessly from the chain. The girl keeps a watchful eye on her as she puts the photo back into her pack. 'Maybe you should eat something. I'm sure they'll give us something to eat in the restaurant in just a bit.'

That must be it.

*

It's not right, said Hans after his first heart attack. We have to tell Bob. We should never have done it that way. She protested vehemently, let's give it some more thought, who knows what we would be destroying in the process? Bob knows nothing, it's not a problem for him. But it is a problem for me, said Hans after his second angioplasty. His misgivings struck terror into her heart, and she lay awake night after night, imagining her son's consternation and the crisis such an announcement would land him in, and how he would turn his back on them, the impostors who had posed as his parents for more than fifty years. I'm not up to it yet, she told Hans through her tears, I have to get used to the idea. How much longer? he wanted to know after his bypass operation. Like a coward, she took refuge behind someone they hadn't been in touch with since they came back nearly half a century earlier. We can't decide without Esther, she said, and her voice crackled with sacred fire, we took an oath, remember? He then visited travel agents and picked up brochures for trips to New Zealand. She pretended to be thinking along with him enthusiastically, and declared them all unsuitable: one trip was too long and the other wouldn't be comfortable enough, they were old and it was doubtful whether Hans would be allowed to fly with his heart condition. Then his heart gave out and he left her behind with the brochures and a problem. His misgivings had taken hold inside of her. She wondered whether it would be a relief to let go of the lie, and to know whether her son would still love her then. But when she saw Bob at family gatherings – so relaxed, his presence such a given – her heart would break just thinking about it. The news of Frank's death seemed to come as a sign. It was time to talk to Esther.

*

To start with, Esther wants to tell her something. Marjorie can feel the blood rising hotly to her cheeks. She would love to take off her black jacket, it's so blasted hot in this country, but the business with her cast keeps her from doing so. 'Here I behaved so well,' says Esther in conclusion, 'and it still resulted in a whole new generation of Jews.' As if she's to blame. Marjorie wheezes. 'Is it my fault?' she snapped. 'I didn't pick Vera out, if that's what you think. I couldn't very well say that he wasn't allowed to marry a Jewish girl. They were at university together in Delft, she had her eye on him then already. And he's such a sweet man, he let her walk all over him.' The truth is that after twenty-five years of marriage, her daughter-in-law can still wrap Bob around her little fingers, and that as an architect she is at least as successful as he is. Bob himself doesn't have a problem with this, he doesn't doubt himself or begrudge his wife a thing, but Marjorie finds it an aggravating notion. Nowadays, women have everything going for them, she says to her women friends, men don't stand a chance.

Next to her, Esther takes a cigarette out of her bag and lights up. Whatever you do, don't bother to ask if I mind, thinks Marjorie. She coughs a few times in succession. Esther pushes her sunglasses further up her nose. 'I could just as well have kept my child,' she says evenly. In an image from a distant past, Marjorie sees her weeping as she sits on the bed with her arms wrapped around Bobby.

Hans nudges her in the back, now, now, *now*.

She plods along, her eyes burning. Far up ahead walks Bob, who is engaged in an animated conversation with his daughter and the boy from here named Kris. He has no idea there's a guillotine hanging over his head and that she's holding the rope. She feels awful. The only thing she can hope for is that he will consider her to have been a good mother. But she's not even certain of that.

'Esther,' she says finally in desperation, 'did we do the right thing?'

The woman in the pinstripe trouser suit next to her shrugs her shoulders and continues smoking her cigarette without speaking.

'I mean, we could tell him the truth.'

'If it would make you feel better,' says the husky voice.

'Not for me, for Bob.'

'Oh.'

'Do you think it would be better for him if we told him?'

A long arm points in the direction of the threesome.

'You're his mother, you know him.'

As if Bob has noticed that they're talking about him, he turns around and looks for her, gives her a cheery wave when he finds her. She waves back, thunderstruck by Esther's response. 'I really don't know,' she says hesitantly. 'What would we be burdening him with?'

'With deception. And a dead family into the bargain.'

His whole life based on a lie. His memories now unreliable. He – who knows nothing – turns back to his daughter and takes off his jacket. His back is slightly stooped from always sitting bent over a drawing board in deep concentration. Hey you, stand up straight, she and Vera and his daughters take turns telling him. He then straightens up obligingly for a moment and immediately slumps back into his natural posture. At this distance, the slight hump on his back moves her, demonstrates his vulnerability.

428

'He looks like a happy person,' says Esther. 'I hope you'll accept the compliment.'

'He has a good life,' she says modestly, as the dents in her heart are pounded out from within.

Alongside her, Esther grinds out her cigarette among the stones on the path with one of those typical Esther-laughs. 'Maybe we didn't do the right thing,' she says, 'but why should he have to pay the price for it? Let *us* do that.'

Esther is entirely right. She is overcome with a wonderful feeling of unselfishness. Of course.

'So we'll leave things as they are?'

'We'll leave things as they are,' says Esther ceremoniously, as if handing out a diploma. Marjorie takes it with a deep sigh of relief. Who would have thought, but there it is.

As they walk past the vineyards she's glad she came to New Zealand. She's almost glad Frank died, if you're allowed to have such thoughts. But there's still a burning question deep inside.

'Esther?' she begins cautiously.

'Hmm?'

'Have you ever regretted our... agreement?'

She answers without hesitation: 'No, never.'

She hadn't expected this and can't believe it.

'Really?'

It remains quiet for a moment. You see? Then comes the deep, husky voice, slowly and deliberately: 'If there's one thing I've always been sure of it's that children were better off without me. A pity for me that's how it was. But regret? No.' And as if to stress this, she says it once again: 'Never.'

Marjorie can hear that she means it. Her beautiful blue house looms up for a moment. But she has no desire to think about all of that. For someone her age, this has been an exceptionally tiring day. All these emotions in this heat and with no afternoon nap. You don't have to take everything in. You're better off letting some things slide right off you, like raindrops off a sheep's woolly coat. In a burst of gratitude, she puts her good arm through Esther's. They continue on their way like this, the two elderly Fates, with their arms linked affectionately and their wrinkles turned towards the sun. For this moment, they appear to be the best of friends.

∗

The mourners stream onto the patio of the restaurant. While they were burying Frank in the ground, professional hands had worked hard and noiselessly. Platters of salmon sandwiches and savoury scones stand ready on the tables beneath the umbrellas, and the pinot blanc waits in the coolers. People awkwardly join each other at the tables and pull up their chairs. The goodbyes still hang in the air, the splashing of the water in the fountain sounds resigned. But Kris goes from table to table like a host, saying: after the funeral we celebrate and laugh, because someone has gone to heaven! Ada closes her eyes for a moment. If You exist, please let him in.

Mozie points proudly at Kris. 'That's our grandson.' His words come out slowly. Although the deep brown velvet of his eyes has turned to faded cotton, the old twinkle still shines through. Next to Mozie sits the quiet woman who sat with Frank. Ada compliments them on their handsome grandson. The woman's face bursts open into a thousand crinkles.

He's very interested in his Maori roots, Mozie explains, much more than we ever were. The Treaty. The rituals. The language. Tribal tattoos. He's got one on his upper arm and he's thinking about getting another one. Mozie would sooner he didn't, but then which young man listens to his old grandad? Kris is the one who found their addresses on the internet. 'That boy has brains,' says the woman. 'He's at the top of his class at the Viticulture College.' 'He'll be the director here someday,' says Mozie.

Kris, with his handsome face and dark eyes, shuttles between the various tables. His friends sit together at one end of the patio. They're dressed in trendy clothing, and say 'sweet, bro' when they're in agreement

430

about something. Kris often lingers at the table where the Dutchies sit together, under the grapevines on the pergola. He and Hannah are bashful with each other, the kind of shyness that can arise between a boy and a girl when they notice how the air between them quivers even before they've spoken to one another.

He pours out the exalted red wine for all takers, the Druivebloed pinot noir. The wine is at its best, he says, and crouches down between Esther and Ada and answers their questions.

*

No-one knows exactly what was going on inside Frank's head. A good wine-maker is always after 'the optimum wine'. He never actually achieves this, nor would he want to. What would you aim for then? Frank de Rooy continued to improve the grape varieties and their growing conditions, continued to propagate and plant. He was an inspired winegrower who lived inside his own dream, and the older he got, the more at ease he seemed to be in the vineyard among the grapevines, and the less at ease he seemed to be among people. A friendly, lovable man, but if you stepped outside his frame of reference, he quickly forgot about you. When he turned seventy, he sold his shares to the board of directors he'd appointed years earlier, and used the money to establish the Druivebloed Viticulture College and the Druivebloed Foundation for scholarships and research on organic winegrowing. Then he started work on the country house. No-one could understand why. It was impossible to figure out what was going on inside his head. He knew exactly how he wanted the house to be, as if he had a blueprint for it. He made drawings, talked with the contractors, and supervised the construction from minute to minute. He brought in a famous interior designer, who started working on the inside of the house after a number of long discussions with him. And then the house was finished and something must have burst inside his head, and blood flowed everywhere and filled the cavities in his brain and caused them to overflow, which pushed his brain to one side and squeezed it together and still the blood kept flowing, it flowed into places where it

431

shouldn't have gone, and wreaked havoc on his brain, until it was damaged beyond repair and he no longer existed. He lived for a time, in a deep coma, and according to the doctors it would be better if he never came out of it.

*

The whole company sighed. 'That house,' says Marjorie. 'What a shame.'

'It will probably be turned into a guesthouse,' says Kris and gets up, because he can't stay too long at one table. Hannah watches him walk away. His shoes crunch over the gravel.

That house. Everyone speaks at once. The splendour. Esther leans towards Bob, the man with the kindly grey-green eyes and the charcoal-grey jacket, the man who is her son, an adult man, the kind of man Sal could have become if he'd been allowed to have a life. As an architect, what does he think of the house?

Bob hesitates. 'Do you really want to know?'

'If he says that,' Hannah exclaims, 'he thinks it's awful.'

Really, these architects always have such strong opinions, Marjorie grumbles. But Esther treats herself to the luxury of a serious conversation about architecture, with this man.

*

'Mozie,' says Ada, when she's plucked up the courage, 'I have a request,' and a short time later he drives her to the big house. It's built on the spot where his caravan used to be, he explains. He himself lives with his wife in Masterton. And Frank's old house is now the shop.

They walk on to the porch. 'There were quite a few women, weren't there?' She tries to say it as casually as she can. Mozie's old man's face breaks into a grin. 'Yes, a lot of women,' he says. 'The lucky bastard, they came one right after the other. I married a girl from my village, well, you know, it was different for me. But him... sometimes they overlapped each other without them knowing about it. The older he got, the longer the relationships lasted. But there would always come a day when the woman

432

would leave the place in tears. Then I knew she'd gone and brought up the subject of marriage and children.'

'Why didn't he want that?'

'He did want it. At least that's what he said. I don't know. They were never good enough. The women knocked at his door, but I don't think he ever let them in. The last few years he kept everyone at a distance.'

He opens the door to the library for her. Once the coffin had been carried out, invisible hands had moved the armchairs back in place. She walks straight to the desk. Only now with Mozie there does she dare to look and see if her eyes hadn't been deceiving her earlier as she leaned over the coffin. She'd seen it right: her old snapshot from the beach stands on the desk inside a silver frame.

He never stopped looking at me.

She picks it up tenderly. A gorgeous young woman, in a swimsuit that shows off her figure in a breathtaking fashion, stands in the middle of the beach looking rather lost. Her blonde hair is blowing in front of her face, she smiles shyly at the photographer, her smile less than happy. Ada can see how beautiful she was then, and her talent for love, the unused potential. I didn't become who I could have been.

Mozie comes and stands next to her. His breathing is raspy, like he has problems with his lungs. She sets the photo back down, next to the yellowed one of the father and mother with their two children, in the East Indies. The palm in the copper pot, the serious faces, the little boy looking curiously into the lens because he has no idea of what's in store. This room, the library, contains his old furniture, is where the mask hangs, and the mysterious oil painting. The only thing that's missing is the creaking leather sofa. This was the beating heart of his house. She can see him sitting here, surrounded by all the people who abandoned him. She bows her head, unable to speak. Mozie's breathing rasps through the room. He puts his hand on her shoulder. 'He was devastated, Ada,' he says. 'It took a long time. I never saw him like that again.'

It hurts. She rubs her face with both hands, as if she has to wash something off. 'I couldn't do it,' she whispers. 'I didn't dare.' He waits patiently. And then, as if reading her mind, he says gravely: 'He always thought it would have worked out with you.'

It hurts.

'Is that what you think, too?' she asks a short time later, as they drive back to the restaurant in the jeep. The vehicle zooms along almost noise-lessly. Mozie pats her knee gently to comfort her. 'That's not how it went,' he says, and when he drops her off at the patio where Bob is pulling back a chair for her and Esther is pouring her another glass of wine, he says it again. 'That's not how it went.'

Then he says goodbye, because he's tired and wants to have a rest. Ada watches him go, the old, brown cowboy, as he walks towards his wife who's waiting for him by the car. He's the only one who lived with Frank all those years. She knows she'll never see him again either.

∗

For the first time in four years, since Hans's death, Marjorie is relaxed, sitting here under the pergola covered with grapevines, which filter the sunlight pleasantly and speckle them with flecks of light and shadow. The pinot noir is heavenly and the platter with the sandwiches just happened to end up within reach. She no longer feels so hot, actually, the tempera-ture on this late afternoon is just right. At the table sits her son, who will remain her son. And her granddaughter, for whom the same applies and who is entertaining everyone with her curious questions about the past. 'They had two kinds of cheese here,' says Marjorie, '"mild" and "tasty". And tasty was *so* tasty that afterwards your taste buds were numb!' 'And Chesdale,' Ada adds. 'They had Chesdale, too.' But most Dutchies didn't like it. 'My gran has completely readjusted to life in Holland,' says Hannah and she wraps her long, bare arms around Marjorie, 'but she should never have left this place.' Ada puts her hand on Marjorie's good arm: 'Why did you go back?'

'Oh, Hans got a wonderful job opportunity.'

Marjorie avoids looking at Esther – although the amber has clouded over, she still has that glint in her eyes – and proclaims in a lofty tone that she's only too glad to be living in Holland because you run such a high risk of getting skin cancer here in New Zealand, what with that hole in the ozone layer.

Ada never stopped being homesick. But their trip to Holland after twenty-five years had been a disappointment. All those visits to relatives tired her out. Her brothers had become materialistic, and they didn't get along with Derk. The church service on Christmas had lacked any kind of atmosphere, no Christmas message, nothing about Jesus, and the pastor performed with a teddy bear. That's when she understood that she would never belong anywhere any more.

Hannah starts talking about the air race. Marjorie waves her good hand. 'It was dull,' she says, 'wouldn't you say? The trip was awful, I was bored to tears. Everything was decided for us, the whole way, all we were was cargo!' Now that they're friends, she leans towards Esther. 'Do you know I still have that silver brooch?' 'That ugly thing with the charms?' So Marjorie didn't mention the rest, that she still has the bon voyage case, and all the newspaper articles, and the magazine with her photograph on the cover.

'We went through a storm,' says Ada, gazing off dreamily. 'That's right,' Marjorie exclaims, 'the storm! I thought I was going to die!' Esther gives them an astonished look, she can't remember any storm. The other two try to refresh her memory. Marjorie tells them how the captain later admitted that it had been almost foolhardy to fly through the storm, that's exactly how he put it: almost foolhardy. Does she remember now? Was that above the Timor Sea? 'Oh, that,' says Esther. 'That wasn't a storm, that was just a little turbulence.'

*

As the sun sinks relentlessly down into the sky, the people around them start to leave. The patio empties out. The table with the Dutchies is the only one left, as if they can't say goodbye to this moment. Kris, his hands on the back of Hannah's chair, assures them it's no problem at all and that they can stay as long as they like. He brings more bottles of Druivebloed. The heat of the day hangs pleasantly beneath the pergola, and the splashing of the fountain is like a soothing song. Ada and Esther and Marjorie don't need to look at each other to know that they're all thinking about the man who travelled alone and who had no-one waiting for him. How he got onto the plane and into their lives. It links them together, like his wine is doing now as well. They surrender to the moment and enjoy his hospitality. The cushions in the chairs are thick and soft, it's as if he's personally arranging them behind their backs, are you comfortable? Do you have enough to drink? There are crab sandwiches, have you tried those yet? The evening breeze could be his hand gently stroking their cheeks. His wine relaxes their muscles and calms their nerves. His wine brings contentment and reconciliation.

'Can I take your picture?' Hannah takes a small digital camera out of her backpack. Esther protests. 'Like this? In this light? Why don't you take this one?' She takes the brochure from the seventies out of her bag, which contains a photograph of herself. 'No,' says Hannah. 'You're much younger there. I want you like you are now.'

'Let me just do my lips again.'

'Like you are now,' the girl repeats. Esther recognizes the determination, sees tiny flecks of amber flash in the green eyes. 'You're cruel,' she jokes. 'With my hair in such a mess? My make-up, my eyes?'

'I promise I won't publish it,' says Hannah, and presses the button. 'Yes, that's nice.' She shows Esther the picture on the display.

'Much too close!' cries Esther. 'You can see all my bags that way!'

'I like it.'

'Oh, dear,' Esther sighs.

'No, really, it's very nice.'

'Come now, I was leaning forward, I should lean back.'

'Okay, I'll take another one.'

This time Esther carefully strikes the right pose. Hannah laughs, a short, throaty little laugh, and presses the button. Esther can't remember ever being so happy, such a liberated kind of happiness. If it wasn't so sentimental and a waste of good make-up, she would cry. Hannah cups her hand around the display so they can see it in the low sun. The photo is even worse than the first one.

'Ugh!'

'You're a perfectionist, aren't you?'

Esther takes the camera and studies the photo from up close.

'Oh, dear, dear, dear,' she sighs.

'All right,' says Hannah, 'one last time then. Your best pose.'

Esther smoothes the deep red blouse, crosses her arms beneath her breasts, positions herself so you can see her profile, and turns her face towards the camera. Hannah presses the button. 'Better,' she says, 'much better, I'll keep this one.' She shows the photo to Esther.

'Oh, you're impossible!'

Hannah looks at it again. 'This one really is much better,' she says, 'admit it.'

'I don't know,' says Esther. And bursts out laughing.

*

The sun is gone from the patio. The staff are clearing the tables around them. Time to go, Bob thinks. He'll drive everyone back to the hotel in the big rental car. The five of them agree to meet in the hotel dining room for dinner after they've had a rest. Ada thinks back to the previous evening in her room and feels the blood of a world traveller pulsing through her veins. It could also be the wine. A little unsteadily, the three women push back their chairs and stand up.

'I do so love the sun,' says Ada. 'My joints bother me less here, too.' Esther puts her cigarette out in the ashtray she's filled all by herself, and knits her brows.

'The wettest place on earth, isn't that what they call Greymouth? Why do you stay there?'

'You know,' says Ada as she puts her arm into the wrong sleeve of her sweater, 'I'd really like a house in Ons Dorp. Have you heard of it? In Auckland.' She recites a sentence from memory, something that has always stayed with her: 'In Auckland, the roses bloom all year round.'

Esther knows what she's talking about, a village full of Dutch pensioners, nothing for her. She walks slowly over the gravel with Ada, arm in arm. Out in front of them, Marjorie is being helped along by her son. 'Yes,' says Ada, 'I'd enjoy the sunshine and being together with all of the others. And being able to speak Dutch.'

'Then that's what you should do. *Hopla.*'

'Derk doesn't want to.'

'Oh, right,' says Esther, because she remembers the stories Frank once told her.

*

The door to the shop creaks open and a bell tinkles. Everything here is made of wood. Ada recognizes the room at once. Although the walls have been removed, she can see from the location of the windows where their bed used to be, and the sofa. She takes a few careful steps and looks around. Cabinets have been built up against the walls and they contain bottles of wine and other merchandise. Then she looks straight into his eyes. The same photo he once sent to her has been enlarged into a poster and hangs behind glass. The founder of the estate, says the girl who let her in. Ada nods, but she's not listening. She's standing in the middle of the room wearing a striped dress. Frank is leaning against the crates, looking at her thoughtfully from beneath the brim of his hat. Ada, he's saying, deep down inside you know perfectly well what you want. It's important that you listen to this.

*

In the car park Marjorie and Esther are waiting for Bob; he's gone to look for his daughter, who is wandering somewhere among the tanks with the boy named Kris, who has now finally, shyly, taken her hand. In his mouth, Kris has the piece of Dutch liquorice Hannah offered him, and even though he thinks it's revolting he's more than willing to eat it for her. Are you coming back? he asks casually. Hannah assures him she will. First she'll travel around for ten days with her father and grandmother, and once they've gone back to Holland, she'll come back. I've got months to go, she says, but I have to earn some money. You can help with the harvest, Kris assures her happily, and he strokes the long, tapered fingers. Sweet.

*

Marjorie and Esther are waiting in the car park and lean up against the car beneath the sign, tired but content. Behind them the fields of grape-vines, draped with white nets. They both agree it was a remarkable day. 'I wanted to ask you something,' says Marjorie. 'I'd like it if you'd look after Hannah a bit. She's still a child, even though she might think otherwise. Invite her to come to visit you sometime, give her a call. Keep an eye on things. Not too much, of course, I don't want her to notice it, well, you know what I mean. Would you do that for me?'

'It would be my pleasure,' says Esther. She's barely able to hide her astonishment.

*

Anyone who knows Marjorie even slightly will have to admit that by doing this she's risen above herself. And if Marjorie can do it, it would seem likely that rising above yourself is within the realm of the possible.

*

Ada hurries to the car park where Esther and Marjorie are leaning against the car and announces her decision, her voice high with excitement. She's not going back to Greymouth. After she's paid a visit to Pete, she'll go and stay with Dan and Bridget in Auckland and from there arrange to move into Ons Dorp as quickly as possible. 'What about Derk?' Esther asks.

Ada considers this for a moment, because she wants to choose the right words.

'Derk is very welcome to come,' she says. 'He has to decide for himself. But I'm going to do it one way or the other.' Marjorie, who still misses Hans every day, raises an eyebrow. But Esther smiles as she strokes Ada on the cheek, like she's a little girl in need of encouragement. 'Time has been kind to you,' she says. 'You're still a beautiful woman.' Ada accepts the compliment as if this came naturally to her. 'Thank you.' 'You're the only one of us who still has a waist. You could accentuate this a bit more. Just a moment...' Esther digs a business card out of her bag and hands it to her: '... when you're in Auckland, come and see me and I'll make you a gorgeous coat dress.' 'I'll do that,' says Ada in surprise. A new dress, that's exactly what she needs.

*

The three of them lean against the car, which is giving off warmth after standing in the sun all afternoon. The wind strokes their faces in parting. Ada feels the pebble's smooth shape in the hollow of her hand. Soon Bob and Hannah will return and they'll drive away from the estate and leave Frank behind. But right now they're still here. Three old brides in black.

A shot sounds behind them. On the path between the grapevines is an automatic air gun mounted on a stand. That's how they do it these days, bird shooting. Esther opens a new pack of cigarettes and lights up. She doesn't need to turn her head to feel the irritation steaming up out of the sensible suit beside her. She blows out the smoke and says contentedly, 'I've got a blood clot in my heart – I could drop dead any minute.'

Ada makes her nervous puppy noise, the one she's made all her life. She wants to know all about it.

Marjorie sighs. Always trying to get attention. She puts up with another two or three clouds of cigarette smoke, which first enter her nostrils and irritate her airways before dissolving into the open air. Then she's had enough. 'Could you possibly blow your smoke in the other direction?'

For heaven's sake, talk about inconsiderate.

*

The sun has dropped behind the hills. Evening is falling over the fields. The car moves slowly over the long, unpaved road as they drive out of the estate between the endless rows of vines. As the car passes, the bird netting lifts slightly.

It's no more than a ripple in the gauzy lengths of white.

AUTHOR'S ACKNOWLEDGEMENTS

When writing about the air race, I made use of the excellent accounts by J. W. Hofwijk for the magazine *Katholieke Illustratie* [*Illustrated Catholic Review*]. In some places I have quoted him almost directly.

First of all, I would like to thank IdtV Film: Anton Smit, Hanneke Niens, Ross Fraser, and Ernie Tee, for providing me with the idea of doing something with 'the great air race', and for the confidence they've always shown in me. My special thanks go to Ross Fraser for giving shape to the idea in its initial form.

My thanks go out to all of the people who were so willing to talk with me about the various subjects dealt with in the book, and who did so with such enthusiasm. I would like to stress how helpful this was to me. In New Zealand, I spoke with passengers from the Liftmaster. They told me their stories and I have used parts of these stories at my own discretion. I hope I have not betrayed their trust.

During my stay in New Zealand, Hannah Story was a wonderful personal assistant, sounding board, and travelling companion.

I owe a debt of gratitude to my patient and discerning readers Elik Lettinga, Liesbeth van der Pol, and Matty Hakvoort. Their comments were invaluable to me.

My very special thanks go out to Andries van Dantzig, my beloved husband, who died in 2005. He knew the characters just as well as I do.

TRANSLATOR'S
ACKNOWLEDGEMENTS

During the translation process, I was helped along the way by many people in the Netherlands, New Zealand, and points in between, people who generously shared of their time and knowledge in their various areas of expertise. I would like to express my heartfelt thanks to everyone, including Maarten Groot, Laura and Peter Watkinson, Mary Siegel, Kathy Voyles, Jane Gower, Jean Anderson, Wilma van den Bosch, Tina Beisteiner, Roy Cumberworth, the BlokEdes, Stephen Higgins, Julie Mhiripiri, Cathy Legried, Brenda Jerome, Ross Fraser, Anneke Fes and Michele Hutchison.

I would also like to thank Laura Barber at Portobello along with Ilona Jasiewicz and Mandy Woods for their warm-hearted professionalism. And finally, thank you to Marieke van der Pol, for writing such a wonderful story.